RELENTLESS

MANHATTAN KNIGHTS 2

EVA HAINING

COPYRIGHT

TO SIMON

Tu sei il sole, la luna e le stelle.
Tu sei il mio amante e il mio migliore amico.
Sei il mio tutto.
Siamo due corpi, ma una sola anima.
Ti amerò fino al mio ultimo respiro.
Tutto il mio amore

CHAPTER 1

ADDI

I THOUGHT I HAD IT ALL FIGURED OUT, LOVE 'EM AND LEAVE 'EM HAS been my motto ever since the day Gavin ripped my heart out and crushed it underfoot.

It was working well, and I've been having a lot of fun with the casual thing, but no matter how hard I try to keep it simple, casual, and uncomplicated with Carter de Rossi, he just won't let it go. He won't let *me* go.

If I'm truly honest with myself, I knew the moment he kissed me that he wasn't a one-night stand, but admitting it to myself and to him has been one hell of a long and bumpy ride.

I don't think my best friend Lily and I could have expected what would transpire when we agreed to attend our friend Jason's restaurant opening. That was the night I met Carter...

As WE STEP OUT OF THE CAB AND LOOK UP AT THE FAÇADE OF LA Cattedrale, I'm overwhelmed with pride for Jason. I've known him my whole life, and when Lily came into our lives, we became like the three musketeers.

2 | EVA HAINING

He's been so busy getting this restaurant up and running, I feel as if I haven't seen him in ages. It will be good to spend a couple of hours with him, although he did tell me that there are going to be some of NY's big dogs here tonight, and he knows I can't resist a hot guy with money for some fun.

As soon as we get inside, we're handed cocktails by a handsome waiter before Jason spies us. After we say hello and congratulate him, he steers us in the direction of a group of investors he wants us to meet. Holy Shit! Even from behind, I can tell these men are hot, rich, and completely fuckable.

I've clearly found my place for the evening. Hello, boys!

Three fine specimens turn to be introduced to us, but as I register each delectable face, Lily stiffens beside me. She looks like she's seen a ghost. Oh My God. Hot guy from the club on Wednesday night at twelve o'clock is giving her the bedroom eyes, combined with a panty-scorching smile. She bumped into him on campus this week, and he clearly wants to *bump* her senseless. If she doesn't let this guy deflower her, I will be *seriously* concerned that she has zero sex drive. Holy smoke!

Lily doesn't know this, but he contacted me yesterday to ask if I would put together an overnight bag for her. He's taking her to the Hamptons tomorrow and wants to be prepared in case they decide to stay the night. I gave him shit for assuming that my best friend would put out on their first date, but he's a pretty smooth talker, assuring me his intentions are honorable and he just wants to make sure she's comfortable in every way possible. I gave him the classic, 'don't mess with her or I'll kill you' speech, but I must say, he seems genuine and he's obviously into Lily.

Considering Xander is off my radar as a potential fuck buddy for the evening, I turn my attention to the other yummy treats available.

Jason introduces the first delicious specimen as Logan Fitzgerald. Tall, blond, and hot as hell with a smile to die for. He extends his hand, which I shake, giving him my sweetest, flirty smile, and it's totally working. He's a definite possibility. Strong, firm hands, and a wicked grin that tells me he has a few tricks up his sleeve. I can tell he's seriously toned underneath his tailored suit. Jason interrupts my mental undressing of Logan to introduce the final hottie of the group. Holy... Mother... Of... Shit...

I don't know how to describe the man standing before me. He is scrumptious in every way possible. I've never seen a man so handsome, intensely sexy, and so freaking beautiful. My instant desire for this stranger is primal—visceral, it's as if I've been pulled into his orbit with no chance of escape.

"Addi, this is Carter de Rossi." I can hear Jason's voice, but I don't see anything except the man standing in front of me, holding his hand out to greet me.

"It's a pleasure to meet you." As he takes my hand, a surge of pure, unadulterated lust ignites inside me, spreading like wildfire throughout my body.

I'm instantly bereft when he relinquishes my hand to introduce himself to Lily, but I can feel his gaze on me as soon as the appropriate pleasantries have been made. I'm vaguely aware of Lily disappearing down the hall with Xander, but I'm too wrapped up in the dark brown eyes staring back at me to think about anything else. His face is tanned—a stunning caramel hue—carved with a strong, sexy jaw and a hint of scruff from a long day. Every one of his features is masculine perfection—his nose sculpted as if Michelangelo himself had created it—lips full, pink, and calling to my very core to lick, bite, nip and suck them. His eyes... God, his eyes are like pools of chocolate, sinful and sexy, leaving me a quivering wanton mess. His hair is short, black, and screaming for me to grab it, pull it and use it to guide his resplendent face down, down, down until I feel it between my thighs.

"Let's refill these drinks shall we." Logan interjects.

I immediately pull myself together and get my flirting back on track. "Sounds good to me, handsome."

He grabs three glasses of champagne from the nearest tray and makes his way over to a small seating area. Carter guides my movements through the crowd with a warm, firm hand at the base of my spine. My stomach tosses and turns at the intimate touch. I find the effect he has on me quite unsettling... I don't like it.

I end up sitting between the two stunning men, chatting, laughing and flirting like a champ. Thank God I managed to shake off my reaction to Carter. That is *not* how it works for me with men. I pick my prey and go for the kill—simple and to the point. I don't need any messy, overwhelming feelings getting in the way.

"So, gentlemen, is this how you roll? Get a girl sandwiched between you, liquor her up and have your wicked way?" I like to play... so I put a hand on each of their thighs and bite my lower lip.

"You like the idea of that, baby?" Logan's cologne tantalizes my senses, his breath warm on my cheek.

I feel Carter on the other side, as he nips my earlobe with his teeth. "I don't think you could handle both of us, sweetheart. I'm not even sure you could handle me." A thrill runs through me at his words.

"You must have me confused with someone else, hot shot. I don't think *you* could handle *me*."

He lets out a sexy little chuckle before darting his tongue into my ear and running his hand up my thigh. "Oh, I could handle you just fine. Better than fine. You'd be begging me for more." I can feel my panties getting wet just at the thought.

I feel Logan's hand grip my thigh as I let go of his. "You're a little tease, Addi. You and I both know you wouldn't take us both on." Logan's voice drips sex—he's right—I don't think I could handle the two of them at once, but I'd give it a good old college try!

"And why is that, pray tell?" My question is directed at Logan, but before he can answer, I feel Carter's lips brush against my ear.

"Because, I wouldn't fucking share you." An almighty shudder courses through me.

I am beyond turned on by the two of them caressing me, their scents mingling, teasing my senses with visions of my wildest fantasies. I need to take back control.

"Anytime, anywhere, boys, but just so you know, I don't revisit my conquests. One-time pleasure is all you'll get from me. I get bored easily, and I doubt the two of you could hold my attention for a second round anyway." I extricate myself from their testosterone sandwich, and head for the bar to get us a round of drinks and catch my breath. When I get back they're laughing and joking, our earlier charged moment forgotten.

The conversation becomes more lighthearted and I get to know them a little better. They're so different from each other but are obviously great friends. From their stories, Logan is practically part of Carter's family. As relaxed as our chat has become, I can still feel an uneasy pull towards Carter, his gaze raking over me as we speak.

The three of us have a great time, and eventually, Lily and Xander reappear, holding hands—I give her an approving wink. The girl needs some serious male attention. Xander is most definitely the possessive type, it's written all over him, but I reckon he could be just what she needs.

I really hit it off with Logan. He's a funny guy when he's not so broody and intense. I'm not a massive fan of the intense male, but I could make an exception for one night. He is so yummy to look at, and I can almost *see* the sex dripping off him. I bet he is *dynamite* in bed. I rest my hand on his thigh, leaning in to hear what he's saying over the music and lively conversation going on around us. Oh wow... he is toned. I was too turned on earlier to fully appreciate it. Normally I would have him halfway out the door by now, but there's something holding me back, and I don't want to admit it, but it's the eyes burrowing into the back of my head.

I casually turn my head to confirm my suspicions, and sure enough, his eyes are ablaze, darting between my face and my hand on Logan's thigh. I can't help myself. "You look a little jealous, Carter. Do you want me to put my hands on *your* thighs?" There's something completely different simmering in his gaze now.

"I want your hands, every-fucking-where. How about you quit the games? We both know you're not going home with Logan tonight."

Holy shit.

"Why? Am I not his type?"

A whisper of a smirk hints at the corners of his luscious lips. "You're every red-blooded man's type, sweetheart... and you know it." His lips graze my ear as he speaks. "You're not going home with Logan, because you're coming home with me. It's *my* name you'll be screaming tonight, begging me to give it to you, again... and again... and again." Every muscle in my body clenches in reply.

His lips feel incredible against my ear, sweeping down to brush my neck with featherlight kisses, his breath hot on my skin. I close my eyes, losing myself to the sensation. "Let's get out of here. I'm going to take you dancing." All I can do is let out a moan of pleasure as he continues to caress my neck, his fingers gently moving my hair to allow him unfettered access. "I'll take that sexy little noise as a yes. Go and tell your friend we're leaving... Now." I'm usually the aggressor when it comes to hooking up, but I'm loving how the tables have turned tonight—but only for tonight.

Lily is getting ready to leave with Xander when I find her, so it's not a big deal for me to skip out with Carter. He assures her that he'll make sure I get home safely... he just doesn't say which home. She pulls me aside and gives me the usual spiel about safe sex, which I find amusing considering she's a virgin.

"I'll be fine. We're going dancing. Don't wait up! Love you, friend." She gives me a swift hug and releases me, heading off hand-in-hand with Xander.

When I turn my attention back to Carter, he's deep in conversation with Logan. "You coming with us or not?" I thought it was just the two of us. Logan is coming, too? This could be interesting. I ponder the delicious mental image for a moment before the reality of the situation is explained.

"Fine. I'll call Alexis and get her to meet us there." That makes more sense, although he didn't seem like he had a girlfriend this evening when he was shamelessly flirting with me—naughty boy!

WHEN WE ARRIVE AT A SLICK LITTLE CLUB CALLED VIPER, WE BYPASS THE queue and head straight for the VIP lounge. A pretty little blonde is standing at the bar, and by the look on Logan's face, she must be Alexis. He walks ahead to greet her, and as soon he makes contact, with a gentle brush of her arm, something passes between them, an unspoken agreement. With her head bowed and her eyes cast to the floor, she senses his proximity. She can identify his touch in a club of thousands. He leans down and whispers something in her ear, her demeanor changing in an instant. She transforms into a loving girl-friend in front of my eyes, as if she's slipping into a role assigned to her. It's strange, but really freaking hot.

"Alexis, this is Addi. Addi, this is my friend Alexis." I shake her hand and exchange pleasantries while Carter orders drinks. When he hands me a French martini and drapes his arm over my shoulder, I noticeably relax, the tension I didn't realize was there, draining from my body as I undergo my own transformation. This man affects me in ways that unsettle me, in ways I haven't allowed myself to feel in a long time. A comforting calm flows over me as I regain my equilib-rium—I become the huntress, not the hunted.

I finish my drink in one long gulp, setting my glass on the bar before taking Carter's hand in mine. I ignore the fire burning my palm from this simple connection. He leaves a bottle of Peroni on the nearest surface and follows me to the dance floor. I find a spot amongst the sea of writhing bodies and turn to face him. Rihanna's *Only Girl* is blaring through the speakers as we begin to move.

In a club full of people, a crowd of hot sweaty bodies, we sway in time to the music, his hands snaking around my waist to pull me flush against his rock-hard, toned body. As I writhe in his grasp, my chest rubbing against him, my nipples harden at our deliciously sexual dance. Every nerve ending in my body is alive with the buzz of a million fireflies. His strong, gorgeous face is the only one I see, his amazing smell intoxicating my senses. All I want in this moment is to lose myself completely, to give myself over to this overwhelming attraction.

He caresses his warm, firm hands up my back, over the exposed skin on my shoulders and up into my hair, holding me firmly in place as his lips find mine in a heart-stopping... mind-altering... orgasmic kiss. They are full and soft, firm and tender, rough and oh so skilled. He doesn't seek my permission—he takes what he wants and I am helpless to refuse him.

Our tongues twist and tangle in a fierce exploration. Carter's hands fist in my hair, pulling me tighter, closer, forcing me to accept him deeper as he fucks my mouth with his tantalizingly talented tongue. I slide my hands up his taut back, his muscles rippling under my fingertips as I make my way up and into his enticing short black hair. It complements his stunningly dark eyes perfectly. I tug it, taking my fill, losing myself in his kiss.

I pull back, panting, struggling to draw breath—to calm my rapid heartbeat as I lock down the raging storm of emotion welling inside me, focusing on the ache between my legs.

"Take me to your place, Carter... I need you to fuck me... hard." The effect I have on him makes me feel powerful and sexy. I grab him by the crotch, rubbing my palm up and down his impressive length, hard as steel and ready for me. I hold his gaze as I tease him... daring him to take me.

Without a word, he wrenches my hand from his cock, circling his hand around my wrist, and pulls me through the crowd. He strides over to where Logan and Alexis are dancing. He has her pinned against his hot, ripped body, holding her wrists behind her back in one hand, the other roaming her body, circling his hips to the music. Her excitement is obvious in the way she moves. I can practically smell her arousal she's so turned on. Logan is oblivious to everyone around him, focusing all his attention on her, giving her exactly what she wants—what she *needs* from him.

Carter interrupts their heated exchange with a hand on Logan's shoulder and a quick word in his ear. A nod of acknowledgement, a panty-melting smile in my direction, and Logan turns his attention back to his date. Carter drags me toward the exit, his breath labored, his warm hand in mine, jolting waves of electricity throughout my body.

The anticipation of how explosive our tryst will be is a tangible entity. It's a mist surrounding us, enveloping us, closing us off from everything and everyone around us as we quickly take a cab to his apartment. I have never wanted someone this badly... *ever.*

CHAPTER 2

CARTER

HOLY FUCK, SHE'S HOT. SITTING IN THE BACK OF THE CAB, I CAN FEEL the sexual tension between us build, ready to rage out of control as soon as I get her inside and all to myself. From the instant I laid eyes on her tonight, I knew… I fucking knew that I would be bringing her here and fucking her seven ways 'till Sunday. She is without a doubt the hottest woman I've ever seen, and just my type—tall, slender, toned. Her leg go on for miles and will look fucking amazing wrapped around my head.

Her hair is beautiful, long and dark, and right down her back, perfect for me to grab as I ride her from behind. Her eyes are filled with hidden depths I could get lost in.

I don't know what bills I throw at the driver as we jump out of the cab, and I don't even care. I just need to get this girl inside… and get *inside* of her. Every move she makes is a turn on—and the dress she's wearing… fuck me. It's strapless, with some sort of puffy skirt that's *seriously* short on her. If I was to slide my hand two inches up from the hem I'd be in the Promised Land, and it's sexy as hell.

She doesn't make small talk in the elevator. Taking charge of the situation, she tells me exactly what she's going to do to me, and I'm rock-fucking-solid by the time we reach my floor.

"I'm going to make you feel... so... damn... good... Carter. I'll have you shouting my name as I suck you off. You'll be begging to go down on me and praying for sweet release by the time I let you fuck me... hard, fast, and just the way I want it." Holy Shit. I've had my fair share of assertive women, but she's in a league of her own.

She is beyond sexy as she talks dirty to me, pinning me with her gaze, biting on her succulent, pouty bottom lip. I'm guessing this is her power play, and most men will gladly acquiesce to whatever she asks of them because they *know* she's going to be worth it. I, on the other hand, plan to show her exactly who has the power in this exchange. She'll be screaming my name and begging me to give her a repeat performance when I'm done.

As soon as I open the door to my apartment, I pull her into my arms and pick her up, pressing her against the wall. I kick the door shut and drop my keys, freeing my hand to hold the back of her head as I lower my lips to hers. She tastes fucking divine, and she feels... fuck, I can't wait to sink balls deep into her tight, wet pussy.

"Oh God, Carter, you feel so big. I want to see you." We start clawing at each other's clothes like animals. She rips open my shirt, the buttons scattering to the floor as I hold her with one arm unzipping her dress with my free hand, all the while, kissing her anywhere and everywhere I can. There is *no* way I will get as far as the bedroom before making her come, she's just too fucking sexy I can't help myself.

I lie her down on the nearest surface I can find and slide her dress off, throwing it behind me as I take in the sight of her, sprawled out on my console table—fucking perfection. She's not wearing a bra, her perfectly pert, puckered nipples screaming for my attention. I cup her breasts, and the sight of her arching off the table, pressing further into my hands is such a turn on. Raking my gaze down the rest of her amazing body, I stop to feast my eyes on the sexy scrap of material that is her panties—deep purple satin, already wet with anticipation of just how good I'm going to make her feel. I want to kiss every, last, gorgeous inch of her... and I plan to.

I can see her hunger as she watches me unzip my fly, dropping my pants and boxers to the floor. That's it, baby, take a good... long... hard look. The fire burning in her eyes has just gone fucking super-nova. This response never gets old!

"See something you like?"

Her sexy grin turns dark and smoldering as she raises her eyebrows, moves her hand down onto her body, and starts to caress herself. Fucking... hell. She is a femme fatale—completely turning the tables on me. That never happens.

"See something *you* like, sailor?"

I'm on her in an instant, ravishing her, licking her, biting, nibbling, fondling, caressing... I can't get enough of this girl. She tastes fucking amazing—like cherries—warm and sweet, her skin soft as silk. It's nice not to be overpowered by some pungent perfume for a change. She is a delight to the senses in every way. I'm looking forward to tasting the effect I have on her, but right now I need to fuck her... so hard. I quickly grab a condom from the drawer under the table and rip the foil wrapper with my teeth.

The surprised look on her face amuses me. "Don't worry, baby. Trust me... you are more than ready for me. These panties of yours are *drenched*. I'm going to slide into that tight pussy of yours, stretch you, fill you, and push you to your limits until you're fucking screaming for me to let you come."

I stand proud, letting her watch as I slide the condom down over myself. I'm not shy. I know I've got a cock that makes women beg. I'm fucking huge and I never get tired of the reaction I get when a woman sees me rock-hard and ready for her. You can see it in their eyes—lust, desire, and a hint of fear that I'm going to split them in two. It's like a drug. I get such a high from it.

I revel in the desire in her eyes. She's hungry for me, ready to let me do whatever the hell I want. It takes me a moment to realize what's different about her... what sets her apart from any other woman I've slept with—there is no fear in her eyes, no uncertainty. This vixen laid bare before me knows exactly what she wants—my cock buried deep inside her while she's screaming my name.

As she chews on her lip like a little temptress, I grab her slender thighs and roughly pull her toward me, impaling her on my cock in one swift move. Holy… Fucking… God… Almighty. She feels phenomenal. Her back arches off the table in response, taking every inch of me, a sexy as hell moan ripping from her chest.

"God, Carter… You feel so good. Take me… hard." I don't need to be told twice, although, I don't think I would tire of hearing her shouting my name and begging me to take her.

I start pounding into her as she wraps her legs around my waist in a vice-like grip. I need to taste her, kiss her, touch her all over. I pull her up and into my arms in one swift movement, never breaking my punishing rhythm. When her breasts press against my chest and her lips collide with mine, I try to think of anything other than the woman in my arms. I swear I could shoot my load just from kissing her. Add that to the fact she has the tightest little pussy I have ever had the pleasure to fuck, and I'm going to seriously embarrass myself if I don't try to calm-the-fuck-down.

She wraps her arms around my neck and twists her fingers into my hair—frantic—grabbing my head, forcing me to take every lick of pure fire that her tongue bestows on mine. My God, she is a phenomenal kisser. Her taste—a hint of alcohol, fruity and sweet, and downright addictive.

She is so responsive, her pussy clenching around me as I slam into her, pushing us higher and higher towards sweet fucking release. I spin us around and push her back up against the wall, my dick drilling into her as I slip my hand between us and flick my thumb over her clit. She is so wet for me—within seconds she's screaming my name, clawing at my back, riding out her orgasm.

"Oh my God… Yes… Carter!" As soon as my name rips from her chest, I can't hold back any longer.

"Fuck… Addi… Fucking Hell." My orgasm is so intense, I feel like my legs are about to give way underneath me. I'm crushing her against the wall to keep myself standing, but she's loving it, milking me for all I'm worth.

I carry her over to the sofa with my cock still nestled snuggly inside her.

"Well... you didn't disappoint, sailor." Her voice is slightly shaky, not the same confident woman from moments ago. I pull her close, taking in the scent of sex and Addi—fucking beautiful. As I caress her face with my hand and move her hair over her shoulder, I can see a change in her eyes, the shutters going down—a steely exterior firmly in place.

"Right, hot stuff, I better get going."

What the fuck? She did not just blow me off after a quickie. And what the fuck is this pain in my chest right now? She is *not* leaving here before I've had my fill of her.

"Come on, Addi. Are you bored of me already? You know you want to stay a while. I'm not done with you yet... not by a long shot." The cogs are turning as she decides whether to bolt, or give in to me... Yes.

"Show me what you've got then." Without hesitation, I'm up and moving toward my bedroom, Addi cradled in my arms, naked and panting as I kiss her with a passion I don't even fucking understand.

I make her scream and beg into the small hours of the morning, enjoying every orgasm I wring from her delicious body, time after time. I haven't even gone down on her yet and I've lost count of how many times her body has tightened underneath me. The slightest touch of my hands on her pussy and she convulses in a whirlwind of ecstasy. I could get used to this... to her.

We collapse in a sated heap of sweaty limbs around 4 a.m. and I feel a strange sense of calm with this girl I hardly know, lying in my bed, curled into my side as if she belongs there.

CHAPTER 3

ADDI

SHIT. SHIT. SHIT. SHITTY... SHITTER! I CAN'T BELIEVE I LET MYSELF fall asleep.

I wake in the arms of the most amazing lover I've ever had. I mean he is like *crazy* skilled when it comes to my body. I had zero control over my own pleasure. I don't like the feeling of having no control, and that's just one of the many reasons I need to get the hell out of Dodge before he wakes up. I'm not really an advocate of leaving like a coward, but I can't face this guy again.

As I extricate myself from his strong, tight, gorgeously tanned limbs, I can't help but torture myself with the musky man smell, mixed with last night's cologne and our sex. I take a deep, lingering breath, watching his striking features in peaceful slumber. He is a vision of male beauty, with a gorgeous tattoo on his shoulder that I'd love to explore if I could bring myself to stay. With one last look, I creep from his bedroom, like a thief in the night, finding my way back to the lounge... and my clothes. I dress as quickly and as quietly as possible, holding my shoes rather than putting them on in case I wake Carter.

I feel bad about ducking out on him like this. He was so amazingly sweet, and rough at the same time. I already feel things that are *not* cool. As I make my way to the door, I spy a notepad on the kitchen island, and something in me just can't leave without some sort of goodbye. I pick up the pen lying next to it and scribble a message.

> *Had a great time, Sailor, thanks for the thrills.*
> *You certainly know how to create waves.*
> *Addi*

I need to sound detached, but I don't want him to think I didn't enjoy myself. What I can't say is *YOU ROCKED MY FREAKING WORLD*. I can honestly say, without a shadow of a doubt, Carter was the *best* sex I will *ever* have. Shit… I need to get out of here before I go back to his room, crawl back into his arms and lose myself to the ecstasy he can bring.

～

AS I WALK DOWN THE STREET TOWARD MY APARTMENT, I AM simultaneously elated and deflated by my predicament. My insides are churning at the realization I won't see him again, or feel the immense connection I felt to him, but at the same time, I know I have a goofy grin on my face and a carefree swagger to my walk at the mere thought of our night together. I don't even notice I'm at my building until I see Lily and Xander on the sidewalk, close to a flashy as hell sports car, which I'm assuming is his. Why am I not surprised that billionaire boy is flaunting the wealth?

"Addi Warner. Doing the walk of shame." Lily gives me a disapproving but loving look as I flash her a massive grin.

"Who said I'm ashamed? I had a fabulous night. Tell Carter I said *Hi* when you see him." I don't even know why I said that.

With a cocky grin Xander responds. "I will pass along your regards, Addi." He sobers, leans away from Lily, and quietly thanks me for helping him out with some preparation for their date today. I give him a playful warning, but he knows that if he hurts her I will hunt him down and break his stupid chiseled face.

I grab Lily into a tight hug and give her some much-needed advice. "Please try to enjoy yourself today, let go, don't think, just feel, enjoy and go with the flow. Okay?" She nods her agreement and my job is done. I leave them to go on their date and head up to the apartment.

When I close the door behind me, a gray cloud descends upon me. I'm acutely aware that Carter will probably have woken up by now and realized I left without a word. To add insult to injury, I left a goddamn note talking about waves. Sometimes I really do hate myself for the dumb things I do.

I try to shake off my funk but it doesn't really happen—the day spent slumming around the apartment, unable to force myself to shower his smell from my body. I'm so freaking pathetic, it's almost funny. I am a walking cliché of womanhood, kicking about in my PJs thinking about a guy. The only difference is that I *chose* to walk away instead of waiting around for him to show me the door.

The guys I usually go for are a sure thing, and I know they will count their lucky stars to spend the night with me, but there was something about him—something about the way he took command of my body, as if it was his to do with as he pleased. It was an incredible turn on, but simultaneously scared the shit out of me. The last time I lost control was with Gavin, and look where that got me, fucked up beyond all recognition. I hide it well... I think, but I will *never* let any man do that to me again.

Everyone thinks Gavin's ultimate betrayal was cheating on me with any college girl who so much as smiled at him... but that doesn't even scratch the surface of what Gavin Jenkins did to me four years ago. I live with it every day. It's always there, and it always will be. I don't let myself wallow in it because that's not who I am, but today, with the smell of Carter in the air, I let myself take a beat to consider how different my life could have been...

I'M SO HAPPY TO HAVE LILY HOME, AND TO BE ABLE TO DISTRACT MYSELF from thoughts of the past. She had some sort of fight with Xander but isn't exactly forthcoming with the details. Instead, I tell her all the gory details of my wild sex with Carter, which she says is TMI, but I like her to know what's out there to be enjoyed. She's almost finished college and she's still a virgin. I want more than anything for her first time to be a great experience, not like mine. I figure the more she knows and the more we talk about it, the more at ease she'll be when she finally takes that step.

After a few bottles of wine and some trash TV, I head to bed, a sense of dread washing over me. I spend the night staring at the ceiling—wondering what, or who Carter's doing right now. The thought of him with someone else makes me nauseous. What the hell? I hate this. I'm exhausted and horny as hell, thinking obsessively about a one-night stand. I seriously need to get my shit together.

I finally give in to my racing, traitorous mind, and slide my hand under the sheets, my fingers dipping down into my wet folds. I'm soaked just at the thought of Carter de Rossi and his toned, masculine body—slick as I push two fingers into my pussy, coating them, ready to give myself the release I so desperately crave. As I pull them from my tight entrance, they glide up and gently caress my clit, already swollen and sensitive. I lose myself to the sensation, remembering the feel of his skilled hands on my flesh—long, strong fingers, teasing me, flicking, fucking me—large, warm palms pressing firmly against me, letting me writhe and beg for more.

I can almost smell his intoxicating scent surrounding me, pushing, driving me toward an incredible climax. My back arches off the bed as I give in to the explosion of sensation unleashed on my body. I stifle the groans, careful not to wake Lily across the hall. My breath is ragged, my heart pounding as I let myself relax and enjoy the warm satisfaction spreading through me.

I have never given myself an orgasm that intense before. Sure, I fantasize about hot guys, celebs, even the odd girl, and I can click the mouse with the best of them, but getting myself off to the memory of Carter's touch is a whole new level of erotic.

As soon as the buzz wears off and sanity returns, I start kicking myself. I hate that this guy has such a huge effect on me after a stupid, amazing, one-night stand. I *do not* let guys affect me like this. I need to get my head in the game and get my exams knocked out this week, and then get this guy out my system by getting under some other willing schmuck. I know it makes me sound like a slut, but hey, I take what I want on my terms, no strings attached. If I was a guy, I would be a freaking hero!

I'm neither a good girl nor a whore, but I tried the one-guy-relationship thing and it completely messed me up, so I occasionally blow off some steam with a stranger. I don't do it all the time, but after Carter, I think I need to get laid sooner rather than later.

My sleep is fitful at best, my dreams clouded by toned Italian skin brushing against mine, murmured words of desire caressing my senses, and an all-consuming passion—pounding, thrusting, taking and giving, spiraling into heavenly oblivion.

CHAPTER 4

CARTER

A FUCKING NOTE? A MOTHERFUCKING NOTE! IT'S BEEN ALMOST a week since I woke up alone and ditched in my own goddamn apartment. I don't know why I'm so bothered, but I've been consumed by fucking rage because of Addi. I don't give a shit about seeing her again, but my male pride has taken a kicking.

We had mind-blowing sex... I'm talking *best fuck ever*! I didn't even scratch the surface of the pleasure I could wring from her tight little body. I was overwhelmed by sheer animalistic lust—I just had to have her. Of course, I thought I'd have plenty of time in the morning to explore every inch of her delectable body, but she vanished without a trace.

I must be losing my touch. I have *never* had a woman duck out on me like that. She didn't leave her number, or even attempt to come up with a lame-ass excuse as to why she had to go.

I'm always busy running the clubs, but I've immersed myself more than usual these past few days. I own five clubs in Manhattan but I tend to spend most of my time working from Cube. I *never* tell the women I hook up with that I own clubs, to avoid any stalker-like behavior. If all my one-night stands knew where to find me, I'm positive it would end badly more often than not. I have been telling myself that Addi would already be in here looking for me if she knew I owned the place.

I've had so many offers this week, and usually I would be all over hooking up with a hot chick, but there hasn't been a single woman in the thousands who have been through the doors of Cube, who could hold my attention for more than five seconds. *Fucking Addi*. I tried to get Logan and Xander to come out tonight and blow off some steam with me—the three of us together is fucking lethal. Women practically throw their already wet panties at us. We're not ugly and we know it —apparently, arrogance is a major turn on to the women of Manhattan.

Xander is already a pussy over this Lily chick. He borrowed the keys to my place in the Hamptons last Friday to take her there for the weekend. It's a bad idea if you ask me—the whole weekend with a girl he just met—it was a bit of a gamble. She could have been a lousy lay and he would've been stuck with her for two days straight. Fuck that! No way am I ever taking a girl up there. The Hamptons is where I go to party with the guys, hook up with bikini clad women on the beach, and just chill out.

Logan is off doing whatever secretive shit Logan does. I swear he's either a serial killer or he's into some serious kink. The women he associates with are always hot as fuck, but the dynamic he has with them tells me there's something going on that I don't know about, and he keeps whatever it is tight to his chest. The girl he's seeing now is nice, don't get me wrong, but it's not love or anything. You know that shit when you see it. I can already see it in Xander, he's pussy-whipped after only a few weeks. I'm going to give him no end of shit for it.

THE CLUB IS PACKED TONIGHT AND THE ATMOSPHERE IS ELECTRIC. THE customers are spending their hard-earned cash getting drunk and dancing their way into each other's beds, but I can't even be bothered finding some random chick to take home.

My phone starts buzzing in my pocket. It's Xander.

"What's up, man?" I need to shout at the top of my lungs in here.

"Hey, Carter. Can you sort out the VIP lounge for Lily and her friends tonight? I want to get out of this student bar and show her a good time."

My mind immediately goes to thoughts of Addi. "How many people are we talking?"

"About ten, nothing major. Just Lily, Addi and a few of their friends who finished their exams today. That cool?"

She's coming here tonight. Perfect. I'm going to make her regret ditching me last weekend. She'll be fucking begging me to take her.

"Sure thing, bro. Head over whenever you're ready. The guys will have everything set up. I'll join you once I've finished with some paperwork."

An hour later, I spy her... gliding through the crowd of sweaty writhing bodies... holy shit, she is even sexier than I remember. Fucking stunning. She's flirting with some douchebag as they make their way up the stairs to the VIP lounge. My fists ball at my sides, an involuntary action to watching some prick with his hand on the small of her back, guiding her up *my* stairs, in *my* fucking club. I need to get a grip before I go up there.

I spend a half hour pacing the floor of my office like a caged lion, before I go in search of Xander. I need a drink. I look around the lounge, but the fucker seems to have disappeared, probably off somewhere fucking Lily's brains out.

I sense Addi before I see her standing at the bar. She's a vision, her stunning features carefree and laughing, her head dropping back as she flirts with the guy from earlier. Before my synapses start firing on all cylinders, I'm behind her, her scent assaulting my senses, her slender body brushing against me. I've got a semi just from this ghost of a touch. What the fuck? She stiffens—she knows it's me—desire burning between us without so much as a glance of acknowledgement.

I slowly slink my arms around her waist, bending down to plant featherlight kisses just below her ear. It's a sweet spot for her and she doesn't disappoint when her body shudders under my touch.

"Tesoro." I continue to tease her, my tongue tracing circles up and down her long, elegant neck. She tastes sublime, like cherries and Addi. It's like a fucking drug.

I feel her body relax back against my chest, her soft, slight, curves, molding to my unforgiving frame. She's a perfect fit, and the realization disturbs me—this is the best I've felt, and the most content I've been since I woke up alone last Saturday.

I run the back of my hands slowly down her cheek, skimming her neck as I trail my fingers down her body, teasing the side of her breasts as I make my way down to her hips. She feels fucking amazing.

I'm rock-solid already and pissed off at the same time. Being a petty prick, I decide to woo her in Italian, whispering sweet nothings to make her melt. It works *every* time.

"*Il formaggio è nel frigo.*" Her badass bravado is nowhere to be seen as she relinquishes her body, languid and ready for me to do as I fucking well please. I can see it in her eyes as I spin her around, she's desperate for me to fuck her. I'm not going to give her the satisfaction so easily. We're going to have some fun tonight.

Her breath is shallow, her heartbeat racing as I pull her flush to my chest and lift her chin, dipping my mouth to capture hers before she can protest. Fucking hell, she tastes good. Her tongue strokes mine, making my cock twitch at the thought of her talented little mouth laving it with undivided attention.

She gives me everything she has in this one unguarded kiss, and as much as I want to lose myself in it, in her, I can't help but feel like a bit of a dick for winning her over with my smooth Italian whispering "The cheese is in the fridge" in her ear. It was a prick move that I usually reserve for the annoyingly dumb girls, but Addi isn't like that. I might not know her very well, but she is sharp as a fucking tack.

I push my guilt aside and give this kiss everything I've got. Her lips and tongue move in perfect symmetry with my own. This is not how I expected to feel when I saw her tonight. I wanted to make her regret putting a dent in my ego, to make her want me, and then leave her hanging.

The reaction she sparks inside me in the middle of my own club is some fucking primitive caveman shit. I want to drag her by the hair into my cave and fuck her into submission. I want her more than I've ever wanted a woman in my life. She *is* going to beg for more when I'm done with her.

I pull back before literally taking her right here on the bar for all to see. The sight of her panting, her full lips swollen from the intensity of our kiss…is so fucking satisfying, and absolutely stunning.

I grab some more drinks and lead her over to one of the sofas, guiding her with my hand on the small of her back, and even this contact has me buzzing all over. Okay, maybe I won't mess with her too much. I certainly won't leave her hanging. I *will* be fucking her tonight and getting her the hell out of my system for good.

Sparks fly as the tension rises, every word from our lips a form of foreplay, teasing each other with a promise of what's to come, but the spell is swiftly broken when Addi diverts her attention to someone behind me.

"You didn't tell me this was the friend you were talking about, *Xander.*" She seems a little pissed.

"I thought you already knew, I mean, you guys have slept together, right?" His feigned innocence is fucking priceless—prick. He knows I don't tell women I sleep with that I own this place. Addi seeks refuge, pressing her face to my chest. I didn't take her for the shy type, but she seems to be surprising me in more ways than one tonight.

"Shut up, man. You're ruining my chances at round two here." He sees the warning in my eyes, gives me a smirk, and heads off to get us all some champagne. Addi relaxes, her soft slender frame melting against me. I'm a little uneasy—the desire to shield, protect, and hold her close becoming a physical ache in my chest. What the fuck? And I thought Xander was a pussy.

After having *a lot* to drink, some great laughs with Xander, and Addi writhing against me on the dance floor, I am ready to get the fuck out of here and get *her* under me. She is dynamite on the dance floor, the way she gyrates her hips, snaking her way up and down my body and the curve of her ass brushing against my already hard as steel cock. She is so fucking sexy and she knows it. Every move she makes, she does with the intent to drive me wild. And it is most definitely working.

When Cube closes for the night, Xander's driver takes us back to the girls' apartment. Lily is a little worse for wear, and not to sound like a dick, but I don't give a fuck what her and Xander are up to right now. I have one thing on my mind and one thing only... being inside Addi, making her scream...

CHAPTER 5

ADDI

MY STOMACH IS DOING SOMERSAULTS AS I LEAD CARTER DOWN THE hallway to my bedroom. Lilliput is completely smashed, but thankfully moneybags is taking good care of her, so I am free to focus on the man candy sending shivers down my spine with the mere touch of his hand and the knowledge that I'm about to have some mind-altering, earth-shattering sex.

I can feel a mixture of nerves and pure desire pooling in my groin as I turn to close the door behind us. My room feels somehow exponentially smaller with *him* in it. I make a move to reach for the handle, but as I do, he's on me, slamming the door shut behind him, grabbing me around the waist and pushing me up against the wall. Holy shit, he's strong. He lifts me with ease, ripping at my dress as his lips crash down on mine.

I hear the fabric tear as he devours me with his tongue, his throbbing erection pressing into me—his hands shredding my clothing along with any doubts I have about letting him consume me a second time. My brain is telling me to stop this, the danger alarm resounding in my head like a police siren, echoing in the darkness, but my traitorous body won't listen. I practically convulse under his touch as he rips my panties leaving me completely naked, pinned to the wall, helpless and vulnerable.

I grab at his shirt, sliding my hands between our bodies to unbutton it, pushing it over his strong, broad shoulders. Our lips are locked, our tongues tangling in a fiercely intense, spine tingling kiss. I'm bereft when he pulls away, his warm sweet breath caressing my face as he struggles to control it. He grabs my ass and pushes me further up the wall before taking my hard, puckered nipple into his mouth. Oh my God!

I fist my hands in his hair, tugging and pulling, forcing his face into my chest, urging him to take me harder. He bites down, sending a jolt of euphoric pain coursing through my body. I lose myself to the sensation of his every touch, his every caress and his hand kneading my breast as I arch into him.

"God, you taste so fucking sweet, baby. I need to get a proper taste." I'm on the bed in seconds, my legs spread wide for him to look, and touch, and taste. His strong hands pin my legs, holding them as far apart as they'll go. He's still wearing his pants, and I have a sudden pang of insecurity. What the hell? I'm not that girl. I *know* I have a rocking body. Every man I've ever been with has told me that, so why the hell am I worried what this guy thinks?

"Fuck me, Addi. You have the sexiest pussy I have *ever* laid eyes on. I fucking love that you wax it all, letting me see those lips, swollen with desire, ready for what I'm about to give you. If it tastes half as good as it looks, I'll be feasting on you for hours."

Every fiber of my being coils in anticipation, turned on beyond all reason as his fingers slide down, caressing the length of my folds with a featherlight touch that sets me ablaze. I shudder, my body giving away how strongly he affects me. I'm already wet, and the satisfied look on his face as he spreads my arousal up and over my clit, is sexy as hell.

"I want to tease you, but I just can't wait…"

His mouth connects with my flesh, tracing the length of me in one slow, languorous lick, until he reaches my clit, flicking it with the tip of his warm, wet tongue. Oh God… the groan that escapes his chest vibrates against my skin, pushing me closer to what I *know* will be a seriously intense climax.

"Fuck... baby... you taste sweeter than sugar." The onslaught of kisses he rains down on me sends me into a tailspin, spiraling into an abyss of pure ecstasy. He's ravenous, grunting and groaning as his light scruff scrapes against my inner thighs, devouring me, heightening my already intense pleasure.

When I think I can't take anymore, he thrusts three fingers inside without warning, propelling me into the hardest, hottest, fiercest orgasm of my life. My body submits, willing to give him anything and everything he wants.

"Oh my God... Carter... fuck... yes... oh God, yes!" I can feel his grin against my pussy, but as I try to scramble away, unable to take anymore, he clearly has other ideas.

"I'm not done tasting you yet. Don't move or I'll have to tie you down." My whole body stiffens. That is *not* going to happen. I begin to panic at the mere mention of it, my limbs rigid and shaking at his words.

He knows something isn't right.

"Relax, Addi... trust me..." I want to run a mile. I don't know this guy and he thinks I should trust him? Not likely! That just gets you all kinds of messed up. As much as my brain is screaming at me to push him away—to get him out of my room and out of my life, I feel a strange sense of calm wash over me as he splays his warm, calloused hand on my stomach, holding me gently in place as he flicks his tongue back and forth, reigniting the flames of desire, fanning them into a raging inferno.

I come hard and fast, writhing against his face, fisting my hands in his hair as he suckles me, letting me ride out the aftershocks of my orgasm, humming his delight as he laps at my juices.

"Holy Shit, Carter, you are a fucking God." Fuck! Damn it, freaking orgasmic brain.

He chuckles against my skin. "Baby, I haven't even begun to scratch the surface yet." Before I have a chance to protest, he increases the pace again, his fingers buried deep inside me, his other hand parting my lips to give him unfettered access. The delicious burn builds in my stomach, heralding a third mind-melting climax.

"Hold on to the bed, Addi... Do it now." Without a thought, I do as he asks. He grabs me, pulling me tight against his face, his strong hands kneading my ass. His fingers brush over my entrance.

Fuck, fuck, fuck!

I buck off the bed.

"Don't, Carter... please, don't..." My voice becomes a whisper "don't..."

His eyes dart up to meet mine—wild and scared, and begging for him not to open Pandora's Box. Tears well in my eyes as he lifts and his head, his eyes reconnecting with mine. My soul is as naked as my quivering body in this moment. My darkest secrets, my worst fears on display as he searches my face for answers, I'm not willing to give.

"I wasn't going to... I would never do anything you don't want, Addi." He stands up at the foot of the bed, his eyes never leaving mine. My heart lurches into my throat, waiting for him to leave and desperately wanting him to stay, but my head won't let me beg.

I lie unmoving, holding his gaze, my heartbeat rapid as his hands move down to his belt. He slowly unbuckles, before unbuttoning his pants and letting them drop to the floor. The sight of his caramel tanned skin, tight over rippling abs and V, teasing me as it disappears down into his boxer shorts, immediately ignites my desire. There's a hint of ink, but I am too aroused to focus on it.

He never breaks eye contact, even for a second, as he hooks his fingers underneath the waistband and slides the fabric over his rock-hard cock, letting it spring free. I can't hold his gaze any longer, drawn to the sight of his throbbing length, craving the feel of him inside me.

"Look at me, baby." His command is laced with tenderness—the tenderness I see in the velvet chocolate depths of his eyes staring back at me. I can't move. I just watch as he crawls onto the bed, straddling my body, his strong toned thighs on either side of me as he stalks me —a lion hunting his prey—lithe, powerful, and impossible to resist.

I lift my hands running them over his warm, soft skin, taut over his broad back, his muscles pulsing under my touch. Even his shoulder blades are sexy, and as I explore his body with my fingertips, he whispers sweetly into my mouth, before claiming it as his.

"Let me make you forget, Tesoro."

His lips are on me, his tongue tangling with mine, his scent invading my senses as his body presses down along the length of me, pinning me to the bed. Every inch of skin that connects with his is alive with lust, desire, and the promise of a phenomenal fusion of two bodies becoming one, for a brief moment in time.

Without a word, he nestles himself between my legs, his hard, thick erection teasing my slick entrance before gently sinking deep inside me.

"Cazzo... Addi... sei così bella." *[Fuck... Addi... you're so beautiful.]* His words are a sweet caress, a seduction of my soul as he begins to move—filling me, consuming me, owning me with every thrust.

All the twisted reminders of Gavin slowly drift away as Carter consumes me. I am stretched and filled to the hilt with the sheer size of him, my body opening to accommodate him more and more as he hammers into me—fierce, but at the same time, tender. This man instinctively knows how to work my body, every touch pushing me closer to the edge of ecstasy. All negative thoughts are a spec in the distance, my focus solely on the pleasure he brings—the storm coiling in my core, ready to burst free and overwhelm my senses.

"Look at me, Addi. I want to watch you crash over the edge." His words are almost my undoing. I lift my gaze, locking eyes with him and the passion I see in their depths is both seductive and terrifying.

He starts to rock his hips as he picks up pace, the base of his thick shaft teasing my clit on every downward stroke. Three delicious, hard, thrusts later and the dam holding my body together is obliterated into a million pieces, my orgasm ripping through me, causing me to convulse beneath him, sending him spiraling into his own intense release.

"Fuck... holy fucking shit, Addi. Look at me."

A fresh wave of ecstasy rips through my body as his orgasm pulses down the length of his throbbing erection. He bites down on my shoulder to stifle the guttural roar fighting to escape his chest. The sharp pain of his teeth sinking into my flesh only enhances my pleasure, forcing me to stifle my own cries in hopes that we don't wake Lily and Xander with the deluge of moans and screams that are fighting to break free.

The swell of emotion as we lie sated and breathless, causes a pain in my chest. Why did I break my one-time only rule for this man? I want to ask him to leave, I don't like having men in my bed overnight, and this particular man is dangerous to the safeguards I've built. But as I look at his face, all rugged perfection, masculine and content, his eyes closed, jet black lashes kissing his cheeks—I know I want him here. I *need* him here... just for tonight... only for tonight... never again.

CHAPTER 6

CARTER

I'M A LITTLE CONFUSED WHEN I OPEN MY EYES. I AM *NOT* LOOKING AT my bedroom walls. I'm in Addi's bed with no sign of her beside me. I don't even remember falling asleep last night. I thought she would be skittish about me staying, but I was just so fucking content that I couldn't move. I don't know what the hell this girl is doing to me.

Usually, I would have taken her at least three times—on her back, from behind, in the shower, but she fucking killed me with the intensity of her release. The way her body was trembling beneath me, clenching around me, tearing my orgasm from me before I was ready. This girl is seriously denting my confidence in the endurance stakes.

I don't generally give a fuck what is going on with the girl I'm sleeping with. I keep it to one-night stands and casual arrangements, it's just easier when I'm so busy running the clubs. Addi is a different story. The look on her face last night, the hurt in her eyes, and the plea in her voice as she begged me not to touch her ass, completely fucking floored me. She obviously has issues with it, beyond just being something she doesn't like. All I wanted to do in that moment, staring into those sweet, broken brown eyes was scoop her up and hold her in my arms. I knew it would have killed her to have any form of sympathy, so I did what she needed—I made her forget, and fuck, she made me forget all my rules about getting too attached. Twice I've slept with her, and twice she has stripped away all my bull-shit, and wrung the most intense and honest orgasms of my life from me.

My golden rule has always been not to get involved with broken chicks. I don't want to take them home, even for one night. Not because I'm a dick, but because I know what it feels like to love a broken woman with your entire being, and it hurts like a mother-fucker. I'm not talking about a lover... I'm talking about Vittoria, my little sister.

Tori is my only sibling, and I would do anything for her—she is the only woman in my life who really matters, besides my mom. She is such an inspiration to me, and I am in awe of how fucking strong she is. But I've seen her broken, with the same look in her eyes I saw in Addi last night, and it ripped my heart out—damaging it beyond repair.

WHEN I WAS FOURTEEN, VITTORIA WOULD HAVE BEEN TEN. WE WERE the best of friends and each other's nemesis rolled into one. God, I hated her at times, but I would do absolutely fucking anything for her. My dad is a pretty big deal in Manhattan. He owns a massive law firm with Xander's dad. They're the major players, but they employ some of their college buddies, and we grew up around these guys, calling them 'uncle' and expecting to see them at all of the family barbecues and parties.

Marcus was my idol. I thought he was the coolest guy I'd ever met, way cooler than my dad. He would always side with me if I was trying to get my dad to agree to something, and he always brought presents —at that age, superficial affection is easily bought.

The summer I turned fourteen my parents threw me a huge party at our house and all the usual suspects were in attendance. The party was in full swing and I was having a great time with my friends when my mom called me into the house and asked if I'd seen Vittoria. I figured she was probably off having one of her moods because I was getting all the attention. Mom told me to go find her and bring her back to the party.

I looked in all the places I thought she would hide, but I couldn't find her and it was starting to piss me off. It was my birthday party and I was wasting time looking for her. As I walked into my bedroom, I heard the smallest, strangled sob escape from my closet. I will never forget that sound as long as I live. My heart was hammering in my chest as I opened the door, sensing there was something seriously wrong.

Vittoria was curled into a ball in the corner, wrapped in my favorite Nicks sweater, sobbing her heart out. I instinctively dropped to my knees and pulled her onto my lap. She was shaking so violently that I remember struggling to keep a hold of her. I don't know how long we sat there. I just held her and stroked her hair to calm her down until she had no more tears left to shed. I couldn't let her see the tears streaming down my face as I watched her break down in front of me.

When I managed to compose myself enough to speak, I asked the question that I knew deep down, I didn't want the answer to... "What's wrong, Tori? What happened?"

If felt like an eternity before I heard the most vulnerable little voice speak the words that would incite an all-consuming rage inside me.

"Marcus... he hurt me... he told me not to tell anyone." I held her tighter, afraid of what she would say next.

"You can tell me, I'm your brother, it's ok... you can tell me anything." She started crying again, the devastation in her eyes tearing a hole in my chest.

"I can't, Carter."

"You need to. What... what did he do, Vittoria?"

"He... touched me, made me... do things, and then..." Her cries were excruciating to hear. "He... he made me cuddle with him. Special cuddles for mommies and daddies. He told me not to tell. He said he would be angry with me if I did."

Even the memory of those words coming from the lips of my sweet innocent sister, make me feel physically sick to this day.

My entire body radiated an all-consuming hatred. I wanted to murder him. I wanted to rip him limb from limb, but I was fourteen and my sister needed me to be strong for her.

I tried to get her to come out of the closet so I could take her to our parents, but she was too scared she would see him. She didn't want me to leave, but I had to go and get my mom and dad. When I finally convinced her it would be ok, I hid her under a pile of clothes, and locked the door to the closet behind me. In that moment I was no longer a boy, my carefree childhood was a thing of the past. I walked the green mile of my youth.

Every instinct kicked in as I picked up pace, bounding down the staircase and out into the garden to find my parents. Before I could reach my dad, I saw Marcus standing swigging a beer without a care in the world, laughing and joking with his friends—fucking laughing. The rage I felt in that moment was indescribable.

I completely lost control, running at him and attacking him like a rabid dog. I remember my dad trying to pry me off, shouting at me, my mom screaming in the background. I was kicking and screaming as he yanked me off of Marcus. And then I said it... screamed it for all to hear.

"You fucking bastard! I will fucking kill you. You raped my sister you worthless piece of shit. How could you do that to her? She trusted you." I was inconsolable as I fell to the ground in a heap.

Everything that followed felt like watching a movie in slow motion. I had never seen my dad get angry before, and this was seething hatred—rage—thousands of years of genetics kicking in to protect his daughter. That day, my father beat one of his closest friends to within an inch of his life before making sure he went to prison. It turned out that Vittoria wasn't the first girl he had done this to. He won't see the light of day outside a prison yard ever again.

My mom was amazing. She went straight to Vittoria and nurtured her, cared for her, and helped to slowly piece her back together. It took a long time, years, but eventually some of the sister I knew before that day came back to me. She is the strongest most courageous woman, and I love her to death.

I'VE NEVER GOTTEN OVER THE FACT THAT I COULDN'T PROTECT Vittoria from Marcus. It has stayed with me all these years, and it always will. I guess that's why I keep women at arm's length. A woman deserves a guy who can protect her from all the bad things in life, and I can't do that.

Up until this point I've never met a woman who awakened a primal desire in me to protect her, and that's why last night fucking terrified me. Something in Addi's eyes called out to me, and I wanted to answer it so badly, so fiercely. I couldn't have walked away even if she'd asked me to.

Where the fuck do I go from here?

I can hear pans being smashed in the kitchen and the girls talking in low, sinister whispers. I need to have a serious conversation with Addi about what happened last night. I don't know if I can handle this... whatever *this* is, but I know I can't just walk away today and never give her another thought.

I quickly grab my clothes off the floor and shrug them on. I hate putting on clothes from the night before, but I'd look like a dick if I went out there in Addi's robe. As I step into the hallway, I bump into Xander. I have never been so happy to see him in my whole fucking life. I need a distraction. We fall into our normal routine, trashing each other as we make our way to the kitchen. The aromas coming at me right now are heavenly. She can cook, too. I am royally screwed.

Watching Xander greet Lily is both endearing and seriously fucking annoying. The look on Addi's face when I walk over to her— you would think I'd murdered a baby. Fuck it... I stand behind her, my chest flush against her back. I *know* I affect her, so I nuzzle into her neck, drinking her in. She flinches at my touch. Shit. She's going to react badly to this.

To my amazement, her entire body becomes fluid, molding to my chest. I take it as a green light to continue nibbling her neck. She tastes so fucking good, and I can still smell sex on her. I'm getting hard from the memory, but her pliancy doesn't last long, and I get the cold shoulder throughout breakfast.

Xander has to leave to organize his date with Lily tonight, and I know I should just go with him, but I want to talk to Addi about what happened last night. Her silence is made worse only by her glacial stare when we're left alone.

The silence is deafening. Eventually, I brave asking if she has plans for the day, only to be cut down with an obvious lie.

"Yes. I'm very busy all day with Lily." From the look on Lily's face this is the first she's heard of it. Fuck, this girl is hard work.

"I better get going, too, then. Walk me out?" I say goodbye to Lily and make my way to the door, my heart pounding in my chest, hands in my pockets, head down. I am a motherfucking pussy, but I don't want to leave her like this.

"So, I'll call you?" I know this is a ridiculous question. She wouldn't spit on me if I was on fire. A phone call from me is not something she'll be waiting for with bated breath. I push my luck for one last kiss and am completely blindsided by her reaction.

She plants her soft, elegant hands on either side of my face, pulling me in, kissing me with a passionate urgency that kills me, floors me, and makes me want to beg for more. As quickly as it began, it's over. She pushes me back and I *know* I have a fucking idiotic sated look on my face, but *fuck me*, that was literally the best kiss I've ever had, and I wasn't even in the driver's seat.

I don't want to push her beyond what she can handle, so I turn and force myself into the elevator without looking back. I can't even turn to face her door as I hear it slam shut. That simple noise stings more than it should.

ADDI IS ALL I CAN THINK ABOUT. SHE HAS CONSUMED MY THOUGHTS this past week. The look in her eyes still haunting me. I can usually spot a girl with issues a mile away, but Addi... she hid it so well, behind charm, sass, and bravado. It was only in that moment of complete vulnerability that she let her guard slip, and there it was... that look. The one that speaks a thousand words. I *know* without a doubt, someone hurt her... really fucking badly.

I'm trying to give her some space, because I realize that Friday night was hard for her, and the trust she put in me to let me carry on, to let me help her forget, was a huge step. Don't get me wrong, I'm not fucking pining over this girl, but she has awakened something long suppressed in me, and I would like to help her if I can. If she ever speaks to me again.

I got her number from Xander yesterday, but I haven't tried to contact her yet. I need a bit of time to figure out what it is that I want to say to her. I'd like to at least offer her friendship. I know I'm not better for much else, but I lived through watching Vittoria piece her life back together, and it is so amazing to see her thriving now. I don't know if she'll ever trust a man enough to have a serious relationship, but she poured all of her strength and focus into dancing. She graduated from Julliard three years ago now and has been touring the world with a prominent ballet company ever since. I am so damn proud of her.

She's going to be back in town soon for a few months which will be great. I miss my baby sister when she's on the road. She's the only one who really understands my reluctance to have a relationship. The only one who knows without a doubt—I don't shirk attachments to women just to be a player. She understands the fear... more than anyone. I could use her advice on what the fuck I'm doing with Addi. I don't want to cause this girl anymore pain, but something is drawing me to her and I can't fucking shake it.

CHAPTER 7

ADDI

I REALLY NEED LILY RIGHT NOW. I NEED TO TALK THROUGH ALL THE SHIT spiraling out of control in my head, but she is so deliriously happy with Xander, and I can't bring myself to dump all of this crap on her. She tried to talk to me last Saturday after the guys left our apartment, but I just couldn't. If I had opened the floodgates at that point, I would have told her things... things about me I could never take back. My secrets are mine, and I will *never* put that burden on anyone else... especially not Lily.

We've known each other since junior high. We're sisters in every way that matters, and Lily has been through more than anyone should have to bear. She had shut herself down to the possibility of love... until Xander entered the picture a few weeks ago. They had a bumpy start, but she's the happiest I have ever seen her. I love her. I would do anything for her, and I won't take this away from her for my own selfish need to purge my dirty, broken soul.

Lily thinks my freshman year boyfriend Gavin cheated on me, broke my heart, and left me angry with all men. She's not completely wrong, but I didn't tell her the whole story, and I never will. I'll live with my shame, keep it as my own, and keep pretending as long as I live. It's the only way to survive.

I spent Saturday locked in my room, trying to block out the night before with Carter. A difficult task when everything in my room smelled of him, reminded me of him, and brought me to my knees in my desire to run into his arms and hold on for dear life. That's not who I am, and it took me a day or two to get over it.

I had a moment of weakness, a single moment in time when he saw into the very depths of my soul, and he didn't run. He stayed, and the way he worked my body... God... the way he touched me... it's the first time since Gavin that I was truly able to forget, to lose myself.

It's Friday night, and Lily is staying at Xander's. I know what I need to do to get out of my funk. I'm going to call the guy who gave me his number in a coffee shop today, and I'm going to go out dancing, drinking and do what I do best. I'm going to fuck him, take what I need and come home to my apartment alone. This is what works, this is what keeps me happy, and anything else is a pipe dream.

An hour into drinks, and I can't handle any more of this guy's insidious rambling. He is so freaking dull, but lucky for him, he has a body to die for and I plan on using it tonight. Colin... I think that's his name... suggests we go dancing at Cube, which gets a resounding *No* from me. I do *not* need to bump into Carter de Rossi tonight. I use my wiles to convince him that Spyder is a much better club and we simply have to go check it out. He doesn't need much convincing. A hot kiss and a grab of his tight ass and he is putty in my hands.

When we arrive at Spyder, the queue is around the block, but it seems to be moving quickly so we wait it out, and when we step inside, it's totally worth it. The atmosphere is electric, music is blaring through the speakers, and bodies are writhing on the dance floor. I need some dancing juice to get past this guy's personality and get down to business. We sling back a few shots before making our way onto the floor.

The guy can move, and now that he's putting his mouth to better use, I'm liking him a whole lot more. He has strong hands, a rock-hard chest, and the way he moves his hips tells me he knows how to use his dick as he grinds his semi against me. His hands are roaming all over my body as I move to the music, finding the slow sensual beat and losing myself to it. It's amazing to drift into the zone—not having to feel, not having to think—just focus on dancing and the desire that's starting to build. Colin caresses me, his lips grazing my neck as I tilt my head to give him better access.

I don't know how many songs we dance to, or how long we stay on the floor, but my body is buzzing as he leads me from the dance floor over to the bar. I down my French Martini in record time, ready to get out of here and take the release I so desperately need from this guy. As I take his hand in mine, leaning in to whisper the filthy things I want him to do to me, I feel a warm, strong hand on my shoulder. As I turn to see who's behind me, my heart sinks deep into the recesses of my stomach. Carter stands towering over me, his imposing frame and stunning features a menacing combination.

"Quite the show you've been putting on tonight, sweetheart." God, his voice does things to my insides that I don't even understand. It washes over me, bathing me in a warm glow, regardless of the words he's saying.

I quickly pull myself together, extricating myself from Colin's grasp—he tries to pull me back toward him but before I get a chance to speak, Carter is in front of me, his glare now firmly fixed on the poor schmuck I came here with.

"Don't pull her like that, man. I would hate to have you thrown out of here."

Colin doesn't seem intimidated by this declaration. "You're the one laying hands on *my* date… *man*. So how about you fuck off, or I'll get you thrown out." Carter throws his head back laughing at this attempt at a pissing contest.

"Yeah, good luck getting me thrown out of *my* club, asshole. I fucking own this place and half the clubs you probably frequent in Manhattan. So, fucking step back and give me a minute to talk to my good friend Addi. How about you run along like a good little boy and go hail a cab so you can get the fuck out of my club before you really piss me off." I should slap him in the face for his outburst, but I am so turned on right now my panties are soaking wet against my pussy.

I turn to Colin to appease the rage I see building on his face. "It's ok, baby. Just go and get us a cab. I'll be right out. Carter's a friend of mine and he obviously has a stick up his ass tonight. I'll be five minutes tops." He reluctantly agrees, but as soon as his back is turned, Carter drags me behind the bar and into his office.

It's a big room, but his presence makes it feel claustrophobic. He pushes me down on the couch, his body looming over me, firmly pressed against mine with his face mere inches from my own. His intoxicating smell invades my senses, his warm minty breath caressing my face as he begins to speak.

"You like playing games, sweetheart? You think it's funny to come into *my* club and parade some fucking douchebag in front of me? I ought to punish you for that, but that would imply I give a flying fuck."

I begin to struggle underneath him as my anger at his words gets the better of me.

"First off, I didn't *know* you owned this place. Second, why would I *want* to parade what I do in front of you? We're not together. I can do whatever and *whomever* I want. And third, if you don't give a flying fuck, why the hell am I pinned underneath you right now feeling your hard-on digging into my leg?"

The fire that ignites in his eyes is so goddamn sexy... all I want is to kiss him and have him ravage me, using his anger to take me hard and fast, right here, right now. We stare into each other's eyes, the knowledge of what we *both* want evident in the crackling tension between us. He leans down allowing his lips a ghost of a touch against mine, the memory of how delicious his kisses are, causing me to arch off the couch, my frustration and desperation for him evident in my movements. He doesn't give in to me, but instead, continues to tease me, before gently whispering in my ear.

"This is how you make me feel, Tesoro. Helpless, frustrated, desperate, and fucking turned on beyond all reason."

As soon as the words leave his lips, I feel the loss of his body pressing down on me. His firm hands are pulling me up to a standing position, and I'm bereft when he turns his back on me, taking a seat behind his desk. He doesn't give me a second glance. He starts looking through some paperwork as I stand, dumbstruck and confused.

"You better run along, Addi. Your date will be waiting outside like the good little lapdog you so obviously need." *What the actual fuck?*

"You are such a dick, Carter. I can't believe I ever hooked up with you. You disgust me."

"Don't kid yourself, Addi. You loved every fucking minute of it, and if I wanted you right now, make no mistake, I would be balls deep inside your sweet little pussy, with you screaming my name and *begging* for more. I bet your panties are already wet at the thought of it."

I slam the door as I leave, my body vibrating from my interaction with King Fucking Douche Nozzle. He is so full of himself, I cannot believe he just said that to me. And the part that makes me *really* angry, is the fact that every word he said was the truth. I would have let him *do* anything to me. I would have *done* anything he asked of me. I crave his touch and I hate myself for it. This is exactly what I wanted to avoid tonight. I make my way out of the club on shaky legs, trying to compose myself, and find Colin waiting outside with a cab ready to take me wherever I want to go…

"Is everything ok, sweetheart?" I hate the sound of him calling me that. I need him *not* to speak.

"Everything is fine. No more talking, okay. Let's go to your place and put that sexy mouth of yours to better use." The grin spreading across his face is gorgeous and sexy, and under normal circumstances it would have me weak at the knees and ready to jump him. He holds the door open for me to slide in, but I hesitate. I don't know if I can do this—but then Carter's words replay in my head and I force myself into the cab. I need to exorcise the hold he has over me once and for all. I steel myself, putting the shutters up—my player persona firmly back in place.

"Are you coming, baby? I plan to… several times. It's just a question of whether you want to come along for the ride." He's beside me in a flash, barking his address to the driver as he reaches for the handle, but before it clicks shut, the door swings back open and Colin is pulled from the cab, a familiar voice shouting at me from the sidewalk.

"Get out of the cab, Addi. What the fuck do you think you're playing at? You're not *actually* going home with this guy." I scramble across the backseat and out onto the pavement, anger and desire building inside me in equal measure for this macho asshole.

He's got Colin by the throat, completely emasculated and forced to submit to the alpha dog.

"I'm doing exactly what you told me to do. I'm getting laid. So back the fuck off, Carter. I got the message loud and clear in your office." His eyes are wild and almost feral with rage.

"Are you fucking kidding me with this bullshit? You would fuck this pathetic excuse for a man, just to spite me? That's fucking low, sweetheart, even for you."

"Who the *hell* do you think you are, talking to me like that? The whole goddamn world doesn't revolve around you, you know! Get over yourself! I'm going home with Colin because he's hot and we're having a great time tonight until *you* showed up, and because I can! GOD KNOWS, I COULD USE A GOOD LAY!"

His chokehold on Colin tightens as my words enrage him further.

"Oh, Addi. If you want a mediocre lay then by all means take this loser home and let him ram all four inches of himself inside you. But if you want to be fucked by a real man who can make your toes curl and have you begging for more, then fucking hop on. I'm ready and waiting, baby."

"You're a dick, Carter. Let him go and leave me the hell alone."

There's a fleeting trace of hurt in his eyes as he releases Colin, shoving him to the ground.

"Have it your way, Addi."

Colin stands up, desperate to save face and assert his strength in front of me. He fists his hands at his sides, his eyes fixed on Carter, who is too busy staring at me with a fierce intensity that has me weak at the knees. He lifts his fist and pulls back before throwing a punch that was meant for Carter's face, but without turning to look in his direction, Carter dodges Colin's fist before twisting to the side and slamming his fist into Colin's face.

"Fuck this shit." He turns and strides back into the club, shaking out his fist and muttering something in Italian I don't understand —asshole.

I quickly divert my attention to Colin, asking if he's ok and apologizing for Carter's ridiculous behavior.

"I don't want to get in the middle of something messy, Addi. I just wanted a bit of fun."

"There's no mess. There's nothing to get in the middle of! I want the same thing you do. One night, no strings, fun."

"Well, alright then." He quickly hails another cab, and this time, Carter doesn't try to stop me. He's done with me, which is exactly what I want... isn't it?

He drapes his arm around my shoulder, moving in to kiss me. He smells of cologne, and it's hot, but it's not doing anything for me. I hate that I'm comparing him to Carter right now. I think I just need a minute to get back in the mood with him.

"Are you okay? Is your lip burst?"

"Don't you worry about my lip, sweetheart, it's fine. Let me show you." His lips crash down on mine and it's good... it's great actually, but it's just not... *him.*

When we reach Colin's apartment building, I follow him in, the silence between us deafening. As soon as the door shuts behind me, I turn the switch firmly off on all of my emotions, unzip my dress and stand naked before him. He is more than pleased with what he sees, his hard-on straining against his jeans as he makes his way over to me. He pulls his shirt off over his head, revealing a great body underneath, before dipping his head and capturing my nipple in his mouth.

"Take me to bed... and fuck me... hard."

He does exactly that, and two hours later when he's sound asleep beside me, I grab my clothes and leave his building without a second thought. I take the coward's way out yet again. I feel cheap and dirty as I hail a cab to take me home. My entire body is screaming at me, telling me I just betrayed Carter. It's ridiculous and stupid, we're not even together, but the harder I try to push it from my mind, the harder it fights back. By the time I reach my apartment I feel physically sick, discarding my clothes in the trash and heading straight to the shower to wash off the scent of my own shame.

MY DECISION TO ERASE CARTER WITH A QUICK ROLL IN THE SACK DID *not* have the desired effect. I've spent the past week being even more miserable than I was before. There hasn't been a day when my thoughts haven't drifted to Carter de Rossi. Our nights together, the sheer ecstasy he can wring from my body, and our fight in his club. I still don't understand why he did what he did, why he said what he said or how he just dismissed me with ease—as if I was nothing—and then *he* gets angry at *me*! It was reminiscent of the way Gavin used to speak to me, and I will be damned if I let any man treat me like that again. There's a part of me that *knows* Carter isn't anything like Gavin, but the way I feel when I'm around him terrifies me. He could hurt me so much more than Gavin ever did—a few intimate liaisons and Carter has me twisted in knots in a way I've never experienced before.

Plan A to forget him was a complete disaster, so I'm thinking Plan B will be in force for a while—stay clear of men altogether and have some much-needed Addi alone time to get my shit worked out.

CHAPTER 8

CARTER

Ten Days Later

RAGE IS NOT THE WORD FOR HOW I FELT WHEN ADDI WAS IN MY CLUB, grinding her tight body against that little prick. He couldn't handle her even on his best day. It makes me feel sick to my stomach every time I remember that dick with his dirty hands all over her, and I can't even contemplate the fact that she got in the goddamn taxi with him. She wanted me... I could see it written all over her face, in the trembling of her thighs beneath me. And then I go to stop her and she throws it back in my fucking face! It did feel fantastic to punch that little shit square in the jaw. I can't believe she let that fucker see to her needs, fanning the flames of the desire I sparked in her. I only have myself to blame—the way I wound her up and then dismissed her. You just don't do that to a firecracker and expect it not to blow up in your face, but I thought she'd come around when I fought for her.

I can't even blame her. I did the same fucking thing twenty minutes after storming back into the club and seeing her on the cameras, leaving with that dickhead. Then I pretty much wrecked my office. It was that or beat the shit out of someone. After composing myself as best I could, I made my way back into the main bar, drank some expensive Scotch and waited for the usual vultures to swarm. Girls in this club can smell money and they fucking target me like a heat-seeking missile. It pisses me off, but it's also a really easy way to get laid. I just sit back and take my pick. I know I'm a dick for saying it, and for doing it, but I don't give a shit.

A pretty little blonde caught my eye and she was up for it the second I opened my mouth and used some of my Italian charm on her. She was more than willing to follow me up to the VIP lounge and into one of my private rooms. I didn't even ask her name before bending her over the plush velvet chair and sliding my hand between her legs. She was soaked and ready for me. It took about two minutes to get her off with my hand before I rolled on a condom and plunged into her. All I could think about was Addi, how much tighter and sweeter her pussy felt wrapped around my dick. I had to shut my eyes —block out the girl I was buried inside and lose myself to the memory of Addi just to get off. It's so fucking wrong on so many levels.

IT HAS BEEN TEN DAYS SINCE THE INCIDENT AT SPYDER AND I'VE BEEN acting like a college dickhead, fucking everything offered to me. I've fucked them in the bathrooms, I've bent them over my desk, and I've let them suck me off in the darkest corners of my club. I even fucked one girl up the ass while her friend ate her pussy, and then I made them switch positions. It was so fucking hot, and yet I still can't shake the memory of Addi. I'd like to say it's because of her mad skills in the sack, but I fear it's more than that. I think I have actual feelings for this girl, and I am so pissed off about it. I've decided to bite the bullet and call her today, and I'm nervous as the dial tone rings out in my ear before it connects and a sultry voice is on the other end of the line.

"Hello?" My heart is pounding in my chest with that one solitary word.

"It's Carter. Before you hang up on me, I just wanted to apologize for the way I acted last week. It was completely out of line. I just saw red when I saw you with that dickhead. Look... Addi... before I say anything stupid, can I take you out for dinner tonight?"

"I don't know if that's such a good idea..."

"Please, Addi. Don't make me fucking beg here. I just want to clear the air. Our best friends are dating and we *are* going to bump into each other from time to time. It doesn't need to be so awkward. Let me make it up to you. I'll pick you up at eight." I need to at least sound confident, otherwise she is going to walk all over me, and I'll let her, which is not how I operate. The silence on the other end of the line is crushing... and then like a fucking lifeline, she speaks.

"Okay. I'll see you then, but only for Lily and Xander's sake. Bye." The line goes dead and I realize I've been holding my breath this whole goddamn conversation. What the fuck is wrong with me?

I get my head down and get to work organizing what needs to be done for the clubs tonight. My PA gets me a reservation at Pink—one of my favorite restaurants—so I head back to my apartment to get ready, before making my way to Addi's to pick her up. On the drive over, I finally feel relaxed, more like myself, ready to work the de Rossi charms on this girl.

As I wait to be buzzed in, I'm already formulating a plan of attack. I know what my proximity does to Addi, and I need to get the upper hand back if I am going to talk to her about what happened the last time I was with her. She completely shut down on me that night, and I want to help her, so if I need to be a bit of a dick to do that, then so be it.

When I make my way up to her apartment, I'm not ready for what awaits me behind the front door... she looks... goddamn out of this world. Not her usual sex siren, but a more demure, sultry, subtle kind of gorgeous. Her body is beyond fucking perfect and tonight it's covered in a flowing full-length maxi dress with a chunky belt around her waist, showing off just how tight her body really is. She's wearing flats which makes me feel like I'm towering over her as I loom in the door frame, drinking in the sight of her, unashamed at my blatant appreciation.

If I didn't know better, I would think she looks a little shy as she gathers her clutch and makes her way back to the door, back to me. I get a hint of her perfume as she reaches me and it's so amazing, I just want to lick her from head to toe and everywhere in between. I can't bring myself to move out of the way to let her pass. Instead I lean in and press my lips to her cheek, lingering longer than I should, my breath growing shallow and erratic as I struggle to compose myself. It's only made harder when I hear her breath hitch, feeling the rapid rise and fall of her chest against my own.

"We should go… don't want to miss our reservation." I rip myself from her orbit and force myself over to the elevator. If I don't put some distance between us right now, I'll be lifting her into the apartment and will have her naked and pinned to the wall in three seconds flat. Normally that would be my goal for the evening, but I need to talk to her, I need to understand how she was able to hide the broken so well. I didn't see it coming and it was a sucker punch to the chest when she let her guard down.

I hold the door for the elevator open and flash her my brightest smile. "After you, gorgeous."

She quietly steps in, graceful and stunning with every move of her body. She is a different girl tonight. I'm not sure how to handle this. I can deal with loud-mouthed, confident Addi—not always in the best way, but I can handle it. The vulnerable woman in front of me is staring at me with a look in her eyes that calls to some base desire inside me to protect her, and I find it harder to deal with.

ON OUR WAY TO THE RESTAURANT WE MAKE SMALL TALK, IGNORING THE elephant in the room—my appalling behavior last week. Addi isn't the type to be overwhelmed or impressed by a fancy restaurant or a flash car, so none of my usual tactics have any effect on her. It's sort of liberating and quite refreshing actually. We order drinks and finally start talking while we wait for our food.

"Thanks for letting me take you out tonight, Addi. I was such a fucking asshole last week I wouldn't blame you if you never wanted to see me again." This groveling is obviously amusing to her.

"You're right, Carter... you were a complete asshole, but I guess I can forgive you. I was a bit of a bitch the morning after our night together at my apartment, so let's call it even."

We chat back and forth about mundane topics until I have to mention what happened between us the last time we slept together.

"You probably don't want to talk about it, but I genuinely want to know what's going on with you? I know that look. The one you gave me when I accidentally touched you in the wrong place. The fear that flashed across your face when my fingers got too close. I've seen that look before and it fucking slayed me to see your sweet face looking so distraught. We don't know each other that well, but we have an undeniable connection, and I want you to know you can talk to me about it... if you want to." I can see her shutting down as soon as the words leave my mouth.

We're afforded a short reprieve when the waiter brings our dinner and tops off our drinks. I can see the cogs turning, watching her decide what to say to me.

"Look, Carter. It's sweet that you're worried about me, and I don't know what you *thought* you saw in my eyes, or on my face, but it's pretty simple. I don't like ass play. It's a one-way street and I don't let any man go there, not even one as sexy as you." She's trying to distract me and I want to believe her, but I just fucking don't. I see something of the same pain Vittoria suffered in her eyes, and she most definitely has not dealt with whatever happened.

"I never wanted to make you feel uncomfortable. I'm just worried about you." She cuts me off before I can say anything else.

"Well, you don't have to worry about me. I'm perfectly fine, and I don't need your pity or your concern. We aren't dating. We fucked a couple of times, and you know absolutely *nothing* about me, so whatever bullshit you *think* you know... just drop it." She stands to leave, her eyes glassy with unshed tears.

"Addison! Sit the fuck down. I was only trying to look out for you. Obviously, I should have known better than to attempt anything deeper. I'm sorry. You warned me when I met you. We fucked... that's it. I was putting my own bullshit on you... sorry. Please, sit down and at least finish your dinner." I know my tone is a little sharp, but apparently she doesn't respond to me being nice to her. At least I know where I stand now.

We stick to superficial topics for the rest of the evening, slipping back into our tried and tested roles as we shamelessly flirt, innuendos rife, and the sexual tension between us growing with every passing minute. This night is taking a direction I didn't expect, but one that I want with every fiber of my being. I want my dick buried deep inside her so badly, I can feel myself harden right here at the table in the middle of the restaurant. She makes me lose all control when I'm around her, and the look in her eyes right now is one of pure lust. It is *so* fucking sexy.

"Take me home, Carter. I want you tonight." I'm conflicted for all of two seconds.

I try to flag down our waiter but I can't see him, so I try to get the attention of the waitress at the next table. "Excuse me, miss. Could we have the check please?" As she turns to answer, my heart sinks. I can see the recognition on her face, and all I want to do is get the hell out of Dodge before it blows up in my face, but it's too late!

"Well, well, well. Onto your next willing victim, I see. At least she's getting dinner before you bend her over, fuck her and then don't call her." Shit, shit, shit. One of my many conquests from the past ten days is standing in front of me looking pissed off and spiteful!

"You can't even remember my name, can you?" She's right, I can't. All I could think about when I was fucking her, was the face of the girl sitting across from me.

"You certainly don't waste any time, do you? Have you already slept with someone else in the two days between fucking me and lining up this poor slut?" Addi is up and making her way out of the restaurant before I can stop her.

"Don't you fucking dare call her a slut. You were *more* than willing, so don't play wounded. If you want a guy's respect, don't offer up your pussy on a platter and then expect to be treated like a princess." I throw a few hundred-dollar bills on the table and make a quick exit to find Addi.

She's marching down the block, forcing me to run to catch up with her. "Addi, wait a minute, let me explain." I try to grab her arm to stop her walking away, but she rips it from my grasp.

"You don't have to explain anything to me, Carter. I know you're a player. I knew it when we hooked up, I just didn't realize you had a conveyor belt going. I don't intend to ride that train again, so I'll be going now. Nice knowing you." *How dare she judge me.*

"Don't get all fucking high and mighty on me, Addi. I wanted you, and you know it. You were the one who ignored *me*, and then turned up in my club letting some random guy grope all over you."

"I didn't *know* it was your club! God. And you were the one who wound me up and then discarded me like I was nothing."

She has some nerve.

"Don't give me that bull, Addi. I came out to get you and you blew me off. Then I watched you get in the cab with that prick, so don't accuse me of being a fucking player. You play the game pretty damn well yourself."

"Yeah, I went home with him, and I fucked him, and it was great... fucking amazing actually. Best sex of my life."

I can't believe we are having this conversation in the middle of the goddamn street but fuck it. "That's a load of crap and you know it. I was there, remember... I KNOW how it felt when I was deep inside you, baby. You fucking loved it, and it scared the shit out of you." I lean in close, my rage threatening to boil over.

"Tell me it wasn't my face you saw while he fucked you. Tell me you weren't imagining it was *my* cock hammering in and out of you, just so you could get off."

"You arrogant bastard." She starts hitting me, pounding on my chest.

"How many women have you slept with since we were together?"

"Why the fuck does it matter? You don't even want me."

"Just answer the goddamn question, Carter."

I know I'm going to regret this. "Seven! Are you happy now? Does it make you feel better, Addi? Since I watched you get into the car with that fucking dickhead I've slept with seven women trying to forget you, and two of them were at the same time! I pictured you every time just so I could shoot my load and get the fuck away from them, because *none* of them made me feel the way you do." I have to hold her hands to stop her from hitting me as she struggles to contain her emotions.

"You disgust me you know that? Don't ever touch me again. Let go of me... now." I do as she asks, the look of defeat and disappointment on her face, stabbing a knife into my heart.

"Addi, this isn't easy for either of us. I don't *ever* let women in. I don't normally *do* the relationship thing, and I don't talk about my feelings because generally I don't have any when it comes to women I sleep with. I know it sounds shitty, but I have my own demons to bear and this is how I've dealt with them. Then you come along and wreck it, making me feel... I don't even fucking *know* what I feel, but I know this much... I want you, I want to be inside you, giving you pleasure and watching the way your body moves as you come apart beneath me."

"Don't spin me another one of your bullshit lines." Now I'm fucking angry. I just poured my heart out and this is what I get?

"It's not a fucking line, Addi. Here's the reality. If you hadn't shut me out after our last night together, I wouldn't have slept with any of those women. I would have been *worshiping* your body, indulging your every desire, *begging* you to ride my cock. But that wasn't the case, and I dealt with it the only way I know how."

A single tear rolls down her cheek as she drops her head in defeat.

"I need to go. Please... just let me go. Whatever this is between us... this attraction... it's toxic, for both of us. I don't want to see you again, Carter. Don't call. Don't try to contact me at all. Let's just walk away while we're both still relatively unscathed... Please." The pain in her eyes kills me, and I know I need to let her go.

"I'm sorry, Addi." I kiss her cheek, inhaling the scent of her, letting it ingrain itself in my memory before I turn and walk away, forcing each step, every stride away from her causing a tightening in my chest that I don't understand. I barely know this girl and yet I'm fighting the urge to turn and take one last look at her. To go back and claim her, to fuck her until neither of us can question the physical connection we share. Fuck, I hate this. I need to talk to Xander and get my head straightened out.

CHAPTER 9

ADDI

THE TEARS STREAM DOWN MY FACE AS I WATCH HIM WALK INTO THE distance. I asked him to do it, but it still hurts to see his strong, broad shoulders getting further away from me without so much as a second glance in my direction. I guess he wasn't as bothered as he made out to be. I can't believe I fell for his bullshit player moves. I practically begged him to take me home, even after the stunt he pulled last week.

I know I did the right thing asking him not to contact me again, because I have a weak spot when it comes to him. Why? I don't know. Everything about him speaks to me on a molecular level, and apparently, I lack any self-control around him. I know it's for the best... so why do I feel like someone just ripped my guts out?

As I walk back to my apartment I soak in the New York atmosphere, letting it wash over me, trying to stop myself from going to my bad place, which I affectionately call 'the abyss.' I think I'm fighting a losing battle as the darkness wraps its creeping tendrils around me, the storm of emotional turmoil quieting like the eye of a storm. I am at the epicenter of all the pain, all of the hurt, and an eerie calm washes over me. Everything I'm feeling ceases in an instant. I no longer *feel* anything. I'm an empty shell. Carter becomes a picture in my mind, with no attachments, no fear, and no sadness. This is how I survive the bad in my life, how I deal with it.

By the time I reach the lobby of my apartment, I am completely numb, ready to paint on a smile, and my signature Addi charms for Lily. If it wasn't for her, I would have succumbed to the darkness bubbling beneath the surface a long time ago.

I'm one of those people everyone sees and thinks I have it all—looks, money, a family who love me, and the best friend a girl could ever wish for. All of those things are true, but unbeknown to everyone around me, the other truth in my life is that Gavin broke me, and fundamentally changed who I am. Carter is just a symptom. He seems like a genuine guy, a bit of a player, but he pulls it off with such swagger that you want him even if it's just for one night. I was under no illusions that I could change him, and I don't want to, that's what is so confusing about the way tonight played out.

I was so upset seeing that waitress and hearing about the women he slept with since we hooked up. Ridiculous, right? I did the same thing with Colin, but I hated every minute of it and wished it hadn't happened the second it was over. I really am a colossal twat.

GRADUATION IS TOMORROW AND I SHOULD BE LOOKING FOR A JOB WITH all of my free time, but my main goal over the past two days has been to eat my own body weight in junk food. I *have* managed to spend some time with Lily, which is becoming a rare commodity now that she's with Xander. Don't get me wrong, I am beyond happy for her, and he's a cool guy, but I could really use my friend at the moment. She's been going for interviews, making plans, and getting laid… a lot. Me? I'm in limbo. I majored in advertising and would like to go into the field, but my motivation is non-existent. I guess I suffer from spoiled rich girl syndrome, along with extreme fucked-up-itis. I just need to get through graduation with a smile on my face and then I can get my drink on with Lil. I need a drama free night, so freaking bad.

I head to bed early with only my dreams for company. The same dream I've had every night since Spyder—I relive our interaction—and every night it plays out the same. There is no fight, no frustration, there is only kissing, fondling, caressing and the fucking I so desperately crave. It is glorious and mind-blowing, but every morning I wake up sweating and damp between my thighs, so frustrated I can't even think straight until I give in and replay the dream with my battery-operated boyfriend below the sheets. I tease my sweet spot, imagining it to be the strong, firm, warm hand of Carter de Rossi. It makes me want him 24/7, and it makes me hate him all the more for it.

I've never gotten myself off so much in all my life… if I don't get over this fantasy soon, Energizer is going to run out of stock! I might even have spent a little extra time with the shower head today, just to alleviate the remnants of my frustration before getting dressed and ready to graduate.

LILY AND I HAVE AN AMAZING DAY TOGETHER. WE CHEER EACH OTHER on as we accept our degrees, and I try my best to run interference between her and her family. She was a little apprehensive about Xander seeing how they treat her, but I know it won't change the way he feels about her. He called me the other day to ask if she had a valid passport, which only means one thing… he's taking her abroad, and you don't plan trips like that unless you're in love with the person, and he is definitely a total goner when it comes to my best friend.

I leave them and make my way to Jason's restaurant with my parents. It's so nice to share today with them, to feel surrounded by the love and acceptance of my family. I didn't realize how much I needed it until my daddy gave me a crushing hug and told me how proud he is. It's comforting to bask in the glow of family and friends.

Jason has decked out the restaurant and spared no expense. It is definitely more for Lily—it has Xander written all over it, but I'll take what I can get. Today has been a perfect day. I have my best friend, my family, my Jason. The drinks are flowing, the food will be phenomenal and we'll be doing some major celebrating later after the oldies go home. Lily found out she got the job she wanted, she's going to be traveling with Mr. Moneybags to somewhere awesome I'm sure, and obviously we were already going to celebrate graduation with some dirty dancing. I'm giddy at the prospect of such a fun evening.

At the sound of the doors to the restaurant opening, I lift my gaze... Shit! I see the imposing, delectable figure of Logan, and realization kicks in... he won't be here alone. As if I willed him into existence, Carter emerges from the doorway and my heart drops like a stone, through my chest, cascading down my body, and smashing onto the floor with an almighty thud. Panic rises as our eyes lock. He looks broken as he registers what must be horror on my face. I can't do this. I can't stare into the depths that have plagued my dreams for days. Self-preservation is all I can handle.

I take my seat while everyone welcomes them. I give Logan a nod of acknowledgement, and can feel Carter's eyes burning into me, begging me to give him a glance, a nod, a smile... anything, but all I can do is stare at the place card with my name on it and pray he can't see my heart hammering against my chest.

After trying to distract myself talking to my parents throughout dinner, I can't help taking a peek when I hear Lily's sisters laughing in a totally obvious way, and very *loudly* flirting with Logan and Carter. I want to rip their tiny little heads off when I see them shamelessly shoving their chests out and twirling their hair. Are we in junior high again with these lame moves? The waiter comes over to take our drink orders while dessert is being served, and I take the opportunity to order the strongest alcoholic drink I can stomach. I need some more liquid courage if I am going to survive tonight.

Unfortunately for me, Lily manages to catch my eye and I know she wants me to meet her in the bathroom—best friend code—a death stare means get to the bathroom now! I steel myself for whatever she has to say, but I am not prepared for her outburst the moment the door closes behind us.

"What the fuck is going on?" I hate lying to Lily, but I can't tell her anything... it would change... *everything.*

She cusses me out for a good five minutes but nothing really strikes a chord until…

"…I'm saying this because I love you. I don't want you to miss out on a great guy because of that douchebag Gavin." I feel like I've been punched in the guts at the mention of *his* name. "Don't let Gavin win." Lily walks out of the bathroom and leaves me in my own personal hell.

I sink to the floor, my chest constricting as the enormity of her words wash over me, a cold shower of emotion, raining down on me, chilling me to my core. All this time—my love 'em and leave 'em lifestyle—I thought *I* was taking control and doing things *my* way. Everything I believed was utter bullshit, and the revelation is unsettling. I can't believe I've been letting Gavin dictate my life all this time without even realizing it. I feel like such a fool.

I can't bring myself to face everyone just yet. I pull myself up off the floor and take a good long look at myself in the mirror. I can see it in my eyes—what Carter saw—the brokenness, the sorrow. He is the only man who has ever seen it, the only man who evokes such strong emotion in me that I can't keep up the façade. I want to give him a chance, I really do, but I don't know if I can I get past the other night and the extent of his man-whoring. I believed him when he said none of it would have happened if I hadn't pushed him away and slept with Colin.

I take a few minutes to compose myself, fix my makeup, and come to the decision that Lily is right. I need to at least give whatever this is with Carter a chance, or Gavin wins… again. I don't know if I can do this, but I'm going to try. I head back out to the party, thank Lily and tell her I love her, before sitting down and letting myself look straight into the eyes of the man who twists me inside out.

As soon as we lock eyes, our gaze is transfixed on each other. My small smile and acknowledgement of his presence gains me a massive shit-eating grin. From that moment on, I am mesmerized by his every move. Even across the room I can feel the tension building between us, desire unfurling in my stomach.

The rest of dinner is a blur, and suddenly I find myself saying goodbye to my family and Lily's mom, before being swept away to Cube with Carter and the others. Xander and Lily make their own way there, which gives me a little time to clear the air with Carter. He is a true gentleman about it. He doesn't make me feel bad, and he doesn't make me grovel for another chance. As soon as I open my mouth to speak, he reads my mind, swooping down to silence my lips with a kiss.

"We'll take it slowly, Tesoro. A fresh start… okay?" The tender smile he gives me before touching his lips to mine is my undoing. I don't know how, but this man just *gets* me. He understands my reluctance, my willingness, and the war that they wage inside me. He takes me by the hand and leads me back into the club. The last time we were in one of his clubs together it didn't go so well and my muscles stiffen, betraying my concern.

"Don't worry, sweetheart. This is going to be fine… *we* are going to be fine. I'm not going to tease you, rile you up, or leave with anyone but you. I will be in your bed, making you moan my name tonight and any night after, if you want me." Okay, that made me a little weak at the knees and he didn't even curse! What happened to him since I last saw him?

We have a fabulous night, and the electricity between us fuels our every move, our every breath, the anticipation of what's to come clouding my every thought. I barely register anyone around me when Carter is in such close proximity. The chatting, drinking, and dancing feels so easy and so… right, between us. I am beyond turned on by the time he takes me back to my apartment, leads me to my bedroom and proceeds to fuck me until I'm a limp heap of overused muscles, powerless to refuse his ministrations. Not that I would ever refuse them. The man is a sex god to rival all sex gods! I think I'm going to start calling him Himeros—seriously—that's how freaking amazing this man is at fucking me.

Carter stays the night, and I don't try to kick him out. I actually kind of enjoy falling asleep in his arms and waking up, making breakfast for us and saying goodbye with a long, sweet, *hot* kiss before agreeing to let him take me on our first official date on Sunday night.

I'm sort of excited about it. I know we've slept together more than once already, but a date is different, and a tiny swarm of fireflies start circling in the pit of my stomach in nervous anticipation.

I get to spend Saturday night with Lily before she sets off for London, which is awesome. We laugh, we eat, we drink and we pass out late after getting her packed for her trip. I spend Sunday afternoon getting showered and shaving all the necessary areas getting ready for my date.

There's a buzz from the doorman at 7 p.m. sharp and I am more than ready to venture out on my first date with Mr. de Rossi. It's been a long time since I've been this excited to go anywhere with a man... and I don't even know where we're going.

CHAPTER 10

CARTER

I'M TAKING A WHOLE DIFFERENT APPROACH WITH ADDI TONIGHT FOR our first official date. No wining and dining, no dressing to impress or dancing the night away. We've done the club thing enough already. She put her faith in me on Friday night and I want to build on that—start to get to know her properly. I know I sound like a dweeb but fuck me, she just brings it out in me. It should probably set the alarm bells ringing and make me run a mile, but I fucking *want* to be around her... I admit it... I'm Carter de Rossi and I'm a pussy-whipped loser for a girl I've slept with three times. I'm worse than Xander!

When I arrive to pick up Addi, I decide it's best if I just whisk her out of her apartment as quickly as possible because if I'm in an empty room with her for more than two minutes, I will have her naked and writhing beneath me, while I fuck her all goddamn night. I think she's a bit surprised when I hustle her out the door. I decide not to tell her where we're going... she'll know soon enough and I hope she likes it. I didn't bring my car tonight, so I just hail a cab to take us to our destination.

As soon as I give the address to the driver, a wide grin spreads across Addi's face. She's so damn cute right now. "Are you taking me bowling?"

"Hell yes, I am! I thought it would be fun. I bet all the guys want to wine and dine you, and you're obviously used to the finer things in life already, so I figured, why not do something fun? Plus, I get to check out that fine ass of yours bending over all night. It's a win/win situation really." She throws her head back and lets out a genuine belly laugh, and a slight snort escapes her. It's so fucking adorable.

"Did you just *snort*?" I can't stifle my own laugh at this point.

"Yes… yes, I did. So what? Don't be a dick. A gentleman would never draw attention to such things."

"Oh sweetheart, you and I both know I am anything *but* a gentleman, especially when it comes to you."

I scoop her off the seat and cradle her in my lap before licking the seam of her plump red lips, eliciting a sexy little moan from her. She opens up, darting her tongue out to meet mine, and it's like fireworks going off as they twist and tangle, stroke and explore. We move in perfect harmony, our mouths and tongues fucking each other, taking what we need, trying to quench the undeniable desire between us. I'm not going to be able to get out of this cab with the raging hard-on I have just from this one kiss.

She can feel the length of me growing beneath her sweet little ass, and she doesn't shy away, instead she starts wriggling on my lap, driving me crazy and making me desperate to impale her on my cock, right here in this cab. The sly grin she shoots me doesn't mask the arousal I see in her eyes. She is just as turned on by me, and two can play at this game. I pull her harder against my lap as I start to grind my hips, forcing her to feel how hard I am, making sure she is positioned so I'm rubbing right over her most sensitive area, the hardness of my jeans adding to her pleasure. A tiny moan escapes her and I know we need to stop, or this evening is going to turn out *very* differently.

"Thank fuck, we're here." The cab stops and I throw money at the driver before jumping out of the cab with Addi still in my arms.

"What the hell? That's not the reaction a girl wants when she's grinding on your cock." I throw my head back laughing at how damn funny she is.

"I'm *trying* to give you a proper date before I slide my cock inside you, baby, but you're making it difficult with your sexy ass and your smart mouth. If you touch my boner with any part of your body one more time, there won't be a date. There *will* be, you and me, and your clothes on my bedroom floor." I give her a swift kiss and set her down on her feet, taking her hand in mine and striding towards the bowling alley.

ADDI FINDS IT HILARIOUS THAT I'VE ARRANGED FOR NEW BOWLING SHOES to be ready and waiting for us when we arrive. I know I said no flashy stuff, and I don't consider this fancy or flashy—it's just fucking hygienic. I plan on licking her from head to toe later and I don't want her pretty little feet inside a used pair of bowling shoes. It's just fucking disgusting. She finds it hysterical and as per usual decides to make fun of me.

"Are you a clean freak germaphobe, Carter? Bad boy player scared of wearing someone else's shoes? Poor baby." This girl really amuses herself, giggling away at her own jokes. She still gladly accepts the new shoes and heads toward our lane to get started. This is going to be fun.

The place is jumping, we have drinks on the way, and Addi is setting up our names on the scoreboard. I take a look up at the screen to find ADDI and PLAYER in big letters staring back at me with a sly grin.

"Nice, Addison... nice. Let's make this game a little more interesting, shall we? How about... some truth or dare? If you get a strike you get to ask me anything you want, or I do a dare, and vice versa." She likes this, I can see the mischief twinkling in her eyes.

"You're on, hot shot. And whoever gets the most strikes, gets to pick a dare for the other person, and you *have* to do it."

Oh, I'm going to enjoy this.

"You have yourself a deal." I hold out my hand to shake on it, pulling her flush against my body as soon as our fingers touch. I run my free hand up her back and into her hair, pulling her head up to just the right angle for me to lick the crease of her lips. "Oh, I am going to enjoy picking a dare for you. It will definitely involve you... naked... and my cock." She licks her bottom lip before biting it, trying to stifle a moan.

"Let's play."

I break contact with her, and as much as it makes my balls ache, I enjoy the bereft look on her face as I saunter past to pick my ball—a big, blue, rock-solid ball... apt for how I'm feeling right now! Thankfully, I get a strike on my first shot, so I don't look like a dick.

"Truth or dare, baby?" I say as I spin around to face her.

"Truth." She looks a little nervous, so I start her off with something simple.

"What's your full name, Addi?"

I see the relief as she picks her ball and brushes past me. "Addison... Stone... Warner."

How does she make her name sound like a sexual treat as it rolls off her tongue and washes over me? Addison... I like the sound of it as I imagine myself shouting her name, grunting it as I spill my come into her tight little pussy. Fuck... I need to distract myself. Easier said than done as I watch her sashay up to take her shot, her perfect ass calling for me to bite it, and claim it. I'm going to make it my mission to show her how much pleasure I can give her.

She's jumping up and down as the pins go crashing to the ground, the screen flashing for a strike. Why do I get the feeling I'm about to get hustled? With a smug look on her face she struts over to me.

"Your turn. Truth or dare?" Shit, I can already see this backfiring on me.

"Truth, but go easy on me... Addison." God, I love saying her name.

"How many women have you slept with?" Holy fuck, straight for the jugular.

"Really, Addi? This is how you want to start our date... thinking about the women I've slept with?"

"I just want to know what level of man-whore I'm dealing with. Should I be worried? Just answer the damn question." I do *not* want to be having this conversation with her. She seems quite playful with it, but I know this is going to kill her good mood. I run my fingers through my hair a few times before I can bring myself to answer her.

"I don't know, Addi. I don't have a little black book of all my sexual conquests, and I don't have notches on my bedpost. I've slept with a lot of women. It's in the triple figures. I'm not proud of it, and I'm not ashamed of it. I have my reasons and that's the way I've lived my life up until now. If I wasn't this way, I would never have been so forceful when I met you, and something tells me you like the way I take what I want…" I leave the words hanging in the air and turn to take my next shot. She's gracious enough to accept my answer and move on.

We have a great time, and Addi totally kicks my ass in our strike competition. I knew she was on the hustle when she was so eager for the end wager. We've found out all kinds of crazy information about each other and even squeeze in some silly dares. She is so much fun to be around, I can't help but smile. She's fucking adorable. I dared her to go get a phone number from a cute blonde girl playing a few lanes over from us. I thought she'd bail and just take a question, but the little minx works her magic and saunters back to me waving a napkin in my face, with not only the girl's number but a pretty pink lipstick kiss on it. I've got a semi from watching her flirt with another girl, and now I *need* to get her back to my place ASAP.

"Read it and weep! You're not the only player in town." She's joking with me, but the image of her leaving my club with that prick comes to mind and makes me want to punch something. I try to shake it off while I order another round of drinks. The waitress who brings them is a shameless flirt and as much as I try to ignore her, she doesn't get the hint and starts touching my arm, completely disregarding the fact that I'm clearly here with Addi. I'm starting to get annoyed trying to extricate myself from her grasp when Addi casually strolls over and parks herself beside me, running her hand up my back, over my neck and up into my hair before giving it a playful tug. All the while, her glacial stare is fixed on the girl touching my arm.

"Best not touch things that aren't yours, sweetheart. That's how you get a broken nose… when my fist connects with it in about thirty seconds if you don't take your grimy little paws off my man." I am so fucking turned on by her possessiveness. My cock is aching as it hardens in my pants, straining against the seam of my jeans. Why is it so goddamn sexy that she's staking a claim on me? Normally I would run a mile if a woman did that. The waitress makes a sharp exit with a disgruntled look on her face, and I am in awe of the woman beside me.

"Tut-Tut, Mr. de Rossi. I can't take you anywhere, can I? Your raw Italian stallion magnetism is just too much for women to resist." A sly grin creeps across her face, and it is so damn sexy.

"You know it, baby. The only woman I want to attract with my 'magnetism' is standing in front of me, looking sexy as hell, and I'm hoping she's ready to get out of here." I pull her close, letting her feel my arousal, and am rewarded with the acknowledgement dancing wistfully in her eyes as I go in for the kill.

Her lips are perfect, so fucking plump, juicy, and ripe for sinking my teeth into. Her breath quickens with my own as I dip my tongue into her mouth, tasting the alcohol, savoring every lick, flick and suck. Everything around us fades into the background as we begin to indulge in this sensual assault—white noise to our growing passion, desire, and urgency to explore each other's naked flesh. I lift her, grabbing her tight little ass, forcing her to wrap her legs around my waist as I deepen our kiss and intensity takes over. When the erotic mist surrounding us lifts for a split-second, I realize I've backed her down onto the scoreboard console. I tear my lips from hers, dragging in a ragged breath, aware of people on the surrounding lanes stopping to stare at the scene playing out in front of them.

I let out a small chuckle before pressing my lips to Addi's ear. "I need to get you home before we get arrested for indecent exposure. As much as I would *love* to spend a night with you in handcuffs, I don't want to share you with anyone. No one gets to see how fucking magnificent you look when you come… except me. Do you understand me, Addison?"

Her breath becomes more erratic, her chest heaving against my torso as I repeat my question. "Do you understand me? No one."

She makes a point of holding my gaze as she gives me the answer I crave. "No one but you, Carter." I know what a big deal it is for her to give me this... even if only for now. I'll take what I can get with her and see where it goes.

"Let me take you home, Tesoro." She nods her agreement, and before I know it, I'm opening the door to my apartment—pulling her in behind me. I'm so fucking fixated on her that I didn't register anything else, from the moment she nodded her head to the moment we arrived here. Privacy and a full night to really explore and enjoy every inch of her delectable body has me buzzing from head to toe with anticipation of the *long* night ahead.

CHAPTER 11

ADDI

M̲Y̲ ᴀᴛᴛʀᴀᴄᴛɪᴏɴ ᴛᴏ C̲ᴀʀᴛᴇʀ ɪs ᴜɴʟɪᴋᴇ ᴀɴʏᴛʜɪɴɢ ᴇʟsᴇ I̲ ʜᴀᴠᴇ *ᴇᴠᴇʀ* ꜰᴇʟᴛ in my life. God... I almost had sex with him in a bowling alley full of people, and I wouldn't have cared as long as he was inside me. It's my turn to take charge tonight. I need to. It's the only way I can reconcile whatever is going on between us without running for the hills. I won our bet, so I can do whatever I want and he has to comply. And right now *all* I want is to see every inch of his gorgeous, naked body, and feel his rock-hard cock hitting the back of my throat.

As soon the lock twists into place, I take charge. "Take off your clothes. I won the wager and I dare you to let me take the lead tonight." He looks a little shocked, but there's an understanding behind his stunning brown eyes. He knows I need this.

A slow, sultry, grin spreads across his beautiful face as the slight scruff from the day begins to cast a rugged shadow along his tanned, chiseled jaw. As he stalks toward me pulling his t-shirt over his head and dropping it to the floor, my stomach starts doing somersaults— Space Mountain has nothing on this guy.

"Your wish is my command, baby."

He holds my gaze as he unbuttons his jeans and pushes them down, along with his boxer shorts. He kicks off his shoes and socks, stepping out of everything else in one swift movement. He stands, confidently, in the middle of his living room, with a wall of floor-to-ceiling windows showcasing the New York skyline, his dick hard as steel as he lets me take my fill, my eyes moving greedily over his body. He has a few tattoos that I've never really had the chance to examine. Against his tanned skin, the black ink is ridiculously sexy. I caught a glimpse in our previous encounters, but I was a little… preoccupied. There is some sort of tribal artwork covering his left shoulder, encroaching onto his defined chest and down his arm to his elbow. I love tattoos on a guy—who doesn't? But on him they're… breathtaking. I want to caress every stunning line with my fingers, before trailing my tongue along each intricate twist and turn of the ink. As I devour the rest of his delicious body, I come to his second tattoo… holy fucking mother of god! This one, I didn't notice before… and it is mouthwateringly hot. It runs between his V muscles. Two lines of writing not in English, so I have no idea what they say, but they look *beyond* amazing on his taut, toned skin. Some of the text is blocked by his raging erection, ready and waiting for me.

He spreads his arms wide. "Do with me as you please, Addison. I'm all yours." My panties are soaked at the sight of him. The way he is so at ease with his body, at ease with being naked, is such a huge turn on for me. He knows how amazing he looks and he's not ashamed to show it.

"Oh, I know, hot shot, and boy do I have plans for you, but first… undress me." His dick twitches at my words and he closes the gap between us.

He doesn't speak, holding my gaze as he lifts my arms above my head, trailing his fingers from the palms of my hands, down my arms, over my sides until he reaches the hem of my silk camisole top. His fingers glide under the edges, his knuckles skimming my naked flesh as he pulls it up and over my head, before dropping it to the floor. A shiver runs through me with the intensity of his smoldering eyes. My breath hitches as he lowers himself onto his knees—fuck—this is one hot sight to behold. He rains featherlight kisses down my stomach while making short work of unbuttoning my jeans and pulling them down, along with my panties. He gently places my hand on his shoulder so that I don't lose balance while he lifts each foot in turn, removing my pumps, sliding my jeans and panties off, and running his hand up the inside of my leg until he reaches the apex of my thighs. I know I'm wet, *so* ready for him, and tonight I feel a little shy at him knowing just how much he affects me.

"Dio mio, *[Oh my God]* Addi. You are so fucking wet, baby." He removes his hand before grasping my ass and pulling my pussy into his face. My stomach comes alive as he takes a deep breath, drinking in the scent of my arousal before flicking his tongue over my swollen, throbbing clit.

"Più dolce il nettare degli dei. So fucking sweet." *[Sweeter than the nectar of the Gods.]*

I have no idea what he just said, but it has my legs buckling underneath me. Carter steadies me as he lifts himself up off the floor, his dick grazing my skin as he pulls our bodies together. His hands move around to the front-fastening catch on my bra, his fingers making short work of it before it springs open, unleashing my now heavy breasts. His mouth claims my nipple, sucking it, teasing it to a pebbled point with his tongue as his hand encompasses my other breast, squeezing it, rolling his fingers over the nipple and pinching it to the brink of pain—a delicious, pleasurable agony. I'm panting and moaning when he pulls away completely returning to his stance in front of me, standing proud as his cock twitches in anticipation.

"You're in the driver's seat tonight, Addison. Tell me what to do." Oh… my… God. I got so caught up in him, I forgot all my rules about taking charge. As much as I hate to admit it—I love the feeling of being at this man's mercy, but tonight I *need* to assert some sort of control, or I know I'll find myself running out of here in the morning, when I want to be nestled in his arms.

"I want you to move over to the windows so I can get a proper look at your body before I lick every last bit of it." I love the excitement dancing in his eyes.

He can't help but keep some level of control as he takes my hand and leads me over into the moonlight streaming though the wall of windows. "Good enough for you to get a *proper look?*" His gaze shifts from playful to a dark and exciting lust, sending shockwaves of desire coursing through my body. I feel a slight tremble in my hands as I place them on his chest, and he covers them with his own.

"Don't be nervous, Tesoro. I am gladly giving you the reins tonight. Whatever you want... or don't want... you decide. I will do *anything* you ask of me, Addi." His sincerity slays me, cutting through my bull-shit issues—speaking directly to my deepest fears when it comes to him. A sense of calm washes over me, my focus now solely on the pleasure I want to give and take from his body.

When he releases my hands, I let them roam, let them feel, let them leisurely explore—each firm, tight muscle rippling under my finger-tips, intoxicating me, fanning the flames of desire stirring inside of me. His skin is soft and firm at the same time. It's the perfect combi-nation. He has a light dusting of hair covering his chest and as I press my lips against him, it tickles my nose. I inhale his gorgeous mascu-line scent. The fresh smell of his body wash is mixed with cologne, and it's a heady assault on the senses. An almost silent groan escapes his lips and it's all the encouragement I need. I kiss and lick my way down his chest, snaking my way around him as if we're on the dance floor.

When I reach his lower tattoo, I follow the lines of it with my tongue, the intricate words winding their way across his skin. I'm on my knees in front of him, and yet I'm confident I have the power as I watch him staring down at me. Tracing each word with my fingertips, I have to ask.

"What does this mean?" I try to spell it out, but my pronunciation is awful. It's written in two lines, from one hip to the other. "Combatti per ciò che si ama. Proteggere o morire." His body stiffens under my ministrations.

"I'll tell you some other time."

Before he has the chance to say anything else, I form a fist around the base of his thick shaft, licking the drop of pre-come beading on the crest of his magnificent cock. His guttural response is such a turn on. I tilt my head to let him watch as I lick his come from my lip.

"Mmm… you taste… delicious." I begin to move up and down the length of him, taking him as deep as I can, moving my hand up and down, feeling his veins pulse against me. He drops his head to his chest, fisting his hands in my hair.

"Cazzo. *[Fuck]* Holy shit, Addi. Don't fucking stop." I love the desperation in his voice as I continue to work him, circling my tongue around his thick length, flicking the tip on every upward thrust. When I feel his release building, the pulsing and throbbing of his cock in my mouth, I pull away ever so slightly.

"Fuck my mouth, Carter, take what you need." I graze his tip with my teeth as I take him back into my mouth, eliciting a roar so feral it causes my pussy to clench in response. His hands are tight in my hair, almost painful as he holds my head in place, pumping his dick in and out, his eyes fixed on where our bodies connect. I look up at him through hooded lids as he begins to increase his pace, thrusting faster and deeper until his cock hits the back of my throat. I gently cup his balls in one hand as the other continues to fist around him.

"I'm so close, Addi. You feel so fucking good." He lets his grip on me loosen, but I take him deeper, sucking him harder, forcing him to climax in my mouth. When his fists tighten, I know he's close and as soon as he feels the vibrations of my satisfied moan on his cock, I'm rewarded with a warm spurt of come hitting the back of my throat. I continue to milk his release from him, savoring every last drop as he shouts my name, over and over again. It is the sexiest thing I have ever heard.

Within seconds of releasing his still hard cock, I find myself thrown over his shoulder as he strides toward the bedroom. The view of his ass is perfection. I just want to take a bite out of it. I get the feeling Carter isn't used to giving up control when it comes to his lovers, and I'm sensing some unease as he drops me down onto his bed. He's struggling to suppress his desire to take over.

"So… Addison. What's next on the menu? Please tell me it involves me ravishing you. After what you just did, all I can think about is licking your divine little pussy." It's clear to me that I'm not really in control right now, but it's too good an offer to refuse. I crawl up the bed and raise myself onto my knees.

"Lie down on the bed. I'll give you what you want, but only if you're a good boy." He complies with a smirk and a quirk of his eyebrow.

I straddle him, my pussy ghosting a touch against his hardening cock before moving up his body. His chest hair tickles my folds as I make my way higher and higher until his grin is splitting his face in anticipation. "I'm going to sit on your face now, and you're going to love every second of it. Tell me how badly you want to taste me, Carter." A surge of power and confidence courses through me.

"You have no idea how badly I want to lick you, suck you, drive you wild, and please you beyond anything you've ever experienced."

I grab the intricately carved headboard as I position myself above him, before lowering just enough for his tongue to reach my pussy. The first flick is... phenomenal. Holy Mother of all that is good and pure! He grabs my ass and pulls me down so I'm pressed hard against his mouth. The little satisfied hum that escapes as he laps at my folds sends liquid fire through my veins, making me so hot for him I feel like I'm going to explode if I don't come soon. I ride his face, fucking his mouth, hard and fast, his scruff only heightening my pleasure as it rubs against my most sensitive area.

"God... Carter... holy fuck... I'm going to come, baby... please... oh shit, please..." A wave of ecstasy washes over my body, radiating from my core and out through my fingers and toes, my entire body convulsing against his face as he continues his ministrations. As one wave subsides, another builds and crashes over me with the same intensity as the first. When I think I can't take anymore, he holds me in place and begins all over again, tracing shapes on my swollen, soaked pussy, until I'm blinded by the pleasure he tears from my body, over and over and over again. When he finally lets go of my thighs, I collapse onto the bed beside him, my breathing labored and erratic.

"God, baby. I could do that all night you taste so fucking good." In seconds, I'm underneath him, his hard, muscled body straddling my own. "Are you ready to let me take the lead now?" I think he's trying to kill me. I can take any more orgasms right now, and I tell him as much! He gives me a mischievous look before kissing and nibbling my neck. "Trust me, baby. You can take more. I'll be gentle, but I haven't had nearly enough of you yet." True to his word, he gently works my body, kissing every single inch of me head to toe, massaging my arms, legs, and back. All the while whispering sweet words of worship—some of them English, some in Italian, and when he finally makes his way up my stomach to my chest, I'm ready for him to fill me, ready to feel his hard, thick cock ride me to a mind-altering climax.

He reads my mind as I lay back and enjoy his attention. "Now you're ready for me. Tell me you want me, Addi. Tell me I'm the only one who can give you what you need." His voice is husky and dripping with desire.

"You know I want you. You are the *only* man who can give me what I need... hot shot." I wanted to call him so many names of endearment, but self-preservation won out. I see fleeting disappoint-ment cross his face before desire clouds all other emotion. He rolls on a condom and lines himself up at my entrance, his throbbing tip, teasing my pussy as I try to take him deeper.

"Patience, Addison. I want to savor you. You're always in such a hurry, always running away from me. Let it happen, Tesoro, è inevitabile come le maree." *[it is as inevitable as the tides]* He slowly eases inside me.

The cry from my chest is something I've never heard before—a satisfied groan that speaks of true contentment as he gradually thrusts every rock-hard inch inside me, stretching me, filling me. When he finally sinks in to the hilt, he lets out a roar that has me on the verge of climax.

He takes his time, rocking in and out of me, all the while, his eyes locked on mine, stripping away all the bullshit between us, leaving only the phenomenal connection we share when we're together. He doesn't pick up the pace or chase his release. Instead, he works us slowly toward the most intense euphoria of my life. I'm screaming his name as mine pours from his lips in a litany of worship.

CHAPTER 12

CARTER

Four Weeks Later

So MANY QUESTIONS ARE RUNNING THROUGH MY MIND RIGHT NOW. I'VE spent two nights with Addi in the past three weeks, and I have the worst case of blue balls known to man.

The night of our first date, something real started between us. The connection we share is primal, explosive, quite possibly caustic, and out of this world fucking amazing. We agreed to take it slow, get to know each other, give whatever this is a try, and for the first week I had her all to myself. Xander and Lily were in London, by all accounts, having a blast, and I got unfettered access to Addi without the added pressure of our best friends analyzing us. We met up for dinner on Tuesday, which turned into me taking her quick and hard in the restroom, before skipping dessert and eating *her* all the night. It was fucking amazing.

We took a trip up to the Hamptons for a long weekend. I know I said I would never take a girl up there, but fuck if she doesn't make me break all my own rules. I don't think we wore clothes for more than half an hour the entire time we were there. We didn't even make it out of the door to eat. I ordered in every meal and ate most of them off her smoking' hot body. The sex was out of this world phenomenal, and the rare moments we spent talking to each other were wonderful. Addi has a warmth and a depth to her that's so endearing, and breathtaking to witness. It's not often that she lets her guard down, but it's fucking beautiful when it happens. Those moments are worth dealing with her bullshit, trying to keep me at arm's length and picking fights when she gets close to expressing a deeper feeling than an overwhelming desire to ride my cock.

I want to try and have a relationship with her, but I don't know how. I've never *had* a "relationship" with a woman, and she is in a league of her own. Every time we are in the same room together, we can't last two seconds without ripping each other's clothes off. It's fucking awesome. I can't get enough of her, and the feeling of being inside her... it is so goddamn intense, and addictive, and just fucking... perfect.

When we got back from the Hamptons everything changed. Addi wouldn't let me walk her up to her apartment, so I dropped her off and headed back to my place, but within the hour her name came up on my cell. I will never forget the sound of her voice...

"Miss me already, sweetheart?" I know I've said the wrong thing when I hear her whimper on the other end of the line. In an instant, my heart is hammering in my chest.

"There's blood, Carter... there's blood." Holy fucking shit.

"Addi, baby... you need to calm down and tell me what's wrong. Are you hurt? Deep breaths for me... please... Tesoro, you have to slow your breathing and tell me what's going on." I am shitting myself right now. This crippling fear is why I've steered clear of relationships all my life.

"Lily... gone... blood." She takes a deep breath and manages to compose herself long enough to speak. "The man who killed her dad escaped from prison last week. They haven't found him yet. My apartment is trashed and there's... God, Carter... there's blood. What if he... shit... if anything's happened to her..." Her panic and terror are killing me. I need to be with her NOW.

"Listen to me, Addi. Don't touch anything. Call the police. I'm going to

call Xander. I'm on my way to you now. I'll be there in ten minutes, okay?"
The line is silent. "Addi? Addi? Are you listening to me?" I can hear her gentle
sobs.

"I... I already called Xander." He must be going out of his fucking mind.

"Right. Just hang tight, baby. I'll call the police. You just wait there
for me."

"Please hurry, Carter... I... I need you with me." I don't want to hang up
the phone, but the sooner I do, the sooner I can be with her.

I don't even remember how I got from my place to her apartment, or
making the call to the police. All I know is that I'm standing in the doorway
looking in, and what I find before me, rips my fucking heart out. Addi is
curled up in the corner of the room, away from the carnage left by Lily's
abductor. She looks tiny with her back to the wall, knees tight to her chest
and her arms wrapped around herself, trying to hold it together. I feel like a
fourteen-year-old boy again, transported back to the moment I opened that
closet door and found Vittoria, helpless and broken. I snap myself back to the
present, remembering the vow I made to myself all those years ago and the
motto I carry around in ink on my body every day—Fight for what you love.
Protect or Die.

It was in that moment, staring at the broken woman before me, I
realized... I'm falling for her. I stayed by her side, comforting her as
best I could, until we got word that Xander had found Lily. She was in
really bad shape but he got to her in time. It was fucking brutal
waiting at the hospital with Addi in pieces and Xander in ruins. He's
like a brother to me, I would do anything for him. Watching him and
Addi waiting to hear if the most important person in their life would
pull through was fucking torture. I held Addi in my arms for hours
stroking her hair, wiping her tears from her flawless cheeks and
offering whatever comfort I could.

After that night, Addi completely shut me out. She said she wanted
space to focus on Lily and her recovery. I didn't like it, but I knew she
needed me to back off. I agreed to give her this time as a breather, but
I told her in no uncertain terms that we *would* be in contact, and when
Lily was feeling better we *would* be picking up where we left off.

~

I HATE TO ADMIT IT, BUT OUR TIME APART HAS BEEN GOOD FOR US. THE fact that we haven't been in close proximity has meant we've actually talked to each other, about real shit on the phone, texting, even PM on Facebook. I'm like a fucking teenager checking my phone every two minutes! There is an honesty in our dialogue that cuts through the bullshit, letting us really get to know each other. It doesn't hurt that she's a goddamn comedian. She cracks me up. Everything about our relationship seems to work when you separate it out. The sex—fucking perfect. Our emotional connection—so fucking deep I don't even understand it. Our personalities complement each other and our sense of humor—exactly the same. I've laughed more than I have in years with her. I even burst out laughing in a coffee shop sitting reading a text she sent me the other day. The people at the surrounding tables were looking at me like I was crazy, but I just didn't give a shit.

I have convinced her a grand total of twice in the past three weeks to meet up with me. The first time, I went to pick her up at her apartment and we only got as far as the elevator before I had her pinned to the wall with my hand up her dress, ripping her lace panties to get access to her wet, hot, sweet little pussy. I had to pull the emergency stop and fuck here right there and then. I came so fucking hard and fast, her pussy clenching around me as she bit my shoulder to stifle her own release. We never left her building that night. We went straight back up to her apartment and fucked until neither of us could stand.

The following week was a similar story. We decided to meet at the restaurant this time so we didn't get... sidetracked. We managed through the appetizers before I was getting her off under the table, feeling her thighs tremble around my hand as I finger fucked her, flicking her clit with my thumb. Her juices are dripping down into my palm. The only thing hotter than watching her come in silence, in public, was watching her reaction as I sucked my fingers clean of her arousal, moaning my delight at the taste of her. I had a whole romantic evening planned for us, but it never happened. Addi grabbed me, pulled me into the restroom, dropping to her knees and giving me a fucking amazing blowjob. She swallowed every last drop and licked her lips before walking back out to the table. I'm beginning to realize that restaurants seem to be a major turn on for us! We can't seem to get through a meal together without having sex in the bathroom.

It's an amazing problem to have—I find it hard to hold a conversation with the woman I'm seeing because we are so fucking attracted to each other that we can't stay dressed or vertical for any length of time. I know I'm going to sound like a pussy for saying it, and I already hate myself for thinking it, but it can't be *just* sex with Addi. I want more. I want all of her, but for now, I would settle for being able to control my sexual urges around her for an hour!

Lily is out of the hospital now, living with Xander and recovering well, so there is nothing to keep us apart. Addi has no excuses, and she knows after weeks of phone conversations, I will fucking call her on her bullshit if she tries to pull away from me.

It's shit or bust time. If I can't find some way to integrate the amazing connection we have when we talk on the phone, with our thermonuclear sexual chemistry, Addi will shut me out because it's her defense mechanism. She won't tell me what happened to her that made her so closed off. All I know is what little information Xander could give me. She dated a complete prick who was a serial cheater back in her freshman year of college. What a dick! Why would you go elsewhere when you have a spitfire in your bed waiting for you? She must have loved him to be this fucked up over him years later. The thought that she has ever been in love with someone who isn't me, makes me so fucking irrationally angry.

I know now, I'm not just falling for Addi... I'm already completely in love with her. I am all fucking in... and it *scares the ever living shit out of me.*

CHAPTER 13

ADDI

THE WAY I FEEL FOR CARTER DE ROSSI *SCARES THE SHIT OUT OF ME.* WE are back on track with our 'relationship' if that's what you want to call it. Our three weeks apart only brought us closer together, and now I know so much more about the man beneath the beautiful. He is kind-hearted, he loves his sister something fierce, and he loves martial arts, training with Xander a few times a week. He also has the best laugh I have ever heard—smooth, throaty and sexy as hell. And the real kicker —he speaks Italian when he's aroused or angry, and he doesn't even realize it.

We have spent so many hours talking and getting to know each other lately. I feel like we've known each other for years. It's a strange feeling for me to be so comfortable talking to him. Sometimes I even think I could tell him the real story of what happened with Gavin, and maybe, just maybe, he wouldn't judge or hate me. Of course, I haven't told him. I'm not ready to run the risk of him being the one to walk away... because he *will* walk away if he finds out.

Carter wants me to meet his younger sister Vittoria. She's a balle-rina and has been on tour for the past six months. She's in town to do a show and then has a couple of weeks off before she heads back over-seas. He says I'll love her if I get to know her. Sister—I can just about handle… parents are a massive No No! She organized tickets for her performance tonight, so I'll be watching my first ballet before going out for a late dinner with Carter and his sister. I'm surprised by how nervous I feel getting ready to leave my apartment—checking my make-up, hair, and outfit too many times to pass it off as anything other than desperately wanting to make a good impression on a member of Carter's family. It's going to be a long freaking night!

As my cab pulls up outside Lincoln Center, I can see Carter through the crowd, my senses awakened by his proximity. He's pacing the sidewalk, an elegant, masculine, primal force to be reckoned with. He's dressed to kill, in a charcoal pinstriped three-piece suit—tailored to perfection. He is quite simply the most beautiful man I have ever laid eyes on… and he wants *me*. As I step out of the cab, electricity starts coursing through me, a magnetic force pulling me toward him. I know he feels it too when his head snaps in my direction and our eyes lock before his gaze roams my entire body.

I'm wearing a Marilyn Monroe style dress tonight. A red flowing multi-layered skirt cinched in at the waist to accentuate my figure, low at the back, the layers of material in the front highlighting the swell of my breasts before tying in a sexy halter-neck. As Carter's eyes settle once again on mine, everything and everyone around us disappears as we find our way into each other's arms.

"Tesoro. You look… breathtaking." His hands make their way up and into the loose waves of my hair, his warm palms cupping my face. As his lips connect with mine my body comes to life in a way only Carter can ignite. "Let's get to our seats. I really don't want to explain to my baby sister that I missed her performance because I couldn't control the urge to fuck my girlfriend." What did he just say? He's never called me that before. He reads my mind. "Yes, I said girlfriend, Addison. Deal with it."

With a sly grin on his face, he holds out his hand to me. I place my hand in his and follow as he strides through the crowd, commanding respect from everyone around him, leading me to our seats, and I realize something as I drink in the sight of him... I would let this man lead me anywhere. It's an unsettling but thrilling thought. As the house lights go down and the curtain goes up, I settle back and attempt to clear my mind of the riotous emotions vying for my attention.

The show is amazing, and as soon as Carter points out Vittoria, I am mesmerized by her. She is beautiful, graceful, and elegant. The depth of emotion she conveys in every sweep of her arms, every move of her lithe body, has me on the verge of tears more than once. I am completely awed by her talent and I can't wait to meet her now. As the crowd applauds each and every dancer, I revel in the pride I see radiating from Carter, his love for his sister evident in the stunning smile on his face.

We make our way out of the theater to wait for Vittoria when I spy a familiar face. "Isn't that Logan over there?"

"Yeah. What the hell is he doing here?" We quickly head in his direction, but he seems to be in a hurry to leave. "Logan!" Carter shouts after him, getting his attention, but the look on Logan's face tells me he's not overjoyed to see us. His looks like he's just been caught with his hand in the cookie jar. As we reach him, his demeanor changes and the suave exterior is firmly back in place.

"Hello, Addi, lovely to see you again." He leans in to give me a kiss on the cheek and the look on Carter's face is hysterical—he's jealous of an innocent greeting. He cracks me up.

"Lovely to see you, too. Is Alexis with you?"

"Something came up at work. She had to leave at intermission." He turns his attention to Carter.

"Hey, man. Did you enjoy the show? I didn't realize Vittoria was back in town." There's a question in there somewhere, but Carter is oblivious and he lights up at the mention of his sister.

"She's in town for a few weeks before she has to go back out on tour. We're just about to take her to dinner. Why don't you join us? I know she'd love to see you." Logan's happy with that last comment, and I realize what's going on. He didn't want Carter to see him here...

because he was here to see Vittoria. Holy Shit. Dinner is going to be interesting!

We wait around, chatting and joking for about twenty minutes before a sweet, sexy voice calls out to the man I've become so attached to.

"Carter!" Before she can say anything else, he sweeps her up into his arms, spinning her around like she weighs nothing.

"You were phenomenal, Vittoria, just amazing. You get better every time I watch you." As he sets her back on her feet, he turns her to face me. My nerves are somewhat settled by Logan's presence. I can sense the spotlight will be firmly off me with him at the table.

"Vittoria, I would like you to meet my girlfriend, Addi." A tingle runs up my spine at his use of *that* word again. I hold out my hand.

"It's a pleasure to meet you, Vittoria. You are an exquisite dancer. I couldn't take my eyes off you." Her blush at my words is so endearing —it reminds me of Lily. I know I'm going to love this girl.

"Thank you so much. The pleasure is all mine. Do you have any idea how long I've been waiting to hear my big brother use the word 'girlfriend' in a sentence?" I laugh at her declaration.

"From what he's told me... I'm guessing a really long time." She glances in his direction, a slight frown marring her flawless features. I watch as an unspoken conversation passes between them. Carter closes his eyes, a pained look on his face as he shakes his head ever so slightly, giving her the answer she needed. I'm desperate to ask what's going on and why it's linked to him calling me his girlfriend, but I can tell from the look on Carter's face that this is not a subject he wants to discuss... with anyone. He seamlessly shifts the conversation to an equally tense topic.

"Look who we bumped into." As her gaze locks with Logan's, the atmosphere becomes charged with the most intense sexual chemistry I have ever witnessed. I mean, I know Xander and Lily have crazy heat, and Carter and I... we are thermonuclear in the same room, but this... what I'm picking up on between Vittoria and Logan, is off the charts. He leans in to greet her, kissing her cheek, lingering for an extra beat when she returns the gesture, her lips leaving a mark. She gently wipes the lipstick from his face, caressing his stubble long after the lipstick is gone. If they keep this up, one of two things will happen —either Carter will kill Logan for looking at his baby sister like he wants to do very naughty things to her, *or*, I'm going to do very naughty things to Carter because I am so damn turned on watching these two.

"It's so nice to see you again, Logan. You look… well." She devours him with her eyes as she speaks.

"It's… nice to see you, too, Vittoria. It was a genuine pleasure to watch you dance tonight. You were breathtaking." I turn my gaze to Carter as this intimate exchange takes place. He looks like his head is about to explode.

"Alright. Enough with the fucking long lost hellos. Are we going to get some dinner or not? I'm hungry." I guess he picked up on their obvious connection too, he'd need to be blind not to have noticed. I take his hand in mine as I lean in to whisper in his ear.

"I like it when you call me your girlfriend." I dart my tongue out, catching his ear before pulling back to gauge his reaction. It's had the desired effect. His playful, sexy, naughty streak is back, and his focus is firmly on me.

"Just wait 'till I get you home… *girlfriend*. I have plans for you tonight that you will definitely… *like*." And there it is, the familiar buzz, coursing through my body, readying me for the promise of an earth-shattering night ahead.

THE RESTAURANT IS STUNNING, THE FOOD SUBLIME, AND THE COMPANY is second to none. The four of us have a fantastic night and I get the feeling that Vittoria will fit in perfectly with Lily and me. She is funny, sassy and she doesn't take any crap. I love her already! Logan isn't the flirty guy I know and love tonight. Instead he's more reserved, his answers are more measured and careful, but he's still great company. I really like him, and he's definitely not sore on the eyes! When Carter asks about Alexis the tension at the table is unbearable. Vittoria looks pained, but we quickly move past it and onto lighter topics.

The wine flows, the conversation has me doubled over laughing at points, and we find ourselves the only customers left in the restaurant come midnight. It's the first time I've eaten out with Carter and managed to keep my hands to myself. Progress! Although, I am desperate to get him back to my apartment now. Watching him laughing and joking with his sister and Logan is a beautiful sight to behold. His carefree laugh is like music to my ears, and the smile splitting his face is just freaking gorgeous. I could watch him forever and never get bored.

When it comes time to leave, Carter plans to drop Vittoria off at her apartment before taking me home, but Logan won't hear of it. "Seriously, Carter, take Addi home. I can make sure Vittoria gets home safely. It's the least I can do after you paid for dinner. I'm buying next time, okay?" I slide my hand up Carter's back, hoping he'll take the hint and get me alone, behind closed doors as quickly as possible.

"Okay. Thanks, man. Take care of her or I'll beat the shit out of you." We all say our goodbyes and I exchange numbers with Vittoria, making plans to meet up with her while she's in town, and as we part ways, I can't help but wonder… what is the history, if any, between Logan and Vittoria? The warm arm snaking around my waist steals my focus to the amazing man beside me. "Are you ready to go home, baby?"

"I'm ready to be alone with you. There are far too many clothes between us right now." The fire in his eyes ignites at my words.

"Fucking right. Give me five minutes to get you back to your place and I'll remedy the problem immediately, and have you screaming my name by the sixth." He stays true to his word… Oh. My. God… does he stay true to his word.

CHAPTER 14

CARTER

Three months later

My life is unrecognizable from the way it was six months ago. Addi and I have been dating properly for months now and it's fucking amazing. I never thought I could feel this way about a woman. I closed the door on that so many years ago, I didn't think it would happen for me. I figured I would probably end up like Heffner, but my reality is so much better. After introducing Addi to Vittoria three months ago they have become really good friends. They're always texting and chatting and fucking Facebook… Oh My God. Sometimes I think I share her with the damn thing, but watching her and Vittoria becoming friends has been amazing. They clicked as soon as they met, and the weeks following our dinner when she was still in town, were great. The three of us spent a lot of time together, and I could see in their eyes that they understand each other in a way only they can. The brokenness I see in each of their eyes… has drawn them to each other. But as far as I'm aware they haven't discussed their pasts—I know Vittoria would never tell anyone—that's the way she wants it and I would never betray her trust.

Addi and I spend the majority of our free time together, either at her place or mine. We rarely spend a night apart, but I know better than to ask her to move in with me. She would freak-the-fuck-out! I've learned to read the signs. I know when to back away from a touchy subject, and I know how far I can push her. She still hasn't opened up about whatever happened with Gavin, but I can be patient. She'll tell me when she's ready... I hope.

I knew months ago how I felt about her, and I'm even more certain now that I am *completely* in love with her. I've bitten my tongue so many times when I've wanted to tell her, but she isn't ready and I don't want to ruin what we have. Everything about her has me hooked. She is funny, sweet, smart and sexy as hell. She's trying to give our relationship a chance and I really admire her for it. I know how hard it must be for her—I struggled myself in the beginning, but the difference between us, is that I've resigned myself to the fact that I want her in every way possible. She still has reservations, but do I think she loves me? Yes... in her own way. Do I think she's in love with me the same way I'm head over heels with her? No, but I'm just fucking hoping that she will be one day.

We've made plans to go to the Hamptons with Xander and Lily this weekend and I've decided it's time to tell her. If I hold it in any longer, I might just fucking burst. If I had my way, she would have been living with me months ago and we would be planning a wedding in the next year. I know that won't happen, so the most I can hope for is to tell her I love her and she accepts it, or best-case scenario—says it back. I've told her she doesn't get to just shut me out anymore, and she knows I fucking mean it. I hate to admit it, but I would be fucking lost without her in my life now. I'm so whipped it's unbelievable, but Christ Almighty, I just fucking love the shit out of her.

Addi got a job in advertising about six weeks ago and her schedule has been crazy. She's loving it, it's what she trained for, but our time together of late has been limited to fucking and sleeping. The sex is still out of this world fucking-fantastic, but I'm missing her crazy sense of humor and the sweeter moments we share. This weekend is going to be a welcome opportunity to spend time with her without the daily distractions of work, and it will be great to hang out with Xander and Lily. They got engaged about two months ago which was awesome—he went all out on the proposal and we organized a big party for later that night. I would be lying if I said I wasn't a little jealous of those two and how open they are about how they feel for each other. The wedding is planned for Italy in two months' time and I can't wait. I have family over there and my folks will be flying in for it, along with Vittoria. I'm going to take Addi on a short trip after the wedding and show her some of the sights I grew up with during my summer vacations.

XANDER ARRIVES AT MY PLACE IN THE SUV WITH ADDI AND LILY already giggling in the backseat.

"It's been too long since we did this, Carter. Let's not wait so long next time."

"Too fucking right, man. Although… it was surprisingly different the last time we were up there. No ladies allowed overnight. Remember that rule? And look at us now, a couple of pussy-whipped losers." Xander throws his head back and laughs at my choice of words.

"We were losers back then, Carter, let's call a spade a fucking spade. I would take being pussy-whipped by the gorgeous woman in the backseat any day." He's right!

"You're a wise man, Xander. I don't think I would be here now if you hadn't talked me around and made me realize what a dick I was after my ridiculous man-whore streak. I really fucked things up, and you were the one who saw the light at the end of the tunnel when I couldn't. Thanks, bro."

"Now you really do sound like a pussy. Get in the fucking car before I make you wear a dress, you sappy son of a bitch." He gives me a friendly shove toward the passenger side with a shit-eating grin on his face. What the hell is Addi doing to me? I'm feeling all this… this shit, and now I'm spouting it to my best friend? I really fucking need to get my girl under me and get inside her—to feel only our passion, desire, and pleasure.

The drive is fun. Lilliput and Addi are a force to be reckoned with for sure. I think we're going to have our hands full with these two this weekend. Xander and I shoot the shit and talk a little business until the girls butt in. "If we hear one more word about work this weekend there will be no pussy for you boys. You got it? NO WORK." Lily looks slightly embarrassed by Addi's statement, but it's funny as fuck and we do as we're told, sticking to talking sports the rest of the way, because I *know* she'll hold out on me if I cross her, just to make a point!

It's a breath of fresh air... literally, when we step out of the car and take in the view of sand and sea. The girls are off like a shot, leaving their shoes behind, running down onto the beach together, and I'm sporting a fucking raging boner at the sight of them splashing each other in the water. Xander and I get the bags into the house and check the fridge is stocked. I grab a bottle of wine, four glasses, and ask Xander to grab a blanket before we head out to join the girls on the beach.

We spend a few hours relaxing, enjoying the weather and the view. With Addi nestled between my legs, her back to my chest and her head resting on my shoulder, I am completely content, watching the waves, listening to the quiet noises that surround us and chatting with my best buddy. It doesn't get much better than this.

After a couple of hours Xander and Lily decide to take a stroll to the nearby cove. I took Addi there the last time we were here, and it was the hottest fucking night of my life. We're not talking romance, we're talking hot, sweaty, fucking. It was amazing to watch her strip for me. She looked like a siren from pirate lore, enticing me into the water just so she could beguile me with her charms. I fucked her in the sea before carrying her back to shore, bending her over a rock and fucking her again and again, thrusting into her with the cold breeze on our hot naked flesh, watching as she came apart beneath me—it was fucking transcendent. My dick is hard just at the memory, and it's pressing into Addi's back.

"Why hello, sailor. What's got you standing to attention?" I start nibbling her neck, the sweet taste of cherries arousing me further.

"I was just reminiscing about the last time I brought you up here, and our little excursion to the cove." I hear the catch in her breath as she takes her own trip down memory lane.

"I'm sure I can give you something even more exciting to think about this weekend." Holy fuck she's hot.

"God… Addi… you might give me a heart attack if you try to excite me more than our little escapade in the cove." Her hand slips between us, finding its way to my now massive erection.

"Oh, baby. You know I love to tease you and take you to the edge. I am going to make you beg before you slide your gorgeous cock inside me."

"And that's why I fucking love you."

Holy shit. This is not how I planned it—just blurting it out.

"Wh… what did you just say to me?" She's out of my arms and on her feet in a flash.

"What the fuck, Carter? You can't just say shit like that. You don't mean it, and it makes things weird between us."

"I fucking *meant* it, Addi. I've wanted to tell you for months. Granted, this is not how I wanted to say it, but there you go. If you're going to be all sexy and fucking adorable all the time, shit slips out." She's pacing the sand.

"You can't mean it, Carter. You *don't* love me. You can't. I'm all kinds of fucked up and you know it. What we have is good, so let's just forget about this and keep things the way they are."

"Goddammit, Addi! Really? I can't fucking *unsay* it, and I won't pretend that I don't love you. It's out there now, you're just going to have to deal with it. I haven't asked you to say it back, and I don't expect you to. I know you don't feel the same, but I'm not going to live a lie so you don't feel awkward. I FUCKING LOVE YOU… GET OVER IT! You're not shutting me out because of this, Addi. Got it?"

"You can't tell me what to do, Carter."

"The fuck I can't!"

"I can't be here." She turns to leave.

"You're not going anywhere, Addi, do you fucking understand me?" I grab her, pulling her close to my chest, letting her feel the rapid beat of my heart hammering in my chest. "Do you feel that? Can you really walk away from me right now?" I position my lips millimeters from hers, letting her feel the intensity of our connection before I continue. "If you can tell me that you don't feel this… that you don't *know* this feeling means something… then do it… walk away and don't come back. Can you do that, Tesoro?" Her lips are on mine in an instant, pouring all the emotion she can't express into this kiss. Our tongues twist and tangle in a visceral, angry frenzy, and before I know what's hit me, she pushes me out of reach and walks away—her walk turning to a run as she disappears down the beach towards the marina.

It takes me a moment to grasp the gravity of what just happened, before I break out into a sprint after her.

CHAPTER 15

ADDI

WHERE AM I EVEN RUNNING TO? I HAVE NOWHERE TO GO. I DON'T HAVE
my cell, my wallet or my keys. Lily is off with Xander for god knows
how long, and I'm running towards a non-existent destination
because the most amazing man I've ever met just told me he loves me.
What the hell is wrong with me? I should be running *to* him, not *away*
from him. God, I hate myself right now, but I can't stop myself from
acting on my survival instinct.

I finally slow to a walk when I feel like my lungs are going to
explode, and I find myself at the marina. I don't know how long or
how far I've run. I *do* know that there is a massive pain in my chest,
and it's not from running. I try to blend in with the crowd, slowing
my breaths and wiping the tears I didn't know were there from my
face. It hits me, I've just blown any chance I had at a real relationship
with Carter. There's no coming back from this.

That's when I hear him in the distance.

I quickly turn to scan the crowd, and there he is, breathless, sweating, and gorgeous. He's running his fingers through his hair as he
shouts my name, striding towards me. When he reaches me, I expect
some sort of grand romantic kiss, or speech, but he just grabs my
hand and drags me through the crowd without a word.

"Let me go, Carter, you're hurting me." The glare he gives me chills me to the bone, but he loosens his grip ever so slightly.

"Hurting you? *I'm hurting you?* Holy fuck, Addi. You have no fucking idea how your actions and reactions affect those around you, do you? You're just off in Addi-land doing your Addi-thing and fuck the rest of us."

"That's not true and you know it. You don't get to judge me because you decided to pour your goddamn heart out, completely out of the blue."

"You really are a heartless bitch sometimes."

We continue on in silence for a moment. I can't argue with him because I know he's right, and I'm ashamed of myself, but I don't know any other way to be. As the crowd dwindles, I notice we're walking down the pier, with yachts lining either side of us. He pulls me in the direction of a stunning vessel with the name "Vittoria" emblazoned across the back.

"Seriously? You want to show off your goddamn boat right now? You are such a fucking swanktard." He turns to face me, pure rage in his eyes.

"What the fuck does that even mean?"

"You're being a swanky bastard at the most ridiculous time possible." Oh God... I just poked the beast. He looks livid.

"When have I ever tried to win you with fucking "swanky" shit? You come from the same background as me, Addison. I'm well aware that none of this impresses you. I thought *maybe* the fact that I'm a good guy who wants to be with you would be impressive enough, but apparently *nothing* is good enough for you." He picks me up, jumps onto the boat, and sets me down, before storming below deck. I follow him.

"Okay... okay... you don't need to get so angry about it."

"*Angry?* You haven't even *seen* angry yet. I'm about to go fucking thermonuclear if you don't sit THE FUCK down and listen to me." I do as he asks. Not because he scares me. I know he would never hurt me. I sit because I need to hear what he has to say.

"Don't mistake me bringing you here for romance *or* love, or me trying to impress you! This is the only place I can take you where I won't get arrested for breach of the peace. I am so fucking angry right now."

"I can see that." Why can't I stop talking? Every word out of my mouth just makes this situation much worse.

"Can you just keep your mouth shut for five minutes, Addi? Si guida pazzesco." *[You drive me crazy]* If he's going to speak freaking Italian, how am I supposed to respond? I have no idea what the hell he's saying.

"I need to say this and you need to fucking hear it."

"In English, please."

"Oh. My. God, Addi. Do you know why I speak Italian so often around you? Because you drive me fucking crazy! You really had no idea I was in love with you, did you?" I shake my head. His use of the past tense isn't lost on me.

"How could you not know, Tesoro?"

"What does 'Tesoro' mean?" His features soften with a defeated sigh.

"It means treasure."

"But you've called me that from the first night we met."

"Look at me when I say this, baby." I lift my eyes as a shiver of nerves run through me. "I may not have realized it then, but you had me snared, hog-tied and besotted with you from the first touch of your hand." I feel like my heart is going to burst right out of my chest. I want to reciprocate and tell him how he makes me feel, but I can't, I'm just too damaged. The silence is deafening. "You seriously have nothing to say to me? I'm not asking for love, or marriage, or even for you to move in with me. All I want is some fucking acknowledgement that you feel anything for me. Am I just a fuck buddy for you? I thought you felt the same intense connection I feel when we're together, but maybe it's one-way fucking traffic." He starts running his fingers through his hair, frantically searching my face for an answer I can't force myself to give. I know this could be the moment he walks away, and I desperately want him to stay, but I know he would be better off without me.

"What do you want me to say, Carter? You know me. You know that this kind of shit isn't my style. We've had a good run, longer than I would usually stick around. Maybe what we have has just run its course."

"If you're going to talk shit, Addi, at least say it like you mean it. Do you remember what I told you in the club that night?" He stalks toward me, looming over me with his imposing frame, his hands gripping the back of the sofa on either side of me. "I told you, you make me feel helpless, frustrated, desperate, and fucking turned on beyond all reason. I feel that tenfold today, baby. Why can't you admit it? Tell me you don't feel the same and I'll walk away and move on. Just say the words."

I can't… it would be a lie. "I… I… I don't know what to say. I can't be what you want me to be."

He runs the back of his hand down the side of my face, a menacing look on his face.

"Okay, Addison. Have it your way. Rather than fight with you for the rest of the weekend, I'm going to fuck you until you not only forget about all this shit you keep spouting, but until you forget your own goddamn name. Don't speak, don't make a fucking sound. Just let me blow your messed up, fucking beautiful mind."

I couldn't speak right now even if I wanted to. The fire in his eyes, the desire emanating from his delicious body, has me dumbstruck.

"Get up and take off your clothes… now."

I open my mouth to protest his curt demand.

"Don't say a word, Addi. I mean it."

I do as I'm told, stripping off my clothes and my underwear until I'm standing before his fully clothed form, completely naked and wet for him. I am so turned on by his angry demeanor, I know that I'm slick and ready for him.

"Wait here."

He disappears above deck for at least ten minutes. I wait, shaking and panting with desire, desperate for his touch, his caress, his beautiful big cock inside me. When he finally returns, I'm so turned on I can barely think straight. He takes my hand and pulls me behind him toward the stairs, snapping me out of my sexual haze.

"I'm not going up there. What if someone sees me? I'm freaking naked here unless you hadn't noticed." He continues to pull on my arm.

"You *will* come outside with me because I told you to. Do you honestly think I would let anyone look at your body but me? You really have no fucking clue, do you? The first night we met, I told you I won't fucking share you. Not any part of you. I already checked, and there's no one around for miles... no one to hear you scream."

"If I have no clue, then why don't I just leave you to it? You can crack one off in the moonlight."

"Don't fucking push me, Addi. What did you NOT understand when I told you I AM going to fuck you until you stop talking shit?" He's so damn full of himself.

"What if I don't want you to fuck me?" He stops dead, turning to face me on the stairs.

"Oh I *know* you want it, baby."

He pulls me up onto the deck before thrusting his hand in between my legs, letting his fingers caress my entrance. His satisfied grin both annoys me and turns me on at the same time. I watch as he lifts his fingers to his mouth, spreading the evidence of my arousal over his lips before darting his tongue out for a taste.

"Your body always gives you away, sweetheart. You're soaking wet for me, just at the thought of how hard I'm going to fuck you. Your breasts are full and heavy, your nipples begging for my attention and your eyes... you can't hide what you're feeling from me. I see you, Addi... I see your joy, your pain, your desire... and fucking hell, the desire in your eyes right now has me hard as a fucking rock." My gaze moves to his crotch and his massive erection, straining to break free from the confines of his pants. "You want it, baby? It is *all* for you. For your tight little body and your smart fucking mouth." As he unbuttons his pants and pushes them down just enough to let his dick spring free, I can't help biting my lip.

"See, Tesoro? I know how badly you want me. You just need to give in to it." He takes his hard length in his hand, stroking the length of it, his breath becoming uneven with each firm pump of his fist. It is so fucking hot. "You like this, baby? Watching me stroke my dick, letting you see how hard you make me?"

I'm mesmerized…

"This is what your hot, sexy little body does to me, Addi. Now, on your knees and I'll give you what you really want." I shamelessly drop to my knees without hesitation, desperate for a taste of him.

He moves closer, his dick brushing my lips before he pulls back. He grabs a fistful of my hair, holding me in place as he speaks.

"Open wide."

I do as he asks, moving forward to take him into my mouth.

"Not until I say so."

He holds my gaze, exerting the power he has over me in this moment and I absolutely relish it. It turns me on and affords me a freedom I didn't know I needed.

"You can take me into your smart mouth now, Addison. And remember, you only get to enjoy this massive cock of mine because I fucking let you." I can tell he is mortally wounded from our earlier fight, and all I want to do is make him feel better. I will do anything he asks to make up for hurting him so badly. I wrap my lips around the swollen crest of his cock, kissing and licking as I go, eliciting the sexiest, husky groan. I take him as deep as I can, using my hand to stroke the remaining length of him. He is so big, and he tastes amazing.

"That's it, baby. Just like that… you fucking love doing that, don't you?"

I nod my head as I continue to work his cock, loving the feel of his skin against my tongue, smooth silk around a solid steel shaft. God, it's amazing. As I start to move faster, working him harder, sucking, teasing and swirling my tongue around him, he tightens his grip on my hair and begins to thrust his hips in time with my movements. I can feel the beginnings of his release pulsing along his thick engorged length, and as his come spills into my mouth, I lap it up, enjoying every drop as I listen to him shouting to the heavens.

"Jesus… Fucking… Christ!"

I sit back on my heels with a satisfied grin, but Carter has other ideas. He picks me up and moves me over into the cockpit, sitting me down on the captain's chair. I watch as he pulls his t-shirt off over his head, his rippling abs glistening with a sheen of sweat and I want to lick every inch of them.

"Spread your legs as wide as you can." His gentle, playful side is gone tonight and what I'm left with is a dominant, desire driven, sexual master.

My legs fall open over either side of the chair letting him see the full extent of my arousal. My folds are swollen with desire, my entrance dripping in anticipation of his touch. I love the look of pure unadulterated lust and appreciation on his face as he drops down in front of me, forcing my legs even further apart as his warm calloused hands push firmly at the apex of my thighs. He slowly runs his tongue from my entrance to my clit in one long, torturous lick. It is heaven and hell rolled into one glorious, erotic sensation.

"Mmm. I wonder how much of this you can stand before you beg me to fuck you." I don't even care that he plans to tease me. I just need his touch... more than I need my next breath.

"Oh God, Carter. I want you... all of you... please!"

"Hold on to the chair."

As soon as I do, his movements become frantic, his scruff rubbing against me in a vigorous, almost painful motion, but the ministrations of his tongue bring a pleasure so intense that I come almost immediately. Screaming his name as I buck wildly against his face. One orgasm is never enough for Carter. He makes me come over and over until I can't control the shaking of my legs or my desperate pleas for him to fuck me.

When I think he's had his fill, he hoists me up, draping me over the captain's wheel, my nipples puckering against the cool polished wood.

"I'm not done with you yet, Addison."

He moves my legs so they're spread wide enough for him to stand behind me, nestled against my naked ass. I hear the rustle of the foil wrapper as he takes the condom from his pocket, but for the first time in my life I don't want any barriers.

"Don't, Carter. Don't use it. I want to feel you." I hear his sharp intake of breath at my request.

"Are you sure?" I can tell he's trying to mask the tenderness I hear in his voice.

"Yes. I have an IUD, it's completely safe. Please, Carter... don't make me beg."

His hands caress my ass as he speaks.

"Maybe I want to hear you beg after the way you've behaved today. Tell me how much you want to feel my cock thrusting inside you... skin to skin." I feel like I'm going to pass out if he doesn't take me soon.

"So fucking badly I can hardly breathe. Take me, Carter... please, let me feel the warmth of your hard, throbbing cock and the wet of your come as it spills inside of me." My words are his undoing.

He grabs my ass and hammers his cock inside me in one deep thrust. It is the most amazing feeling as our bodies become one, and as he starts to move I don't even recognize the moans escaping my chest.

"Holy Fuck, Addi. Tu sei l'altra metà di me. Sei stata fatta per me. Tell me you know. You have to fucking know what this means." Tears well in my eyes. I'm overwhelmed by the love I feel for him. I love him. I'm completely and utterly in love with this man.

I'm screaming as he rides me harder and harder, bringing us to a stratospheric climax together.

"I know, Carter... God... I know!"

As we struggle to get our breathing under control, he slumps over me, his naked chest against my back. His tender side reemerges as he gently caresses me with his fingertips, kissing down my spine, his dick still pulsing inside me as I clench around him.

"Remember how this feels... how I feel inside you, how we feel together. Remember it the next time you want to walk away from me, Addi. Take a fucking minute and think about this moment for both our sakes."

He continues to feather kisses all over my neck and shoulders until I feel him harden again. He pulls out of me agonizingly slowly, leaving me bereft, before taking my hand, leading me back below deck and onto the bed. Without a word, he crawls on top of me, spreading my legs and pushing his hard length inside me. He brushes my hair out of the way with his fingertips, before tracing the lines of my face as if he's trying to memorize each and every detail. My breathing is shallow, my heart pounding in my chest as his lips crash down on mine. He gently starts to swivel his hips building us toward a deep, intense, soul destroying climax. He completely shatters all of my defenses, leaving me naked and vulnerable in his arms, and there is nowhere else I'd rather be.

I don't know how long we stay on the boat, enjoying the silence, lying in each other's arms as we gaze at the sky above. If I could ever know true serenity, this would be it. It could have been hours for all I know, but the minute my stomach rumbles, Carter has me up and in his arms.

"Let's get you home and fed, Tesoro." I wish I could speak Italian. It sounds so beautiful as it rolls off his tongue.

"What did you say to me back there, when you were inside me? You spoke Italian." I see a fleeting look of indecision cross his masculine features before he speaks.

"I said, you are the other half of me. You were made for me. You felt that, didn't you? When we were joined, skin to skin, with no barriers between us, tell me you felt it, too?" His eyes are asking me so much more than his question, but I answer him all the same, hoping that one day I can say the words he needs to hear.

"Yes, Carter… I felt the same way." It's all I can choke out past the emotion crushing my windpipe, but it's enough for him. It's enough for us… for now. He tucks me under his arm as we walk back to the beach house in a sweet, comfortable silence—perfectly content.

CHAPTER 16

CARTER

WHEN I TOOK OFF AT A SPRINT AFTER ADDI THE OTHER NIGHT, THE only thought in my head was 'don't let her go, don't let her leave.' Everything that happened after was a blur of pure emotion, a build-up of anger and off the charts lust. She makes me so fucking angry sometimes, but this was a whole new level of rage. I knew she would react badly when I finally said the three words she's so terrified of, but I fucked up, telling her the way I did, and she supremely fucked up when she decided to run. I didn't see that coming. I thought she would yell and shout, but to *literally* run away from me... fuck, her issues go much deeper than I thought. I know for a fact that she feels the same way. She loves me, but she would rather sabotage what we have, than admit it. I couldn't protect Vittoria from Marcus, but I *will* protect Addi from herself and her past, even if it kills me.

We've had a great weekend with Xander and Lily. She's good for him, and the more I get to know her, the more I like her. Their relationship seems so easy in comparison to Addi and I. They love each other fiercely and they're not afraid to show it. They obviously have complete faith in the relationship, and their feelings for one another. I'm seriously beginning to doubt if things will ever be like that for us. In all honesty, I think I would get bored if things were too perfect, but fuck me, I wouldn't mind it being a hell of a lot easier than it is right now.

Addi has been quiet and a little detached since our showdown on the yacht. Fair play to her, she really knows how to flip the switch and put on a brave face when she needs to. I don't think Xander and Lily have any idea what's been going on with her. I don't hide it half as well.

Xander and I decide to head out for a jog on the beach before we go back to the city, and the first thing he does is call me on my mood.

"What's going on with you and Addi? You're like a bear with a sore head this morning, and I only know one person who gets you this twisted up. What happened when Lily and I left you guys yesterday?" He can read me like a book and I hate it!

"It's so fucked up, man, I don't think you would believe me if I told you."

"Try me. Just don't cry on me like a pussy." He thinks he's so funny.

"Shut the fuck up. When have I *ever* cried? I have balls remember. Big… Italian… balls." I take off running, needing a few minutes to breathe in the fresh sea air before I explain what's going on.

"I told her I loved her."

"That's great, Carter. I'm happy for you." I can't help but laugh.

"Don't be. She did a runner on me. Literally. She fucking ran away when I said it, and I had to go after her." I glance in his direction to confirm the shocked look I know is there.

"Seriously? What happened when you caught up to her? It can't have been that bad, you're still together."

"Xander… I have never known anyone like her. She has some serious shit to deal with. I can see it in her eyes. It's the same look I've seen in Vittoria's eyes all these years." He comes to an abrupt halt, grabbing my arm to get my attention. I turn to see the recognition in his eyes.

"I'm so fucking sorry, Carter. I had no idea. Lily never mentioned anything." He knows what I'm talking about. He was at my fourteenth birthday party, and he's the only friend I have who knows what happened to Vittoria.

"I don't think Lily knows. Fuck... I don't know exactly what happened to her, but I know it must be pretty bad. She just fucking shuts me out as soon as shit gets real. It tears me up to see her so broken. I swore I would never get seriously involved with a woman for this very reason, but I can't walk away. I love her, but I can't help her if she won't tell me what happened. It's so fucking frustrating."

"You know she's crazy about you. It's obvious to anyone who's been in the same room as you two. The chemistry between you guys is off the fucking charts. She'll come around, you just need to hang in there." He doesn't realize how fucked up last night was, but I'm not going to go into the details with him. I don't understand it myself, so I wouldn't even know where to start.

"It is what it is. I've told her I won't let her run again and I fucking meant it. Anyway... are we here to shoot the shit or are we going to run?" Xander knows me better than anyone, and he gets the message. He takes off running, and when I catch up to him we clock up the miles in silence, at a good pace. It's exactly what I needed before going back to the city.

One month later

OUR CRAZY NIGHT IN THE HAMPTONS WAS ALMOST A MONTH AGO NOW, and things with Addi are better than ever. She still plays her cards close to her chest, but I feel like she's opening up, little by little. I haven't used the 'L' word since in case she freaks out... again. I need her to feel safe enough to let me in. I've tried talking to her, but she's a master at evading the question and changing the subject. She's told me little snippets here and there about Gavin and how he cheated on her. She thought he was the one, he said he loved her, and she gave herself to him body and soul, and he fucking crushed her. He slept around behind her back until she walked in on him with another girl, and that was the end for her. She obviously suspected he was playing around, but until she saw it with her own eyes, she gave him the benefit of the doubt. Listening to her talk about him makes me want to find him and beat the shit out of him. He broke her, and for what, to get some extra pussy? If I ever met this guy I would fucking kill him, without blinking.

Work has returned to the usual, endless mayhem. Addi is working all the hours under the sun, and I've just acquired a new club on the Upper East Side. I now own and run six of the hottest clubs in Manhattan. I'm ecstatic that business is going through the roof. I've always lived and breathed my clubs, but lately I'm beginning to think it might be a good idea to take a step back. I would like to hire someone to oversee my growing empire, so that I can actually enjoy the money I make and have some fun! Tonight is opening night of the new club, Vortex. All of my clubs are high-end, expensive, and plush with the best quality VIP lounges in the city, but Vortex is a different breed altogether. The entire club is one big VIP lounge. A playground for Manhattan's rich and famous. The staff have all signed NDAs so that whatever happens in Vortex, stays in Vortex. When people pay this much to have a good time, they expect to be able to let loose in a way they can't anywhere else.

I've been at the club all day, making sure everything runs smoothly. All that's left for me to do now is grab a quick shower and get changed. I'm going to head over to Addi's apartment, get ready, and bring her back with me. Xander, Lily, Logan and his latest arm candy, will be joining us later for the celebrations. I can't wait to show them around this place. The private rooms are off the charts luxurious, with a little kink for those who so desire it. It's probably right up Logan's alley. I'm certain he's a deviant of some sort... dirty bastard! He's such a fucking smooth talker when it comes to women, they just lap it up. They probably beg him to take them to the dark side! I guess I shouldn't really judge... I'm not exactly a saint myself. A lot of the shit I've done with women could be considered deviant behavior, and I loved every fucking minute of it, and there are some things I miss. Don't get me wrong, I love Addi, and the sex is hot, but I would love to explore anal play with her. I'm getting hard just thinking about it—

slipping my fingers inside her, readying her for my cock driving between her perfect cheeks, all the while pounding her pussy with a vibrator. The screams I could elicit from her would be fucking sublime, but shit... I need to stop torturing myself with this fantasy. I think about baseball for a few minutes, letting my raging hard-on subside before I leave the club and make my way to Addi's place.

THE CLUB IS A LIVING ORGANISM TONIGHT, ALIVE, PULSING WITH THE rhythm of the music. The DJ is on fire, the staff are working together perfectly to provide an impeccable service to our clientele, drinks are flowing and everyone is enjoying the party. I manage to check in with Addi and the guys a couple of hours into the night, but Addi is such a fucking distraction when I'm supposed to be working. She had to drag me from her apartment earlier because she looked so goddamn hot, I would have sold every club I own to stay in with her and fuck until neither of us could see straight.

She's wearing a short, black, one-shouldered dress. It's simple and sexy, with a killer pair of heels that make me want to strip her and fuck her while she digs them into my back. She's sexy in a pair of jeans, but when she really goes all out for a night on the town... fuck me! I want to rip her fucking clothes off right now.

I can sense her, wherever she moves, whatever she's doing, I can *feel* her. It's been tough watching an endless stream of guys obviously trying to impress her while I do my due diligence with the high-profile guests. There are a few A-list actors and actresses in tonight, some big names in the music business and plenty of Manhattan's socialites. I feel like I've been manhandled by hundreds of women by the time I make my way over to spend some time with Addi. I pull her tight to my chest, letting the smell of cherries wash over me for a moment before I let her go.

"Nice to see you, too, sailor. Your henchmen here have been keeping the men away with their death stares. Did you give them that instruction?" She cracks me up.

"No, I didn't, but they know me well enough by now to keep the pricks away from you so that I don't get arrested for assault with a deadly weapon. You're mine, baby, and no one touches what's mine."

She rolls her eyes at me. "Under normal circumstances I would cuss you out for referring to me as an object… but…" She runs her hand down my chest. "You look so goddamn sexy tonight, I might let it slide… as long as you *slide* into me later." She leans in close to my ear, her breath a sensual caress. "And I can assure you I am *more* than ready for you."

"Holy shit, Addi. I have a massive hard-on right now." Her hand slips between us, grabbing my cock through my pants.

"You really… are… massive… Mr. de Rossi." Fuck, I need to get her home.

"Baby, you *need* to stop doing that or I'll take you into one of the private rooms and ravish you for the rest of the night."

"Is that supposed to deter me? I would say it's an incentive to keep rubbing your cock. Maybe it's like a magic lamp… if I rub it enough I'll be granted three wishes!"

I'm laughing as I respond. "Rub my cock like that, Tesoro, and I'll give you anything your heart desires." She takes great delight in pushing me away with a smirk on her face.

"Now come and say hello to your friends before you go back to schmoozing the elite, and later I might grant *you* a wish or two." She takes my hand and leads me over to where everyone's sitting.

Xander and Lily are cuddled up as close as two people can possibly get without fucking, laughing, drinking, and just… enjoying each other. Logan is here with a new girl, I didn't even bother remembering her name. I'm sure she'll be history by the next time we all get together. She's gorgeous, slim, and petite—and behaves exactly the same way as the rest of the women I've ever seen him with—compliant. They hang on his every word, doing whatever he asks. He must be hung like a fucking horse. As soon as they see me, I'm met with a round of applause before they all stand up to congratulate me on my new venture.

Xander is first to comment. "You've outdone yourself with this place, Carter. It's perfect for those of us with more money than sense! Seriously, though, fantastic job. Can't wait to get Lily alone in one of those plush private rooms." I laugh as he steps aside to let her give me a hug and her congrats.

"This place is amazing, Carter. I love it. Congratulations." I thank her and turn my attention to Logan who already has a shit-eating grin on his face.

"Carter… those private rooms are fucking amazing. I've already spent a little time in one with Cheryl-Ann. She particularly liked the chaise in there." The look on his face tells me it wasn't so much the chaise, as whatever they were doing on it.

"Do I need to disinfect that room already?"

He throws his head back and laughs. "What can I say, man? There's a reason her nickname is Cat. She purrs like a fucking kitten when I'm licking her…"

"Stop! I don't want to know. That's a $10,000 piece of furniture you just defiled!" I try to say it with a straight face, but I can't help laughing.

He doesn't seem like himself tonight. He's definitely a little drunk. He's not normally so forthcoming with information regarding his conquests, and he tends to hold his liquor pretty well. I pull Addi aside. "What's going on with Logan?"

"Nothing that I know of. We were all having a laugh earlier, I was telling Lily how Vittoria is getting on with her latest tour. I showed them all some pictures of her on Facebook with the dance company, and her with her new man candy. We had some drinks and then Logan disappeared with Cat for a while. He's just a little drunk, Carter. I'm sure he's fine." The look in her eyes tells me she knows more than she's letting on, but a tap on the shoulder from one of my staff means I have business to attend to.

The rest of my night is spent taking care of the A-List guests, and it's not until the club is closed and the last of the revelers have left that I catch a glimpse of my girl, carefree and dancing with her best friend, laughing and joking. Xander has the same fucking goofy look on his face that I'm sure I have on mine. I just love seeing her happy, without a care in the world, and it makes my night to see the smile on her face right now.

She doesn't notice me until I move in behind her, snaking my arms around her waist, letting her grind her perfect little ass into my groin.

"Ready to go home now?" She nods her head as she continues to grind against me.

Xander comes over and lifts Lily off the floor. "Let's get you home, sweet girl. I have some not so sweet plans for you."

"Thanks for waiting with Addi, bro. I really appreciate it."

"No worries. These two are impossible to separate once you let them loose in the same room. But I do need to get my girl home and remove this ridiculously small dress. Later, bro." Lily shouts her good-byes as Xander drags her out the door, desperate to get her alone. I can understand that. All I want to do right now is lose myself in Addi.

"Your place or mine?"

"Let's go to your place. I like your bed better than mine now." I need to bite my tongue to refrain from asking her to move in with me after her innocent admission.

"Your wish is my command… now about you rubbing my cock for wishes?" She slaps me in the chest before cuddling into my side as we head out to my car. It's such an affectionate gesture from her that most people would take for granted, but not me. I know the little things are a big deal for Addi, and I appreciate every indication that she's trying to move forward with me. I hold her close, silently thanking my lucky stars.

CHAPTER 17

ADDI

WHEN WE ARRIVE BACK AT CARTER'S APARTMENT, THE CHARGE THAT always sparks between us is there, but tonight it evolves into something softer, something more sensual, something... more. Our usual frenzied tearing at each other's clothes, fumbling to get to the nearest surface so we can fuck, is replaced by a sensual seduction. Carter silently leads me to his bedroom, before delicately undressing me. His touch is gentle and calculated, as if I might break if he holds me any tighter in his grasp. Every inch he uncovers is met with a soft kiss from his plump, delicious lips, his tongue darting out to taste me, to tease me, his satisfied hum vibrating against my flesh. Desire unfurls in my stomach with every touch.

I return the favor, gently removing each item of his clothes, caressing every inch of him with my fingertips. When I flick my tongue over the tip of his rock-hard cock, he steps back, lifting me to my feet and placing me on the bed with the utmost care.

"Not just yet, baby... later. Right now, I want to feel you, to watch you come apart beneath me, while I slowly thrust inside you, owning you, claiming you with every deliciously slow rock of my hips. Filling you until you can't take it anymore. I want to watch the look of bliss on your face as I come deep inside you." His words alone have me wet and ready for him.

He holds my gaze, and the intensity of this one look, so many unsaid words passing between us, has me panting in anticipation. He grasps his beautiful cock, guiding it to my entrance, before slowing, sensually, sliding inside me, one long torturous thrust until I am completely full of him. His pelvis hits my clit at the perfect angle, spreading a delicious, quiet ripple of sensation throughout my body.

We continue this slow dance together, enjoying every movement of our bodies together as one. I can't take my eyes off him, scared I will break the spell and he'll disappear if I so much as blink. Sex has *never* been like this for me. This is so much more than just sex. The eroticism and emotion of this one moment is devastating in its intensity. I'm close to tears as he slowly worships my body, and his tender words are my undoing.

"Tesoro… ti amo." *[I love you.]*

I can't help the tears trickling in a constant, silent stream down my cheeks at his whispered words of adoration. As he moves slowly inside me, filling me, claiming me, and loving me, a sob escapes my chest.

"What's wrong, Addi? Did I hurt you?" He searches my face for a sign. "Please… mia bella fidanzata… talk to me." *[My beautiful girlfriend]*

He stills inside me, our bodies connected in the most profound of ways as the words I've held in for so long spill forth.

"No one has ever made love to me before."

He holds his weight on his elbows, raising his fingers, gently caressing the tears from my eyes.

"I love you, Addi. You deserve to be loved and adored… and made love to, every single day of your life. You mean so much to me. I've been making love to you for a long time now… tonight is just the first time you've realized it."

"I… I never thought I would *ever* feel this way, Carter. Not after Gavin." The full force of it all hits me square in the chest. A stark contrast to the man in front of me. The difference between Carter's love for me, and what *he* called 'love' is glaringly obvious to me now.

I feel bereft as Carter pulls out of me, breaking contact, but only for a split second before he scoops me up into his arms and nestles me safely against his chest. He moves with me as if I weigh no more than a feather, positioning his back against the headboard of his massive bed, before pulling the covers around us.

"Tell me what happened, baby... please... if you can."

I've never told anyone what really happened behind closed doors between Gavin and me. But now, in this moment, I need to relieve myself of the baggage and burden I've been carrying around for far too long. Carter doesn't push me or speak another word. He simply strokes my back as I listen to his steady heartbeat, taking comfort and courage from it. He gives me the time I need to formulate the words I've never said to another living soul.

"Gavin didn't *just* cheat on me." My voice is small and almost unrecognizable, even to me. "When I met him, I was a naïve girl straight out of high school, in love with the fantasy of my new life at college, and what better way to complete the pretty picture than by dating the most popular, dreamy guy on campus. All the girls loved him. He had a way about him, no matter who he was talking to, he made them feel like the only person in the room. When he asked me out on a date I was so excited, every freshman girl wanted to be me.

We started dating and for the first few months my life was close to perfect. We'd said, 'I love you,' we made love, and everything about him drew me in, made me believe he was 'the one.' As time went on, he started to change. He wasn't quite so attentive, and I'd notice him looking at other girls, not even trying to hide it. Then he started asking for things in the bedroom that I just didn't want to do. At first, he just sulked about it, was nasty to me, or just plain ignored me for a few days. Then..."

The words begin to choke me, the memories suffocating as I gasp for air. I can feel Carter's heart hammering in his chest as he tries to give me the space and time I need to continue. "It's ok, baby, I'm right here." His words give me the strength to continue.

"Then... one night, I caught him kissing another girl. He chased after me, professing his love, and telling me it was all a big mistake. I wanted *so* badly to believe him. I let him take me home, but when he tried to kiss me, I burst into tears, hurt by his betrayal. The look in his eyes was pure disgust as he watched my heart break in front of him."

I take a deep breath.

"That was the first night he hit me."

Carter's grip tightens, his whole body rigid, his toned muscles corded and ready to fight.

"The slaps became punches, and the punches turned into beatings. Never where anyone would notice. He was too smart for that. He stopped even *trying* to hide the fact that he was making out with other girls, and by that point I'd started to believe his bullshit lies. I thought it was all my fault. I was too emotional, too frigid, too uptight. If I just did the things he wanted, he wouldn't need to find other willing girls. He started asking for anal sex, which never really appealed to me, but I was desperate to keep him and make him love me again. The night I finally gave in to his demand, it wasn't a request by that point. I thought things would get better between us, back to the way they were when we first met. It was one of the worst nights of my life.

"I could have been anyone. He didn't care how I felt or how rough he was being with me, slamming into me with no warning, no build up. It was... excruciating... and humiliating. He pinned me to the bed, rutting into me like a rabid dog, over and over, so harsh and punishing, pushing my face down into the pillow to muffle my sobs. When he was done... he beat me pretty badly, telling me I better not cry the next time. I was bleeding, sore, and torn from how rough he'd been. I was so used to the other bruises on my ribs, arms and legs. They barely even registered with me at the time.

"He took me that way on numerous occasions, every time leaving me broken and bruised, but I still wasn't enough for him. I walked in on him in bed with another girl. I'd convinced myself that he was just fooling around with other girls, and that he would never *sleep* with them, especially after I gave him what he wanted. It was the last straw for me to see him naked and bucking wildly inside another girl... I took my final hit that night when he caught up to me. It was the worst beating of them all. I ended up in the ER, alone and too ashamed to call Lily or my family. A week later, after I'd recovered, I filed a restraining order against him. I didn't tell the police about the attack, I didn't have to. I had enough evidence in texts and threatening voice messages to have the order enforced with immediate effect. I haven't seen him since."

The silence is deafening as Carter's body vibrates against me, and when he finally speaks, his voice is a low whisper, hoarse and more menacing than I've ever heard.

"He fucking... raped and beat you." I can hear the pity in his voice and see it in his eyes. He thinks I'm completely broken.

"He didn't rape me... I... I let him do those things."

He stops me, his tone stern.

"He sexually assaulted you. You didn't want it, he knew that and he did it anyway. And then he fucking beat the shit out of you. Fucking hell... I need a minute. I'm so sorry, Addi."

I knew he would pull away when he realized just how damaged and fucked up I am. My heart shatters into a million tiny shards. "I understand. I'll go." I move to find my clothes and leave the safety of his apartment, unable to stomach the way he's looking at me.

"What are you doing? Where are you going?"

"I'm leaving. I can't stand to see the pity in your eyes."

"*Fucking pity?* Are you shitting me right now? I only asked for a minute to process everything you've just told me, to stay calm for you, and you want to run away... *again?* It's not pity you see, Addi, it's fucking seething rage, it's fucking undying love... I *love* you... so hard it hurts to take a fucking breath. The idea of anyone hurting you is nauseating... it's fucking abhorrent to me, Addi. Can't you understand that? I... LOVE... YOU...ADDI... I'm so fucking in love with you."

His words are a balm to my broken soul, soothing me, healing me, giving me the strength to speak the words I need to say.

"I... I love you, too, Carter. I'm *in love* with you, but I'm terrified of that feeling."

"So am I, Tesoro. So am I. But I'm *more* terrified of losing you, of losing what we have. Please… trust me. I won't *ever* hurt you like that. I *promise*." He cups my face in his warm callused hands, entreating me with his gorgeous brown gaze. "Trust me. Let me help to make this better for you, claim you back from him. You're mine now, Addi. Let me love you the way you deserve. The way I know you *want* to be loved." I can only nod my acceptance. I'm at a loss for words. Nothing I could say would possibly be enough to express how I feel for this man.

"Wrap your legs around me, Addi." I do as he asks, our naked flesh flush against one another, my breasts tight to his hard, muscled chest.

"I want to show you what it can feel like, to be claimed… everywhere." I understand what he's asking, and his face is telling me it's completely my call. He won't push me.

"Do you trust me, Addi? I've wanted to do this with you for a long time, but now it seems so inconsequential to me. I don't need it to be happy with you. I won't think of you any differently if you don't want to do it. But I *do* want you to feel that every part of your body is *yours*. Not marred by anyone else. Every inch of you is beautiful, Tesoro… inside and out. I want to help you claim back what's yours."

I dip my head down into the safety of his neck, inhaling the scent that gives me such comfort. "I want that, too, Carter, but I'm scared. Please… be gentle."

He plants the softest kiss on my lips. "I will always be gentle, Addi, with your heart and with your body. I won't ever do anything you don't want."

He deepens the kiss, letting me lose myself, feeling only his lips on mine. The desire I felt earlier returns as his hands begin to roam my body. We remain face to face as he lifts me up, letting me lower myself onto his throbbing erection. It feels divine as I seat myself to the hilt, taking all of him inside me. Our bodies slowly begin to move in time, Carter letting me ride him, savoring every upward movement, his eyes closing as I lower myself back down. His fingertips dance across my sensitive flesh, leaving a trail of desire in their wake.

As his hands begin to massage my ass, my body tightens in fear. "Trust me, Tesoro. I will only give you pleasure. You can say stop at any time." He lifts his finger to my lips. "Suck." His face searches mine, concern evident through the desire I see in his flawless features.

"Credetemi, io ti proteggerò… sempre." *[Believe me, I'll protect you… always.]*

He removes his finger from my mouth, replacing it with his tongue, twisting, tangling and teasing as he slides his fingers down my spine. I try to stay relaxed, but it's almost impossible to tame the storm raging inside me. His finger wet with my saliva moves down, teasing at my forbidden entrance.

"Keep moving, baby, use my cock, get yourself hot and sweaty riding me. Let me worry about the rest."

I move my hands up to grip his shoulders, slowly working the length of him, pumping up and down, creating a steady rhythm for both of us. It feels incredible.

"That's it, Addi. Feel how hard I am for you. Feel what you do to me, only you. I'm so close, baby… but I need you to come first. Tell me when you're close."

I ride him, slowly increasing my pace, losing myself to the exquisite ecstasy, giving myself over to the unfamiliar sensation of him teasing my rim. I never thought I would experience pleasure this way, but my nerve endings come alive under his gentle caress, sending a jolt of electricity straight to my pussy, forcing it to clench around Carter's impressive length. I delight in the familiar pull deep in my core as I grind up and down, taking what I need, chasing my release.

"I'm almost there, Carter, I'm going to come… oh my God… yes!" As I reach the peak, ready to crash over the edge and down into the sweet abyss of euphoria, he gently eases his finger inside, holding my body tight to his chest.

"That's it, Tesoro. Take what you need. You are so fucking beautiful when you come for me."

His words together with the sensation he creates, sends me into tailspin. I ride him harder, letting him press his finger all the way inside me, filling me in a way I've never felt before. It only intensifies, the climax radiating from every nerve ending, from every fiber of my being.

"Oh my God, Carter... please... come with me... yes... yes... yes!"

He continues to fill me in every way possible, his tongue owning my mouth, his finger claiming me, and his cock hammering into me as he rears up off the bed, taking me as deep as he possibly can. The guttural roar that tears from his chest is primitive, sexy, and so full of need... for me. I fall in love with him all over again in this moment.

"Addi... fuck... sei mio. Si può sempre e solo essere mio *[you are mine. You can only ever be mine.]* ... Holy Shit!"

We stay wrapped in each other's arms kissing, nuzzling, nibbling at each other. Our bodies slide together with the soft sheen of sweat our lovemaking has created—it's heaven. I could stay like this forever and die happy. It's a long time before either one of us speaks.

"Let's get cleaned up."

Carter stands up with me still wrapped around him, his semi-hard cock still deep inside me. He walks us to the bathroom, sitting me down on the cold granite countertop before pulling out of me and moving to fill the tub, adding some bubbles for my benefit. He lifts me as if I might shatter into a thousand pieces if he's not careful, lowering us both into the tub. He positions my back to his front, wrapping his strong muscular legs around me. I rest my head against his chest, content... for the first time in... forever.

"Ti amo, Addi." He kisses my head, wrapping his arms around me.

"I love you, too, Carter."

I can breathe again...

CHAPTER 18

CARTER

Two Weeks Later

I AM IN AWE OF ADDI. HER COURAGE, HER BRAVERY, HER VULNERABILITY, and her willingness to open up to me, has completely floored me. I am so proud of her. It's a major step forward for her, telling someone, telling *me* what happened. I watched Vittoria go through it, and how hard it was for her to trust people again. It shows an inner strength I knew was there, but until she recognized it herself, no one could help.

That night with Addi was a combination of the most intense rage I've felt since I was fourteen, and the greatest elation I have *ever* felt. I've had to rein in my anger and curb my instinct to hunt down that son of a cunt, Gavin. I would fucking bury him in a shallow grave if I followed my gut. I'm trying to focus on what is important in the here and now—Addi. I'll protect her from any threat, with every breath I take.

In the moments when I feel like my anger is going to swallow me whole, I take a minute and replay the other revelation she shared with me that night—she loves me. It took her a long time to realize it, and to admit it to herself, but when she did, it was the sweetest sentence I have ever heard spoken.

We put her demons to bed, and I claimed every single part of her body as mine. She looked so fucking beautiful riding me wildly as I eased my finger in and out of her, owning her in every way possible. I feel like such a dick for moaning about not being able to do that with her before. I never could have imagined her reasons for not wanting to, and when it finally happened, it was all about her, all about *us*... and nothing at all to do with my sexual gratification. It was an epiphany for me. I've always wanted to make a woman feel good when I'm with her, but it's always been to inflate *my* ego and to enhance *my* enjoyment. That all changed as soon as Addi opened up to me. All I want is for her to feel pleasure in every way possible. To love her body, and everything that we are when we're together, and all the pleasure our bodies can bring to one another. It is the least selfish I've ever been during sex, and at the same time, it gave *me* the greatest satisfaction and pleasure of my life.

Things between us have been amazing since then. We are only going to get stronger, growing together as a couple, and I will *never* get tired of hearing those three little words tripping off her sexy little tongue.

TONIGHT IS XANDER'S NON-BACHELOR, BACHELOR PARTY. HE WANTED to be a complete killjoy and just go out for dinner with the girls, but Logan and I convinced him that we would forever rename him 'Xanadu' if he didn't man up and at least have a guys' night out. This will be the last time the three of us get the chance to hang out like this. I know we'll still see each other, but it won't be the same after he's married, and hopefully, one day, Addi and I will make the same commitment to each other, embarking on our own life adventure together. As for Logan, I don't think he'll ever settle down. He seems to tire of women after a really short period of time.

First, we grab a quick bite at Jason's before heading to one of my clubs for drinks, and to meet up with some of his other friends. Spyder is jumping, just the way I like it. I must be making a killing tonight. It's one of those nights when it really pays to be the owner. I don't think a regular Joe will be getting served a drink for at least half an hour as they fight their way through a sea of people to get the attention of the bartenders. I've had one of the private rooms set up with a pool table, a private bar and our own, female, bartender. Logan is flirting shamelessly within two minutes of setting foot in the door. I don't blame him though, she's hot, and I would have been all over her in my attempts to get her under me, before I met Addi. She's a great worker and a really sweet and funny girl. Logan could do a lot worse, but I know he's only looking for an easy lay tonight, and I get the distinct impression from the way she's looking at him, he's found it. She remains professional, despite Logan's obvious attempts to get her to slip out with him for a little while. Xander and I are busy trying to wipe the floor with each other at pool when Logan finally drags himself away from the bar… and the bartender.

The rest of the night goes by in a blur of booze, pool and possibly some dancing. I don't remember much after Logan insisted on shots. Scotch, beer, and tequila are not the best combination. I vaguely remember him leaving with my bartender, and I have a hazy recollection of hailing a cab to take Xander and I back to my place. I'm almost positive there was more Scotch after that and then I woke up in my bed this morning fully clothed and stinking of booze.

I need coffee.

Dragging my sorry ass out of bed, I strip off last night's clothes and step into a hot shower, my head resting on the tiles to keep myself upright. I stand for at least ten minutes letting the water beat down on me, slowly bringing me back to life. When I feel semi-human, I get dressed and go in search of Xander.

Oh my God. He's already sitting at my breakfast bar, coffee in hand, freshly showered, new clothes and a bag of fresh bagels waiting to be eaten.

"What the fuck, man? How is it that you're up and looking like you had an early night last night?"

He chuckles. "I took two aspirin and a tall glass of water before I went to sleep. Maybe you should have done the same... asshole! I had David bring me clothes and bagels. I might not be hung over, but I'm fucking tired and I couldn't be bothered going out for breakfast."

I tuck into the bagels and coffee. It's my fucking lifeline this morning. After two cups of strong coffee, I feel ready to tackle my day. We spend some time talking about arrangements for the wedding, which is only two weeks away now. I'm the best man, so I have certain things I'm going to have to take care of before we get on a plane to Italy. When I've made a list, and assured Xander a million times that I won't forget anything, he moves on to dissecting my love life.

"So... things seem to be going well between you and Addi these days?" It's a statement and a question rolled into one.

"Yeah. Things are fantastic with us right now. I've never been happier."

"What changed?"

"She finally opened up about her past... and it let us move forward. She's fucking amazing. She's been through so much and now that I know, I can totally understand her reaction when we first got together. I've never felt anything so fucking intense before in my life. It's like a force-field, drawing us together, charging the air between us every time we're in the same room. Fuck, even talking to her on the phone gets me hard."

"That's great, Carter. It's nice to see you guys happy. She obviously loves you and you don't need to be a rocket scientist to see that you're crazy, head over heels in love with her... you big pussy."

I burst out laughing, remembering all the times I've given him shit about Lily. "I guess I deserved that one."

"No shit, Sherlock! She's the one?"

It brings a smile to my face just thinking it. "Yeah, man... she is. I'm going to ask her to move in with me when we get back from Italy." A fleeting look of worry passes across his face. "She's a different person than when we met. She's not afraid to tell me she loves me. We spend every night together at her place or mine, and her shit is already taking over my apartment. It's more of a formality than anything. I wouldn't ask her if I didn't think she was ready."

"Well then, I'm really happy for you both. I know Lily is thrilled to see Addi so happy, and she's always been rooting for you to be the guy who got past the façade. When we get back from our honeymoon, the four of us will need to celebrate. It's a big step I never thought I'd see you take... not after Vittoria."

The atmosphere changes, the gravity of what he's just said, hanging in the air.

"I know. I never thought I'd be able to get past it, but Addi is worth the fear. She's worth the heartache. It'll always be there in the back of my mind, the concern that I might not be able to protect her... but I'm not fourteen anymore, and I will fucking die trying to keep her safe from anything that could hurt her." I hate the knot that forms in my stomach at the mere thought of anything happening to her. I need to stop thinking about it or I'll drive myself crazy.

"I need to lighten the fuck up right now. Let's go get our girls and take them out for the day."

"Great idea."

We text the girls and tell them to be ready in twenty minutes for a day of adventure. They spent the night together at Addi's apartment, so it makes it even easier to grab them and go. We have a great day laughing and joking, excited about our trip to Italy for the wedding of the century... that is... until I marry Addi!

CHAPTER 19

ADDI

Two Weeks Later

As we step out onto the tarmac at Verona Airport, I want to drop to my knees and kiss the ground. I've always been a great traveler, but the flight here had me breathing into a vomit bag for most of the journey. As soon as we took off, my stomach lurched up into my throat and stayed there the entire flight. Lily and Carter were fussing over me, rubbing my back, telling me to put my head between my legs, giving me sips of cold water but nothing seemed to help. I've never been happier to be back on terra firma. I still feel like I'm going to barf, but a nap at the hotel and a proper meal, and I'll be ready to get my maid of honor freak on!

I spend the drive to the hotel with my head in Carter's lap, and not in a good way. The streets are cobbled, bumpy, and not at all helpful to my fight to keep down the breakfast I ate fifteen hours ago. When we finally stop, and I thank Jupiter that I made it here in one piece, Carter lifts me from the car, carrying me into the hotel lobby. I beg him to put me down so he can check us in, but he ignores me, cradling me in his arms while he organizes a key to our suite. He carries me into the elevator and up into our room, only putting me down when he reaches our bedroom.

"You need to rest, baby. A few hours and you'll feel much better." He kisses my head as he lowers me to the bed. "I'll go organize our bags and see if Xander needs me to do anything. I'll be back in a little while, but if you need me, just call." As the door clicks shut behind him I close my eyes and give in to the exhaustion my body is crumbling under, the room spinning as I drift into a fitful sleep.

I JUMP OUT OF BED, RUNNING TO THE BATHROOM, JUST MANAGING TO lift the lid before puking my guts out. I hear footsteps behind me as I hug the bowl.

"Are you ok, baby?"

I take a moment to assess the situation. "Other than the fact that I'm hugging a toilet bowl that isn't my own, I actually feel much better." I slump onto the floor, the cold tiles soothing my clammy skin. "A *lot* better."

He scoops me off the floor, sitting me on the edge of the tub while he rifles through my toiletries. He brings me my toothbrush and toothpaste, shower gel and shampoo. With the utmost care, and the sweetest furl of concentration on his brow, he sets to work pampering me, slowly bringing me back to the land of the living. First, he brushes my teeth, before holding a cup in front of me. "Spit."

"I can walk over to the sink and do this myself, you know."

He kisses the tip of my nose. "Just let me take care of you, Tesoro. I've been sitting here helpless and worrying for the past sixteen hours."

"I've been asleep for sixteen hours? Holy crap! I'm supposed to be helping Lily."

He gently strokes my hair. "I've got your back, baby. I told Xander to take Lily to see Juliet's balcony before the rest of the guests arrive and he doesn't get a minute alone with her. I'm sure he's been enough of a distraction for her today."

"Devious and gorgeous. I'm one lucky girl."

He starts the shower, stripping out of his clothes, holding my gaze as his pants drop and his thick, hard cock springs free. "I won't argue with you there, baby. You are pretty lucky to have all this at your disposal." His hands roam his body as he makes his way over to me, carefully undressing me before lifting me into the shower.

The water cascading over my body is a welcome, refreshing, glorious feeling made even better by the presence of a hot, naked, and very wet Carter. I reach down to run my hand over his cock when he grabs my wrist. "No, baby. You've been ill. I just want to look after you."

"But I think this would *really* help me feel better." I make him laugh as I pout and bat my eyelids at him, shamelessly stroking his cock at the same time.

"You're something else, you know that?"

"Yes... and that's why you love me!"

His eyes turn from playful to smoldering in an instant. He grabs my ass, lifting me off the floor and pressing me up against the tiles. "I do love you... and you love me. It's all that matters, Tesoro."

"I love you, Carter de Rossi. Make love to me. Own me... fuck me." There are no more words, only desperate kisses, clawing, caressing, and loving. We lose ourselves to the sensations that swirl around us, between us, through us. We find each other in the calm that comes from our union—the eye of the storm.

An hour later, after a handful of toe-curling orgasms, I feel so much better, and I find myself ravenous. The sound of my stomach rumbling has Carter dressing me, somewhat grudgingly, and treating me to a fantastic meal in the Piazza Vicino. We watch the crowds as they get ready for a night at the open-air opera in L'Arena. This is where my best friend will marry the love of her life in two days' time, and I can't imagine a more perfect setting for their fairytale to become a lasting reality.

I've eaten my own weight in pasta and had a few glasses of the best Chianti I've ever tasted. Carter orders everything in fluent Italian, chatting and laughing with the waiter as if he were meant to be here.

He's in his element, and it's a beautiful sight. I could get used to Italy… with Carter.

I FIND MYSELF CREEPING OUT OF BED AS QUICKLY AS I CAN WITHOUT waking Carter. I make it to the bathroom, closing the door behind me and sinking to my knees… again. Last night's pasta is *not* good when you're seeing it in reverse. As soon as I've emptied my stomach of its contents, I feel one hundred percent better. I've never had a bug like this before. Yeah, I've puked, and I've felt awful for days at a time, but I usually feel like crap the entire time. The fact that I felt amazing last night, and starving too—it's just not like me. Realization dawns… oh shit.

Oh shit.

Oh Shit.

Oh shit, shit, shit, shit!

This cannot be happening to me. I have a goddamn IUD fitted. I can't be pregnant. As a war wages inside my head, I already know I'm fighting a losing battle. I know this feeling…

I've felt it before.

A knock on the door startles me. "Addi, baby, are you in there?"

I scramble to my feet, flushing the toilet and quickly brushing my teeth. "Yeah. I'll be out in a minute."

"Are you ok? You're not sick again, are you?"

I don't want to lie to him, but I have to. "I feel great, Carter. Stop worrying. I just want to get a head start on today. Lots to do." I open the door and rush past him, eager to get out of this room. It feels so oppressive all of a sudden. "Got to go meet Lily and do the final prep for tomorrow. Then I need to make sure everything is set for the rehearsal dinner tonight."

He slinks up behind me, snaking his arms around my waist as I pull on my jeans. Running his hands down to stop me from zipping them, sliding his hand inside. "I'm sure Lily could wait a half hour." He starts kissing behind my ear, which he knows will weaken my resolve… but not today.

"I really have to get going. I'll make it up to you later. I have *so* much to do."

"And I don't? I'm the fucking best man, Addi. I just wanted to spend a little time with you before it gets crazy." I can't cope with this right now.

I do the only thing I know how to, my go to setting. "Boo-freaking-hoo. Cry me a river so I can float the fuck away."

"What the hell is your problem today, Addi? I swear to God you can go from being the sweetest person I've ever met, to being a complete bitch in two seconds flat." I've hurt him, and it's the last thing I wanted to do, but I need to get out of here before I freak out. "Go do whatever bullshit you think is more important than me. I get that you want everything to be perfect for Lily. I feel the same way for Xander. He's been my best friend since I was born, but don't use it as an excuse when there's obviously something else eating at you."

I reach out to touch him, to offer some sort of comfort, a small apology for my outburst. But he flinches, and my heart breaks a little at the sight of it. "Just go, Addi. I have shit to do, and I don't have time for your games today. I'll see you later." He grabs his clothes and heads into the bathroom, locking the door behind him.

I feel like a colossal bitch right now… because I am one. Carter has been nothing but amazing to me, so understanding of my hang ups and insecurities. If only I had told him the full story when I had the chance, maybe this would be easier. Me being me, I had to make it harder. I couldn't just lay it all out for him and see what happened. First thing's first, I need to go and buy a goddamn test to see if my suspicions are correct.

EVERYTHING RUNS SMOOTHLY AND I MANAGE TO KEEP MY HAPPY FACE firmly in place throughout the day. Lily asked a few times if I was okay, but I just played it off as a little jet lag, nothing to be concerned about. I managed to slip away at one point when Xander was being a naughty boy, chasing Lily around this gorgeous town. It worked in my favor though and I quickly found the nearest pharmacy, bought a pregnancy test, and shoved it to the bottom of my oversized bag.

I only have a half hour before the evening's events kick off. I rush to my room to find that Carter is already gone, and he left a sweet little note for me:

> *Tesoro,*
> *You know I love you more than words.*
> *I'll be waiting for you downstairs with love in my heart,*
> *a smile on my face, and a hard-on in my pants.*
> *Sorry about this morning.*
> *Carter xxx*

I have no idea why he's apologizing, but I love him for it. He can make me smile with the smallest gestures. I really don't deserve him.

I quickly rummage in my bag for the test, ripping it open to pull out the instructions... damn it! My hands are shaking so violently that I can't even keep hold of the box. I drop it on the bathroom floor, the test stick falling out of the packet and onto the cold, hard tiles. I'm immediately transported back in time to when I last had to take a pregnancy test.

I break out in a cold sweat, unable to face the seemingly inconsequential task of peeing on a stick, the outcome of which could change my life forever.

I gather up the contents of the box and shove everything back into my handbag. I can't deal with this right now, so I resolve to take the test first thing in the morning and concentrate on getting ready for a night of smiling and pretending that everything's fine.

The rehearsal dinner is a complete success. Xander and Lily are the picture of a happy couple, and it warms my heart to see Lily so in love. It was a difficult road for her to find Xander, but she's a tough cookie, and I love her more than I could ever express.

When I find Carter he's his usual cocky self. "Hi. Are you *my* Addi?

She loves me so much it's embarrassing at times. She practically worships the ground I walk on. She's fucking adorable, but she has this crazy evil twin who appears sometimes and *she* acts like she wants to rip my head off and spit down my neck. Which one are you? You're both smoking hot, so it's hard to tell the difference."

I throw myself into his strong, safe arms. They feel like home, and I know this is where I want to be.

"There's my girl. I missed you today, Tesoro." He cups my face, planting a gentle, reverent kiss on my lips. He tastes amazing—Carter and Scotch. "You ready to say hello to my parents now? They have been *dying* to meet you since we arrived. I can only hold my mother back for so long, baby."

I feel ok about meeting them. This is a major step forward for me, and considering my current predicament, I can only assume it's a good thing. Carter has shown me time and time again how much he loves me, and would do anything for me. He didn't judge when I told him about what happened with Gavin. His opinion of me didn't change, he just kept on loving me. When I take the test tomorrow, I'm just going to tell him. I think we can handle it. It's not the way I would have planned it, but I love him, and want to spend the rest of my life with him.

"Okay, let's go meet your parents."

"I've already met them, baby. I've known them my whole life." He thinks he's so funny, and I know he's trying to ease my nerves.

"Ha-freaking-ha. You know what I mean."

He leads me over to where I see Vittoria talking with an older gentleman who bears a striking resemblance to Carter. Wow. If this is how he's going to age, I am definitely sticking around. Next to him is a stunning, petite woman, with black hair, tanned skin, flawless complexion, and an air of sophistication you just can't fake. I love her instantly.

"Ciao, Mamma. I'd like you to meet my girlfriend, Addison Warner." He kisses her on either cheek before presenting me to her. She looks me up and down before pulling me into a heartfelt hug.

"Ciao, Bella. You are very beautiful, Addi. I have heard so much about you from Carter and Vittoria. It is a pleasure to finally meet the woman who has captured my son's heart." I blush at her words.

"The pleasure is all mine, Mrs. de Rossi." She's shaking her head at me.

"Mrs. de Rossi is my mother-in-law. Please, call me Ria."

Carter is already turning me in the direction of his father. "Ciao, Babbo. This is Addi."

He holds me firmly by the shoulders, kissing each cheek before he speaks. "It is wonderful to meet you, Addi. We were beginning to think you were a figment of Carter's imagination, but I don't think even he could have dreamt of someone as beautiful as you."

"Why thank you, sir. I do believe I know where Carter gets his charm."

He turns to Carter with a wide grin. "This one's a keeper, son. Don't let her get away."

"Don't worry. I don't plan on it." He pulls me to his side, wrapping his arm around my shoulder.

I chat with Ria and Vittoria for a while, catching up on what Tori has been doing on tour. I've missed seeing her, but we keep in touch and have become really good friends.

Ria watches as we laugh, joke and swap funny stories. "It is lovely to see how easily you have become a part of both my children's lives. When you have kids of your own you'll understand just how much it warms a mother's heart."

Carter butts in on our conversation. "Calm it down, Mamma. There will be NO children in the near future, if at all. Let us be. We're happy just the two of us."

My heart sinks… drowns… as the words fall from his lips. The lips I love, the ones I thought would welcome a child who is a part of me and of him into the world. I never even considered the fact that he might not want kids. The room starts to spin, my legs giving way beneath me. Carter catches me before I fall. "Addi… are you ok? What's wrong?"

I steel myself to answer him, unable to tell him the real reason for my collapse. "Just feeling a little lightheaded. It's really hot in here, and I think I may have had a glass of wine too many." He helps me over to one of the tables, kneeling in front of me as I attempt to stop the spinning in my head. "Could you get me a glass of water, please? And don't let Lily see me. She'll worry over nothing."

He does as I ask, returning quickly with a concerned look on his face. "You haven't been right since we got here. Maybe we should get you to a doctor."

"No! I'm fine... honestly." I'm silently begging him with my stare.. "I'm still a little run down after the travel sickness, that's all. I'll get a good sleep and be fine tomorrow. Stop worrying."

He bends down, kisses my head and looks deep into my eyes. "I will *always* worry about you, Tesoro. I love you. You're all that matters to me."

I close my eyes, savoring his words, knowing my time with him may be limited. He doesn't want kids, and if this test comes back positive, I *know* I can't get rid of the baby—our baby. I can only pray that I'm wrong, that the test will be negative and I won't lose the only man I've ever truly loved.

CHAPTER 20

CARTER

I CAN'T BELIEVE XANDER IS GETTING MARRIED TODAY. WE'VE BEEN BEST friends all our lives, literally, since birth. He's not just my friend, he's my brother. Life couldn't be better. He's marrying the girl of his dreams, who happens to be best friends with the girl of my dreams. Although, if my girl doesn't get her ass out of the bathroom sometime soon, this day isn't going to happen at all. I've already had Xander texting me asking where I am, and Lily has been texting Addi's phone, which is sitting next to the bed while she hogs the bathroom. It's not like her to lock the door, but I figure she's a little stressed with the whole maid of honor gig.

"Addi, are you ever coming out of there or do I need to tell the bride and groom that we're changing the location of the wedding to the executive suite bathroom?"

"Fuck off, Carter. I'll be out when I'm goddamn ready."

"Open the fucking door, Addi. Now." I wait, ready to kick the fucking thing in if I have to, but I hear the click as she unlocks the door and brushes past me. "What the fuck is going on? Wait... have you been crying?"

"Leave me alone, Captain Obvious."

"What the fuck have I done now?"

"Nothing. My best friend is getting married today. I'm allowed to be a little emotional for crying out loud."

"Yeah, I understand that. But you haven't been yourself since we got here, and you're starting to piss me off." I just poked the bear.

"Piss you off? Well why don't you save us both the trouble of wasting our time and just leave me already? We'll call it quits and be done with it."

"Have I just walked into the fucking twilight zone? Where the *fuck* did that come from? I'm not going anywhere. This... what we have... is not a waste of time. I'm *not* quitting on you... because I love you! Get with the program, will you?"

She breaks down, crumpling to the floor like I've never seen her before. So fragile, and I don't even know why. All I can do is offer her some comfort. "I'm not going anywhere, Tesoro. It's just you and me. Okay? No one and nothing will come between us. It took me this long to find you, I'm not about to let anything get in the way of us being together. Will you please believe me when I tell you, you are *it* for me? All I want... is you."

She sobs against my chest as I rock her body back and forth in my lap, trying to sooth whatever it is that has her spooked. The rocking turns into kissing, the kissing turns into caressing, and before I know it, Addi is the one begging me to make love to her. I don't hesitate. I can see the need in her eyes, and want to reassure her that I'm here, and I will give her anything she needs. I would do anything for her. Lifting her off the floor, I take her to the bed and make love to her, my eyes never leaving hers. The connection between us is a physical presence in the room. It's the first time that we've come together in quiet moans of appreciation with the intensity of our joint release held tight between us, inside us, around us.

∾

WHEN ADDI AND I FINALLY WENT OUR SEPARATE WAYS TO GET THE BRIDE and groom ready to tie the knot, I had a knot of my own, deep down in my gut, a feeling of dread I just couldn't shake.

Xander called me on my mood while he was standing at the altar, waiting on Lily. I felt like a total bastard, having him being concerned about *me* on *his* wedding day. But, it all paled into insignificance when I saw Addi walking down the aisle, a beaming grin on her face, her eyes fixed on me, looking so breathtaking I just wanted to run to her, touch her, to check that she was real.

The ceremony went off without a hitch and everyone is having a great time at the reception. Addi and Vittoria have spent a lot of time together, Xander and Lily have been completely wrapped up in each other, and I've been shooting the shit with Logan. He seems distracted, but I've given up trying to understand him lately. Besides, I'm pretty distracted myself as I watch Addi across the room. Her carefree laugh, her mischievous grin and her smoking' hot body teasing me with every move.

When it comes time for the bride and groom to make their exit, I find Addi in the crowd, her eyes moist with unshed tears. "You ok, baby?"

"Yeah, I'm just so pleased for Lily. She deserves to be happy more than anyone." I hold her tight to my chest, feeling her sweet little body melt against mine.

"*You* deserve to be happy, Tesoro, more than anyone I've ever met. Let me make you happy. Travel around Italy with me." As she lifts her eyes in surprise, Xander and Lily pounce on us.

"You didn't think we would leave without saying goodbye, did you?" Lily envelopes Addi is a tight hug as they both let the tears flow.

"We'll see you in a few weeks. Thanks for everything, brother." Xander pulls me in for a man hug/slap on the back.

"I'm really happy for you, Xander. Have a great honeymoon. We'll catch up with you guys when you get back."

He turns his attention to Addi, giving her a hug. "Look after my boy here. He loves the shit out of you." She gives him a small smile and a nod, before tucking herself under my arm.

Two minutes later and they're gone, but the party is still in full swing.

"Dance with me?" I hold out my hand, happy to feel Addi's warm, elegant fingers slide into my palm. I lead her onto the floor and begin to sway, holding her hand against my chest, nestled between us, my other hand skimming her lower back. As she rests her head on my shoulder, I feel myself relax for the first time today. "Will you let me show you Italy, Tesoro? New York will still be there in a couple of weeks. I already checked to see if you could take the time off. I hope you don't mind. I thought we could use some time together, just the two of us. No work, no pressures, just us. What do you think?"

She slinks her arms up and around my neck, pulling me down into a tender kiss, her intoxicating scent invading my senses. "Sounds perfect. Thank you." Her voice is small, and she sounds choked with emotion as her words tumble forth. "I love you so much, Carter, you know that, don't you?"

I stop moving, my hands coming to rest on each side of her stunning face, my eyes fixed on hers. "I *know*, Addison. I *know* you love me. We can work through anything as long as we're together. Just you and me now. Tu sei tutto quello che vedo il mio, Tesoro."

"What does that mean?"

"It means you are *all* I see." Her lips find mine in an urgent kiss. A fervent plea for… what… I'm not sure. But I will find out, and I *will* make it better for her.

"Make love to me all night. Show me you love me, Carter." Without another word, I lead her from the dance floor, the beginnings of Bruno Mars *Just The Way You Are*, playing in the distance.

We walk through the cobbled streets of Verona, hand in hand, the tension rising as the streets close in on us, shielding us from the outside world, from reality. We're trapped in a Shakespearian tragedy of love and loss. A feeling of desperation wells up inside me, the dread from earlier rearing its ugly head. I won't be able to breathe if I don't touch her, taste and feel her… now. As if reading my mind, she stops mid-stride turning to face me.

"Touch me, Carter. Here… Now… Fuck me the way I need you to." Her eyes beg me, and I can't refuse.

I pull her down a quiet cobbled alley, only realizing at the last minute, we're at Juliet's balcony. It's deserted at this time of night, and completely secluded. A perfect place for a lovers' tryst. "Take off your panties and lift your dress for me, baby. Let me see how wet your sweet little pussy is."

She does as I ask without question. "I'm so wet for you, Carter." Spreading her legs wide, she props one foot up on the statue of Juliet, opening herself up to my roving eye. I make short work of the distance between us, dropping to my knees, grabbing her ass and pulling her pussy into my mouth.

"You taste so fucking sweet, Addi. I could eat you all night… and I intend to, but for now a quick taste will have to suffice until I can get you back to our bed."

I flatten my tongue against her folds, licking from her entrance, dripping with arousal, up the length of her until I reach her clit, swollen and ready to be teased into a quick, frenzied orgasm. I slowly circle the bundle of nerve endings that bring her an intense kind of ecstasy, before sucking it gently into my mouth. Her skin is so fucking soft and tender, I just want to kiss these lips the same way I kiss her mouth—for hours—enjoying the tantalizing taste of her. Her mouth tastes like cherries, but these lips are like a sweet liquor, addictive and able to make a grown man drunk. I move my tongue, spelling out her name as I flick, suck, and nibble on her clit. Her soft moans spur me on, her breaths growing frantic as she begins to lose control.

"Vieni per me, il mio amore… come for me, my love." I hold her tight against my face, letting her ride out the aftershocks of her orgasm, her body trembling beneath my hands.

I press her against the wall, a shrine to lovers past and present who have scrawled their names as an offering to Juliet, seeking her blessing on their love for one another. I quickly unzip my pants, pushing them down just far enough to let my cock spring free, throbbing and ready to sink into her warm depths. I stroke myself from root to tip, enjoying as she watches in anticipation. "Is this what you need, Addi? Tell me you need me."

"I *need* you, Carter. I *want* you to fill me, possess me, claim me."

I lift her, positioning myself at her slick entrance. "Hold onto me, baby."

I pound into her with a punishing rhythm, pressing my hands against the harsh stone, shielding her silky, smooth skin as I hammer in and out of her with every delicious thrust of my cock. She's screaming my name in seconds, her teeth sinking into my shoulder to stifle the noise reverberating around this enclosed alley. I enjoy the painful bite as I chase my own release, thrashing into her over and over until I feel myself spilling inside her. My breathing is labored and sweat trickles down my back as I press my forehead to hers, drinking in her scent as I allow my racing heart to calm.

"Let me take you back to the hotel and make love to you properly. I want to taste you all night long, feeling your juices dripping from my chin as I take my fill."

I fix her dress, before making myself presentable enough to walk the remainder of the way back to our hotel without being arrested. I don't really want to call my dad to bail me out with the polizia for having my cock out! My mom would have me saying Hail Mary's for years.

In this moment, I feel like everything has fallen into place. I'm in the country I love most in the world, the birthplace of my father. I have the girl who makes me want to be a better man tucked under my arm, her hand resting around my waist, and a future ahead of us, full of possibilities. As long as we're together, I don't give a fuck what happens. If I lost all of my clubs tomorrow and all my worldly possessions, everything would be fine as long as we're together.

I am true to my word. I spend the night savoring every sweet inch of Addi. Tasting, teasing, worshiping her, and wringing as much pleasure from her body as she can possibly take before we collapse in a sated heap as the sun rises over the city that inspired the greatest literary love story in history. If you ask me, Romeo was an idiot. He should have fought harder for Juliet when he had the chance. The tragedy of their story should be a lesson to lovers. Everything falls apart when you don't communicate with someone, when you let misunderstandings get in the way. When you don't fight for what you want, for what you *need* to live and breathe.

As I watch her fall asleep in my arms, she is more breathtaking than ever. She is glowing, gentle, and soft as silk. She is my Venus. I will always fight for her, for what we have, no matter what life throws at us.

CHAPTER 21

ADDI

YESTERDAY, I SAT IN THE BATHROOM FOR WHAT FELT LIKE HOURS, waiting and watching a small stick that would determine my future. When the plus sign appeared, I think a part of me died. Five days ago, I would have been terrified but excited at the prospect of becoming a mom and bringing Carter's baby into the world. Now that I know he doesn't want kids, it's the worst possible outcome for the life I thought I would have. I could never terminate this pregnancy, and understanding that this heralds the end of my relationship with Carter was a devastating blow. I sat silently sobbing for the longest time, the world around me disappearing in a cacophony of white noise whooshing in my ears.

Today, I'm getting ready to spend two weeks alone with him. To savor everything about him—about us. It's more than I thought I would have, but it will never be enough. I love him with everything that I am, and that's why, when we get home, I need to leave. He doesn't want children, and I won't force him to live a life he doesn't want. He would do the right thing by me, I know he would, but months or maybe even years from now he would resent me for it, and I couldn't bear to see that look in his eyes. I also can't get rid of our baby. If I hadn't fallen pregnant, I would have lived a happy life with

Carter without kids. But I *am* pregnant, and I love this baby, and I'll do my best to protect him or her until the day I die. I *want* this baby. I just wish it was what we *both* wanted. I've seen what can happen when a man is cornered with this responsibility. I *won't* do it to him. I *can't*.

Carter and I have decided to embark on a vacation all around Italy. He's going to show me all the places he enjoyed growing up and we have no one to answer to but ourselves for fourteen days. Real life can wait, and I can pretend that the future is bright for us, just the way I want it to be. I'm going to make sure this is a time we both remember and look back on with fondness in the years ahead. It's going to be excruciating when I have to leave, and Carter will put up a fight. He'll think I don't love him. But hopefully, over time, he'll look back at the time we're about to spend together and realize that I love him more than I could ever possibly express.

THE CLOSEST BIG TOWN TO VERONA THAT I'VE ALWAYS WANTED TO SEE, is Venice, and it doesn't disappoint. Carter organized a convertible Lamborghini Gallardo Spyder, in trademark bright orange, for us to travel around in the next few weeks. These boys don't do anything by halves. The drive from Verona to Venice wasn't a long one, but every bit of scenery here is breathtaking. We have to park the car outside of Venice which is such a strange concept. There are no roads! An ancient city down in the depths below, steeped in the history of so many lives lived. As we walk through the train station and out into the sunlight, I am completely speechless at the beauty before me.

"E'così bello qui." [*It's so beautiful here*]

"I hardly ever know what you're saying, but it sounds amazing. I could listen to you speak Italian all day. It's super sexy."

He grabs me around the waist, letting me feel his length hardening against me. "Voglio che gridare per me, il mio amore. Solo per me. Tu sei più bella per me di tutta l' Italia. Ti amo più della vita stessa." [*I want you to scream for me, my love. Just for me. You are more beautiful to me than the whole of Italy. I love you more than life itself.*]

I melt into his arms, completely beguiled by the unknown words of seduction rolling off his delectable tongue. "You had me at 'voglio.'"

He smirks against my lips. "Seriously? I seduce you with my mad Italian skills and you give me a cheesy Jerry Maguire rip off?" He starts to tickle me relentlessly, making me convulse in the middle of the street.

"Stop. Stop, stop! I take it back. I love your mad skills."

He continues to torment me. "And?"

"And...... I love you. Mercy, please, mercy!"

His lips find mine, his hands no longer torturing me as they slide down my sides to cup my ass. "Don't you forget it, baby."

We spend the rest of the day walking around Venice, taking selfies on the Rialto Bridge, buying venetian opera masks in the gorgeous little markets dotted throughout the city, and finally enjoy an amazing dinner in Piazza San Marco. Our hotel looks out over this famous square, and with such a magnificent backdrop, we make love into the early hours before I curl up cocooned in Carter's warmth and strength. but my mind wanders as soon as his breathing becomes shallow and even. I stare at him for what feels like hours, trying to capture everything about him and lock it away to keep close to my heart. My tears drip down onto the dusting of hair on his chest, and as I wipe them with my fingers, the familiar charge I feel whenever we are connected, sparks and ignites a new wave of desire deep inside. I begin to kiss and nuzzle his hard, toned, tanned flesh, seeking a comfort I will never find.

"Not had enough of me yet?" A sly grin creeps across his stunning features, his eyes still closed.

"I will *never* get enough of you, Carter. Remember that." My eyes twinkle with unshed tears, my voice laced with melancholy.

He tilts my chin toward him, pinning me with his gaze. "I will. I'm yours, Addi, for as long as you'll have me... I'm yours." A tear breaks free, making its way down my cheek towards my lips. Carter catches it with his tongue. "What's wrong? Why so sad?"

"I'm not sad... I'm happy. I just feel so overwhelmed by how beautiful this city is, how beautiful you are when you're here, and how lucky I am to have met you." Before the extent of my despair spills from my mouth, I capture his bottom lip with my teeth, savoring the taste of him. It's all the encouragement he needs to ravish me.

We spend the next day in bed, recovering from our night of passion. The only time I leave the bed is to be sick in secret. I managed to convince Carter to go and get us some food while I 'freshen up,' but by the time he returns half an hour later, I'm wiped out, asleep on the bed. I think he assumed it was exhaustion from our sexathon, but the truth is, my body is changing, my energy being redirected to nurture the baby growing inside me, and constantly lying to him has me completely and utterly emotionally drained.

As the week progresses, we work our way down the countryside, seeing so many quaint, authentic Italian towns most tourists will never know even exist. We visit olive groves, churches, museums and beaches. I want to experience anything and everything with Carter. The water here is so clear and blue as far as the eye can see, the beaches white as snow. It's not the season to be out sunbathing, but it doesn't detract in any way from my appreciation of such wonderful surroundings.

Today we're driving to Florence. Not only is it an amazing city, full of culture, art and some of the best shops a girl could ask for, it is also where Carter's family are originally from. He still has family living on the outskirts of the city and he wants to take me to meet them. I'm apprehensive at first, it's a big deal to meet so many members of his family at once. I don't speak the language, and when we get back to New York... the spell will be broken, and I will become a distant memory to him in the months and years ahead. I make the decision to learn everything I can about Carter, his heritage, and his family here in Italy. This will be part of our child's identity, and I want to be able to teach him or her everything I can about where they come from, and the amazing man who fathered them. By the time we reach a little town called Campi, twenty minutes outside of Florence, I am almost excited at the prospect of meeting everyone.

~

CARTER'S AUNT THERESA KEEPS TRYING TO OFFER ME DRINKS. "NO WINE for me, thank you." I think this is the fourth time I've refused her in the three hours since we arrived.

She turns to Carter. "Why she no drink? Bambino? Carter!"

His face tightens as he admonishes her. "No, Zia. Cazzo fai madonna. Non spaventarla." *[No, aunt. What the fuck? Don't frighten her.]*

I don't need to speak Italian to know that he's not happy with her assumption. My heart sinks a little further into my ever-present despair. When he finishes cussing her out in Italian he moves over to sit next to me. "Are you ok, Addi? Now that I think about it, you haven't really had much to drink since we touched down in Italy."

I manage to force a smile. "Trust me. If you had the same travel sickness I had on the way here, you wouldn't be drinking much either. The thought of most things, including alcohol, still make me feel a little queasy." He accepts my answer and goes back to catching up with his family.

There must be about twenty cousins here and five or six sets of aunts and uncles—I have trouble keeping track of everyone. It's nice to watch Carter in his element, the whole family crowding around, loving him, full of affection. He speaks so fluently and with such ease, it's a joy to witness, even when I have no idea what he's saying. He tries to translate as much as he can, but I don't want him to miss out on enjoying time with his family because of me. The evening passes quickly with lots of laughs and twice as many stories of Carter as a young boy, getting up to mischief with his cousins here in Italy during the long summers. I ask so many questions, gathering information to salt away and remember for our baby in the future. Carter watches me, with a massive, panty-dropping smile as I interact with his family. My face must mirror his as I observe him play with his cousins' children. They range from eighteen months to nine years old, and they all love him. He's adorable with them, and I can't reconcile the man who doesn't want a family of his own, with the man in front of me, surrounded by family and loving every minute of it. I guess having this level of extended family is more than enough for some people.

We stay in a gorgeous hotel in the center of Florence for a few days, with a view of the Duomo. We spend a lot of time with his family, but he carves out time for the two of us to explore the city together. He takes me around all the famous museums. I stand in awe of *The Birth of Venus* in the Uffizi and am completely dumbstruck in front of *The David* in the Galleria. Having said that, *The David* is nothing compared to the sculpted perfection holding my hand as I walk the streets of Florence. We leisurely stroll up and down the Ponte Vecchio, Carter making me wait outside while he ducks into one of the jewelers. I take the opportunity to savor the sights and sounds of this magical place, watching as couples from all over the world enjoy the romance this historic city inspires. He comes back out twenty minutes later, empty handed, telling me they didn't have what he was looking for.

I'm a little sad when we leave Florence and his amazing family behind, but I'm happy that it'll just be us for the remainder of our trip. With the top down, a breeze in my hair, and Michael Jackson's *Love Never Felt So Good* blasting on the radio, we're headed for Rome, and for a brief moment in time, I feel perfectly carefree. Just a woman, completely in love with the man of her dreams, an endless future of possibilities sprawled out before us like the vast expanse of road ahead. If only it could stay this way.

CHAPTER 22

CARTER

I WISH WE COULD STAY HERE FOREVER. ITALY FEELS LIKE HOME TO ME, and having Addi here, and all to myself without the hassles and pressures of work has been amazing. Every day I spend with her, every hour that passes, I fall even more in love with her, if that's even possible. If there was any doubt in my mind that she's 'The One,' it's been completely eradicated by our time here.

I've brought her to Rome for the final four days of our vacation. It won't be enough time to show her all the beautiful treasures this city has to offer, but it will give her a taste, and we'll be back in the future. There's a myth that if you stand in front of the Fontana di Trevi, with your back to it, and throw a coin over your shoulder, if it lands in the water you'll return to see it again. I do it every time I visit, and plan to take Addi to see it while we're here.

THE VIEW OF ROME FROM OUR SUITE IS PHENOMENAL—A PANORAMIC vista of the ancient city. But the view behind me is even more breathtaking. Addi is asleep on the bed, rosy cheeked and rumpled from our afternoon of love making. She's radiant. The sheets have pooled at her waist, her gorgeous breasts, plump and begging for my touch.

As the sun spills through the windows, kissing her skin, I can't help but do the same. I crawl onto the bed, lowering my lips to capture her sweet budded nipples into my mouth, applying as little pressure as possible, suckling her, flicking my tongue over the hardened tip. My hand runs from her waist up and over her other breast. She stirs beneath me, her voice sleepy and so damn sexy.

"Mmm. I could get used to this as a wake-up call." Her hands fist in my hair, holding me against her luscious breasts.

"Baby, the Italian diet agrees with you. I swear your tits look even better than usual. So fucking firm and plump. Ripe for me to taste."

She flinches ever so slightly beneath me. "I'm hungry. Let's go get something to eat." She tries to push me away.

"What's wrong? A minute ago you wanted me as your human alarm-clock and now you're shoving me away."

"Nothing's wrong. I just want to get out of here for a while and grab a snack." She gives me a saccharin sweet, if not somewhat forced smile, and I know better than to push her when she doesn't want to talk.

We enjoy a delicious meal in one of the many piazzas Rome has to offer and Addi seems to have gotten over her funk from earlier. After dinner, we take a leisurely stroll around the city, seeing the sights by moonlight. It feels different at night, but equally as amazing as it is during the day. The atmosphere is filled with romance, couples enjoying their surroundings and each other. I throw my arm around Addi's shoulder and hold her close, leading her down a non-descript cobbled alley, but the astounding landmark at the end of this dark little street is why I brought her here. I watch closely, my eyes fixed on her as I pull her out into Piazza di Trevi. Her eyes are aglow, wide as saucers, and glassy with unshed tears. I would give up everything I have to see the smile splitting her face right now every day, for the rest of my life. She's so fucking beautiful.

I pull her tight to my chest, whispering in her ear. "Do you like la

Fontana di Trevi? La fontana è solo la metà bello come te, il mio tesoro." [The fountain is only half as beautiful as you, my treasure.]

I revel in the shiver that courses through her body as my words caress her senses.

"It's so beautiful, Carter. I've never seen anything so remarkable in my life. I could stare at it forever and never get tired of how magnificent it is."

"I know how you feel, baby. I feel the same way… about you." She turns in my arms, her eyes diverted from the masterpiece in front of her and locked on mine.

"I love you more than I can ever tell you."

Her declaration renders me speechless. And that doesn't happen very often. "Addi…"

Her fingers dance across my lips. "Don't say anything. Just kiss me. I want to remember this moment when I'm old and gray."

"I'll remind you, cara mia."

I move my hands up into her silky black hair, gripping it, holding her in place as my lips descend on hers. I want to give her everything her heart desires, and if she wants to remember this kiss, then I will pour every ounce of love, passion, and desire I feel for her into it. I nibble on her, relishing her taste and how her breath hitches as my lips brush against soft skin. I lick the seam of her lips, a plea for her to give me what I want. One touch of her sweet little tongue and a familiar spark ignites inside me, spurring me on to deepen our kiss, to claim her as mine. Desire takes over and I find myself devouring her, ravishing her mouth with my tongue. Within seconds I am rock-hard, my cock straining against my pants, desperate to feel her warmth surrounding it. I finally pull back, aware of the fact that I don't want to have a piazza full of strangers watch me lose control and fuck her until she screams, right here, right now. I swear, sometimes I think I might not be able to curb that deep, dark desire I feel for her. It's like a freight train when it hits, an unstoppable force between us, connecting us in a way I've *never* felt with anyone else.

"Will you remember this, Tesoro? This kiss, this moment, this immeasurable love between us?"

"Every delicious, earth-shattering detail. Always."

OUR TIME HERE IN ITALY IS COMING TO AN END. TOMORROW WE HAVE to get on a plane and fly back to our real lives in New York. This has been the best two weeks of my life. Xander's wedding seems like a lifetime ago. So much has happened, and my time with Addi has been phenomenal. I've wanted to ask her to move in with me so many times while we've been here, and there have been perfect moments, romantic moments, but every time I've wussed out. I've played every scenario out in my head. Will she freak the fuck out like she did in the Hamptons? Or will she freak out in a good way? Will she think it's too soon? Will she think it's an amazing idea? If I knew the answer, I wouldn't be so fucking scared to. I've decided to wait until we're back in New York. I don't want her to think it's a knee jerk reaction to us spending all our time together over the past few weeks. It's easy to be with someone 24/7 when you're on vacation, and I need her to know that I want day to day real life with her. The crabby days when she's a hormonal bitch, the tired ones when she's wiped out from work and just wants to crash on the couch, the lazy ones when all we want to do is hang out together at the apartment, and even the angry days when we piss each other off. But most of all I want *every single day* with her. To love, protect, and just... *be*, with her.

For our last night in Rome I have a little something special planned for Addi. She once accused me of being a 'swanktard,' and even I would say the surprise I've organized tonight warrants the title! But here's the thing... I don't give a fuck! I *know* she doesn't need anything flashy or extravagant, and that's *why* I wanted to do something special. It's been a long road for us to get to this point, and it deserves some sort of fucking celebration!

I wanted to keep it a secret, so I told Addi I had some errands to run and left her with strict instructions to be ready in an hour. I've just been to make sure that everything is set up the way I want it, and it looks fucking perfect. All I need now is to go get my girl.

When I open the door to our suite I'm astonished by the angel before me. Addi is a vision in flowing white silk, a roman goddess in the flesh. Her skin is flawless, her hair cascading down her back with effortless elegance, and she flashes me the sexiest grin.

"Like what you see... sailor?" I must have such a goofy look on my face.

"It's been a while since you've called me sailor. It takes me back to when you wanted to bust my balls all the fucking time." I laugh, remembering how different things were between us eight months ago.

"I'm sorry, baby. You just annoyed me with all your holy hotness back then!"

"What changed?"

"Your cock is just SO BIG, I decided to put up with you." Addi's out to play tonight.

"Wow. If you didn't look so fucking angelic right now I would torture you for that comment. I'll give you a pass this once, but only because my dick really IS THAT BIG!"

She slaps my arm playfully before pulling me towards the door. "Come on, before your MASSIVE... ego... stops us from getting out of the room." I fucking love her.

As we make our way through the streets of Rome I take off my jacket and hand it to Addi shivering beside me. "Why didn't you bring a coat?"

"It would've ruined my outfit."

I will never understand women. "But my oversized suit jacket sets it off perfectly? You crack me up."

"Why thank you... Player."

"Oh come on, baby. Surely I'm past that label now? I'm reformed. A new man. I met a ridiculously gorgeous girl and she saved me from turning into the next Heffner."

"She must be quite a catch. I'd love to meet her sometime."

"Sorry, baby, I can't let you. It would go to her head if she knew how awesome she is. I can't risk it. Her massive... ego... might make her forget that she loves me."

Her face becomes solemn, our funny banter forgotten as she caresses my cheek with her delicate fingers, tracing my jaw, along the scruff that's grown since this morning. "She would never forget how much she loves you." There's something in her eyes, something that gives me pause, a deeper meaning behind her softly spoken words. I try to shake it off, this uneasy feeling in the pit of my stomach, continuing our signature witty banter as we make our way to our destination for the evening.

When we arrive at the Colosseum, Addi is giddy with excitement. "It's stunning, isn't it? I wish we had managed to go on the tour while we were here. All the sex distracted me from the once in a lifetime opportunity to see one of the most amazing, iconic, historical wonders the world has ever known. You and your mad skills have a lot to answer for, mister."

"I'm flattered that you chose my particular... 'skills' over some ancient ruins." She's about to give me no end of shit for calling something so magnificent 'ruins,' but I stop her with a chaste kiss. "BUT... you don't have to choose between us. I want to give you everything within my power to give." I turn her in my arms, her back to my chest as I direct her gaze to the entrance, which is brightly lit, with an attendant standing outside. "Your evening awaits, il mio bel Tesoro—my beautiful girl."

She is speechless. I can't believe I've rendered the mighty Addi speechless. "Come on, baby. Let me show you history, the way it's meant to be seen."

As we approach the main entrance the attendant greets us, ushering us up into the main walkway around the amphitheater. It is *exactly* how I pictured it. There are candles everywhere, delineating all that's left of the gladiatorial holding cells. The walls are steeped in so much history it's a physical presence, coming to life to tell its stories. Addi remains silent beside me, clutching my hand so hard I'm starting to lose circulation.

"Are you okay? Is this okay?"

She bursts into tears. "Oh my God, Carter. Of course it's okay. It's better than okay. I can't believe you did all of this... for me. No one has ever… I mean… I haven't ever… not for me… not all this just for me." Fuck, I don't know what's happening right now, but I *think* they're happy tears and happy ramblings.

"Addison. Listen to me. This is a drop in the ocean of what you deserve. You are the strongest, most amazing, funny, intelligent woman I have ever met. You need to know that you deserve every good thing that happens to you. Don't you know how much you're loved? Your parents worship the ground you walk on, Lily would die for you, and I would do fucking anything for you Addi… *anything*. Tell me you understand." She nods, her shallow sobs tugging at my heart. "This is not the reaction I was expecting."

She smiles. "I'm so sorry, Carter. I don't know what's wrong with me. My period must be due or something. Freaking emotional much?"

I pull her close, eager to lighten the mood. "You mean God's high five to men the world over every month? You girls think we get upset that you're crabby and teary for a few days, when it's actually the opposite. We're just so fucking relieved that we haven't gotten you pregnant, we'll put up with any level of crazy!"

She stiffens in my arms, and again, I'm perplexed, but I'm on a mission to make her laugh, and I won't stop until I hear that beautiful sound.

"Does this put my big dick in jeopardy of *not* being ridden like a stallion later?" My girl is back with an all-out belly laugh, and it's music to my ears. "Seriously! I give you the Colosseum for a night, I have an amazing dinner planned, and I've got another trick up my sleeve. I really need to know that I didn't do it all for a night of spooning." I can't even get the last words out without laughing.

"You'll be sleeping out in the hallway if you keep this shit up." Only Addi and I would be trash talking each other at a time like this, in the most romantic setting on Earth, in a fucking fairytale moment. It's why I love her so much.

"Oh My God. Can I at least feed you before you throw me out on my ass?"

She gives me a sly grin. "Well, okay then. If you must!"

We have a magical evening. The food, the surroundings, and most of all the company is perfect. We laugh and joke, Addi even manages to say some really sweet things to me, and as our evening draws to an end, I remember the one thing we have left to do. "We need to go back to La Fontana di Trevi."

"I won't say no! But why do we *need* to go back? You've got me intrigued."

"We didn't throw money in the fountain."

She looks at me as if I've just escaped from the asylum. "And?"

"It's easier if I just show you." I take her hand and run through the streets of Rome.

"Hey, hotshot. Next time, you get to run on freaking cobbles in five-inch heels! Slow the hell down."

"Sorry, baby. I just really want to do this with you."

I can see her mind working and the glint of mischief in her eye. "Oh, are we having filthy fountain sex?"

"I fucking wish, but no… dirty girl." We walk out into the piazza, busy and beautiful in the moonlight. "We need to throw coins in."

"You're an idiot. You know that, right?"

"Just follow me." I lead her to the edge of the fountain. "Turn around."

"If you push me in, I'll kill you. Just so we're clear."

"So, you would let me fuck you in front of all these people, but if I pushed you in the water it would be a deal breaker? You're definitely my kind of woman. Now do what you're told for once in your life. Turn around with your back to the fountain." She finally does as I ask. She's as stubborn as a fucking mule sometimes. I hand her a coin. "Now hold my hand and throw the coins over your shoulder. If they land in the fountain it means we'll come back here together someday."

Her hand tightens around mine. "That would be a dream come true." She fucking melts me.

"On the count of three. One… two… three." We toss the coins over our shoulders, turning quickly to watch as they splash into the water. "The fountain has spoken. We'll be back here one day, Addison Warner. You and me, together." She doesn't say a word. She just holds me, snaking her slender arms around my waist, pushing her face tight to my chest.

We stand this way for a few minutes before a man playing the violin tries to serenade us. I would usually tell these guys to get lost, but something about the way Addi clings to me makes me want to have this clichéd moment with her. I slip the guy a few Euros and tell him to play *A Thousand Years* by Christina Perri. Addi loves those shit vampire movies and I know she'll appreciate the gesture.

"Dance with me." It's a profound moment, dancing with her, in this place, the music playing gently in the background as our bodies sway in time. I can sense that my life will never be the same.

When the music stops, I lift her into my arms and carry her back to the hotel. By the time I reach our suite and open the door, she's asleep in my arms. I try to lie her down gently on the bed, but her slender frame clings to me as her sweet voice whispers against my chest. "Make love to me, Carter. One last time... in Italy." Who am I to deny her? I slowly strip her naked, savoring every inch of her beautiful body, unwrapping her like the gift that she is to me. Then, she watches as I slowly remove my clothes, dropping them to the floor before climbing on the bed beside her.

"Tell me what you want, Tesoro."

"You, Carter. I'll only ever want you. I need to feel you inside me, please." My heart aches in my chest at the yearning in her eyes. I straddle her, positioning myself at her entrance, coating myself in her arousal before leaning down to kiss her sleep swollen lips. As our kiss deepens I slide inside, my breath catching at the exquisite pleasure it brings me, every hard inch of me sinking deeper inside her. The sexy little moan that escapes her makes my dick twitch, causing her warm, wet walls to clench around me, and it feels fucking fantastic.

We move together, enjoying every slow, tantalizing thrust, savoring how our bodies fit as if we were made for each other's pleasure. She falls apart beneath me in wave after wave of intense orgasms, her body so attuned to my own. When I feel the beginnings of my own release, I don't chase it, I take my time, working Addi into a frenzy for one last mind-altering climax. When she crashes over the edge, my name a prayer on her lips, I crash right along with her. I feel like it goes on for hours as I ride it out, groaning her name as I claim her lips with my own. It is so fucking intense.

I fall asleep happy and sated with Addi in my arms, her whispered words of affection a perfect lullaby.

"I love you, Carter."

CHAPTER 23

ADDI

One Week Later

I've been putting off the inevitable for a week now. We arrived back from Italy last week, and life has just felt so perfect, aside from my early morning secret bouts of hugging the toilet bowl. I've gotten hiding it from Carter down to a fine art. We've spent most of this week at his place, thrown back into the daily grind of life and work in Manhattan, but the few short hours we've had together at night have been intense, passionate, and filled with tenderness. It's difficult to go from being with someone 24/7 for over two weeks, to hardly seeing each other. I had planned on making a clean break when we got back, but I've been a coward, and I've been selfish, telling myself that one more day with him would be enough. But it will *never* be enough. The words have been on the tip of my tongue so many times, and so many times I've tried to convince myself that he'll come around to the idea of having a child, and that he won't resent me for it. Deep down, fear twists in my gut, unfurling like a dark, black cancer, stopping me from saying those three little words. *I am pregnant.*

I'm getting ready for dinner with Carter. I know that tonight is the night I need to break up with him. I can't just disappear or leave him a note. We've been through too much together, and I love him too much to leave him with questions, or any hope that we'll work it out. As I stare at myself in the mirror, applying the finishing touches to my makeup, the questions tormenting me are simple—how do you convince someone you love more than anything in the world that you don't love them anymore? That you never loved them? That the magical time you spent together meant nothing more than great sex?

I tell myself I only need to convince him for tonight, just long enough for me to leave New York, because he *will* realize that it's all a lie. When he sits contemplating our time together, he will *know* without a shadow of a doubt, that I love him deeply. By that point, I will be long gone. I don't know where I'll go, or what I'll do, but I know I need to do it alone. If I tell Lily just now she'll convince me to stay. She'll convince me to tell Carter what's really going on, and his life will be irrevocably changed in a way he doesn't want.

When Carter arrives to pick me up, my heart lurches into my chest at the sight of him. His lush black hair, drops forward onto his brow, still wet from the shower. I study every line and contour of his resplendent face, because I *need* to remember everything about him. His eyes are alive with love as a sexy grin spreads across his flawless features, perfect lips calling to me for one last kiss. After two weeks in Italy his skin is a delicious mocha brown, enhancing his ripped physique, making me wet just looking at him. His tan is made even more noticeable in stark contrast to the crisp white shirt he's wearing, open at the collar to reveal a smattering of hair, peeking out, teasing me with the memory of how sensual it feels against my lips as I kiss his chiseled chest. His tailored navy pin-striped pants showcase his strong muscular thighs and tight ass to perfection.

"What are you staring at, cara mia?" The rasp in his voice turns my insides to jelly, desire shooting through every nerve ending in my body.

I struggle to rein in my desire as I ready myself for the task ahead. "I'm almost ready. Just let me grab my bag."

He strides towards me, stalking me, making me feel like his prey, and I am desperate to be captured by him. "Now is that any way to greet your lover?"

His hands slide readily into my hair pinning me in place, his scent invading my senses, washing over me like a cool breeze on a summer day. Cologne, shower gel, and Carter. As our lips connect, an explosion erupts inside me, every ounce of love I feel for this amazing man, pouring out of me, through me and into this one kiss. I fist my hands in his shirt, desperate to hold onto him for one more moment. Tears prick at my eyes, and I squeeze them tightly shut to block the torrent of emotion fighting to break free. Once the dam bursts there will be no going back.

"Now that's the kind of hello I could get used to." He showers my face with featherlight kisses before letting go and taking a step back. I feel the loss of his body against mine, and an ache forming in my chest. "You look amazing. This dress makes your curves pop in all the right places."

I'm wearing a simple teal shift dress tonight—very Audrey Hepburn. It clings to my curves, which are already starting to change ever so slightly. "Thanks. I thought I would make an effort."

"I almost don't want to take you out for dinner, when I could be stripping you out of this dress and making love to you for hours instead."

"We're *going* to dinner. I'm starving." He pouts as I grab my purse and lead him from my apartment and out into the city I will no longer call home as of tomorrow.

"You've hardly touched your dinner, baby. Are you feeling ok? I thought you were starving? I can order you something else if you want?" His quiet attentiveness and constant concern for my well-being is killing me. I can't break his heart like this. I know I'm a coward, but I just can't do it.

"It's fine. I don't need anything else. I'm just not feeling hungry all of a sudden."

He takes my hands in his. "Would you like to go for a walk? We can get out of here and do whatever you want... or we could just go back to my place?"

"A walk sounds good." If I go to his place, I will never leave.

As we walk hand in hand through the city, the weight of what I'm about to do is choking me from the inside out. I feel like I'm suffocating. I don't even register where we are until Carter pulls me into the lobby of the Empire State Building. "Let's go up. It's such a clear night, the view will be exquisite." I would follow him to the ends of the Earth if things were different.

When we reach the observation deck, we take a moment to admire the view of Manhattan sprawled out before us. A city full of possibilities. And as I stand contemplating the future, Carter stands behind me caging me in, his arms on either side of my body, holding onto the railings. His lips caressing my ear as he speaks.

"You know I love you, Addi. You make me feel like I'm on top of the world. I want to give you everything this city has to offer and more. I want to be with you every minute of every day."

He pauses for a moment, taking a deep breath, nerves evident in his voice as he continues.

"Will you move in with me, Tesoro?"

My heart stops beating, the world around me closing in, a crushing weight on my chest as I realize this is the moment I need to break his heart. I want so badly to twist in his arms, claim his lips with my own and cry a resounding 'yes.' I am an awful excuse for a human-being. I've been too selfish to break up with him, and what I've been left with, is an opportunity to do the right thing, in completely the wrong way. I hate myself before a single word passes my lips.

I slowly turn, taking a moment to try and steady my thundering heartbeat. His beautiful face worried and nervous, his eyes searching mine for the answer he so clearly desires, but his expression changes as soon as our eyes connect. It's now or never. I push against his warm, hard chest. "Why would you ask me that?" The quiver in my voice betrays me. He doesn't move, his eyes boring into me. "Why would you think this is what I want? Have I *ever* given you the impression that I want to live with you?"

He opens his mouth. "Addi…" I cut him off, the hurt in his eyes too much for me to bear.

"I can't do this, Carter. I'm not this person. I thought you knew that. I don't want this." I duck under his arm, trying to get away from his imposing presence, but he grabs my arm.

"Wait a goddamn minute, Addison. You don't get to say something like that to me and walk away. Not after everything we've gone through to get here, everything we mean to each other. I know you… and this isn't you."

"You obviously *don't* know me, Carter. I warned you more than once, but you're fucking relentless. I'm not the girl you fall in love with or live happily ever after with. I'm the girl you screw before you find *that* girl." His grip tightens as I try to make a break for the elevators.

"That's bullshit and you know it. You're scared, I get it. I even expected it… but this… I don't know what the fuck is going on right now, Addi. You need to explain this to me." My heart splinters in my chest, wreaking havoc on my body, tearing me to shreds.

"What do you want from me? I'm not the settling down type. We've had a great time together, Italy was amazing and I will always cherish it, but we both know deep down this is never going to last. Let's just part ways now before it gets complicated and ugly."

"I thought we were on the same page, Addi. This isn't just a fling for me, and I don't think it is for you either. Something has you spooked, way beyond me asking you to move in. Whatever it is, you can tell me, we can work it out. As long as we're together, nothing else matters. Remember what I told you, Tesoro. Just you and me now." He lifts his hand in a tender gesture to stroke my face, his movements careful and wary as if trying to soothe a lame animal.

I flinch at his touch, watching his heart break at my reaction. "Don't make this harder than it needs to be. I'm sorry I hurt you. It was never my intention." I turn on my heels making a hasty retreat to the elevators, but just as I enter the open doors, I find myself spun around to face Carter, his arms tight on my biceps.

"You can't just fucking walk out on me like this. You don't get to make that decision by yourself. I told you I would fight for you, for us, even when you aren't willing to."

The elevator attendant steps up. "Is this man bothering you, miss?"

"Yes. He won't let go of me." The look on Carter's face is pained, tortured and devastated, and I hate that I'm the one causing it.

"Take your hands off the lady, sir, before I call security."

He lets go, stumbling back in shock.

"Addi…"

As the doors close between us, I leave my shattered heart at the top of the Empire State Building, with the only man I've ever really loved, my name a strangled plea on his lips.

"Addi… please…"

I take a deep breath, tears flowing freely down my cheeks as I wait for the doors to open onto the lobby. When they finally do, I hurry from the building, but a strong arm grabs my wrist. The voice of a broken man behind me.

"Why are you doing this to us, Addi? Talk to me."

"I've said all there is to say. It's over. Please, just let me go. I'm not this girl."

"You're MY girl. Tesoro. I *know* you love me. Tell me you don't and I'll let you go, I'll never bother you again."

I can't look him in the eye. "I don't love you, Carter." There is no conviction in my voice and he knows it.

"I don't believe you. Fucking look at me and tell me you're not in love with me. Tell me that when we're together you don't feel the most intense connection you've ever felt to another person on this whole goddamn planet." He grabs my face forcing me to look at him, his eyes wild with fear and desperation. "You can't say it, Addi, because it isn't true."

I gulp down the lump in my throat, steeling myself for the biggest lie I will ever tell. I let out the breath I've been holding for what seems like forever, firmly putting the wall in place that I've cultivated over the years. A blank expression betraying the agony raging inside me.

"I don't love you, Carter. I'm sorry I let it go on this long. You deserve so much more, and I can't give it to you. I got carried away with the idea of it all, but... I'm not *in love* with you." I lean in to kiss his lips. My last selfish act toward the man who taught me what true love really is. His taste will be forever emblazoned in my memory, his smell a lasting imprint on my senses, his touch a permanent mark on my soul.

As I pull back to bask in his beautiful eyes for the last time, my heart is broken into a million pieces, scattered to the ends of the Earth, his chocolate brown depths begging me to stay. The last words he says to me as I pull out of his grasp will forever haunt my dreams. His low, rasping voice thick with emotion.

"I will always love you, Addison, but if you walk away now, don't come back, because I can't do this again. Not with you, Tesoro. I *won't*."

As I walk away, the only comfort I have as my world crumbles around me, is that a piece of him is growing inside me, a part of him that I will keep, cherish, and love until my dying breath.

I CAN'T STAY IN THE CITY ONE MORE NIGHT. IF I DO, I'LL END UP AT Carter's door, begging him to forgive me, to take me back. I'd plead with him to *want* this baby. I furiously throw anything and everything into a suitcase. I can barely see what I'm picking up through the tears that sting my eyes. Sobs wrack my body, my eyes swollen and bruised from hours of crying. My breath is labored as I pack up my life. The life I love with Lily, and Carter. I haphazardly stuff my toiletries into the case before zipping it up and wheeling it out into the hallway.

As I reach the door to my apartment I take a moment to reminisce about all of the special moments I've had in this wonderful place, my home. I grab a notepad from the console table and scribble a note for Lily before closing the door behind me. I know the first thing she'll do when she finds out I broke up with Carter—she'll come looking for me, and I need to let her know that I'm okay, or at least I will be… one day… maybe.

I hail a cab and head for the airport. I don't know where I'm going, but I guess I'll find out when I get there.

CHAPTER 24

CARTER

Four Weeks Later

THE SUNLIGHT BURNS MY EYES AS I AWAKE IN A HAZE. I STINK OF BOOZE and I'm not sure where I am. I'm not surprised or worried, this has become my life recently—par for the course.

Every day is the same. One long endless void, flowing into the next. I work, I drink, and I sleep. Sometimes I sleep with whichever random woman offers herself to me on a slutty platter. Basically, it's back to the good old days for me. As the room slowly comes into focus I realize I'm in a cell. Holy Fuck, what did I do last night? I'm too out of it to care. I don't care about anything anymore, so I close my eyes and drift off, only to be startled awake by banging on the bars next to where my head is resting.

"What the fuck, Carter?" Xander? What the hell is he doing here? And why the fuck is my back killing me?

I slowly lift my pounding head, my vision skewed as I take in the disapproving look on my best friend's face. "Why are you here? Shouldn't you be on your honeymoon?"

"I got back three weeks ago and I've seen you since then. You're just living in a permanent drunken haze and can't fucking remember it. I need to post your bail so we can get the fuck out of here." He returns fifteen minutes later with an officer to open my cell. I get my keys and wallet and head out into the far too bright morning light. He immediately gives me shit. "What are you doing? You need to snap out of it."

I see red. "Oh really. Is that all I need to do? I didn't realize it was so fucking easy. I'll get right on that."

"Shut the fuck up, Carter. I'm trying to help you." He opens the door to the car, but I just can't be around him, so I start walking. I associate him with Lily, and everything about Lily is a stark reminder —Addi is gone.

"Why don't you just go back to your perfect life with your perfect wife and leave me the fuck alone, Xander? I don't need to see the fucking pity on your face."

"Just get in the fucking car. Lily and I are worried about you. She wants to see you. She asked me to find out where Addi is… and I heard back from my investigator this morning. I know where she is man. Just come back to my place and we can decide what to do."

He's staring at me expectantly, waiting for me to get in the car. Just the mention of her name is like a knife in my chest. "I don't give a flying fuck! She gave up on me. She doesn't love me, so why the fuck would I give a shit about where she is?" I'm shouting in the middle of the street, but I can't rein in the fury I feel roiling inside me. "Just leave me the fuck alone."

I start walking in the general direction of my apartment, listening as Xander yells my name, but I just don't care. Half an hour later I find myself standing outside Cube. It won't be open for another twelve hours, but there's a couch in my office with my name on it, and a bottle of Jack in the cabinet that will numb the ache in my chest… at least for the next few hours.

THE PULSING BEAT OF THE PACKED CLUB JUST OUTSIDE MY OFFICE DOOR wakes me from my stupor. I feel like hammered shit as I shuffle into my private bathroom, and the man staring back at me in the mirror looks even worse. Every movement is a major effort for my weary muscles as I drop yesterday's disgusting clothes to the floor and step under the shower head, letting the water cascade over every inch of my aching flesh. I rest my throbbing head against the cold tiles, easing the banging of the marching band that's taken up residence in my brain. I can feel something on my back, remembering it was sore before I fell asleep, and as I run my hand over my shoulder blades, I have a flashback to the night before sitting in the chair of a tattoo shop. I rip the covering from my skin, pain and dread creeping through my veins. The night begins to come back to me in a movie reel of events. I left the club early after drinking far too much Scotch and stumbled into the tattoo shop. Oh fuck. The memory of my slurred request is like a bucket of ice water in the face—*Tesoro. I want you to write 'Tesoro' on my back. Big and black and broken, just like my fucking heart.* Jesus… I'm such an idiot. As if my tormented soul wasn't enough of a reminder, now I have a permanent testament to the biggest mistake I ever made.

How did I not see it coming? I thought she loved me back. I thought that she wanted me, that she needed me, just as much as I need her.

As I slide down the tiles to the floor in a crumpled mess, I drop my head, broken, battered and bruised… my body, my mind and what's left of my useless shell of a heart. Grief takes over. I would have given her anything and everything she wanted in this life, if only she could have loved me. I failed again, on an epic scale. I couldn't protect *myself* from Addi, and I obviously didn't protect *her* from the demons who continue to plague her. I'm so disappointed in myself. I swore after Vittoria that I would always protect the ones I love.

The rest of the evening comes flooding back as I curl into the corner of the shower, my arms around my knees as I try in vain to hold it together.

"Hey, handsome, mind if I join you?" I'm propped up at the bar of a

complete dive, the sting of my new tattoo distracting me from the other ache that's now a constant presence in my life.

"Fuck if I care."

"You sure know how to sweet talk a girl."

Who the fuck does she think she's talking to? "Do I look like I need to sweet talk a woman into bed? They willingly drop their panties for me like the good little sluts they are. Is that what you're looking for, baby? Hop the fuck on."

"Asshole."

She turns and walks away, but I'm too drunk to care, or to keep my mouth shut. "You're right, honey, I act like a complete fucking asshole. Do you know why? Because women like you let me! Dumb whores who can't bend over quick enough for me."

I've attracted an audience now. Four big guys are standing between me and the girl. "I think you need to apologize to the lady."

"Pft! Lady? Don't make me laugh."

The bartender leans over the bar. "I think it's time you leave before you get yourself into trouble."

The guys now surrounding me seem to be getting larger. "Listen to him... dickhead. Get out before we throw you out on your ass."

"I'd like to see you fucking try." My fist connects with his jaw before he knows what's hit him. I'm fighting all four of them, punch after punch, taking blow after blow. I'm holding my own with these guys, but I'm out numbered and I'm drunk. Two of them grab a hold of my arms, one on either side of me as a third guy gives me a swift knee to the stomach. I drop to my knees, and just before his fist slams into my face, I hear a siren in the distance. The door opens and in walk two police officers. I slump to the floor when the guys holding me let go, before being I'm hauled to my feet, cuffed, and taken out into the back of the squad car. That's the last I remember.

The water turns cold, jolting me back to the here and now. I stare at my body, noticing the bruises, the tell-tale signs of the night before. No wonder I feel like shit. As I step out the shower and grab a towel, I can see my back in the mirror. There in big black scroll—TESORO—in permanent ink between my shoulder blades. Fuck! I will *never* say that word out loud again. It physically hurts. How is it possible to love someone so goddamn much, and hate them in equal measure at the same time? I don't know how many times I've gone over that night in my head. What could I have done differently to make her stay? If I had never asked her to move in, would we still be together now? So many questions I can never answer. And even if I could, it wouldn't change the outcome. I wasn't enough for her. I wanted to build a life, and a future, and a family with her, and she didn't want it… she didn't want… me.

I quickly dress in a pair of black jeans and a white t-shirt that I keep here at the office. I don't even bother with boxers because they'll just be in the way later, when I find a hot chick to bang. Addi doesn't want me, but there's plenty of willing pussy in this city for me to lose myself in, and that's exactly what I plan to do tonight.

HER TONGUE SLIPS INTO MY EAR SENDING A JOLT STRAIGHT TO MY DICK as I grind against her on the dance floor, her nails digging into my ass, pulling me closer. I swear she's trying to get off on my leg right here in the middle of the club.

"Let's take this to my office, baby." Her eyes light up, her teeth biting into her bottom lip as she nods in agreement.

"You can take me any-where-you-want, sailor." I flinch at the term of endearment, but quickly shake it off. I drag her through the crowds, praying she'll keep her mouth shut while I fuck her. As soon as we're behind closed doors she's tearing at me like a deranged animal.

"You hungry for me, baby? Why don't you wrap those lips of yours around my cock?" She immediately drops to her knees, unzipping my jeans, pulling my cock free. "That's it. Open wide, sweetheart."

She doesn't expect any preamble or pretense of romance, she just does exactly as I ask, fisting the base of my cock before taking it fully into her mouth. She quickly starts pumping and sucking me until I'm rock hard against her tongue. I close my eyes, distracted by her blonde curls bobbing up and down in front of me. As she picks up pace I can feel myself getting closer, until visions of Addi on her knees flash into my mind. Her luscious lips wrapped around me, her silken black hair flowing down her back as she teased me with her tongue, long torturous luxurious licks, the scent of cherries intoxicating me as she worked me into a frenzy. She felt so fucking good. Her tiny satisfied moans vibrating along the length of me.

"That's it, Tesoro, take me as deep as you can. Do you feel how hard I am for you, Addi?"

"My name's Amy, but…"

"I don't fucking care what your name is, sweetheart. I just want to fuck you. Are you okay with that?"

"Yes." She flicks her tongue over the tip of my cock, moaning her delight.

"I like 'Tesoro,' you can call me that."

As her lips return to the head of my cock, I'm shocked and disgusted by myself. How could I call her Tesoro? As much as I need to shoot my load right now, this girl's mouth is not going to cut it. I push her away.

"Just get out."

"I'm not done. Let me make you feel good."

"GET THE FUCK OUT!"

She gets up from kneeling on the floor for a fucking stranger and grabs her bag. Before she slams the door, she gives me the death stare. "You're a fucking psycho. I feel sorry for Addi… whoever the fuck she is."

I pick up a glass from my desk and hurl it at the closed door. "FUCK! FUCK! FUCK!" It shatters all over the floor. I run my hands through my hair, feeling completely out of control of my own fucking life. "Why the fuck did you do this to me, Addi?" I grab a new bottle of Jack taking a long swig before it joins the shattered glass on the floor. "I fucking *loved* you. I still fucking do. You ripped my goddamn heart out. Why can't I hate you?"

I start throwing anything and everything I can get my hands on. My computer and iPad, even my fucking stapler crashes against the wall as I unleash all the pent-up rage from the past month. I have been so fucking numb, unable to feel anything beyond the crushing noth-ingness that the loss of her has left inside me.

"I JUST WANT TO FUCKING HATE YOU!"

I tip over my desk before picking up a chair and hurling it toward the bathroom door. It smashes to pieces, the door following suit. I don't even recognize the strangled roar that escapes me as I drop down onto the only piece of furniture left in the room—the couch.

I take in the devastation surrounding me, a perfect representation of the agony I feel, every minute of every day. I want her back so badly. With my elbows resting on my knees, I cradle my head in my hands, lost in my own despair. A captive of my own heartbreak. A prisoner of my godforsaken soul. A tear drips down onto my palm, and I finally give in, letting myself feel the crushing loss of, with only a bottle of Jack for comfort. It's hours before I finally pass out in the oblivion of a drunken sleep, a sweet release from the torment awaiting me in my waking hours.

CHAPTER 25

ADDI

Meanwhile

It's been four weeks since I left everything behind in New York —my job, my apartment, Lily, and worst of all... Carter. I thought it would get easier as the days and weeks pass by, but it hasn't. Every day I miss him more, and every day that I don't hear his voice, a little part of me dies inside. A sick part of me hoped he would fight for me, that he would text or call, or something, anything. I haven't had a single message, voicemail or even a missed call from him. It hurts like hell, but I don't know why I would expect anything different. I ripped his heart out and handed it to him on a platter before walking away from everything we had. It was one of the worst nights of my life.

The driver is talking to me, but I can't understand what he's saying, he just sounds like white noise in the distance. I feel both numb, and completely overwhelmed by the depth of my heartbreak. I'm sobbing uncontrollably, fighting every instinct I have to go running back to Carter, groveling on my knees for his forgiveness. My cruel words play over and over on a loop, and I hate myself more than I ever have. The familiar pull of the abyss is calling to me, where I don't have to feel anything. A dark lonely place where neither love nor hate can exist. It's been my safe haven over the years. A coping mechanism to stop the negative from pulling me under like a riptide. There have been a handful of times in my life over the past four years when I've contemplated what it would be like if the world stopped turning, if I jumped off the crazy train... if I just... stopped.

When we pull up at the airport, I grab my bags and slowly make my way inside, taking one last glimpse around me, at New York, before I find a new place to call home for a while, or maybe forever. Airports are crazy places, filled with so much joy and so much sadness. People saying goodbye to their loved ones as they embark on new adventures, and people welcoming their loved ones back with open arms and happy tears. It's a lonely feeling when you're surrounded by so much love, and none of it is for you. No one is going to come and wish me well on my journey. No one even knows I'm here, or where I'm going. I don't even know. As I reach the desk I realize just how bad I must look. All puffy eyes and mascara smudges.

"Are you alright, miss?"

"No... I mean yes, thank you. I'm just sad to be leaving."

"And where are you traveling today? How can I help?"

"I don't really know. Where is the next available flight going?" The recognition I see on her face kills me. "Within the U.S."

"Let me check for you." She quickly taps away on her keyboard, deciding the course of my life, without even knowing it. "The next flight leaves in half an hour, going to Delaware."

"What about the next flight after that?"

She gives a light chuckle before going back to her screen. "Texas. Boarding in one hour."

"I'll take it."

"Wouldn't you like to know where in Texas? It's a big State."

"Not really. It doesn't matter. I'll take a one-way ticket, please."

Her professional smile fades a little as she completes my request and hands me my boarding pass. "I hope you find what you're looking for, miss. Enjoy your flight."

"Thank you." I move at a snail's pace amongst the sea of people bustling through the airport, eager to reach their destinations.

It feels like the longest hour in the history of time, waiting to board. I am at war with myself the entire time, knowing that until I set foot on the plane and watch it taxi onto the runway, I still have time to change my mind, to try and repair the catastrophic damage I've caused. I find a corner to sit in, so as not to draw attention. Silent tears roll down my cheeks. I torture myself thinking about Carter. How is he feeling, what is he doing? Has he found someone to warm his bed for the night? I know that's what he did when I slept with Colin. Things were so different back then, and the depth of feeling between us now is... was... so much more profound. I contemplate whether I will ever be able to see him again. If the baby looks like him, I'll never be able to return to New York. If he was anyone else, maybe I could, but he's not. Lily is married to Xander, and Carter's been his best friend since birth. If he found out that the baby's his and that I kept it from him, he would never forgive me. And rightly so.

Should I just be selfish and tell him? He says he doesn't want kids, but maybe it would be different with me? Maybe he would thank me in years to come for giving him something he didn't even realize he wanted? My heart begins to quicken, a kernel of hope in my spiraling confusion. And then his words come flooding back to me.

"There will be no children in the near future, if at all. Just let us be. We're happy just the two of us."

"No, Zia. Cazzo fai madonna. Non spaventarla."

"God's high five to men the world over, every month. You girls think we get upset that you're crabby and teary for a few days, when it's actually the opposite. We're just so fucking relieved that we haven't gotten you pregnant, we will put up with any level of crazy!"

Bile rises in my throat and make a mad dash to the restrooms. I barely reach it in time before watching the contents of my stomach spill over into a disgusting public toilet. I think I've hit rock-bottom. I really hope my life can't get any worse than this. If I could curl into a ball and wait for death, I would. But the churning sickness in my stomach only serves to remind me that I'm not just responsible for me anymore. I need to do what's right for my baby, for Carter's baby. He or she is all I have left of him, and I will cherish that with every beat of my heart, with every breath I take. I pull myself up off the floor, wash and freshen up, and then put my well-practiced mask firmly in place to get me through the flight.

When I arrive in Texas, I'm weary. I feel it in every bone of my body, in every fiber of my being. I switch my phone on just long enough to check Google for a decent hotel in the area. I hail a cab and make my way to the local Hilton, upset that my phone had no messages, and I know it's selfish. Once I've checked in and gotten my key card, I make my way up to my modest room. As I open the door, it hits me just how different this is from my time spent with Carter in Italy. We were surrounded by beauty, love, and laughter. Now I'm alone, pregnant and broken-hearted. I let the full impact of what I've done sink in, crawling up onto the bed, using all my energy to pull back the crisp white sheets and cocoon myself inside of them. I've never cried so much in my life. I stay in the room for a week, without setting foot outside the door. The only time I leave the bed is to puke or open the door for room service. My face is permanently red and puffy, my eyelids are almost swollen shut, my nose hurts from endless tissues and I have a constant headache from the sheer exertion of crying. It's only after a week of this that I find the strength to drag myself into the shower and take a good long look at myself in the mirror. I can see the small changes in my body, the slight swell of my normally flat stomach, and the fullness of my breasts. It's then that I pull myself out of my pity party and make a plan.

I need a job, an apartment, and a life.

THE NIGHT I LEFT, I SENT LILY A TEXT TELLING HER THAT I WOULD BE traveling for a while and not to worry. She was still on her honeymoon and I didn't want to worry her or ruin it for her. As soon as she got back and found out from Carter what had happened between us, she inundated me with phone calls, texts, and countless voicemails begging me to contact her. When she found the note in my apartment, she left me a message sobbing her heart out, begging me to come back and sort things out. I haven't been able to call her. It's too painful, and still too raw. If I heard her voice right now I would confess everything and she would have me back in New York before I could blink. But I can't ignore her, she's my best friend, so I've taken to short emails, letting her know I'm doing okay, and that I've made a friend here who keeps me sane with her brand of insanity. Her name is Sarah. She works at the same bar I've been working at since I arrived. She's really nice and she knows a little of my situation, but never judges.

I don't know why I chose Texas—maybe because Lily grew up here before she moved to New York... or maybe because it was the next flight out after Delaware! Either way, I feel like I still have a part of my best friend with me as I take in the sights and smells of the city, wondering what her life was like here with her dad.

She always replies to my emails within ten minutes of receiving them, always signing off with the same heartfelt plea. *Please come home, Addi. I miss you and I love you.* It makes me cry every time, and it doesn't help that my hormones are all over the place.

I'm three months along and the pregnancy is going well. I'm eating healthily, nurturing our baby growing inside me in any way I can. I've found a nice local doctor who's been monitoring the progress of me and the baby, giving me regular check-ups and my first ultrasound. Seeing the baby for the first time on the monitor was unbelievably emotional, being able to see what Carter and I created together. I feel so close to him when I lie my hand on the almost imperceptible bump of my stomach. I find myself lying for hours at a time, remembering his touch, his voice, the way he loved me with everything he had. It's gotten easier to let myself remember. At first I was so distraught I couldn't hold onto the memories for any length of time. I worried I was forgetting everything, except the hole in my chest where my heart used to be. The heart I left in New York, with *him*. Not thinking about him was worse than thinking about him, so eventually I let myself feel, let myself remember, and now those quiet moments are what I cherish most.

I have a cute little one-bedroom apartment close to the bar. It's not a palace by any stretch of the imagination, but it has everything I need. The town is small, and everybody knows everybody. I grew up knowing that these sorts of towns exist, with populations barely reaching into the thousands, but this is the first time I've actually experienced it firsthand. It's comforting to be taken in and accepted by everyone, especially when you're on your own and trying to make a home for yourself. My co-workers are great, Sarah and I are usually on shift together so we have some laughs to pass the time. We've become quite the team now, and the regulars love our crazy banter. Sarah helped train me, teaching me how to pull the perfect beer, how to make cocktails, and pretty much everything else that comes with the job. Having never worked a bar before, I am so grateful they took a chance on me. I'm a quick study too, so I had it all down pat in less than a week.

My manager Hank is an eternal flirt, quite a bit older, and super protective of me and my bump. Gladly I'm not really showing yet, but I thought it best to tell him straight off the bat. He's like my own personal bouncer. Whenever a customer gets a little over friendly, or the place gets a bit rowdy, he's there in a heartbeat, watching over me, looking out for me. He's become like a brother in the few weeks I've known him.

When I'm not working, I'm reading up on pregnancy, the do's and don'ts, and what to expect when it comes to the birth. It's sad reading about the things you and 'your partner' can do together, knowing that I will have to face the biggest moment of my life alone. It terrifies me. It makes me want to run back to Carter, beg for his forgiveness and confess the real reason I left. But every time I find myself staring at his number, I remind myself why I did what I did. I wanted him to have the life he wants, the life he deserves. Kids were never part of his plan, and I couldn't corner him and force it on him. I tried that with Gavin and look how that turned out. Two days after Gavin found out I was pregnant, I wasn't pregnant anymore... just the way he wanted it.

I lie awake at nights thinking about my angel baby. What he or she would've looked like, whether it was a boy or a girl, and would they have looked like me? Questions I will never know the answers to. I was young and naïve, not strong enough to stand up for what I wanted. I wasn't ready to be a mom, but I would have worked it out. I would have done my very best to be a great mom for my baby, but I never got the chance. That's why I just couldn't terminate this pregnancy. I never planned to have kids, especially after what happened with Gavin, but as soon as I knew a life was growing inside me, a life that Carter and I created together, in love, I felt like a mom.

The hardest thing I have ever done, was walk away from Carter. Any of life's trials that may come my way from this point on will never be as brutal as that moment. I would take a thousand beatings from Gavin before I would want to relive telling Carter I didn't love him. I needed for him to believe me, but at the same time, I wanted to scream at him, *how could you doubt my love for you even for a second?* It's something I've struggled with every night as I lie my head down on the pillow, next to an empty space, where *he* belongs. Every night is the same, falling asleep with tears dripping down onto the soft cotton sheets, as I let myself remember his touch, his smell, and the way I felt when I was in his arms, warm, safe and content.

CHAPTER 26

CARTER

"THIS HAS GOT TO FUCKING STOP... NOW."

"You don't have to shout, Xander. For fuck's sake."

"I'm not shouting. You're just so hung over that a fucking fly would sound loud to you right now."

I open my eyes to take in my surroundings. Shit. I completely trashed my office last night and then slept on the goddamn couch. Could I be any more pathetic?

"Come on. You're coming back to my place."

"You don't have to do this, man."

"Well, apparently I do. You don't seem to be getting your shit together by yourself, so hurry the fuck up and let's go."

"I need to clean this place up first."

"No, you don't. I've already organized for one of the staff to do it, and I've offered them double pay to keep it quiet."

My body sags, exhausted from trying to deal with everything alone for the past month. "Okay. Thanks, Xander." I follow him out, a living breathing zombie. A shadow of my former self.

His car is parked out front and I literally crawl into the back of the big SUV, passing out as soon as my face hits the cool black leather seats. It must only be a ten-minute drive to Xander and Lily's apartment from the club, but I'm jolted awake by the door opening and the sun streaming in.

"Fuck."

I stumble into their building, Xander propping me up in the elevator to stop me from collapsing under the weight of my own body. When the door swings open, I'm greeted with the sight of Lily pacing the floor, worry etched on her brow. She turns to see me, limp and pathetic at her husband's side.

"Oh my God, Carter." She rushes over and pulls me into a tight, heartfelt hug. "I've been so worried about you. Are you okay? Come and sit down. I'll make you something to eat."

My voice is a gruff whisper. "I can't eat anything right now. Maybe I could just have a shower and crash for a bit? Sorry to put you out like this."

Her tiny, warm hand cups my cheek, caressing it with her thumb. It's a tender gesture and I appreciate the show of affection. "You're not putting us out. I'm glad you're here. Anything you need, Carter, honestly. I'll go get some towels and put the shower on in the guest bathroom for you. It'll just take a minute. I'll be right back."

As I watch her scurry off down the hall, my heart aches, remembering her and Addi together. She's hurting, too, and it's my fault. I pushed her best friend to leave everything behind. She couldn't even stand to stay in the same State as me. I should have been the one to go. To let her keep her life and her friends here in New York. I hate to think of her, wherever she is, alone, with nothing of her former life to hold on to.

Xander comes over with an espresso held out to me. "Think you might need this. I'm not coming in the shower with you to keep you upright. I love you, man, but I draw the fucking line at washing your junk."

I manage a small laugh before gulping down the steaming hot shot of coffee. "Understood." Lily appears, telling me the room is ready and that she's laid out some of Xander's clothes for me to change into after my shower. "I can't thank you enough, Lil. I really appreciate everything you guys have put up with from me over the past few weeks."

"We're not just friends, Carter, we're family. Don't ever forget that." With a nod and a strained smile, I head down the hall and into the guest room.

I strip off my clothes, thinking I should just burn them after last night. The thought of that girl all over me, and calling her *Tesoro*—fuck—it makes my skin crawl. I throw them into the laundry bin before stepping into the shower. No amount of water can wash away how gross I feel. I've fucked a lot of women in my life, for a lot of different reasons, but I have never tried to pretend they were someone else. And I have *never* called anyone Tesoro before. It was special, just for Addi, and last night I turned it into something dirty and meaningless.

As I let the water wash over me, I think back over the past four weeks. I've done and said so many things I'm not proud of—used so many women. Let everything around me, including my friendships, crumble. I am a fucking sorry excuse for a man at the moment. No wonder Addi ran away.

I don't even bother to dry off. I just drop face first onto the bed and fall asleep, completely naked, on top of the covers, sunlight still streaming in through the windows. It's a small comfort to know that I'm not alone in the apartment. This place might not be my home, but it feels like *a* home, and the low hum of people I love talking and getting on with their lives in another room is a welcome sound as I drift off into a dreamless sleep.

WHEN I WAKE IN UNFAMILIAR SURROUNDINGS, I DON'T HAVE THE SAME panic that's plagued me of late. I'm not drunk, and I know where I am. I can hear familiar voices coming from the living room. Xander, Lily and... Vittoria? What is she doing here? I quickly dress in a pair of jeans and plain fitted black t-shirt of Xander's that Lily left out for me. I doubt he'll want these jeans back after my junk has been commando in them. I'm certainly not wearing his fucking boxers. It would be tantamount to rubbing our junk together. Fuck that! I'll buy him a new pair of jeans. I grab the cons I was wearing last night and make my way out to the living room.

"Feeling any better?" Lily looks concerned, and it warms my heart to know she still cares about me after I drove her best friend away.

"I feel a million times better. Thanks, Lil. It was nice to wake up in a bed for a change. And thanks for the clothes. I think I'll just incinerate what I had on yesterday." She looks at me with a confused frown. "The less said about that the better. Some things I just don't want to know."

"Come sit down with us. I think it's time we had a conversation."

"Oh fuck. Are you guys doing an intervention? I've really hit an all-time low now."

Xander laughs. "It's not an intervention. Calm the fuck down. We're all worried about you, and I have some information that I think, if you're honest with yourself, you'll want to know."

"I remember you said you know where she is. She doesn't want me, man. I need to start coming to terms with it without giving myself liver disease. She moved away from everything she loved to get away from me, and if she wanted me to know where she was, she would have contacted me by now." I slump down onto the couch next to Vittoria.

"Hey, Tori. It's so good to see you. Wish it was under better circumstances, but it's great that you're here." She cuddles into my side, wrapping her arms around my waist.

"I love you, Carter. You've always been there for me, and now I'm going to do the same for you. Addi and I were close before she left. She and I... understand each other. I know you saw it in her, the same brokenness that I had... have. There's more going on here, I can feel it."

I pull her tight to me. "I appreciate that, sis, but she made her decision. I pushed her too far and she snapped. She didn't love me. End of."

She wrestles out of my arms, rearing up, exasperation on her delicate features. "She loves you. How could you lose sight of that? There is *obviously* something else going on here, Carter. She *needs* you. I know you're hurting but you need to go and get her back. Bring her home, where she belongs, with you."

Lily cuts in. "She's right, Carter. I have never seen Addi *so* in love with someone. She is head over heels for you. I know it! I don't know what she was thinking, or what's going on, but I need you to go and bring her home. Please. She belongs here with you, with us."

"I don't know, Lil. She had a lot of issues after Gavin, but she told me everything that happened with him and I thought we'd moved past it."

"What happened with Gavin? It's obviously more than him just cheating on her. Isn't it?" Her voice is distressed, her mind probably racing, contemplating the awful possibilities.

"Yes, is the short answer. I think she was ashamed and didn't want you to think less of her. I can't go into more detail. It's her story to tell and I can't break her trust. Maybe if she had confided in you, you would have been able to help her in a way I obviously couldn't."

"It's not your fault." Vittoria interjects.

"I thought she trusted me enough to tell me *anything*. I was wrong. I failed her, Tori. The same way I failed you."

Vittoria grabs my face in her hands, forcing me to look at her.

"You listen here, Carter de Rossi, and listen well. You did not fail me! You were fourteen years old for God's sake. There is no way you could have known what was going to happen. There was no way *any* of us could have known what he was capable of. You..." Tears fill her eyes as she continues. "You saved me, Carter. So many times, I could never possibly repay you. Every night you sat with me, wrapped me up in blankets and rocked me to sleep, singing to me to chase away my demons. I could *never* have lived through all of that without you. You have been my rock, my constant. I know you've carried your own demons from that day, and that it's effected your relationships or lack thereof with women. Do you have any idea how happy it made me to see you with Addi? You love her with complete abandon, one hundred percent all in. I know what it took for you to do that, and how hard this must be. But think, Carter... think? Please, look back at your time with her before the night she left, and ask yourself honestly, do you really believe that she doesn't love you? That she never loved you? Siete due corpi, ma un'anima sola." *[You are two bodies, but one soul.]*

In an instant, every memory of Addi flashes before my eyes. All the times she said she loved me. The way our bodies moved so intuitively together, molded as if by fate. A perfect fit. And then it slams into my chest like a Mack Truck. How did I not see it before? There were so many times in Italy when she was trying to tell me, pleading with me to remember no matter what, that she loves me. Holy fucking shit! *She was planning to leave me when we were in Italy.* This had nothing to do with me asking her to move in. Vittoria's right. There's something else going on. A rush of adrenaline courses through my veins, jolting me back to life for the first time in a month.

My voice is low and measured.

"Xander... where's my girl?"

CHAPTER 27

ADDI

I'M WORKING TONIGHT, AND I'M ALREADY COMPLETELY AND UTTERLY exhausted. I've been sick more than usual today but I've dragged myself out of bed to make my shift on time. I know Hank would have given me the night off, but I need the distraction and routine that working in the bar provides. I still have access to all my accounts and Daddy's money, but I need to start taking responsibility for my own life. When things settle down, I'm going to try and find an advertising job in the city, but for now the bar is just what I need.

Once I'm up and dressed I feel marginally better, taking the time to do my hair and make-up. It always acts as a little pick-me-up. That's what my mom always told me, and I swear by it. Or at least I used to. As I sit and stare at my reflection I don't even recognize the girl staring back at me. My eyes are sunken and tired looking, the sparkle that once glimmered brightly is gone. My hair is always scraped back into a ponytail. It's easy for work, and I don't have any desire to spend hours styling it to keep it straight, for no one to see. I don't fit any of my favorite clothes. I've had to buy new jeans and tops, and a few skirts. There isn't exactly much choice around here, but I managed to get some stuff delivered from the city. It's bad enough I have nothing that's familiar to me and my ass is apparently growing exponentially, I am *not* giving up my favorite brand of jeans just yet, damn it!

As I pull into the parking lot of Joe's, I have a strange feeling that someone is watching me. I look around the lot, but there's no one there. I must be imagining it. I slam the door on my rental and head in to start my shift. I'm met by a warm welcome from the regulars and staff. It's Saturday night and the place is packed, so I quickly don my black uniform t-shirt with 'Joe's' emblazoned in big red letters across my chest and throw my bag in one of the lockers. On my way out to the bar, Hank shouts me into his office.

"Everything okay, Addi? You look pretty beat. You sure you don't want to take the night off. I can call in one of the other girls to cover for you." He's always so sweet to me.

"No, I'm good. Just couldn't sleep last night, but I *want* to work. Trust me, I'm better off here than I am sitting in my apartment moping and feeling sorry for myself."

"Okay, sweetheart. But if you feel bad at any point tonight, just come and tell me and you can go."

I give him a real, honest smile, which doesn't comes naturally to me these days. "Thanks, Hank. You're the best."

"I know. I'm fucking awesome." I take my leave, laughing all the way down the hall and out into the bar.

It's jam packed tonight with all our regulars and some out-of-towners who were here for one of the high school football games. I'm still not up to speed on everything that goes on in this town, but I know the team is the center of the universe for most people who live here. I get to work, taking up residence at the bottom end of the bar while Sarah works the top. The hours tick by quickly, serving drinks non-stop. I don't even have time for my break, but I don't mind. Anything that distracts me from Carter is a good thing.

Every now and then throughout the evening I get that same feeling I had in the parking lot, like someone is watching me. I scan the bar several times, but don't see anyone looking at me, or anyone who looks out of place. I tell myself it must be my crazy hormones and overactive imagination playing tricks on me.

About an hour before closing, the party is still in full swing and I'm dead on my feet, serving drink after drink, so I'm in no mood for the douchebag who pulls up a stool in front of where I'm serving. "Hey, baby. Can I buy you a drink?"

"No thanks. I'm working. What can I get for you?"

"A beer, and your phone number." Everything about him makes my skin crawl.

I open a bottle of beer and place it down in front of him. "Here's your beer."

"You forgot your number."

"No, I didn't. I'm flattered, but I'm not interested."

He's obviously had plenty to drink before sitting down to the beer I've just served him.

"What's your problem, baby? You frigid? Need a guy like me to show you how to have a good time?"

I turn to walk away but he rears up over the bar and grabs my arm.

"Let go of me."

"Don't be so uptight. No one likes a frigid girl." I am frozen to the spot, déjà vu of so many similar moments with Gavin flashing in my head. I would normally rip a guy like this to shreds, but that was the old me. I'm a complete wreck, emotionally and physically drained, and I panic. I start frantically searching the bar, as if by magic, my knight in shining armor will appear... my Carter. Before I know what's happening Hank is ripping the guy's arm off me, most likely breaking it in the process.

"Are you okay, sweetheart? Are you hurt?" I throw myself at him, clinging for dear life, my whole body shaking from the shock of what just happened.

"Thank you so much." I begin sobbing, standing behind the bar while everyone stares at me.

Hank scoops me up into his arms and lifts me out into the hall, away from prying eyes. My hands are wrapped around his neck, my cheek burrowed into his chest, the tears flowing freely down my face. "Carter... I just want Carter."

Hank kisses the top of my head. "I know, sweetheart. I know." He places me on the couch in his office. "Stay here. I need to go and deal with that schmuck."

I let my muscles relax, slumping further into the sofa cushions, emotionally exhausted by what just transpired. I try to shut it all out, to flip the switch and let myself become numb, but it doesn't work. Not anymore. *He's* always in my thoughts, the permanent ache in my chest a constant reminder of what I've lost.

I can hear the commotion from all the way back here, and when Hank returns, he tells me some guy no one knows started pounding on the douchebag who grabbed me, shouting and swearing at him. Apparently, he won't be talking, drinking, or trying to intimidate women anytime soon. They had to send for an ambulance because his face was so messed up. My unknown protector left before anyone could get his name or thank him for standing up for me. I figure he didn't want to be asked any questions about what happened. An assault charge would be a hell of a price to pay for someone you don't even know. I don't think I'll ever hear the end of it from Sarah. She says the guy was like Hercules—a demigod, gorgeous, muscled and chivalrous. She makes me laugh when she says her panties literally disintegrated at the sight of him, and then a heavy weight settles on my chest. I'm flooded by visions of a perfect God-like body, the most stunningly handsome face I've ever seen, and a soul even more beautiful. He crowds my thoughts as I fall apart. I'm so devastated by my own self-inflicted loss that I begin to wail, long, pained, soul-wrenching sobs. Sarah and Hank chalk it up to hormones and a traumatic night, and I don't tell them any different. To say it out loud right now, would be more than I could bear.

My life is a mess, my heart broken beyond repair, and the only person in the world who can fix it, the only person I want to be with more than anything right now, is the one person who hates me. I miss everything about him—his face, his smile, the way he held me close and made everything around us disappear. He made me feel so safe and loved, but that's gone now, and I'm completely lost without him.

CHAPTER 28

CARTER

As soon as Xander told me where she is, I headed back to my apartment, packed a bag and booked the next flight out to Dallas. I have an address and the name of the bar where she works—Joe's. How fucking original. The flight feels endless, and I'm a little on edge by the end of it, desperate to get to my girl.

I don't even bother going to my hotel when I arrive, instead opting to drive straight over to her apartment in the rental I picked up at the airport. When I pull into the small town, I just can't imagine this being somewhere that Addi would choose to live. She's sophisticated and refined, and she definitely enjoys the finer things in life. I would say this place isn't big enough to hold her attention, but what the fuck do I know? This entire scenario just seems like a work of fiction to me. If someone explained the last six weeks of my life to me, I would swear blind they made that shit up.

I have no idea what I'm going to find when I come face to face with Addi, or what I'll say to her. I was so focused on getting here, on being in the same State as her, I didn't take the time to work out what I want to say. I can't exactly just say *Hey, Addi. I know you really love me. I've come to take you home.*

I try her apartment first, but there's no answer, so I quickly drive all of two blocks to the bar, but as I pull up, I'm frozen to the spot when I see her slender frame getting out of a car in the parking lot. My heart lurches up into my throat, constricting my air supply. She looks fucking breathtaking. She's too far away to see me, but I know for certain it's her. I could spot her in a crowd of thousands. I can't make my hands move to open the door handle, so I just take a moment to watch her.

She turns around, scanning the lot as if she can *feel* my eyes on her. It sends a shiver down my spine, knowing that I still have an effect on her, even if she doesn't know it. When she finally makes her way inside, I feel bereft. Just the sight of her was enough to fill at least some of the void I've been living with for the past month.

I stare at the door now for half an hour at least, but I can't seem to make myself get out the goddamn car. Fucking pussy. My phone vibrates in my pocket, and when I check the display I see a message from Xander.

Xander: *Found her yet?*

Me: *Yes and no. Outside the bar.*

Xander: *She at work?*

Me: *Yeah. Saw her go in. Been sitting outside for 30 mins. Being a pussy.*

Xander: *Grow a pair and go get her.*

Me: *Fuck off*

Xander: *I'm wounded*

Me: *Maybe I should write her love letters for days and see if that works?*

Xander: *Fuck off*

Me: *Later, Jackass. I'll keep you posted.*

He's so fucking annoying sometimes, especially when he's right. I get out of the car and make my way over to the entrance. When I pull back the door, I'm greeted with a cacophony of voices. The place is packed, with what seems to be football fans. Addi is behind the bar, working endlessly, with a swarm of customers around her end of the bar.

I decide to find a spot in the corner where I know she won't see me, and I can just watch her for a while, until she takes a break, or it calms down a little. I find myself sitting for hours, but time means nothing to me. I could stare at her 24/7 and never get tired of seeing the way her body moves, and her smile, God, her smile fucking kills me, but she looks tired though. She doesn't have the same vibrancy that once oozed from every pour. I can tell, from one hundred feet away, she's not the same girl I fell in love with.

At regular intervals throughout the night, she scans the room. I'm not sure if she's looking for someone, but I like to think she can feel my presence. Maybe it's wishful thinking, but we used to be able to sense each other in a room full of people. It didn't matter where she was in my club, even at full capacity I could still sense her. She's like a magnet I'm inexplicably drawn to, with a force I just can't fight against. I don't *want* to fight it. I just want her to remember how it feels between us when I whisper in her ear, or when I touch her. The way I make her body shake with an intensity and euphoria that only I can give her.

I'm quickly distracted from my reverie when I see one of the guys sitting at the bar obviously trying to flirt with her. My fists ball at my sides. I know I need to calm the fuck down, but I *hate* the idea of anyone being close to her, when I can't be. And then it happens… he almost throws himself over the counter to grab at her when she tries to walk away.

All I hear is a buzzing in my ears as my blood begins to boil. A red mist of pure rage descends, clouding my vision. Everything and everyone around me becomes insignificant. They are mere obstacles in the way of me getting to Addi. Adrenaline courses through me, readying my muscles for a fight. I start shoving people out the way, pushing through the crowd… and then I stop. A big guy, probably about fifteen years older than me storms out and appears beside Addi behind the bar. He throws the asshole to the ground, and she turns to him immediately, burying her face in his chest. He holds her with a ferocity and a tenderness I recognize well. I watch, helpless and broken as he scoops her up, her arms wrapping around his neck, her face seeking comfort against his shoulder as he carries her out of the bar, and away from me.

She's moved on. *She's fucking moved on.*

She doesn't need me to rescue her. She doesn't need me at all.

She really did leave because she wasn't in love with me.

I feel like I've been hit in the chest with a sledgehammer. I had a glimmer of hope when I stepped in here tonight. A small sliver of a chance at the future I so badly wanted with her. And now it's gone. I see the guy who practically assaulted Addi stumbling to his feet, and I set my sights on him as the target for all my rage, all my disappointment, all my heartbreak. I quickly make my way to where he's hanging onto the bar and as my fist connects with his face, I feel a marginal amount of relief wash over me. I *need* this, and he *needs* to pay for laying a finger on Addi.

"What the fuck, man?"

"Don't you ever fucking look in her direction again, understand?"

"Fuck you. It's none of your goddamn business. Who the fuck is she to you? Some cock tease, piece of ass."

"Say goodbye to eating solid food, you fucking piece of shit. You don't deserve to breathe the same fucking air as her." I start beating him so hard my knuckles bleed.

"What. Is. She. To. Me?" I spit out between blows.

"She's my fucking world! My fucking everything!"

No one even attempts to pull me off this guy. Obviously Addi is held in high regard already. The guys who surround me as I continually lay into this pathetic excuse of a man, are chanting and shouting for me to hit him harder, hit him again, to show him what happens when you mess with a lady in this town. I don't stop until I hear his nose crack underneath my fist. I back off, leaving him cowering like the little pussy he is. His face is unrecognizable, his eyes black and blue, covered in blood and already swollen shut. His nose is plastered across his face, and his lips are bleeding. I stare down at my hands, cut and bloody from my own brutality. I can't fucking breathe. I stagger through the cheering crowd and out into the parking lot, bending over with my hands on my thighs, struggling to pull in a lung full of air. What the fuck just happened?

I hold it together just long enough to get over to my car and slump into the driver's seat. I don't know how long I sit in silence, thinking about Addi, so close, and yet further away than ever. I start slamming my hands against the steering wheel, my frustration nowhere near exorcised by the beating I just gave Joe-fucking-Handsy back there.

I hang my head in defeat. "Come ho potuto essere così fottuta-mente delirante? Fanculo! Perchè, Addi, perché lui? Perché non ero abbastanza? *[How could I be so fucking delusional? Fuck! Why, Addi, why him? Why wasn't I good enough?]* I love you more than he ever could."

I'm startled by a rap on the window and turn to see a pretty little redhead staring back at me. I instinctively lower the window, even though I have no desire to talk to anyone right now.

"Everything okay?" She gives me a sultry smile and I can tell she's hot for me. "I just wanted to make sure you were okay. I saw what you did back there, defending Addi. It was really... chivalrous of you. Do you know her?" I ponder her question for a moment, thinking about the girl I fell in love with, and the girl I just saw swept up in the arms of another man.

"No. I don't know her. I just don't like dickheads who think they can take what they want without permission. No woman should have to put up with that." I'm just trying to be honest, but I can see it's affecting her. She lets out an almost inaudible moan before biting her bottom lip, her breath becoming shallow and erratic as I stare into her forest green eyes. "Do you know her well?"

"Yeah, she's great. She hasn't been here long. Arrived from New York last month running away from some guy apparently. They wanted different things, so she split and ended up here. But enough about her. Can I get you some ice for your hand... or... anything at all?"

Her tongue darts out to wet her lips and I already hate myself for being this guy. I don't want to be a player anymore, but it's who I am, and right now, I need to lose myself, and try to forget about Addi. I switch on the charm, and ignore the nauseating feeling in the pit of my stomach.

"I'm sure I can think of something."

I open the door and step out of the car, looming over her petite frame, watching as her breath catches just from the brush of my hand over the swell of her breasts and down to her waist. I pull her tight against my chest and lowering my head to her ear.

"Do you like the idea of fucking a stranger in an alley, sweetheart?" She simply nods. "Does it make you wet? Make you feel dirty?" She's panting as I continue. It's just too fucking easy. "How badly do you want me to fuck you?"

Her voice is a breathy whisper as she answers me. "So fucking badly. Anything you want, baby… please." I take her hand in mine and lead her down the dark and dingy alleyway behind the bar.

"You got protection?" She pulls a condom packet from her pocket with a sultry grin. "Of course you do." I drag her into the darkest corner I can find before crashing my lips down on hers. She tastes like tequila as she swirls her tongue, teasing me, biting on my lip.

I quickly unzip her jeans and push them down her legs, together with the trashy G-string she's wearing, spinning her around to face the wall so I don't have to look at her while I fuck her.

"Bend over, sweetheart." Without hesitation, she offers herself to me, bracing her hands on the wall for purchase. I ram my fingers inside of her, feeling how wet she is already.

"Oh God, baby! Yes… that feels so good." I pull out of her, moving up to spread her arousal over her clit before shifting round to cover her ass.

"Just how dirty are you?" I press my fingers between her cheeks and she backs into them without flinching.

"You can take me anywhere you want, honey." Fucking perfect.

I rip open the foil packet with my teeth and slide the condom over my rock-hard cock, before spreading her cheeks and pressing into her, one hard inch at a time. When I'm seated to the hilt, I thrust two fingers into her pussy, massaging her clit with my thumb.

"Oh God… you're so big."

"Yeah… you like that? Enjoy the fucking ride." I hammer into her, taking what I need, telling myself over and over that this is who I am. This is what I want—dirty, hot sex, with no strings attached.

It doesn't take long for her to spiral over the edge into an intense climax, her pussy clenching around my fingers, her ass tight as a fucking drum around my cock. I chase my own release, pounding into her over and over again as she begs me for more. When it comes it's sweet fucking relief. All of my pent-up anger and heartbreak, momentarily forgotten.

As soon as I'm done, it all comes crashing back and I'm ready to get the fuck out of Dodge, but she has other ideas.

"What's your name?"

"None of your goddamn business, sweetheart. If you didn't need to know it *before* I fucked you in the ass, you don't need to know now." I give her a swift kiss on the lips before striding out of the alley without another word.

I hate what I've become. I'm not a player anymore. Over the past month I've become something much worse. I'm a completely different person. Before I met Addi I slept around, but I always treated women with respect and was very upfront about what I wanted. Now I'm just another dickhead who uses women and discards them for kicks. I've turned into… Gavin.

The realization rocks me to my core.

I'm disgusted by my own depravity. I've become the one thing I promised Addi I would never be. I don't fucking deserve her… I never did. She was right to leave me, to move on, to find someone who is incapable of sinking to the depths that I just did.

When I get back in my car, it's at least fifteen minutes before my body stops vibrating and I'm able to put the key in the ignition and leave the love of my life behind, in the arms of another man. A better man than me.

I CHECK INTO MY HOTEL JUST LONG ENOUGH TO WASH OFF THE BLOOD that's covering my hands, and the stench of the redhead from the alley. I change my clothes and put my t-shirt in the trash. When I'm satisfied I don't look like a homicidal maniac, I check out and make my way to the airport to catch the next flight back to New York, which doesn't leave for five hours. It's torture to be so close to Addi and know that I can never have her.

Time passes so slowly, I think I'll lose my sanity, everything about the past few hours playing over and over in my head. The image of Addi in the arms of another man is burned into my retinas. I can't escape it, and I can't bear to keep reliving it. I think about the last month of my life and how I can't keep doing this to myself and to the people around me. As much as I want to lose myself in the bottom of a bottle of Jack, I need to at least *try* to hold it together. I know I can't move on. It will never be an option for me, but I can put on a front. I can stop drinking. I can stop womanizing. I can make it seem to the outside world like I'm doing okay, and maybe one day years from now I might start to believe it myself.

When I'm finally sitting in my window seat on the plane, I watch as Dallas becomes a spec below me. The possibility of the future I came here to salvage, lost beneath the clouds. A dream that was never meant to be.

CHAPTER 29

ADDI

Two Weeks Later

My heart swells in my chest as I read and reread the email Lily sent me a few weeks ago. She's been working flat out in her free time writing her first novel, and it's finally ready to release. Of course, she refused Xander's help to get it published, instead opting to submit it to some of the contacts she's made through her new job. She handed in the manuscript under a pseudonym so as not to curry favor, and also because she knew the name Rhodes would get instant attention. She's so amazing. I really miss her. I miss talking, watching silly chick flicks, just laughing and joking the way we used to. I don't know if it will ever be the same after the way I left without a word or an explanation.

Her email arrived the night after the incident in the bar, and I burst into tears as soon as I saw her name in my inbox. Needless to say, I continued crying when I actually read it. Her book has been picked up by a small independent publishing house, and it's in production as we speak. The release is in two weeks and Xander is throwing a party to celebrate. It's so his style and I freaking love him for it. He loves her without apology, and I really admire him.

I've read the same message every single day for two weeks, her plea for me to come home if only for the release party. This is what she's worked toward for so long, what she's always wanted to do, and I am so proud of her, but I don't know if I can do what she's asking of me. If Xander is throwing the party, then he will most definitely be inviting Carter.

I'm not showing enough at this point for anyone to notice, and my morning sickness has stopped. Thank God! I want to see Lily so badly it hurts. We've never been apart this long since the day we met. I can't avoid her forever, and I don't want to. If I miss this major moment in her life, I will *always* regret it, and she will *always* resent me for it. You can't go back and fix things after the fact, and I understand how much it can eat away at you. If I could go back and change the way things happened with Carter, I would, in a heartbeat.

With my mind made up and my phone in my hand, I make the call I've been longing to for six weeks. It only rings twice before she answers.

"Addi?" God, I've missed that voice. It warms my heart and soothes my soul in an instant.

"Hi, Lily."

TWO WEEKS AFTER SPEAKING TO LILY, I'M HERE IN NEW YORK, standing in my old apartment, which my parents decided to keep, praying I would come home. It feels so empty without Lily and haunted by memories of Carter. I can barely breathe.

I had to go and buy a new dress for the party, because nothing in my wardrobe even remotely fits me now. I decided to go with something sexy and fitted, because if I go for anything else, people really would start talking. I've opted for a black Audrey Hepburn style dress, covered in a layer of the finest black French lace. I think I can pull it off, the black concealing the small rounding of my belly. I have a killer pair of peep toe heels and my hair is straight and sleek down my back which is no easy task! My make-up is minimal tonight, mainly because I'm exhausted by the time I'm done showering and styling my hair.

I'm ready just in time to leave for the Four Seasons—Xander's venue of choice. I told them I could just grab a cab and meet them there, but they insisted on sending David to pick me up. Lily asked me to fly in yesterday so that we could spend some time together, but I just couldn't do it. If I had seen her one-on-one I would have broken down and told her everything, and it would have ruined her big moment. I promised her I would stay for a few days, and I will, but tonight is her night, for her to revel in her achievement. Tomorrow I'll sit down with her and explain what's going on. The only thing I can't tell her is who the father is. It's best I keep that piece of information a secret... from everyone.

When the doorman calls to tell me David is waiting downstairs, I feel like my body is on fire, my stomach lurching up and into my throat. I know I'm going to see Carter tonight, and I have no idea how he will react to me, or how I'll react to him. I grab my bag and head downstairs, my heart beating so fast I'm scared I'll go into cardiac arrest. David is ever the professional, greeting me with a smile, opening the door for me, and driving me to the party without another word spoken. It gives me far too much time to worry about what tonight will be like, around everyone that I love for the first time in two months. My parents, Lily, and Carter. While I'm lost in my own world, the familiar streets of New York pass me by, and suddenly the door next to me swings open.

"We're here, Miss Warner." My brain just can't process the fact that all of the people I love most in the world are no more than two hundred feet from me.

I step out of the car, making my way up the steps and into the lion's den. I feel like I'm walking the green mile, heading for the gas chamber, my body vibrating with nerves. I'm directed to the ballroom by a member of staff, and as I step into the crowd, I immediately *know*... he's here. I can still sense him, scanning the room until my eyes stop—frozen—staring across the room into the chocolate-brown depths that I see every night in my dreams as they glare back at me. I can see his breath catch at the same time as my own and all I want to do is run to him, but I know I can't make the first move. I broke everything we had, and he has no idea why. I can't force him to speak to me, but I'm praying he will. I desperately want to hear his rough, low, gorgeous voice. As I stand, willing him to stride toward me with the lithe elegance I love, he shifts his gaze to the pretty blonde trying to get his attention, turning his body away from me. It's a blow to my already tenuous confidence. I'm not sure I can manage through this evening without breaking down.

I'm out of place and lonely, in a room full of family and friends, until I feel a warm hand on my shoulder and turn to see my mom and dad, the widest grins on their faces as they envelop me in a Warner family hug. Normally I would be embarrassed, but in this moment, I have never been happier to be at the center of my parents' affection. "Oh, sweetheart, we're so glad to see you." My dad's voice sounds shaky. "How are you, baby girl?"

I squeeze them both a little tighter, hoping that my voice doesn't betray me. "I'm okay, Daddy. I'm so happy to see you both. I'm so sorry I worried you." My parents still don't know I'm pregnant, but I told them I needed to get away after my break-up with Carter. I told them it was my doing, because I didn't want them to think badly of him, and they accepted it, never pushing me for more information.

"We're just glad you're okay, sweetie." My mom's voice is thick with unshed tears, and my heart hurts knowing how badly my actions have affected everyone I care about.

"Why don't I go get my girls some drinks?" My dad turns to head to the bar.

"Just an orange juice for me, Daddy. I have an early start tomorrow." He nods, thinking nothing of the lie that so effortlessly trips off my tongue.

"I better go find the woman of the hour and say hi. I'll catch up with you guys in a bit."

"Okay, sweetheart. We'll see you later. Please, don't leave without saying goodbye."

"I won't, Mom. I promise. Love you." I have to walk away before I start crying. The fact that they feel the need to beg me not to leave without saying goodbye to them is gut wrenching. What have I done to everyone? I hate myself for all the pain I've caused.

I slowly make my way through the crowds, nodding, smiling and saying the odd hello when a familiar voice grabs my attention. "The guest of honor is this way." It's Xander. I can see every emotion flit across his face—anger, pity, and confusion. "Please don't ruin this for her, Addi. She's worked so hard, against all the odds. She's been a wreck since you left. She's worried about you. We all are." The small admission that he doesn't completely despise me after what I did to his best friend is an olive branch I never expected, and it brings a lump to my throat.

I choke it back before I speak. "I won't, Xander. I promise I won't cause any trouble. I just wanted to support Lily tonight. I'm so proud of her. You know I love her like a sister."

He gives me the smallest smile. "I know, Addi, and she can't wait to see you."

There's a circle of people surrounding Lily, but when Xander's imposing frame appears, her eye is drawn to him like a moth to a flame, and it's then that she sees me by his side. I don't know how I thought she would react, but I'm elated when she practically starts shoving people out of the way to get to me, a massive grin on her face and tears in her eyes. She pulls me close, wrapping her arms around me, holding on as if she's afraid I'll disappear at any given moment.

"Addi... God, I'm so happy to see you." It's all she can manage before the tears spill out. "I've missed you so much."

I hold on to her as tightly as she does me. "God, Lily, I'm so sorry. I've missed you, too, more than you could ever know." We just stand, crying in each other's arms, oblivious to the party going on around us.

Xander steps in after a while, almost prying us apart. "This is supposed to be a happy occasion, ladies. Let's not forget, my amazing wife has just become a published author."

We stand, wiping our mascara streaked tears from our eyes, laughing at how ridiculous we must look to everyone around us right now.

"He's right, Lil. This is your night. We're not spending it blubbering like a couple of idiots. Let's get this party started. I'm so freaking proud of you, Lilliput. I always knew you would make your dream a reality." We give each other a happy hug before we join Xander and all of the other revelers in celebrating this amazing woman, my best friend, Lily Rhodes—author.

I can feel his eyes on me the entire night, but as the hours tick by, I realize he has no intention of speaking to me. I still can't stop myself from glancing in his direction every so often, and whenever I do, he's staring at me, studying me, his eyes raking my body from head to toe. It's thrilling, chilling, and devastating all rolled into one. I would give anything to feel his touch one last time, to breathe in his addictive scent while he ravishes my body.

I try to distract myself, making the rounds of friends I haven't seen in months, exchanging small talk and pleasantries, everyone avoiding the white elephant in the room. I can see it on each and every one of their faces—the unanswered question—*why did you disappear, Addi?* Gladly no one has the guts to ask, and I'm not going to offer up that information any time soon, or ever.

I'm finding that one of the major downsides of pregnancy is having a bladder the size of a pea now, and I've lost track of how many times I've had to use the restroom this evening. Returning from what I can only assume is my four hundredth trip to the restroom, I'm accosted by Carter in the lobby.

"Addison." The cool, detached way he says my name knocks the wind out of me.

"Hello, Carter. I… It's…"

"Save it. I think you've said all you need to say to me, but there are a few things I need to say to you."

His eyes devour my body as I stand no more than two feet away from him. His smell invades my senses, even more masculine and arousing than I remember. My memories are a cheap imitation of the real thing. My entire body aches at his proximity, and the gulf that's formed between us.

"Addi, I understand you don't love me. I'm not here to try and change your mind."

"Carter. Please. Don't."

He continues. "It's painfully obvious to me now. Why you left and why we could never work." My splintered heart can't take much more of this. "But you're punishing everyone else around you. Lily and your parents. I don't want that for you. My failings and what happened with us shouldn't come between you and the people you *do* love."

"Stop." My voice is a hoarse whisper, painful as I speak past the lump in my throat. "You don't understand."

"I understand perfectly."

"No, you clearly don't understand anything."

Anger flares in his eyes. "Now just wait a fucking minute, Addi. I'm trying to help you here, even though you dumped me and fell off the face of the planet in the blink of a fucking eye."

"Like you even cared. You never tried to call. You never texted me. You obviously weren't that heartbroken." I regret it the moment I say it. I'm just grasping at anything to stop myself from confessing everything to him right here in the lobby.

"What the fuck, Addi? *You're* upset because I didn't come groveling to you after you told me you didn't love me, and that you never had? Did I bruise your delicate fucking ego? I'm ever so goddamn sorry. MY... MOTHERFUCKING... BAD!" He runs his fingers through his hair in frustration.

"I'm so sorry, Carter." I'm overwhelmed with emotion, and all I can do is the same thing I always do when faced with a situation I can't deal with, I run. I turn on my heels and flee for the exit, my hand outstretched to hail a cab as soon as the cool night air hits my face. I can hear Carter behind me.

"Addi. Wait! I didn't mean that. Don't fucking run. Addi... Addi!"

A cab pulls up and I grab at the handle, shaking as I jump in and beg the driver to move, to get me away from here. As I look behind me with blurred vision, I see Carter, standing in the middle of the road, his arms in the air.

"Cazzo. Addi. Fuck!" I hate myself even more than I did before, if that's possible. I've learned nothing. I ran away... *again*. What the fuck is the matter with me? I broke my promise to my parents that I wouldn't leave without saying goodbye, and I broke my promise to Xander that I wouldn't cause any trouble tonight. As soon as Lily realizes I'm gone, she's going to be upset, and yet again, with *my* selfishness, I've ruined everything.

I don't deserve to be a mom. What hope does this baby have with me as its mother? This unbearable epiphany has me sobbing my heart out in another New York cab, driving away from Carter... again.

CHAPTER 30

CARTER

I'M BANGING ON THE DOOR TO ADDI'S APARTMENT AFTER CONVINCING the doorman to let me in without calling up to her first. "Open the door, Addi. We need to talk." There is silence for what seems like forever. "I know you're in there. I watched you come up."

"There's nothing to talk about, Carter. Please, just go away."

"I can't do that and you know it. You at least owe me this." The door slowly opens, her tear streaked face like a knife to my chest. She gestures me inside, reluctance evident on her face. "Is it so repulsive to you to be in the same room with me now, Addison?"

Her voice is a whisper. "That could *never* be true and you know it."

"Why would I know that? You walked out on me without so much as a second thought for how you made me feel or what I wanted, and you started a new life somewhere else. I tried to speak to you tonight and you fucking ran, Addi... you *ran*. It's classic you. I don't know why I'm still surprised by it."

"I guess I deserved that. But don't *ever* think that I never gave you a second thought. I was devastated when I left."

I can't hide the distain in my voice. "I highly fucking doubt it."

"You don't know what you're talking about."

"Well, fill me in, Addi, because I was left without a fucking clue that night."

"I left for you. So you could have the life you wanted."

"You're not even making sense, Addi. Don't fucking kid yourself that you did any of this for me. You did it for yourself, because you wanted something I obviously couldn't fucking give you. If you loved me... you never would have left."

"That's not true."

"The fuck it isn't! You're like a fucking grenade. You explode without any consideration for the people who might get caught in the crossfire. Do you have any idea what you did to me when you left? *Do you?*" Her tears begin to fall, but I've held it in for so long, I need her to know how I feel. "You fucking killed me, Addi. You shredded my heart, ripped it out of my fucking chest, and stomped all over it."

"I know." Her words are laced with remorse.

"I don't think you fucking *do*, actually! You have *no idea* what it took for me to open up to you, for me to love you, for me to trust you, and you fucking threw it away like it was nothing, like it was *less* than nothing."

"Carter... I need to explain."

"Maybe you should have done that sooner. I don't need to hear why I wasn't good enough for you now, Addi. It'll just add insult to injury."

"What do you want from me then? Why did you come here?" Her defeated tone makes me want to pull her into my arms and tell her it'll all be okay, but it's not my place now. My hands fist at my sides, fighting the urge to reach out and touch her.

I feel sick to my stomach as I choke out the reason I'm here.

"When are you going to tell, Lily?"

"Tell her what?"

"That you're pregnant."

Her face falls at my words. She knew this was the reason I came to confront her. She's not that naïve.

"What? How? How do you know?" Maybe she *is* that naïve, or

maybe she never fully understood how much I worshiped every inch of her body.

"You don't think I remember every curve and line of your body? I fucking memorized it and it's on a permanent loop in my head, tormenting me, night, after night, after night." I feel bile rising in my throat as I continue. "Is it his?"

She looks shocked. "What are you talking about? Who?"

"The guy I saw you with in Dallas."

Realization dawns. "You came to Dallas? When? Why?"

"Yes. Like the fucking idiot that I am, I came to bring you home to be with me. It was about a month ago. Xander found out where you were and as soon as he told me, I took the first plane out. I didn't even bother checking into my hotel before I came looking for you." Her face is distraught as I continue. "I watched as a customer was coming on to you. *He* came to your rescue before I could. It broke my heart all over again to see you cling to him for comfort. It fucking slayed me, Addi. I *did* however beat the ever living shit out of the guy who had been grabbing at you like a piece of meat. Then, I bought a ticket on the next available flight and came back to New York a fucking empty shell."

I watch as the tears spill from her eyes. "That was you?"

"Yes."

"I had the strangest feeling that night. It was as if I could feel you everywhere I went. Oh God, Carter. I'm so sorry."

The lump in my throat is too much to swallow down. I choke out possibly the hardest words I've ever had to say. "I'm happy for you, Addi. You'll make a wonderful mother and he obviously adores you. I just wish it could have been with me."

"What?"

"I said I'm happy for you."

"No! The other part."

"I just wish it could have been me. That *we* could have had a family together. It was my dream for us."

"But you said you didn't want kids."

"When?"

"At the rehearsal dinner, to your mom. Then you were horrified at the mere suggestion by your aunt in Florence. You called a period a fucking high five from God. What was I supposed to think?" She looks so distraught. It's killing me not to go to her.

"Addi, you had to have known that I was only saying those things so I didn't scare you off? How many times had you run from me? Look at how you reacted when I told you I loved you for the first time. Of course I wanted to be the father of your kids. I wanted everything with you. The house, the wedding, and the children who would be just as beautiful as you."

She sinks down onto the couch. "Oh my God! What have I done?" I crouch in front of her, desperate to touch her, to comfort her. "What have I done, Carter?"

"Talk to me, Tesoro. What is it?" Her sobbing makes me ache.

"It's yours. The baby. It's yours, Carter."

What the fuck?

"I don't understand."

This can't be real.

"I found out I was pregnant the morning of the wedding. I was terrified to tell you. I was ninety-nine percent sure the night of the rehearsal dinner, but I still had to take the test to confirm. When your mom brought up the subject of kids, I was devastated when you said you didn't want any."

"Holy Shit, Addi."

"I couldn't get rid of it, Carter. As much as I love you, and as much as I wanted to build a future with you, I couldn't get rid of it. I didn't want you to be trapped living a life you didn't want. A life you would end up resenting me for."

She breaks down completely, sobs wracking her fragile body. I can't hold back anymore. I scoop her delicate frame into my arms and carry her into the bedroom. I lie down on the bed, pulling her tight against my chest, my heart thundering against her back. Eventually the sobs turn to whimpers, and the whimpers fade until she finally passes out, her breathing becoming even and peaceful. I take this precious moment to move her hair out of the way, tracing the lines of her face ever so gently with my fingers.

"I wanted it all, Tesoro. I wanted you to trust me, to love me, to be the mother of my child, to be my lover and my wife." She stirs at my touch. "I love you so much, Addi. I failed you, but I won't fail our baby."

She turns in my arms, awake and staring at me with the softest, sweetest eyes I have ever seen. "Touch me. Please. I need to feel you. I've missed you so much, it's a constant ache in my chest." I can't resist her. I've wanted this for so long—for her to *want* me.

Without a word, I capture her mouth. Two months of devastation and longing are obliterated by this one small but overpowering connection. She tastes of cherries and Addi, just the way I remember, only sweeter. I suck and nibble at her lips, begging her to let me in, and as her tongue darts out to meet mine, an explosion of sensation erupts inside me. It's a heady feeling and it fuels my desire in a way I've never felt before. I lose all control. We grab at each other's clothing, ripping it, tearing at it, until only our naked flesh remains.

The feel of her skin against mine is divine, her slightly larger breasts pressed against the hard muscles of my chest, the beginnings of her rounding belly against my abs. Knowing that it's my baby growing inside her, that it's my seed causing these changes to her lush body, is the most erotic... sensual feeling in the world. I shift her onto her back, running my hand down her curves, learning the contours of her new body. My hand stops on her belly, gently caressing it. She tries to push me away.

"I know I'm getting fat. It's disgusting."

I move her hand and continue my ministrations. "Nothing about you is disgusting, Addi. Your body is more beautiful now than it has ever been." I kiss every inch of her stomach enjoying how it feels on my lips, soft and supple, her naked flesh quivering at my touch. As I make my way up her body, her breath becomes shallow, her moans the most amazing sound to grace my ears in what feels like forever. As I take her nipple into my mouth, my own groans reverberate against her skin, causing her back to arch off the bed, pushing herself further

RELENTLESS | 209

into my mouth. "Fuck. Addi. I've missed this. I've missed everything about you." I flick my tongue over the puckered tip, taking hold of her other breast in my hand. "Oh God. You feel amazing." Her breasts are fuller, heavier, and just fucking perfect.

"I've dreamt of this every night we've been apart, Carter. Please... don't wait any longer. Please, make love to me. I need you." I want so badly to take my time and savor every moment, but her words stir the urgency inside me.

I grab my cock, positioning myself at her entrance. "God, baby, you're so wet for me. I need a taste of you. I've been starved of you for so long." I pull her hips up, grabbing her ass and lowering my lips to her glistening folds. Oh My God. She tastes even better than I remember. Her moans and gentle whispers of my name are divine. As I continue to lick and suckle her clit, she falls apart beneath me, her orgasm a moment of pure bliss, not only for her, but for me. I've been lost without this connection, without her.

I drop her hips down to the bed and slowly inch myself inside her, my eyes rolling back in my head. I'm struggling not to come as soon as I feel her warm, wet flesh pulsing around my engorged tip. "You're so damn tight, baby." It takes me a few minutes to calm down before I can sink all the way inside her, seating myself to the hilt, stretching her to her fullest.

"God, Carter. You feel so amazing." Everything about this feels right, her voice, her body, the way I fit her so perfectly. I can't get enough. I start to move with long, slow thrusts inside her. It's a sweet kind of torture, achingly magnificent. I lower my mouth to hers.

"Taste yourself on me, Tesoro. Taste what I do to you. Remember it, and *never* forget it." She sucks my bottom lip, biting it gently with her teeth, savoring her own juices. It's so fucking hot, and I need to move faster, harder, but always careful not to let my body weight press against her stomach. As she grinds into me, meeting me thrust for thrust, I lose myself to the sensation, lust and desire taking over any rational thought. I just need to feel her. I lift her off the bed, cradling her close to my chest as I bring us up into a seated position.

"Ride me, Addi."

She immediately responds, anchoring her hands on my shoulders as she begins to move up and down the length of me, her clit brushing against the base of my cock as she picks up pace.

"God, Carter, I'm close. I need you to come with me. Oh… God."

"I'm right there with you, baby. Just let go."

Harder, faster, she looks fucking perfect riding me like she owns me, and she fucking does. I watch her beautiful breasts as they bounce up and down with every thrust, taking first one and then the other into my mouth. When she starts to tighten around my cock, I run my hands up her back, fisting them in her hair, holding her so I can watch as she falls over the edge.

"Look at me, Addi. I need to see you come." She bucks wildly against me, chasing her release and catapulting me into mine. "Holy fuck. Yes… cazzo… mia dolce bella ragazza… Addi." *[Fuck… My sweet beautiful girl]* We come together with an intensity and passion that's been haunting my dreams for months. It feels too fucking good, and I know she feels it just as much as I do.

"Carter! Oh God, Carter. Fuck… yes… yes!" As I spill myself inside her, hot spurts straight to her core, she cups my face, kissing every inch of stubble, licking along my jaw before darting her tongue into my mouth. "I love you, Carter de Rossi. I always have and I always will."

I gently lower her onto her back, our lips locked in a sweet and reverent kiss.

"Say it again."

"I love you, Carter. I always have… and I always will."

"Do you know how badly I've wanted to hear those words dripping from your gorgeous lips?"

She pulls me down onto her. "Yes. As badly as I've wanted to say them for two months." We lie together, our limbs entwined as we enjoy the sound of each other breathing, content in the silence, happy just to be together, until…

"Carter. Was that safe for us? For the baby? I know you must have been with other women while I was gone, and I don't blame you, but I'm just worried. Could the baby catch an STD?" My world comes crashing down around me… again. This is what she thinks of me? That I would put the health of my baby in jeopardy for my own sexual gratification? I'm out of the bed, gathering my clothes before she speaks again. "What are you doing? What did I say?"

"What did you say? This is exactly the problem, Addi, this is why we're in this mess in the first place. You don't fucking trust me!"

She's frantically scrambling to get to me. "Of course I trust you."

"No, you fucking don't. If you think for a second that I would have unprotected sex with you while you're pregnant with *my fucking child* if I wasn't one hundred percent sure it was safe, then you don't know me at all."

"I'm sorry, Carter. I didn't mean it. Please, don't go. Stay. We can talk about it." She's breaking my heart all over again.

"What do you want to talk about, Addi? All the women I fucked after you broke my fucking heart? I can't give you a number this time, baby, it wasn't fucking seven, that's for sure. I spent the first month after you left drunk and banging any woman who wanted me, because I needed to feel fucking wanted."

She moves to comfort me, but I recoil from her touch. I just can't bear it right now.

"Here's the ugly truth for you. I don't remember the names of any of the women I slept with while you were gone. And when I came to Dallas and saw you with that guy, I fucking snapped. I fucked a girl in the alley behind the bar and then I walked away from her like she was nothing. I fucking hated myself, Addi. As soon as I got home I got tested, I stopped drinking, I stopped using women to try to forget you and started trying to remember who *I* am. I never wanted to be *that* guy. I just wanted to be *your* guy."

I pull her naked body up and into my arms. "Addi. I love you more than you could ever understand. But we are… toxic. You can't trust me to look after you and do what's right, and I can't trust that you won't run away again. I don't know if we'll ever be able to trust each other, and maybe we can do that to each other, tearing each other apart trying to hold onto a love that is so phenomenal, all-encompassing, all-consuming, and that burns so brightly it will become caustic. I would do that for you, Tesoro. I would tear myself apart and give you my broken heart a thousand times over. But it's not just us now, Addi, we have a baby to think about. A baby I want so badly it hurts. It's a part of me, and it's a part of you. I can't be selfish. I've obviously failed you, or we wouldn't be standing here having this conversation, and it's breaking my heart all over again. I won't fail our baby, Addi. I can't live with that kind of failure."

Tears are streaming down her flushed cheeks as she chokes out her plea. "Don't do this, Carter. Please. I can't do this without you." I grab her face in my hands, forcing her to look at me.

"You will *never* have to do this alone, Tesoro. I will *always* be here for you and the baby, but the only way I can do that, is if we're not together right now." Her face drops to my chest. "We'll work it out, baby... somehow. I promise. It will take time, and we'll learn together, how to be a family, but we need to take it slow. Do you understand why I need to do this, cara mia? Why I need this time? Why *we* need this time? Tell me you understand."

"I understand. I just don't know how to live without this." She places her hand on my chest... over my wildly beating heart. "The last two months have been a living hell." She rests her head against my shoulder. "You're all I'll ever want or need, Carter."

"Tesoro. You are the love of my life. You will *always* be everything to me. That's why I can't fail you again." I kiss her head, my chest aching at the sound of her muffled cries. We stand like this until she has no more tears left to cry. "You need to rest, baby." I lift her into the bed, pulling the covers around her.

"Please don't leave. Stay with me. At least until I fall asleep."

I can't deny her.

"Of course I will." I lie on top of the covers, her head resting on my chest.

"Carter..." Her voice is a whisper.

"Yes, baby."

"I noticed the tattoo on your back." The silence is deafening as I wait for her reaction. "Why would you do that, after I treated you so badly?"

I stroke her hair as I give her an honest answer. "Because even in my darkest hour, I never stopped loving you… and you never stopped being my Tesoro."

She cuddles into me a little tighter. "Ti amo, Carter." My heart swells in my chest.

"I know, baby. Now try to get some rest." She falls asleep almost instantly, but I find myself unable to leave, lying with her for hours, staring at her stunning face, watching the rise and fall of her chest, wondering how the hell I'm going to do this. I've never had to put someone else's wants and needs above my own, but I need to now. Our baby needs to have a stable home, and all the love and attention they deserve. Addi and I will never be a stable force if we continue to tear each other apart with the depth of our love for each other.

We were meant to be, but sometimes, love, passion, and a connection so fierce it's a physical presence in the room around us, just isn't enough. Especially not when it will affect our baby.

It is 3 a.m. before I can bring myself to leave her, my sleeping beauty, destined to be mine, but always just out of my reach. I'll do my best to bring us back together, so that maybe, just maybe, we can have the future together that I so desperately crave with every fiber of my being.

CHAPTER 31

ADDI

I open my eyes, slowly coming around from the best sleep I've had in months, with the smell of Carter still lingering on my pillow, aware of a presence in the room with me. In my sleepy haze, I remember asking him to stay with me until I fell asleep last night, and I'm so happy he stayed. There was an awful moment when I thought he was going to leave and never come back. I turn to face him, but I'm more than a little surprised by the face staring back at me.

"Holy shit. Fuck a duck, Lil."

"Morning, sunshine." She's amused with herself. I'm just confused.

"What are you doing here?"

"Em… I used to live here, and you're still my best friend." I can see she's holding something back.

"Spit it out, Lil, you're a terrible liar."

She gives me a sympathetic smile. "Carter called last night and told me that you might need your best friend today. He wouldn't tell me anything more than that, said it wasn't his place, but he didn't want you to wake up alone. I came over a few hours ago and you looked so peaceful, so I just crawled in next to you like old times. I hope that's okay?"

"Of course it is. I don't deserve you, you know that, right?"

"You *deserve* a smack in the face for leaving me without a word. I've aged about ten years in the past two months worrying about your crazy ass."

I drop my head, completely ashamed of myself. "I'm so sorry, Lily. Truly. If I could go back and change it, I would."

She pulls me into her arms. "Please, just tell me what's going on, Addi." Her delicate perfume and the familiar scent of her shampoo gives me so much comfort. I fall apart in her arms. "You're scaring me. What's so bad that you had to run away?"

I take a deep breath and say the words that scare me half to death.

"I'm pregnant." She crushes my body against her own, as if somehow, I'll become a part of her if she squeezes me tight enough.

"Holy shit, Addi. I can't believe you've been dealing with this on your own. Is it... Carter's?" I push myself out of her grasp.

"Of course it's Carter's. Why would you even ask that?"

"Because you just packed up your shit and left him behind. Why wouldn't you tell him?"

"He knows now. I told him last night."

"No wonder he sounded like shit when I spoke to him. God, Addi. You have no idea how much that man loves you. He was a mess when you left."

"I didn't tell him, because he said he didn't want kids. I didn't want to trap him."

She's shaking her head, a sad, disappointed look on her face. "Addi, people say stupid stuff all the time. You should have given him the benefit of the doubt. He loves you more than anything. You should have trusted him."

"I know that now. When I told him, he explained the only reason he said he didn't want kids was so that I didn't get spooked and run away from him again. I'm such a freaking idiot, Lily. I know I should have trusted him. I've ruined everything."

"What happened when you told him?"

"He was angry, and disappointed that I didn't confide in him. We talked, we made love, I messed things up again."

"Wait... what?"

"I asked him if it was safe for the baby that we had sex without a condom. I know he must have slept with a lot of women while we were apart and I was worried."

"Oh, Addi. Come on. You know him better than that. He would *never* put you or the baby in danger. He might be a man-whore when he's heartbroken, but you are *everything* to him."

"I know, okay, I screwed up. He said he can't trust me, and that I don't trust him. He agreed to try and give us another chance, but he wants to take it slow. I can't mess this up again, Lil. I want to make it work with him and the baby. I want us to be a family."

"Well stop running, Addi. It hurts everyone who cares about you. If you do it again, he's not going to be so forgiving. You *broke* him when you left."

"What happened?" She takes a moment to think before she answers.

"Normally I would tell you to ask him, but I don't think it will help either of you right now. So I'll tell you."

She fills me in on everything that happened while I was gone—the drinking, the women, the complete disregard for his own wellbeing and even his night in jail. My heart breaks all over again realizing just how much I've hurt him.

"When he came back from Dallas, he just shut down. He cleaned up his act. There were no more women and there was no more drinking, but he was lost, Addi. Really fucking lost. Xander was worried he wouldn't get over you... ever. You know I love you, you're my family, but I was so damn angry at you for leaving this shit storm behind. You can't treat people that you *say* you love like that."

"I'm so sorry, Lily. I fucked up." She pulls me close.

"Yeah, you did, but you're back now, and we all still love you... including Carter. You're not alone in this. We're all going to be here for you and the baby. You need to prove to Carter that you can be trusted with his heart, and you need to learn to trust him with yours. He's completely and utterly head over heels in love with you, Addi. Embrace it and cherish it."

"I will. I promise. Thank you, Lil. I love you."

"Love you, too, friend."

We spend the rest of the day together, catching up on the two months we've been apart. I get to hear all about Lily's book and what's been going on with her and Xander. Now that she's focusing on writing, Xander has finally convinced her to give up the blogging job and he's planning to take some time off so that they can travel together.

Lily is already insisting she won't be going anywhere anytime soon, especially not before the baby is born. A better friend would argue with her, but I'm selfish. I want her with me through this and I know Carter will appreciate having Xander to talk to as we try to find our way back to each other and prepare to become parents.

When I finally curl up in bed, I can still smell a hint of Carter on the pillow. I lift my phone from the nightstand, debating whether or not it's a good idea to send him a message so soon, but in the end, I can't help myself.

Me: *Thank you for sending Lily. It was exactly what I needed.*

Carter: *You're welcome, Tesoro. I only wish I didn't have to leave you lying there looking like an angel.*

Me: *Why did you?*

Carter: *Because I want this to work. I want you so badly it hurts. I don't want to ruin it by jumping straight back in where we left off.*

Me: *I understand. I just miss you.*

Carter: *I miss you, too, cara mia. Now get some sleep, beautiful girl. We'll talk tomorrow.*

Me: *OK*

Carter: *I love you, Tesoro. Never doubt it.*

Me: *I love you, too. Night x*

Carter: *Buonanotte x [Goodnight]*

I snuggle down into my covers, a smile on my face, and a glimmer of hope in my heart.

CARTER AND I SPEND THE REST OF THE WEEK SPEAKING ON THE PHONE and texting. The day I went to visit my parents and tell them I'm pregnant, he left a package with the front desk so that when I got back I had a box full of my favorite candy and potato chips. I called him as soon as I opened it… well, maybe not right away… I may have wolfed down an entire bag of Hershey's kisses like a complete pig, and then I called him! We spoke for hours, and I admitted the Hershey incident, which had him laughing his head off at me and calling me his little piggy for the rest of the night. As long as I'm his, I don't care if I'm a girl, a piggy or a flying horse.

He assured me that my mom and dad will get over the initial shock and be happy for us. After all, we're giving them their first grandchild, but they're idealists and pretty old school. They were hoping I would have the big white wedding, followed by the pitter-patter of tiny feet. I don't think it was their dream for me to get pregnant by my boyfriend and then dump him and move to another State. My heart constricted in my chest at Carter's words to me.

"You can tell your dad that I would make an honest woman of you tomorrow if I didn't think I would end up like Richard Gere in *The Runaway Bride*." He was joking around, but I could tell there was a serious note to his comment, and it made me feel even worse about the way I've treated him. All I could do was try to lighten the mood.

"Wow… did you watch that movie with your boyfriend?" It did the trick and I took advantage of the reprieve, changing the subject. We made plans for Saturday, to go on a second chance, first date.

I'M NERVOUS AND EXCITED AT THE PROSPECT OF SEEING CARTER tonight, excited to spend time with him and nervous in case I mess it up. I'm starting to show now. It's like my belly just popped out in the past few days. I'm blaming the baby, but it could definitely be all the food I am constantly shoveling into my pie hole! Nothing fits, and I feel disgusting.

By the time the doorbell rings, I've shoehorned myself into a pair of black three-quarter length pants and a black lace tank top, mainly because it's stretchy and goes over my little bump. I've gone for some chunky purple accessories and soft waves in my hair. It's not classic Addi, but it'll have to do.

I open the door and the look on Carter's face is so damn sexy. His delicious chocolate-brown eyes rove all over my body, stopping dead when they reach my stomach. I defensively fold my arms across my front. In a heartbeat, he's in my space, invading my senses, pulling my arms apart and pinning them to my sides.

"Don't hide from me." I feel shy all of a sudden as he drops to his knees, letting go of my arms and ever so gently placing his large, warm hands on my belly. His gaze lifts to mine, a stunning smile splitting his face. "You are… breathtaking, Addi." He presses his lips to my stomach, right on my belly button. "So fucking amazing."

I can feel the tears pricking my eyes, and I start blinking them back, annoyed at my new, permanent state of emotional *defcon one*.

"Don't cry, cara mia." He gets up off his knees and stands in front of me.

I drink in the sight of him—tall, lean, muscular, and sexy as hell. He looks dangerous tonight, like the bad boy I met in Cube that first night. He's wearing dark blue jeans, faded in all the right places, a white fitted t-shirt highlighting every deliciously defined muscle of his torso to perfection, and to finish the look, a black leather jacket. His hair looks like he's freshly fucked, and all I want to do is grab it in my hands and guide his head to where I'm aching for him.

He wipes the tears from my cheeks. "How can you be crying, and at the same time, looking at me with such wild desire in your eyes?" I feel myself blush.

"Crazy pregnancy hormones." I'm expecting a laugh from him, but his eyes are fixed on me, on my lips. I can hear his breath quickening, his tongue darting out to wet his sinfully gorgeous lips.

"I want to take this slowly, Addi. I don't want to mess it up." He runs his hands through his hair, his eyes never leaving my lips. I mirror his action, darting my tongue out to wet my lips, inviting him to kiss me. The groan that escapes his chest, makes me weak at the knees and awakens the fireflies in my stomach, sending them into a frenzy of want and anticipation.

"We better go before I throw you over my shoulder, take you into the bedroom, and play out every fantasy I've had of you over the past two months."

"Would that be such a bad thing?" I watch the desire drain from his eyes, and I'm devastated.

"We can't just pick up where we left off, Addi. I'm sorry. As much as I want to make love to you… and believe me, I really fucking want to, too much has happened for us to just sweep it under the carpet and act like it doesn't exist."

"I understand."

"Do you? I want you so badly right now, my dick fucking aches. Do you know that's how much I want you? Do you know that's how much I need you? Do you understand how much it hurt when you left me?"

"I'm so sorry, Carter." He cups my face in his hands.

"I don't want you to apologize again. I don't want you to think that I'm punishing you by withholding sex, which is what the look on your face suggests. Please… believe me when I tell you this is torture for me, but that's how much I love you. I'm in this for the long haul, Addi. I am *all* in. I need you to trust me and I need to be able to trust you, but *never*, *ever*, doubt that I want you more than my next breath. I'm so fucking in love with you it's ridiculous."

I crack a smile.

"I love you, too."

"Good. So, are you going to put me out of my blue balls misery and distract me with dinner and a movie?" His mischievous grin is back, something I haven't seen in a long time, and it's a beautiful sight to behold.

"Well, just because you put it so eloquently… let's go, Casanova." He leans down, giving me a chaste kiss, before opening the door for me.

"Romance is my middle fucking name."

Our laughter echoes in the hallway as we enter the elevator and head out into the safety of surrounding ourselves with strangers. It doesn't always work for us, but Carter is fighting our overwhelming passion for each other, his noble intentions winning out over animalistic desire. I don't know how long I'm going to be able to stand it. I want to do as he asks and take it slow, but it's hard when every fiber of my being is screaming at me to seduce him, to make him mine again and let him take me as his own, claiming me, only for him.

CHAPTER 32

CARTER

Six Weeks Later

THESE PAST SIX WEEKS HAVE BEEN FUCKING TORTURE.

I'm trying to be the good guy. Thinking with my head rather than my cock, for a change, but I swear I'm getting calluses on my right hand from my frequent meetings with palm and her five sisters. I haven't jacked off this much since I was thirteen. I'm going to end up with carpel tunnel at this rate.

Every time I see Addi, she looks even more beautiful. Her breasts are fucking amazing, growing and filling out, readying her for motherhood. Her stomach is rounded and it's plain for all to see, she's carrying my baby. It's such a turn on I can't even describe it, knowing that I did this to her. I'm the only man who will ever do this to her. It calls to my most primal urges and desires when it comes to her.

We've been trying to take it slow, but we're talking about me and Addi—slow has never really been our style. There have been a few nights that I just couldn't leave. I couldn't resist my desire for her. We've made love, we've fucked and we've devoured each other on a few occasions. I know Addi doesn't want to take things slow, she's said as much, and when she sets her mind to seduction, I'm a fucking goner.

I'm starting to notice a change in her. I feel like she's beginning to trust me—really trust me. I don't want to get carried away because we have a long road ahead, and plenty of time before the baby is born for her to completely freak out and try to shut me out again.

Vittoria is back in town, and anxious to catch up with us, although, truth be told, I think she's more excited to see Addi than her big brother. I've invited Xander and Lily to come over to my place tonight, and Logan with whoever his latest victim is. Vittoria's seeing someone, some mystery guy. I told her to bring him, but she said he's out of town on business. Loser is probably scared to come and meet me, and rightly so. I would have no problem beating the shit out of any guy I don't think is good enough for my little sister, and that's pretty much every fucker who looks at her.

Before I can spend the evening with Addi and Vittoria, I need to go and interview a prospective manager to oversee the running of my clubs. I toyed with the idea a few months back, and now that the baby is on the way, I figure it's the perfect time to take a step back and enjoy some time with Addi and the baby. I hope this guy is better than the last one I interviewed. I swear I wouldn't have let that guy manage his own bowel movements. If today's interviewee can tie his own shoelaces it will be a step up!

WITH A NEW MANAGER HIRED AND MY GIRL HERE BESIDE ME, MY DAY just keeps getting better. Addi is making herself at home, cooking up a storm for everyone while I shower and shave. When I walk back out into the kitchen, it's the best damn feeling in the world watching her treat my apartment like it's her own.

Her sweet baby bump is perfect, making her even more beautiful as she dances around my kitchen singing along to my iPod, ingredients covering every available surface. It's like watching an angel, a dream—my dream. This is what I want for us. A home together, a family, and just… normal, everyday life. It takes her a few minutes to notice me, but she doesn't stop, doesn't miss a beat. She simply gives me a mischievous grin and a wink of her eye. It's adorable.

When the doorbell rings, I'm reluctant to let anyone else intrude on my time with Addi, but when she eyeballs me for ignoring it I give in and open the door.

"Hey, cock blocker!"

Xander starts laughing. "Nice to see you, too."

Lily just stares at the two of us. "You guys are weird. I'm going to go see if Addi needs any help." She kisses Xander, and I observe them, envious of just how easy their love is. I hear his breath catch as she turns and makes her way over to Addi.

"You're a lucky son of a bitch, Xander." He has a stupid grin on his face.

"Don't I know it." Lily reappears with two beers, holding them out to us before leaving without a word. "Fancy a thrashing on the Xbox before dinner?"

"Sure. I can take twenty minutes out of my day to kick your ass."

"You wish." We head down the hall to the game room.

This is my hideaway, my man cave. A massive plasma screen, with surround sound, and every console on the market. I rarely get to come in here with the clubs taking up all of my time this past year or so.

I don't even get a shot fired on *Call of Duty* before Xander starts in on me.

"So how are things with you and Addi?"

"We're taking it slow. I told you that."

"Yeah, and I know you. You're a moody bastard when you're not getting laid."

"Fuck off." He pauses the game and turns to look at me with a serious scowl.

"What are you waiting for, Carter? You say you want to take things slow, but I can see it's tearing you up. You can't bullshit me, man, we've known each other since we were born. You're holding back. Why?"

"Of course I am. Look what happened the last time I let my guard down with her. She ripped my fucking heart out and left me for dead."

"If you can't get past it, there is no fucking hope for you two. You need to let it go and give her a real chance to prove she's changed. You want what's best for the baby? You and Addi working your shit out, *that's* what's best for the baby."

"I know but give me some fucking time man. I can't go through that again. The women, the drinking, the getting arrested, I can't ever be that guy again. I'm going to be a dad. I need to get my shit together and *keep* it together. Addi and I are the fucking polar extremes. I can't seem to find the middle ground with her. We're either so loved up that we make you and Lily look tame by comparison, or..."

"Hold the fucking phone! Tame is not a word that will *ever* be used for Lily and me."

"Fuck off, Xander. I know you guys are fucking perfect and your sex life is fucking amazing. I was just making a point. Sue me!"

"You're a dick."

"You're right, I have a HUGE dick! Anyway... the point I was making before you so rudely interrupted, was that Addi and I are either ripping each other's clothes off or ripping each other's heads off. How the fuck do I channel such an all-consuming, crazy level of passion, and stop it from becoming completely toxic and poisoning what we have?"

"I think you're looking at it the wrong way. You don't need to channel anything. What you feel for Addi, isn't just physical, it's much more than that. I get it man, it's overwhelming and sometimes it feels like you're on a rollercoaster that you can't get off. I hated how I acted when I met Lily, I still hate how goddamn possessive I feel of her every minute of the day. I swear sometimes I can't concentrate in meetings because of how badly I want to be with her. I know she could rip my heart out and leave me completely broken, but I trust that she's not going to do that, because she loves me the same way."

"I get it. And that's amazing for you guys, but Addi *did* leave, and she *did* rip my heart out. I took the leap of faith when I first fell for her. I put it all out there at her mercy. I don't know how to do it again. I want to, so fucking badly, but how do I do it?"

"Just close your eyes and jump. She loves you, Carter. She's the mother of your child, and for what it's worth, I think she's learned her lesson. She doesn't want to lose you again. You didn't hear this from me, but she's really struggling with you guys taking things slowly. She's scared you're not all in man. I know you shouldn't have to be the one to trust first, after everything that happened, but she needs you to step up."

I sit running my hands through my hair. I'm really fucking scared to jump.

"You know I've always got your back, Carter. I want you to be happy, and I think Addi is a big part of that for you."

A familiar voice booms from the door.

"I knew it. I leave you two alone for a few months and you're butt buddies." It's Logan. We haven't seen him since the wedding. He's been traveling a lot for work, dealing with some British band he wants to bring over to the States.

"Hey, dickhead! How the hell are you? Long time no see!" He plops himself down in one of the chairs, with a beer in his hand.

"I'm good. Your sister's here and colluding with your women while you guys have been busy having your love fest in here."

"Vittoria's here? When did she arrive?"

"What am I, her damn keeper? I don't know. I just got here."

"It was a simple question. You need to get laid, loosen up a bit. Where's your latest victim? She out talking to the girls?" He flinches, but quickly composes himself.

"No. I didn't bring her. It's… complicated."

"Complicated? Does she actually have opinions, instead of blindly doing whatever you ask?" He starts laughing.

"You have no fucking idea!"

Xander's retort makes me laugh. "Have you met my wife and his girlfriend? Opinionated, bull headed, and complicated as hell. Welcome to the club!"

Addi appears in the doorway, her sweet smile doing strange things to my insides. I want her so badly.

"Are you boys coming to have dinner or are you going to sit in here playing with your joysticks?" There's the smart mouth I love so much.

"Coming, baby." She gives me a sly grin.

"Oh, you definitely will be later. I can guarantee it."

My dick twitches in my pants as I watch her, following her blindly, my friends all but forgotten.

I hear Xander and Logan chuckle, speaking in unison behind me. "Pussy-whipped."

I turn and give them a wink. "I *do* love to whip a good pussy."

Addi smacks me in the arm before dragging me over to the dining table, where my baby sister is sitting with a massive grin on her face, but it's not directed at me. She's looking straight past me... at Logan.

When I glance back at him, I see the same shit-eating grin on his face, and I wonder how I could have been so blind all this time. They have feelings for each other. What the fucking fuck? I am going to kill him.

DINNER WAS AMAZING, IT ALWAYS IS WHEN ADDI IS COOKING, BUT I'M distracted and she knows it. I've been watching Logan and Vittoria. They seem to be acting the way they always have—friendly but distant. But, every so often, a look passes between them, and I know there's something I'm missing.

The girls are deep in conversation when I hear Addi ask the question I want the answer to.

"So, Tori, tell us about this hot new guy you're seeing. We need details."

"Nothing to tell really. We rarely get time to see each other, our schedules are pretty crazy."

"Oh, come on, you can do better than that. You told me last week that he gave you, and I quote, 'the most phenomenal orgasm you've ever had.'" I need to jump in here.

"What the fuck, Addi? Brother in the room here. I don't want to hear shit like that. Lucky the son of a bitch couldn't make it tonight." I turn my gaze to Logan. "ANY man who lays a finger on my sister, better be prepared to take a severe fucking beating from me." He just stares me down, but I know he understands exactly what I'm saying.

"Oh, shut up, Carter. I'm a grown woman and you can't punch every guy I date."

"Of course I can, and I will, happily." To my surprise, Logan speaks up.

"If Vittoria's happy, surely that's what matters?" Everyone turns to look at him, waiting for my response. We all know what's really happening here.

"No. What matters is that this new guy is *clearly* not good enough for her. He couldn't even be bothered to show his face tonight."

"Or maybe, he's trying to respect her wishes."

"And why are you such an expert on the guy, Logan? Do, fucking, tell!"

"Goddammit!" He stands from the chair and strides around to where Vittoria is sitting. "Because it's me, but you already worked that out, so let's not play games."

Vittoria stands, wrapping her arms around his waist.

"I want to see where this goes. Please don't make it harder than it needs to be. I want you to be happy for me."

"Happy? One of my closest friends has been fucking my little sister behind my back, and I'm supposed to be happy about it?"

Logan squares his shoulders, holding Vittoria in a protective stance. "Don't talk about her like that, Carter. You know this is more than that, or I would never have let anything happen. We both travel all the time, but we've kept in touch since the wedding, and we've only seen each other twice since then. There are no guarantees that we can make this… arrangement… work, but I want to give it a chance. I would never do anything to intentionally hurt you. You're like a brother to me. And I certainly would *never* hurt Vittoria."

I am so fucking angry right now.

"Well, if I'm your brother, that would make her your sister, and *that* makes your 'arrangement' just fucking sick."

He moves Vittoria out of the way, before stepping up to face me.

"Say one more word, Carter, and I won't be responsible for my actions." His voice is low and menacing, but I'm not scared of him. I could take him down without breaking a sweat. He's not the only one who can sound threatening.

"Get the fuck out of my house… now!" He takes Vittoria's hand, striding toward the door.

"Tori. Don't you dare walk out of here right now, especially not with *him*." She gives me a sympathetic look before she speaks.

"I have to go with him, Carter. If you can't at least try to be happy for me, then I guess we won't be seeing each other much for a while. Please… don't make me choose." Everyone else sits in stunned silence as I watch my sister walk out the door with Logan.

It feels like hours before anyone speaks, Xander's voice cutting through the tension in the room. "I think Lily and I should go and let you wrap your head around this."

Addi ushers them out, saying her goodbyes and apologizing for the abrupt end to our evening. When she walks over to where I'm leaning on the countertop in the kitchen I can sense her disappointment.

"Well, that was a great way to handle it, Carter. Drive your sister and Logan away. Why can't you just be happy for them?" She puts her hand on my shoulder, but I shrug it off.

"You have no idea what she's been through. He's no good for her. You've seen how he is with women. He uses them, controls them, and then discards them. He'll hurt her, and she's been hurt enough to last a lifetime."

"I know you want to protect her, but you need to give them a chance. You need to give Logan a chance to prove himself to you. You weren't exactly a boy scout when I met you, but look at you now. Don't you think that he could change for Vittoria?" I slump down onto the bar stool next to me and think about it for a moment.

"Logan is like a brother to me, but I don't want to take the risk that he *doesn't* change, and he breaks her heart. People's hearts can only be broken so many times, Addi. There comes a point when one more break would shatter it for good, and nothing could piece it back together."

She forces my legs open, positioning herself in between them, her little bump resting against my chest as she pulls my head against her, enveloping me in a tender embrace.

"We're not talking about Vittoria now, are we?"

"I guess not."

She weaves her fingers through my hair, pulling my head back until I'm looking up into her tear-filled eyes.

"I'm so sorry, Carter. I wish I could go back and change what happened, change what I did, but I can't. I can only stand here and promise you I will do my very best, every single day, to make you trust me again. To make you trust in the love I have for you. I'm scared, too. I don't think I could cope if I lost you again. It was the hardest thing I have ever done, and I thought I was doing it for the right reason. I was wrong."

She dips her head to kiss my lips as tears rolling down her cheeks.

"It's torture. Being together, but we're not really together. I want to be all in, Carter. I want us to really make a go of this. I understand you wanting to take it slowly, but I don't know how much longer we can go on like this. Our connection is too intense, too passionate to temper. It creates a physical ache in my chest, trying to hold back all the time, never really having all of you."

She places my hands on her growing belly, on our child.

"*We* want all of you, Carter. Please… please… forgive me. I'm here. I'm not going anywhere, and I just want to love you, to give myself completely to you, and to have all of you in return. I want us to be a real family."

She kisses me with everything she has, melting my heart, cutting through all my bullshit fears and hang ups. Her lips taste so sweet and I feel myself relax into her touch for the first time since she came back into my life. With every kiss comes a whispered plea from her cherry lips.

"Please."

"God, Carter, please."

"I need you."

"I want you."

"I want to be yours."

The control that I've been exercising for the past six weeks is completely annihilated with those final words from her beautiful mouth. In one swift move, I'm behind her, spreading her legs, pushing myself in between them to get closer to her.

"You *are* mine, Addi. You've always been mine. You will always *be* mine." She bends over, bracing her hands on the counter edge, offering herself up to me.

"Take me, Carter, please. Make me yours again."

CHAPTER 33

ADDI

I KNOW WHAT I WANT. I KNOW WHAT I'M ASKING OF HIM. HE KNOWS
what this means to me.

"Are you sure, Addi?" He pulls my hands away from where they're
clutching the countertop, turning me to face him. "Are you asking
what I think you're asking?"

"Yes. I want you to make me yours... there." His eyes frantically
search mine.

"Why? Why now? I don't want you to do this because you think
you have to. I know things have been strained between us, but we're
going to get through it. You don't have to do this for me, Addi."

I cup his face in my hands, stroking his cheeks with my thumbs.

"I know that. I feel safe with you. I want you. I want you to claim
me in every way possible. Please." I implore him. "I want this... with
you." He scoops me up as if I weigh nothing, and strides toward the
bedroom with purpose.

"I'm not taking you this way for the first time over a fucking
kitchen counter." He lays me down gently on the edge of the bed,
before dropping to his knees in front of me.

I watch as he slowly removes each of my shoes, taking a moment
to massage each foot. Next, he slides his hands up my calves, tantaliz-

ingly slow, teasing me as his fingers glide over my skin. A thrill of anticipation runs through me as his hands make their way higher and higher until I feel his fingertips graze the aching flesh between my thighs. The lace of my panties is wet, soaked in my own arousal, desperate for the touch of this strong, beautiful man kneeling before me.

"I love you, Tesoro. Tell me you know that." I lift my ass off the bed, allowing him to pull my panties off, giving him unfettered access.

"Yes, I know, Carter. I love you, too. I don't think that you believe me, though."

He stands up and crawls onto the bed, positioning himself behind me. I feel his fingertips trail down my back as he unzips my dress, and with a gentle push, the straps fall from my shoulders, letting it pool around my belly. He unclips my bra and pushes the straps firmly down my arms, discarding it on the floor.

I watch as his lithe body moves around me, sexy and sleek, and deadly. He stands, pulling me to my feet, gently pushing my dress over my bump and watching as it drops to the floor. I am completely naked and vulnerable in front of him.

He drops back down onto his knees, his lips tenderly pressing against my stomach.

"Do you have any idea how much I worship you, Addi? You are so beautiful... radiant perfection." His hands roam my body, leaving me burning with desire, and desperate for more.

"Watch me, cara mia."

My eyes are transfixed as he starts to undress. He is in perfect physical condition. Muscular, lean, tanned, and completely mouthwatering. When his erection springs free, my nerves awaken and throw my body into chaos.

He takes his thick, hard length in his fist pumping it up and down. I watch as he grows bigger in his hand, his pleasure evident on his face and in the tiny groans that escape him.

"Are you sure you want this inside you, Addi?" I close my eyes, trying to calm the storm raging inside my chest. My entire body vibrating with the need to have this man.

"Yes." He let's go of his throbbing length, fisting his hands in my hair and taking me in a fierce kiss.

"I want you so fucking badly, baby." I grip his firm back, feeling his muscles rippling under my touch.

"Take me. I'm yours. All of me." I hear his breath catch, heavy and erratic.

"Climb onto the bed. On all fours. Show me that pretty little ass of yours. Show me how badly you want it."

I'm shaking as I crawl onto the bed, positioning myself in the middle on my hands and knees, utterly exposed to his gaze.

"You look so beautiful, Tesoro." The bed dips as he moves, climbing on behind me, spreading my legs to accommodate his imposing frame.

He places featherlight kisses on my back, sending a shiver down my spine. His hand snakes around my body, finding my sweet spot. I'm wet and ready for him. His fingers start tracing small circles, driving me wild, building a pleasure inside of me so desperate to escape, to find release. It doesn't take much for him to push me over the edge, and I'm screaming his name as the waves of my orgasm crash over me.

"You are so responsive. The slightest touch and you fall apart for me. It's so fucking sexy." He dips his fingers into my pussy, feeling how wet I am. He thrusts two fingers inside, letting me push back into him and ride him hard. "That's it, baby. Take what you need." I do exactly that, riding him to a second quick and really intense release. My head slumps down onto the pillow as I struggle to hold myself up on shaky arms.

Carter slowly pulls his fingers from me, sliding them back to coat my rim with my own arousal. He presses the tip of his finger inside, letting me adjust to the feeling.

"Do you like this, Addi? Do you like feeling my fingers inside you?" The fear I had the first time he did this is gone. I feel only pleasure, only love.

"Yes, but I want more." He slides his finger out, before two thrust back inside.

"Oh God, yes!" His other hand caresses my ass, kneading, fondling and squeezing it.

"Your ass is like a peach, Tesoro. I just want to take a bite." His voice is dripping with need, and thick with desire. "Are you ready? I need to hear you say the words." I turn my head, so that he can see my eyes when I answer him.

"I'm ready." He pulls his fingers out of me and grips his cock, positioning the head between my cheeks.

He slowly pushes inside. Gently stretching me, he lets me get used to the feeling before pushing any further. As I take each glorious inch of him, the feeling of being filled is overwhelming. It's unlike anything I've ever felt before. When he's seated to the hilt, he stops moving, letting me adjust and set the pace.

In this moment, I feel completely safe and loved. I start to move my hips, encouraging him to move, to thrust, to claim me. He answers me with a languorous rhythm, steadily thrusting in and out of me, the intensity of it overwhelming. He holds me firmly in place with one strong hand wrapped around my hip, the other moving between my legs.

He quickly thrusts two fingers inside my slick entrance, making me feel fuller than ever before. The friction of his fingers curling against the back wall of my pussy is electric, the divine feeling of his cock and fingers together working me into a frenzy. I can't hold back any longer when his thumb skims over my clit, applying the lightest of pressure. My body explodes, my vision clouded with stars as I lose myself to the sensations coursing through every nerve ending in my body. I'm bucking wildly beneath him as he thrusts into me, chasing his own release. Growling my name.

"Fuck. Addi... Addi!"

It's liberating, like the weight I've been carrying around for years has been lifted. I finally feel like I belong to Carter in every way possible, and I love it.

He slowly pulls out, before moving me onto my side and curling in behind me, kissing my back, shoulders, and neck.

"Are you okay?" I twist in his arms, eager for him to see just how great I feel.

"I've never been better. Honestly. That was amazing." He kisses the tip of my nose.

"You are so damn beautiful, Addi." I don't know what to say. I simply bask in our love. "I'm sorry this has been so hard on you over the past six weeks. It's been killing me trying to keep my distance." His eyes close, unable to look at me as he continues. "I'm scared, Addi. I'm really fucking scared. I want to just take a leap of faith and give you one hundred percent, but I know what it feels like when it's pulled from under me, and I don't think I would survive it a second time."

I take his hand in mine, grasping it tight, holding it to my heart, which is hammering in my chest. "I'm scared, too. I don't want to let you down again. I don't want to screw this up. I'm scared to jump, in case you don't want me the same anymore."

"I will always want you, Tesoro."

"Then let's hold onto each other and make the leap together. What do you think? Will you jump with me, Carter de Rossi?" His eyes soften and my heart swells.

"I want that more than anything, Addison Warner. Let's jump. Me, you, and the bump."

"I love you."

"I love you, too. Please, don't break me." He pulls me close, nestling his face in the crook of my neck, and my heart breaks to see my strong, alpha male, pleading with me not to hurt him... again.

"I won't." My voice is thick with unshed tears. "It's just you and me... and the bump."

After being pampered with a luxurious shower, washing every inch of my body with the utmost care, Carter lifts me back to bed and crawls in beside me, turning me around, so he can cuddle his chest to my back, wrapping his arm around my belly, resting his warm hand protectively over our baby, our future. I fall asleep, happy and content, for the first time since we were in Italy. I will never take this feeling for granted again.

CHAPTER 34

CARTER

Four Weeks Later

My life is the definition of perfect. I have the most beautiful girlfriend in the world, and a baby on the way. The new manager I hired for the clubs is great, allowing me to make up for lost time with Addi. She doesn't have a job here in New York, and I convinced her that it was okay to take some time out and think about it later, after the baby's born.

We have been living in our own little world, spending every waking hour together at her place or mine. We never spend the night apart, and that's just the way I like it.

Since we put our cards on the table last month, I think we have both relaxed and realized that it's safe to trust each other again. People take trust for granted, but once you lose it, it really is a hard thing to get back. Addi and I are lucky. I guess Xander was right. The intense passion we have didn't need to be channeled, it just is. It filters into every part of our relationship.

It feels amazing to just enjoy being together again. I'm not second-guessing everything she does or worrying about whether she's going to run out on me. To have my love reciprocated and for Addi to finally understand how strongly I feel for her is great, and life is good.

TODAY IS ADDI'S BIRTHDAY. I WANTED TO TAKE HER AWAY FOR THE weekend, and she wanted to have a party at Cube. I had to put my foot down on that idea, because I would definitely end up in prison for beating up anyone who so much as brushed against her belly. I managed to persuade her that a ridiculously packed club was not the place to spend your birthday when you're almost seven months pregnant.

Eventually we agreed on a dinner at Jason's restaurant. What she doesn't know is that I've arranged for a small dance floor and one of my DJs to come and give her a private club for the evening. She gets to dance the night away with Lily, and I don't have to murder anyone. It's a win/win.

I'm picking her up at seven, which gives me just enough time to shower and change after spending the day setting up at the restaurant and getting her present. I ordered it weeks ago, but I picked it up this afternoon—a Cartier platinum locket. I got the store to insert a picture of Addi and me in Verona on one side, and a tiny ultrasound picture of the baby on the other side. I figure we can get a picture of the baby put in after he or she arrives. The front of the locket has a ruby in the center, with our initials engraved on either side. I really hope she likes it. I wanted to get her something personal to let her know what a sentimental schmuck she's turned me into!

When I arrive at the apartment, she is a complete knockout, in a sexy black dress that hugs every one of her curves, accentuating her beautiful pregnant belly. I can't get enough of her like this.

"Tesoro. You are a vision tonight." She sashays over to me, putting a little extra sway in her hips.

"Why thank you, Mr. de Rossi. You look quite dashing yourself."

"Pregnancy definitely agrees with you. You are sexy as hell, and all mine." Her sly grin lets me know she enjoys the compliment, even if she seems a little shy about it.

"Let's go and celebrate the birth of the most amazing woman I have ever met."

"Oh, I didn't realize it was a joint party."

"Don't be coy, Addison. You know I'm talking about you and that I mean every word. Get used to it."

"Okay then. Let's go celebrate the awesomeness of me!"

"That's better. Come on, birthday girl."

We grab a taxi and arrive at Jason's ten minutes later. Addi is a little flustered, and I have a raging hard-on after getting a sneak peek at the black satin panties she's wearing under her dress. I say peek, but I really mean a sneak feel. I fucking love to feel how wet she is for me, ready and waiting for me to take her. I need a minute to think about baseball and laundry, anything to get my mind off of all the dirty things I want to do to her right now.

Everyone is here. Xander and Lily, my parents, Lily's mom and sisters, Addi's parents, and some of her friends from college. Logan and Vittoria are both traveling for work right now, which is probably for the best. We haven't spoken since my outburst at dinner. I know I need to apologize to both of them, but it doesn't mean I want him seeing my sister, but I've had bigger things on my mind, like the woman I can't take my eyes off.

Dinner is delicious as usual. Jason has made a real name for himself with Manhattan's elite. La Cattedrale has become a new hot spot. Addi seems to be having a great time, chatting with everyone, and eating enough food to feed a small village, but I think it's cute. When the last plates are cleared and everyone is ready for drinks, the DJ starts playing *Treasure* by Bruno Mars and Addi jumps up from her seat, throwing her arms around my neck.

"Thank you!"

"You're welcome, baby. I knew you wanted to go to the club, so I thought I would bring the club to you." Lily is over dragging Addi onto the dance floor in seconds. I don't even get the chance to steal a kiss.

I stand back with a smile on my face and a beer in my hand, watching my girl dance and enjoy herself. Everyone is having a blast, and I'm just happy to sit back and soak up the atmosphere. I get up to dance with Addi a few times, spend some time chatting with Xander and Jason, but Addi—she's determined to dance till she drops.

Around eleven o'clock my phone starts ringing in my pocket. It's my new manager. I head down the corridor toward the restrooms to get away from the music. We talk over some problems at Spyder and Cube tonight, nothing that can't be fixed, but he's new, and I'd rather talk him through how I like things to be handled.

I was so deep in conversation that I didn't notice one of the waitresses standing right next to me until I ended the call.

"Sorry, am I blocking the door?" She gets a look in her eye that I've seen so many times before.

"No. I was waiting to talk to you."

I don't want to be rude, but I can't be bothered with this shit. "Is everything okay with the party? Is there something I need to do?" She places her hand on my chest, which I quickly remove.

"Actually, I think there's something I can do for you."

She makes a move to kiss me, but I move out of the way before she gets the chance. "What the fuck are you doing? You *do* know this is my girlfriend's birthday party... my pregnant girlfriend?"

"So? We can still have some fun. She doesn't need to find out." She tries to touch me again and I can't fucking stand it.

"Nothing is going to happen between us. I'm *not* interested." I turn to walk away, but as I do, she grabs my arm and slides her number into my pants pocket. I grip her hand, annoyed by her persistence and lack of respect for the fucking guest of honor. I lean in close so she can hear every word. "Don't touch me again, or I'll have you fired. Why don't you try NOT being so fucking desperate, and maybe, just maybe, you won't get labeled a whore for the rest of your sad little life."

As I turn to rejoin to the party, I see Addi. She's just standing watching this play out. I quickly make my way over to her.

"Sorry you had to see that, baby. She's a stupid little bitch who can't take no for an answer apparently." The waitress storms by, flashing Addi a smug grin.

"Doesn't look like she got a *no*! It looks like she got exactly what she was after."

"You are kidding, right?" You don't seriously think anything happened with her?"

"Don't insult my intelligence, Carter."

"Nothing happened! I would never cheat on you."

"Yeah, that's what Gavin used to say, too. I believed him like a chump and look where it got me."

"Don't you dare fucking compare me to that piece of shit."

"If the shoe fits! You're a player, Carter, and once a player, always a player." I can't believe she's comparing me to him.

"Are you kidding me with this bullshit? Let's talk about a leopard changing its spots then, shall we? When we were first together, you purposely pushed me away, then brought another guy to my club, and took him home to let him fuck you, just to spite me."

"That's not true."

"It fucking *is*! Okay, so you didn't know it was my club, but when you were beneath me in my office, I knew you wanted me, I could see the desire in your eyes, I could feel your heart hammering against my chest. You wanted me, but you let some douchebag, random guy, fuck you. By your standards, should I be worried about you doing that now?"

"I would never do that to you." Her eyes fill with tears.

"But you think I'm heartless enough to do it to you, and do it when you're pregnant with my child? Wow. You have a high opinion of me, Addi. Thank you for the vote of confidence."

"What do you want me to think? You disappear for fifteen minutes and when I find you, some waitress has her hand down your pants."

"I want you to *believe* me. I was on the phone dealing with work, and when I ended the call she was there, trying to get me to notice her. I told her I wasn't interested. I tried to walk away. She didn't fucking listen and shoved her number in my pocket. How is that my fault?"

Her angry exterior softens. "You're right, I'm sorry. I'm just not feeling very sexy right now, and hot girls throwing themselves at you makes me crazy. I believe you."

I pull her into my arms, but I can feel her reluctance. "Thank you. You know I love you, Addi. Only you. And you are the sexiest woman on the planet to me." Her body relaxes as she snakes her arms around my waist, allowing me to comfort her. "Now can we get back to your party, and celebrate what a lucky son of a bitch I am to have you?" She nods against my chest but refuses to look up at me. I lift her chin, forcing her to make eye contact, and when she does, I'm upset to see tears in her eyes. I wipe them away with my thumbs. "Don't cry, cara mia. C'è solo te, sarà sempre voi." *[There is only you, it will always be you.]* I claim her mouth in a fierce kiss, entreating her to keep faith, to *trust* me. We make our way back to the party, but Addi never really gets back into the spirit of things, and by one o'clock she's asking me to take her home.

THE RIDE BACK TO HER APARTMENT IS TENSE AND PAINFULLY QUIET. I hate it when things are like this between us, and the deafening silence continues until I close the door behind us. Addi is on me in a second, clawing at me, kissing me, begging me to make her feel better.

"Please, Carter. I need to feel you. I need to know that I'm yours, only me." I fist my hands in her hair as she pushes my back against the door.

"You're it for me, Addi. There is *no one* else." I ravage her mouth as she grinds her body against mine, moving her hand down to rub my already rock-hard cock, so turned on by her desperate need for me. I savor every touch of her hands as she starts to unbutton my pants and push them down my legs, along with my boxers, letting my erection spring free. I am so ready for her, to claim her as mine, again and again and again.

As my pants hit the floor, my keys fall out of the pocket, crashing onto the hardwood floor. We both startle at the sound, looking to see what caused it, and that's when my stomach lurches at the sight before me. Along with my keys, there's a napkin on the floor with a bright red lipstick mark, and a crude message on it:

I want to taste your big hard cock. Call me 555-6981 Angel x

You have got to be fucking kidding me. How could I forget to trash it? Addi quickly swipes it off the floor before waving it in my face, fury marring her flawless features.

"Thought you'd just hang onto this, did you? What are you waiting for? Angel is obviously ready and waiting to 'taste your big hard cock,' Carter." She throws it at my chest and storms off, leaving me with my pants at my ankles.

I pull them up, not even bothering to zip them before striding over to her. "What the fuck, Addi? I forgot to take it out of my pocket. It's not a big deal. Do *not* read into it. I was busy with you and I just forgot."

She spins around to face me, frantic and distraught. "Have you slept with a lot of other girls while we've been together?"

"*What the hell?* That's a fucking leap. So, I've gone from getting a number I *didn't* want, to fucking her at your birthday party, to sleeping with multiple women while I've been dating you?"

"You're avoiding answering me. How many?" Her detached, cold tone devastates me.

"None! I don't know how else to say it. Zilch, nada, zero… fucking NONE!"

"Don't fucking lie to me, Carter! I see the way women look at you. You click your fingers and they come running, with their panties at their ankles."

"Oh my God! I don't *want* anyone else, Addi. Goddammit!"

"So you've miraculously transformed from a man-whore who likes fucking two women at once, to being a stand-up family man, content and completely satisfied with just me? Not fucking likely! I'm not *that* good a lay, and I'm not going to sit around here with our baby while you're off fucking whoever you damn well please at the club every night. I'm *not* going to be that person again."

I am fucking dumbstruck.

"I can't stand here and listen to you tear me apart for no good reason. This is all on you. If you can't trust me over something as easily explained as this, then there's no hope for us. I actually feel sick to my stomach that you could think, even for a second, that I would cheat on you. It's even worse that you think I would do it when you're carrying my child. My enemies hold me in higher esteem than you do, Addi." I start pacing the floor, feeling like the walls are closing in all around me. "I can't do this." She's breaking my fucking heart all over again. "I will be there for you and the baby one hundred percent, whatever you need. But us... I don't think there can *be* an 'us' anymore. Too much has happened. We're not good for each other. We're toxic together. Explosive in the best and worst possible ways. I need to put the baby first now, ahead of my own wants and desires. And God, do I want you, Addi. Never doubt that. But if you can't trust me, then we have nothing."

Tears fall from her eyes, and all I want to do is hold her and tell her everything is going to be alright.

"There are three people in our relationship, Addi. You, me... and Gavin. You can't live your life expecting every guy to be like him. He was a dick who didn't deserve you. I'm the guy who would throw himself under a bus rather than hurt you like he did. I would give up everything I have to be with you, to have you trust me, to have you trust that what we have is special."

She takes a step toward me but I can't let her touch me, not just now.

"You're ripping my heart out all over again." My voice is thick with the agony forming a ball in my throat, closing off my air supply. "You promised me. You asked me to take the leap with you and trust you. I did that. *You* are the one who can't be trusted, not me. I've never given you any reason not to believe in me. You on the other hand, have pushed me away and run away from me more times than I can count.

I'm not made of steel, Addi. You can't just keep doing this to me and expect me not to break."

I scrub my hand over my stubble, struggling to contain my devastation.

"You walked away from me when I put my heart on the line for you, and it damn near killed me. I can't trust you not to do it again, not with your clear lack of faith in us. I need to walk away from this before you break me beyond anything I can come back from. I can't become that guy. I don't *want* to be that guy. I'm going to be a father."

I close the distance between us, pulling her close, kissing her forehead. Reaching into my jacket pocket I pull out her birthday present, still clinging to her as I find her hand and close it around the box. "If you ever doubt where my heart and my loyalties lie, look at this, Tesoro. You *are* my heart, but you can't be trusted to cherish it the way *I* cherish yours." I try to pull away, but she holds on tight. "I need to go. I'm sorry." I pry her hands from around my waist. "I'll be in touch soon to help you get organized for the baby. Anything you need, you just have to ask. You will always be the love of my life, Addi. Nothing will ever change that. I'm just hoping one day you realize it."

She lets me leave without a word. She doesn't put up a fight. She has *never* put up a fight for me, and that's part of the problem.

CHAPTER 35

ADDI

CARTER AND I HAVEN'T SEEN EACH OTHER SINCE THE NIGHT OF MY birthday party, when I let him just walk out the door without asking him to stay. I don't know why I let him leave. I've asked myself every day since it happened. I love him more than anything in the world, but I let the part of me that's ruled by my past, by Gavin, take over. I just shut down.

When Carter left, I sat for at least an hour staring into nothingness, before I opened his gift. The most stunning locket I've ever seen, engraved with our initials on either side of a gorgeous red ruby. Inside, there's a picture of us together in Verona and one of our baby. It's the most thoughtful, heartfelt gift anyone has ever given me.

I immediately put it on and I haven't taken it off since. When I touch my hand to the cool metal, I remember his words to me. *If you ever doubt where my heart and my loyalties lie, look at this, Tesoro. You are my heart, but you can't be trusted to cherish it the way I cherish yours.*

I know he's right. I don't deserve his heart. I've done nothing but batter, bruise, and break it beyond repair, since the moment we met. I've cried so many tears, I'm surprised that my eyes haven't dried out yet. From one day to the next I go from inconsolable, uncontrollable sobbing, to a steely determination to win Carter back, to earn his trust, and make myself worthy of his love again.

I've wanted to pick up the phone and call him so many times, a text, an email, anything to be in contact with him, and every time, I stop myself, unsure of what to say, scared that he will reject me. I'm terrified he'll dash what little hope I'm hanging onto that I can make things right.

After six days of staring at my phone, I finally plucked up the courage to text and ask him to come to my OB/GYN appointment with me. He was the one who suggested we go out for lunch first and have a talk about where we go from here. I know he meant what we're going to do about the baby, how it will work because we're not a couple, but I'm hoping I will be able to change that, because this past week has been unbearable. I've missed him every minute of every day. I have some serious freaking groveling to do, but I will do anything it takes to make things right between us. I really messed up last week. I let my insecurities get the better of me, and I punished Carter for Gavin's mistakes... again.

I'm nervous as hell about seeing Carter today. After our fight last week and our breakup, I feel like this is my last chance. Maybe that ship has already sailed, but I need to at least try.

I've not been feeling so great since I got up this morning, but I'm putting it down to nerves. I haven't been able to eat anything, worrying about what I'm going to say to Carter when I see him. I've been getting shooting pains in my stomach, but they pass quickly. I'm not particularly worried about it, I'm thirty weeks along now and the midwife said I could start getting Braxton Hicks contractions around this time.

I'm excited to let Carter feel the baby kicking. It's been a quiet little thing for the most part, but today it's kicking the hell out of me and I can actually see my belly moving. It's amazing and mind-blowing, and I want to share it with him. I want to share everything with him.

Time seems to drag this morning. I'm ready way too early, hair and make-up flawless, with a pretty maternity dress to accentuate my bump, just the way Carter likes it. The only thing left for me to do is take my daily pregnancy vitamins. I head into the bathroom to get them from the cabinet, when an agonizing pain rips through my body.

I manage to grab hold of the edge of the sink, curling my fingers around it so tight that my knuckles turn white. I'm trying to breathe through the pain, but it's stealing my breath away as I try to take even the tiniest of gasps. I feel like a red-hot knife has been thrust into my abdomen and is being dragged from one side of me to the other.

My vision goes blurry as my knees buckle under the intense pain, and I drop to the floor, twisting onto my side, trying anything to alleviate this unbearable torture wreaking havoc on my body. I don't have my phone with me, it's sitting on the kitchen counter. I know I need to get to it and call Carter, but I can't move. Tears stream down my face as I rock myself, breathing through the overwhelming agony.

My brain starts playing tricks on me, taking me back four years to the last time I felt anything even close to this level of pain. I can hear Gavin's voice, cold, cruel, and evil—taunting me, scaring me, threatening me. I snap back into the present wish a gush of warmth between my legs. I can see crimson liquid running down my legs and onto the floor tiles in a stark terrifying contrast to the cold white marble.

"Oh God, No. Please, not again. Not our baby. Not Carter's baby."

With every move I make, there's a searing, burning agony, crushing me from the inside, but my instincts kick in and I force myself up onto my hands and knees, my body shaking against this brutal internal assault. I slowly crawl toward the bathroom door, but the energy I expel to make it six feet to the entrance is too much for me, and I slump against the heavy wooden door frame. I shift my gaze to where I've just come from, and all I see are thick streaks of dark red blood.

An anguished sob rips from my throat. Something is very wrong. My baby is in danger and needs my help. I cling to that thought, using it to dull the excruciating agony, channeling what little energy I have left into moving my muscles, making my arms and legs work together to pull me out into the hallway.

The distance between where I am and the kitchen seems like an insurmountable task. My phone is high up on the counter—an impossible goal. The feeling of blood trickling down my legs is a constant reminder that I need to keep moving. I need to get help. I need Carter.

Every move forward is a victory, every look back, a defeat. The trail of blood behind me is petrifying. I'm starting to feel drowsy, my head dipping, my consciousness teetering on the edge. I can't see straight, through the torrent of tears filling my eyes and coursing down my cheeks.

"Carter. Please. I need you."

Through my silent pleas, I know he'll be expecting me. He'll wonder why I haven't shown up. The fear that he'll think I just ran away the same way I always do, is a devastating blow.

"Please, have faith in me."

I am hoping beyond hope that he *will* come to my rescue. That he *will* come looking for me.

I hear my cell ringing, vibrating against the countertop. I'm so close, and yet so far away from the help on the other end of the line. I feel like every ring is mocking me, provoking me, making me angry that I can't reach it.

"Goddammit. Why is this happening to me?"

When I finally make it to the kitchen, I'm hysterical, laughing and crying that I've made it this far, but I need to take a moment to gather some strength. I need to stand up and grab my phone. I try to steady my breathing, but my heart is racing. It's going too fast, but I don't know how to slow it down.

The smeared trail of blood behind me causes bile to rise into my throat, a physical manifestation of my horror and fear. I manage to pull myself into a sitting position, my back against the cabinets, my head resting against the hard, unforgiving wood. I close my eyes, just for a second, trying to focus on my breathing, but when I try to open them again, I feel like I have weights attached to my lids, making it almost impossible for me to lift them.

"Carter."

My world starts to spin, fading in and out, my body slowly slumping toward the floor. In my head, I'm screaming at myself to get up, knowing that every downward movement is taking me further away from my phone, further away from the help I so desperately need, further away from *him*.

The apartment is so quiet. I'm all alone. I can feel the life draining from my body, and I am helpless to do anything about it. My body is consumed by an overwhelming cold, a bone deep, chilling exhaustion. I try to fight against it, but I can't. I'm just one woman, and I don't have any fight left. Maybe if I let myself rest for a little while... just a few minutes and I'll have enough energy to get up.

I curl my hands around my stomach in a last act of protection.

"It's ok, baby. Daddy will be here soon. Daddy will find us. I love your daddy so much. Daddy will save you...."

I feel a rush of relief as I give in to the cold darkness. The pain dissipates and my body stops shaking. I can feel my breathing grow shallow and my heart rate slowing down. The single thought that keeps me from letting it completely consume me, is the image of Carter, holding our baby in his arms.

I want to see that... I want to be a part of it... I want to live...

THUD! THUD! THUD!

"Addi!"

CHAPTER 36

CARTER

ADDI WAS SUPPOSED TO MEET ME AN HOUR AGO. I WAITED IN THE restaurant like an idiot, just hoping she would turn up with some crazy story about why she was late. Instead, I stared at my phone, willing it to ring, while the waiter looked at me as if I'd had a death in the family. This is exactly what I'm talking about. This is why we can't work. I can't even trust her to show up! I love her so much, and I keep waiting for her to prove me wrong, but it's becoming glaringly obvious she doesn't *want* to trust me, and that I *can't* trust her.

I take a cab over to her apartment, running through every possible scenario of why she would blow me off like this. I'm so pissed right now, but I'm trying to stay calm because she's pregnant, and I love her more than life itself.

When I arrive at her building and step inside the elevator, I feel a sense of urgency, I just *need* to see her... now.

I stand knocking on the door for a few minutes, thinking maybe she hasn't heard me. "Addi. Are you in there? It's me. You never showed up for lunch. I was worried... and fucking annoyed! The appointment with the OB/GYN is in forty minutes."

Still nothing.

"Goddammit, Addi. I don't want to play games with you. I thought we were past this."

I can hear something. It's faint, but I'm sure I can hear her voice. I press my ear to the door.

"Addi."

"Help... me." Holy fuck. She's in there.

"Open the door, baby."

"Help." I can barely hear her over my own pulse hammering in my eardrums. I try to open the door but it's locked.

"Can you get to the door?"

Silence...

"Stay back, Addi. I'll need to break the door down to get to you."

Silence...

Nothing else matters except getting to her. I stand back, readying myself to kick the door in with every ounce of strength I have in me. One almighty kick and it bursts inwards, the wood splintering where my foot makes contact.

I immediately scan the apartment looking for Addi, and that's when I see a trail of crimson.

"Addi?"

The red marks seem to have come from the hallway and they disappear behind the counter. I run over to the kitchen, dread and fear choking me from the inside out.

"OH, FUCK!"

I drop down onto the floor.

"Shit. Addi, baby, can you hear me? Talk to me."

She's completely surrounded by the deep red liquid pooling on the floor, covered in it from the waist down. I've never seen a person so pale. I try to pull her close to me, but she's a dead weight, unconscious and completely limp in my arms.

"Addi, baby, you need to wake up."

Her head slumps down onto her chest.

My brain finally kicks in and I grab my phone from the inside pocket of my jacket to call 911.

"I need an ambulance. My girlfriend is pregnant and she's covered in blood, she's unconscious and I can't get her to wake up." I quickly give them the address and they assure me that the paramedics will be with me in minutes.

"Sir, I need you to check for a pulse."

This can't be happening. She text me this morning. She was fine. My hand is shaking as I press two fingers to her throat, terrified that I might not feel anything. I'm so relieved when I feel the faintest flutter on my fingertips.

"She's alive, but her pulse is weak. Please, hurry."

I hang up the phone and scoop Addi's fragile, blood stained body onto my lap, holding her close to my chest. She feels so cold. I scramble out of my suit jacket, careful not to move her too much. Draping it over her shoulders, I pull her tight against the warmth of my chest stroking her hair, rocking back and forth trying to calm the panic—the complete and utter terror.

I start rambling. Talking to her in the hope she'll wake up and say something so ridiculous and completely Addi-like to me, and I can tell her how wrong I was. I want her to know we *need* to be together, no matter what.

"Stay with me, Tesoro. Mi stai spaventando ora. Ho bisogno che tu resti con me. *[You're scaring me now. I need you to stay with me.]* You can't leave me, baby." I can feel her breath getting shallower as we wait for help to arrive.

"I need you, baby, more than I need air. Tu sei tutto per me. Il sole, la luna, le stelle, e tutto il resto. *[You are everything to me. The sun, the moon, the stars, and everything in between.]* We're supposed to be a family, Addi. You, me, and our baby."

I feel tears trickling down my face, dripping onto her beautiful hair as I cling to her.

"Siamo tenuti a invecchiare insieme. Non puoi lasciare dietro di, Addi, io non ti lascerò. Tu sei mia e io sono tuo, per sempre. Io non sono pronto a dare che fino. Non posso. Abbiamo ancora molto da fare insieme il mio dolce, bella Tesoro." *[We're supposed to grow old together. You can't leave me behind, Addi, I won't let you. You're mine and I'm yours, forever. I'm not ready to give that up. I can't. We still have so much to do together my sweet, beautiful treasure.*]

She lets out a long, labored breath, and I wait for her to breathe in but it doesn't come. This can't be happening. She can't...

I quickly lay her down on the cold tile, pressing my ear to her chest, but I can't hear a heartbeat.

"Fuck! Please, don't do this to me, Addi."

I quickly straddle her small frame, linking my hands together and locating the point on her chest where I know I need to start compressions. The room has become a vacuum. There is no sound, there is no air, and there is no... life.

I start pumping her chest the way they teach you in first aid, stopping to breathe air into her lungs after thirty compressions. Her lips are turning blue. I can feel her slipping away, and with her... the life of our child.

"Please, baby. Please fight. Goddammit, Addi... you need to fight! This can't be how it ends for us. The baby needs you Addi. I need you!"

I keep up the compressions, praying to God that she'll come back to me.

"FUCKING BREATHE. HOLY SHIT... BABY... I NEED YOU TO... BREATHE. FOR. ME."

Time has stopped. Life... has stopped.

I feel an arm pulling on my shoulder, but I shrug it off as I continue my efforts to get Addi's heart started.

"Sir. I'm a paramedic. Please, step aside and let me work on her. Let me help."

I turn to see the man talking to me, two others standing beside him with bags and boxes that might just bring her back.

"I don't know how long it's been. She's not breathing. She's thirty weeks pregnant."

"Sir. I need you to move. Now."

I remove my bloodstained hands from her chest and slump down onto the floor beside her, letting them move in to try and bring her back to me.

"Please. Please, help her. She's… she's… everything."

Time is ticking by in slow motion as I watch them try to revive my reason for breathing. I don't think I take a single breath until I hear the words that give me a sliver of hope.

"I've got a pulse. It's faint, but it's there."

I grab her wrist, needing to feel the life pulsing through her veins. That tiny flutter is the best thing I've ever felt. She's alive.

"We need to get her to the hospital, sir. She's lost a lot of blood and she needs immediate medical attention."

I let go of her hand, bereft, and desperate to be by her side as they lift her fragile body onto the gurney. I follow them into the elevator, down through the lobby, and out into the waiting ambulance. They allow me to ride with her, but I can't get close. They're working tirelessly, trying to keep her as stable as possible until we get to the hospital. The sirens blaring as we speed through the streets in a race against time, in a fight to keep her and the baby alive. When the doors fly open and a team of doctors swarm her, I know that she's far from out of the woods. Getting her pulse back was a small victory in the war that has been waged on her body.

I run in behind them, following until one of the nurses turns around, stopping me in my tracks.

"I'm sorry, sir, you need to stay out here. You need to let the doctors do their job. I'll come and let you know when they've stabilized her." She turns to head into the emergency room with the rest of the doctors and nurses.

"Please, miss. Please keep her alive. I need her. The baby needs her."

She places her hand on my arm, giving me a sympathetic smile. "We will do everything we can to help her and the baby. She has the best doctors working on her."

"Thank you."

As she disappears behind the double doors, I catch a glimpse of Addi, her small body laid out on the table, her dress cut open, her arms hooked up to all kinds of tubes and needles. There's a mask over her face, forcing oxygen into her struggling lungs. She looks so small and helpless, her perfectly rounded bump protruding with monitors covering it, searching for signs of life from our baby. How can this be happening?

I drop down into a chair, my head in my hands, trying to breathe, trying to comprehend the gravity of the situation. I reach into my pocket and dial Xander.

"Hey, Carter. How was lunch with Addi?"

I don't even recognize my voice as I tell him what's happening. "She's bleeding, Xander. Blood. Everywhere. She stopped breathing... she wasn't breathing, man."

"We're on our way now. What hospital?"

"Mount Sinai." I drop my phone to the ground, a numbness taking over my body. I start to shake, the image of her lifeless body ingrained in my brain. My hands are covered in her blood, my shirt is drenched in it. No one can lose this much blood and survive, can they?

I HEAR LILY BEFORE I SEE HER.

"Oh my God. Carter." She drops down in front of me, her face etched with despair as she takes in the sight of me.

"Is she?" She can't even bring herself to say the words.

"They're still trying to stabilize her. They haven't told me anything."

She pulls me into her arms, clinging to me for dear life. "She's going to be okay, Carter. She's a fighter." I grab onto her, the only person who loves Addi almost as much as I do.

"She has to be, Lil. She just has to be."

Xander strides over to the reception desk, demanding that someone comes to speak to us as soon as possible. It's the first time I've been truly grateful that he's a pushy bastard. Normally I'm the same, but I'm so fucking scared right now, I almost don't want to find out what's happening. If they walk through those doors and tell me they couldn't... that her and the baby... I can't even think it. It's too horrific.

A few minutes later, the doors swing open and a solemn looking doctor walks toward us, her scrubs covered in blood. As I stand to speak, I feel like the ground is crumbling beneath my feet. My world is falling apart.

"Are you Addison Warner's family?"

"Yes. She's my wife." I don't care if it's a lie. As far as I'm concerned at this moment in time, it's a fucking technicality. Xander and Lily are silent at my side, not even a look of surprise at my declaration. They know as well as I do, that if Addi makes it through this, I will fucking marry her and chain her to my side for the rest of her very long life. "How is she?"

"We've managed to stabilize her enough to get her up to the OR. She has extensive bleeding, we've transfused five units already, but she'll need more. We have to go in and find the source of the bleeding."

"What about the baby?"

"The baby is alive, with a strong heartbeat, under the circumstances."

"Thank God."

"I don't want to give you false hope, sir."

"Carter. Call me, Carter."

"Okay, Carter. Our priority at this time is to stop your wife's bleeding. We are aware that she's only thirty weeks into the pregnancy, but there is a strong possibility we'll have to deliver the baby today. Addison's body is struggling at the moment. If we can put off delivery, we will, but it all depends on what we find when we get her into the OR."

"I understand. Please do whatever you have to. Just keep them alive."

"I will do my absolute best. I need to go and scrub in. There's a waiting room up on the surgical floor. The receptionist can give you directions. Someone will keep you updated."

"Thank you, doctor."

As soon as she turns to leave, I sink back down into my seat. Holy Shit. The baby is so premature. There is no guarantee it'll survive being born at this point. Addi will be devastated if we lose the baby. *I will be devastated.* Above all else, today, I *need* Addi to pull through. If she doesn't...

"Come on, Carter. Let's get you cleaned up and then we can head up to the waiting room. Addi's parents are on their way and so are your mom and dad."

"I don't need to get cleaned up, man. I'm not leaving here." Xander pulls me into a hug.

"I know, brother. I'm going to go pick you up some fresh clothes and I'll be back in twenty minutes. Lily is going to stay here with you. Look after her for me. You two need each other right now."

I watch as he comforts his wife, her eyes red with tears for her best friend. It makes me ache for Addi. The one person who could offer me any kind of comfort, is the one person I can't be with.

When Xander leaves, Lily and I find out where we need to be and head up to wait. It's all we can do now... *wait...* and hope.

CHAPTER 37

ADDI

I'M VAGUELY AWARE THAT I'M NOT AT HOME ANYMORE. THERE ARE people all around me, unfamiliar voices, frantic and shouting orders. I don't really understand what they're saying. I hear snippets of words that scare me—blood... critical... stat... the baby. Oh my God. The baby. My baby. Our Baby.

I was supposed to meet Carter for lunch, but the last thing I remember was going into the bathroom to take my vitamins, and then I was consumed by a blinding pain. I ended up on my hands and knees trying to crawl to my phone, to get help, to get Carter. The pain was so intense, like being crushed from the inside out, I must have passed out before I could call for help. I think Carter found me. I have flashes of him calling my name, intense pain, and then nothing.

Now I'm here, alone, in a room full of strangers.

"Carter." I manage to whisper.

A soothing, almost ethereal voice answers me. "Addison. I'm Doctor Field. We're going to take you into the operating room now. You've lost a lot of blood and we need to get it stopped. We're going to do everything we can for you and your baby."

"Carter." I croak.

"Your husband is outside waiting for you. I'm afraid he can't come in here." I can feel my panic rising.

There's a hand on my shoulder. "You need to stay calm, Addison. For the baby. We're going to take good care of you. I promise."

I open my eyes, but all I see is black. "I can't see. What's happening to me? I'm blind."

The voice in the darkness returns. "Your blood pressure is dangerously low right now, Addison. It can cause temporary blindness, but as soon as we get it back up, you'll be fine. That's why you need to stay calm, honey. I'm here with you." She grabs my hand and squeezes.

"The baby? How is my baby?"

"She's fine. She's a fighter."

"She? It's a girl."

"I'm sorry, Addison. I should have asked if you already knew the sex. Yes… it's a baby girl."

In my darkness, a ray of light. "I'm having a baby girl."

"Congratulations, Addison."

"Addi. Just Addi."

"Do you have any names picked out, Addi?" Slow, silent tears course down my face.

"I always wanted a girl. Verona. I wanted to call her Verona."

"That's beautiful. Is it Italian?"

My fear chokes me as I try to speak. "Yes. Her daddy is Italian. He'll be an amazing father. Please tell him I wanted to call her Verona."

"You can tell him yourself. When you wake up from surgery *you* are going to tell him."

"What's your name?"

"I'm Laurie, and I'm going to be by your side throughout surgery, Addi." It gives me a small amount of comfort.

"I'm scared. I don't want to die. I want to be a mommy, and I want to tell Carter I'm sorry, and that I love him."

"You need to fight, Addi. For Carter, and for Verona. You hear me?"

A sob escapes me. "Yes. Please, promise me, though. If I don't make it, please tell him I love him. He's my whole world. Him and Verona." I take a deep breath, trying to swallow the lump in my throat. "If it comes down to it, save her, save Verona. Please. Promise me."

Although I can't see her, I feel her stroking my hair. "I promise." She continues to hold my hand as other voices begin to speak, telling me that they're going to put me to sleep now. A cold sensation creeps up my arm as they inject me with something. My head starts spinning almost immediately.

"Count back from ten for me, Addi."

I try to choke it out. "Ten."

My brain is racing, my survival instincts pushing me to stay awake. "Nine."

I don't want to die. I *want* to wake up from this and be a mommy. I want to raise my daughter.

"Eight."

I might never see her beautiful face. She has to survive. I couldn't save my first baby, but Verona needs to survive.

"Seven."

An image of Carter holding a gorgeous baby girl, our baby girl, fills my mind, soothing my fears. He'll look after her. He will protect her, and love her, and give her everything she needs. Even if I can't.

"Six."

My body is numb, my thoughts fragmenting with fleeting images of Carter, Verona, and a baby who never had a chance. A baby I couldn't protect. A baby I never had the chance to love and cherish. My heart breaks for that little life, and for the baby I've felt growing inside me these past few months. All I can do is pray she fights to survive… that she fights to live.

"F… i… v… e…"

I feel myself being pulled into the darkness, into my worst nightmares…

Four Years Earlier

. . .

I RUN OUT OF HIS DORM, THE TEARS PRACTICALLY BLINDING ME AS I TRY TO make my way through the crowded halls. I feel like I'm going to be sick, choking down the sobs and screams that want to break free from my throat. I knew he was messing around a little, but fucking another girl? Have there been others? I feel like such a fool. I really thought if I did everything he wanted, I would be enough for him—that he would love me again.

I'm almost out of the building, when a familiar hand curls tight around my wrist.

"Where the fuck do you think you're going, baby?"

"Let go of me."

"Don't tell me what to fucking do."

"Please... Gavin." He drags me back through the crowd and down into the basement boiler room. The fear that grips me in this moment is like a vice around my chest. It's dark and eerily quiet. No one knows we're here.

I know what I need to do. I need to tell him why I came over tonight. It will change his mind about whatever he has in store for me now.

"Don't ever run away, Addi. I fucking decide when you come and when you go. Got it?"

"I'm sorry, Gav. I was upset. Seeing you with... her." He grabs my face in his large, strong hand, gripping me so tight that my teeth are digging into my cheeks. I taste blood.

"That's none of your fucking business. You're MY girl. None of those girls mean anything. You're the one I love, baby." He lets go of me.

"There have been others?" My voice is barely a whisper. My heart broken into a thousand pieces. The back of his hand connects with my face before I have a chance to shield myself.

"NONE OF YOUR FUCKING BUSINESS! You really are a dumb cunt sometimes."

"I'm sorry... I'm so sorry, Gavin. Please, forgive me. I love you." He pulls me into his arms, stroking my hair.

"I forgive you. Just don't fucking question me again, I don't like hurting you."

"Okay... I won't. I have something I need to tell you." I hesitate.

"You can tell me anything, baby."

I take a deep breath and say the words out loud for the first time. "I'm eight weeks pregnant." I feel his body stiffen against me, his delicate strokes on my hair becoming painful as he curls his hand into a fist, taking my hair with it.

"Is it mine?" I have never heard his voice sound so cold and void of all emotion. It's terrifying.

"Of course it is, Gavin. I've always been faithful to you. There's only you." He pushes me away.

"You really are a manipulative little bitch, aren't you? Getting pregnant on purpose to fucking trap me! Is that what you thought? That you could TRAP ME?" I'm speechless as I stare into his wild eyes. "ANSWER ME!"

"No... N... N... No. It was an accident, I would never try to trap you. I love you. And I love our baby." His face slowly twists into a repugnant smirk, pure evil radiating from every pore. I instinctively wrap my arms around my stomach.

"There is no 'OUR' baby. We are not having a fucking baby together. Not now... not ever. You're just a piece of ass I keep around because you're like a little lap dog, eager to fucking please me, and you'll do anything I ask, no matter how much of a fucking slut it makes you."

I choke down my fear, steeling myself to say the words he needs to hear, finding a confidence I didn't even know I had. "I'm keeping the baby, Gavin. With or without you."

"That's not your decision to make."

"It's my body." My pulse is racing in my ears, every instinct I have telling me to get out of here.

"The fuck it is! It's MY body. And you are NOT having a fucking baby." The look in his eyes is chilling.

I make a run for the door, for freedom, for safety. I reach out my hand and manage to grab hold of the handle. One twist is all it needs. It's all I need to get away from him.

"Oh no, you don't. Fucking whore." He drags me away from the door by my hair. Tearing some of it out with his brute force. "Who the fuck do you think you are? You're just a stupid little bitch. You're nothing." I scramble

away from him on my hands and knees, trying to find somewhere to shelter me from his wrath.

He grabs my leg, pulling me toward him, my face and stomach smacking onto the hard, concrete floor when I lose my balance. I try to grab hold of anything around me, but nothing can stop him now. He flips me onto my back, pulling me up by my shirt until his face is an inch from mine, his spit hitting my face as he speaks.

"You're going to be sorry you tried to run away again, Addi. I warned you. But you never fucking listen." The first punch connects with my cheek, making my head spin. He doesn't hold back.

"Please stop, Gavin. Please."

My words fall on deaf ears. He's lost to the anger, the rage, and the bloodlust I see in his eyes. I curl into a ball, shielding my stomach with my arms and legs in the hopes that I can keep my baby safe from this animal.

The world around me goes quiet as I shut down. I shut off my emotions, shut out the pain... and I try to wait it out. Punch after punch, followed by his boot kicking into me, my ribs, my legs, and my back. With a final kick straight to my stomach, to our baby, he spits on me and leaves me for dead. Death would be a sweet relief from the pain, humiliation, and utter terror I feel.

I laid there for an hour before I found the strength and the courage to move. I waited until I knew the halls would be empty enough to leave without being seen. I took myself to the ER where I told them I had been mugged and attacked by a stranger. They wanted to call the authorities, but I told them I didn't want any police involved.

While I sat in that sterile white room, waiting on a nurse returning to give me a few stitches to a cut on my arm, the worst happened. I started bleeding. It didn't stop. Two days later my baby, was gone. Its father punched and kicked it to death... and I couldn't do anything to stop him.

In that moment I stopped feeling, stopped caring, and stopped loving. The day my baby died, a part of me died with it.

CHAPTER 38

CARTER

IT'S BEEN AN HOUR SINCE THEY TOOK ADDI INTO SURGERY. THE longest hour of my life. I've been pacing the waiting room, pacing the halls, feeling like a caged animal, helpless and terrified. Xander came back with fresh clothes, and I forced myself to take five minutes to get changed and cleaned in the bathroom. He's been trying to keep Lily calm and positive, telling her how Addi will be back busting our balls in no time. I want to believe his words so badly it hurts.

Addi's parents and mine are here now, waiting and hoping with the rest of us, and together there is a collective gasp when the door swings open and a doctor enters the room, still in surgical scrubs.

"Mr. de Rossi?" I'm standing in front of her in a flash, desperate for any news she can give me.

"Yes. How's Addi?"

"I'm Doctor Field. I've been working on your wife since she came in today." She looks around the room, a question in her eyes.

"It's ok, doctor, we're all family. Please, just tell us how she is." Her eyes lock with mine, her expression grave.

"It's not looking good." My world just fucking stops.

"We had to deliver the baby. She's small, but she's fighting. They've taken her up to the NICU."

She? I have a daughter?

"Addison has extensive scarring on her uterus from her previous pregnancy, and the placenta was attached to an area of scar tissue. It ruptured, causing the hemorrhage." Previous pregnancy? Why didn't she tell me? "We're struggling to stop the bleeding at the moment. She's losing blood as fast as we're transfusing it. If we don't manage to stop it soon, she's not going to pull through."

All I can feel is my heart hammering against my ribcage, trying desperately to burst out of my chest. She can't die. She... I... we... there's so much I want to say to her, so much time we're supposed to have.

"Our only option at this point is to perform a hysterectomy. I know she's very young for this, but it's her only chance of survival, and even then, I can't guarantee she'll make it through the surgery. Her body is very weak. If we remove her uterus, it will give her a 50/50 chance."

I feel Xander's hand on my shoulder, and realize that everyone is standing around me, waiting for me to speak. I look at Addi's parents, their faces distraught, devoid of color, their lips set in a grim line as they give me an imperceptible nod.

"Do it. Do whatever it takes to save her. Please."

"We will. I can promise you that." She makes her way to the door, turning just before she disappears from sight. "I would urge you go and see your baby, Mr. de Rossi. She's fighting for her life and hearing her daddy's voice will be a big comfort to her." She leaves me to deal with this chilling revelation.

I completely fucking lose it.

"Cazzo! Fuck!" I lash out, punching straight through one of the walls in the waiting room. Xander is behind me, holding onto me, like he's the only thing holding the broken pieces of me together.

"I'm so fucking sorry, Carter." He pulls me back and into his arms. "She's a fighter. She's going to fucking fight to come back to you. To you *and* the baby."

I cling to my best friend, my brother, hoping to garner some strength from him. "I can't do this without her man. I need her. She's fucking everything to me. This can't be how it ends." Tears well in my eyes. My desperation thick and heavy in my voice. "The last conversation we had, I told her I couldn't trust her and that it would never work between us. I told her I would be there for her and the baby but that our relationship was over. It can't be the last thing I ever say to her."

"She knows you love her."

"I didn't fucking mean it, any of it. I was hurt and scared. I thought it was for the best. Now it just seems so fucking stupid. I love her, and I need her more than my next fucking breath. A world without her in it isn't comprehensible to me. It just isn't right." Lily comes to wrap her arms around us both.

"Lily, I'm so sorry. If I had never pursued her we wouldn't be sitting here right now, and Addi wouldn't be... dying on an OR table. I only ever wanted to protect her, to love her, to build a life and grow old with her."

"She's going to get through this, Carter. Addi is going to get through this. Fifty percent is more than enough odds for my girl to kick death's ass. She loves you and she wants this baby more than anything. She's not going down without a fight."

I squeeze her close. "I hope you're right."

I hear my mom's voice close by. "You need to get your hand seen to. You'll be no use to Addi or the baby with a mangled hand." I'm suddenly aware of the pain coursing through my hand, looking down to see blood and shards of sheetrock protruding from my skin.

"I don't want to leave here in case they come back to tell us what's happening with Addi."

"It's going to be at least another hour before they come back with any information. Go. Get your hand seen to, and then come back."

"Okay. But call me the minute you hear anything." Xander assures me that he'll come and find me if there is any news, and so reluctantly I head down to the ER to find out what I already know. I've broken my hand.

The staff are very understanding of my situation, fast-tracking my X-ray and getting my hand put in a cast up to my elbow in record time. It hurts like a motherfucker, but it's nothing compared to the pain of waiting to hear if Addi is going to live… or die.

Now is the time that I need to man up. I'm a father now, and my baby girl needs me, too.

As I step through the doors of the NICU, head to toe in scrubs, my body is vibrating with nerves and fear. I'm about to meet my daughter for the first time. This is not how I envisaged this happening. I thought, like everybody does, that Addi and I would be together, welcoming our baby into the world after nine months of waiting. Instead, Addi is fighting to stay alive, and so is our daughter. She's ten weeks premature, and the nurses have already warned me that she's tiny, weighing no more than a bag of sugar.

"This way, Mr. de Rossi." A kind looking nurse leads me over to the corner, where I can see an incubator, surrounded by beeping machines and tubes attached to my baby girl.

"She's doing really well considering how premature she is. You've got a little fighter on your hands."

My voice is a whisper. "Just like her mommy."

Nothing prepares me for what I see as I stand in front of the clear box that is keeping my baby alive.

She is so incredibly tiny. She could fit in the palm of my hand, fragile, and breathtaking. She is covered in tubes and needles, with tiny bandages holding them in place. I watch the rise and fall of her almost transparent skin as the machines breathe for her, and the tiny flutter of her rapid heartbeat. My own heart swells in my chest, overwhelmed with a love I never knew possible.

She has the smallest little hands and feet I've ever seen, perfectly formed, and oh so beautiful. Even with most of her features obscured by tubes, it's clear to me that she looks like Addi. A little princess, my tiny treasure. I press my hand to the glass because it's the closest I can get.

"Hi, Tesorina. I'm your daddy. You have no idea just how much I love you. And your mom? God, she hasn't been able to come say hi yet, but she desperately wants to meet you. She is going to be so in love with you. We're going to be so happy together, the three of us. Us against the world. So, you just keep fighting for me, baby girl, okay? For your mom. We need you."

I stand and stare at her in awe for the longest time, praying she's strong enough to survive this. She's so small. I have never been so consumed with love for someone in my life. I never knew this kind of love existed, until I looked into her tiny face and it hit me like a freight train. I can't do this alone... I need Addi... our baby needs her mother.

The nurse appears at my side. "Mr. de Rossi, the doctor needs to speak to you about your wife. She'll meet you up in the OR waiting room now."

My heart stops beating, the gravity of what I'm about to hear weighing down on me. I'm terrified, but I need to know. I turn to my daughter, taking one last long look, before steeling myself to go and find out about Addi.

"Ti amo, Tesorina. I'll be back soon."

I can barely put one foot in front of the other as I make my way up to the waiting room, and when I finally open the door, everyone is looking at me expectantly, disappointment evident on their faces.

"Where's the doctor?"

Xander stands up. "She'll be here any minute." He pulls me into a hug. "Did you go to see the baby?"

I manage a small smile as I remember her stunning little face. "Yeah. She's so fucking tiny, and beautiful, and amazing. She looks just like Addi. She's got tubes coming out of her all over the place, but she's hanging in there... waiting to meet her mommy."

The door swings open, and Doctor Field walks in, looking exhausted and drained.

"Mr. de Rossi." A high-pitched whistling sound is all I hear, my body fighting against the possibility of hearing that Addi didn't make it. That she's... gone. "Your wife made it through surgery. She's a tough woman." I drop to my knees, my legs unable to support me. "It was touch and go there for a while. We had to perform the hysterectomy, but she's going to pull through. We've transfused her to replenish the blood she lost, and she'll need time to heal, but most of her recovery can be done at home. She's a very lucky woman. The paramedics told me you administered CPR at the scene... you saved her life, Mr. de Rossi. We couldn't have done any of what we did today if you hadn't stepped up when she needed you."

"Doctor, I can never thank you enough for what you've done for her, for all of us. I really didn't think she was going to make it. God... I thought... I was going to be raising our daughter alone. I can never repay you for giving my daughter her mom. For giving me back my wife." Addi's mom and dad drop to the floor beside me, throwing their arms around each other, and me.

I hear Lily's sobs of joy in the background and Xander soothing her. My mom and dad express how happy they are that she's going to make it, that she's alive, that her beautiful fucking heart is still beating in her chest.

Relief isn't the word I would use for how I feel right now... I don't think there *is* a word that could do justice to how I feel. She did it... my girl fucking fought... even when she was broken beyond repair... she fucking fought it, and came back to me, and I will *never* let her go again.

I'VE BEEN SITTING NEXT TO HER BED SINCE THEY BROUGHT HER BACK from surgery. She's still under anesthesia, but just being here, beside her, holding her hand this past hour, has been more than I thought I would get with her when I found her earlier today. It's been less than twelve hours since I walked into her apartment, but it feels like weeks. Endless hours of worry, despair, and paralyzing terror. The image of her on the floor in the kitchen will haunt me as long as I live.

I'm thankful for every breath she takes, but I realize that when she wakes up I'll need to tell her she will *never* have any more children, and that we have a daughter who is fighting to survive. I'll need to tell her I know that she was pregnant before. Of course, that can wait until she's ready to bring it up.

I can't believe after all this time, after all we've been through together she felt she couldn't confide in me. I know it's one of the reasons I told her we couldn't work, but I just don't care anymore. If she doesn't trust me, then I just need to work harder to prove to her that she *can* trust me, with anything. If she wants to run, I'll convince her to stay. I will do *whatever* it takes to make this work between us. I love her too goddamn much not to.

Her hand twitches in mine. Her eyes fluttering open.

"Carter." Her voice is croaky and so quiet I can barely hear.

"I'm here, Tesoro. I'm here." I gently kiss her hand, her face, anywhere I can, without hurting her.

"The baby? Is she okay?"

"She's hanging in there, just like her mommy."

Her eyes look pained as tears begin to fall. "I'm a mom." She's sobbing as I try to carefully lift her into my arms. "I didn't think I was going to wake up from the surgery. I thought I would never see you again, and that I would never get to meet our daughter." Her fragile body shakes in my arms, tearing me up inside to see her so distraught.

"You're here, baby. You stepped up today and came through for our daughter, and for me. I thought... I thought I'd lost you. I'm so sorry, Addi... about everything. I love you."

She's groggy from the anesthesia, and her speech is a little slurred, but the words I cling to, the words that I never thought I would hear again, fall from her beautiful lips.

"I love you, Carter."

CHAPTER 39

ADDI

I FEEL LIKE I'VE BEEN RUN OVER BY A STEAMROLLER. MY BODY ACHES, and I have never been so tired in my whole life, but none of it matters today, because I'm alive and Carter is coming to take me up to meet our daughter in a few hours. It's been three days since she was born, since I had surgery to save my life, and now I've got enough of the needles removed from my arms, which look like pin cushions, the doctors have agreed to let me make the journey to the NICU in a wheelchair.

I've been pretty out of it on painkillers over the past few days, so this morning was the first time that I really had a proper chat with Dr. Field. She told me what happened. The scarring on my uterus from Gavin's attack when I lost the baby was the reason that I started bleeding out. I asked if she had informed my family of the cause, and my heart sank when she said she had told them. It was the only way to explain what had happened, and now they all know. Not one of them has mentioned it to me. Carter knows, and he has been nothing but amazing. If he's not with me, then he's spending time with our daughter. He only leaves the hospital long enough to get a fresh change of clothes, or to eat.

It's been a hard few days. The day after surgery, Carter sat with me and explained that the doctors had to perform a hysterectomy to save my life, and consequently I will never have any more children. I cried for hours. Crying for the lost possibilities of the family we could have been, crying because my baby is struggling to survive, and if we lose her… it doesn't bear thinking about.

Carter was amazing, soothing me, telling me that I'm all he needs. Me and our baby girl. Nothing else matters. I know it will probably hit me hard when I'm healthy, happy, and feeling like it would've been nice to have more children. I'm devastated, but I'm so grateful to be alive that I can't focus on that pain right now. I need to focus on getting better, on my daughter and the fight that she faces, and on *living*. It's a gift we take for granted every day. A gift that can be taken away in a heartbeat.

Carter's got a broken hand, but he hasn't complained once. I asked him about it and he looked so upset at the memory. All he said was that he needed to punch something to keep from losing his shit altogether. I didn't press him. I can't imagine how difficult it must have been for him to wait, not knowing what was happening to me or the baby.

I'm deep in thought when he walks into my room, his commanding presence like a cool breeze on a summer day. I breathe him in, savoring everything about him as he presses his lips to mine.

"You ready to go meet our baby girl?"

"I've never been more ready for anything in my life." He ducks out of the room and brings in a wheelchair from the hall. Not just any wheelchair, it's been pimped out with balloons and glitter and pink!

"Your chariot awaits, my queen."

MY PALMS ARE SWEATING AS WE ENTER THE NICU. I'M SO EXCITED, and at the same time terrified to meet my daughter for the first time. Carter and the nurses have warned me not to be scared by all the tubes and machines, but I can't help feeling that it's my fault she's in here fighting for her life.

Carter wheels me into the corner, next to an incubator with Baby Warner written in neat handwriting on a pink card attached to the bottom of the Perspex box.

"Addi, meet our daughter." As I peer inside I see the tiniest little hand with perfect little fingers. My eyes slowly take in every detail, until I reach her face. A sob fights to burst out of me, but I clasp my hand over my mouth, scared I'll frighten my baby girl. It takes a moment to regain my composure.

"Oh my God, Carter. Look at her. She's so beautiful. I can't believe we made her."

His arms wrap around my shoulders in a sweet and tender gesture, his cast rough against my skin and his lips soft on my ear. "Thank you so much, Tesoro. You've given me everything I ever wanted. I love you both so much." I grab ahold of his forearm, nestling into his warm embrace. He feels like home. At this moment, with him by my side and my baby alive in front of me, my life finally feels... real. When he lets me go, I lean forward to take a good long look at my daughter.

"Hi, baby girl. I'm your... mommy."

Tears are streaming down my face as I gaze at her stunning face. Carter told me that she looks like me, but I disagree, I think she looks like her daddy. She has a cute tuft of black hair, the sweetest pouty little lips, and the smallest nose you ever saw. She's so tiny. It breaks my heart knowing that I should still be taking care of her, letting her grow inside my belly until she was ready to be born, happy and healthy.

"I'm so sorry." I drop my head into my hands, only to have them gently pulled out of the way as Carter kneels before me, cupping my face in his hands.

"You have *nothing* to apologize for, Addi. You did amazing. You fought when so many people would have given up. Do you realize that you kept our girl alive, even when you stopped breathing? You came back to us when your body was broken and too weak to function on its own." His voice is thick with emotion, his eyes full of pain. "God, Addi, they told me... they said... it was 50/50. I have *never* been so scared in my entire life." His head rests on my lap as I stroke his hair, my gaze falling between him and my baby girl. We sit in silence for a few moments before he lifts his gaze to mine. Even after everything my body has been through in the past few days, his stunning brown eyes can make my stomach do somersaults. I'm filled with so much love for this man. "What shall we call her? Baby Warner is cute and all, but she deserves a beautiful name."

"I did have a thought before they put me to sleep. They told me I had a daughter, and I thought Verona was nice, but if you don't like it we can pick something else."

A slow, genuine smile tugs at the corner of his lips. "Verona Warner. I love it."

"No. Her name is Verona de Rossi." I have never seen a smile so beautiful, so real, and filled with such all-consuming love.

"You mean it?" I nod my head, delighting in his reaction. "I don't know what to say. Thank you, baby. Thank you so much." His lips press tender kisses all over my face, every inch caressed by his gentle touch until he reaches my mouth. We share a heartfelt kiss, slow, soft, sensual and emotional. "I love you, Addi."

We spend an hour with Verona, talking to her, looking at her, and just watching her breathe. The nurse came by at one point, and told us she's doing well, and they're feeling positive about her chances. I know it's still early and anything could happen, but I can just feel it. I know she's going to pull through this. She's a little fighter. The only reason I agree to leave her and go back to my room is because I'm in a lot of pain after sitting up for so long, and Carter insists. He lifts me back into my bed, and I just want to cling to him and never let go.

"You shouldn't be lifting me with a broken hand."

He lets out a small chuckle. "You weigh about sixty pounds, Addi. I think I can handle it."

"Don't make me laugh, it hurts."

"Sorry. No more fun. I promise."

Once I'm settled in and he's rearranged my pillows and covers about ten times, he sits beside me and takes my hand in his.

"Carter. I never thanked you."

He looks puzzled. "For what?"

"For saving my life." He furrows his brow, obviously uncomfortable thinking about what happened. "The doctors and nurses told me what you did. If you hadn't stepped up and refused to give up on me, I wouldn't be here. There is nothing I will ever be able to do to repay you for that. You gave me the opportunity to meet Verona and tell her I love her. To tell *you* how much I love you, and how eternally sorry I am for all the heartbreak I've caused." He lifts my hand to his lips, planting a firm kiss on my palm.

"Addi, the fact that you're alive is all I will ever need. A part of me died when your heart stopped beating. My world became silent. It became meaningless without you. I never want to feel that way again."

"I'm so sorry, Carter."

He squeezes my hand a little tighter. "Don't ever apologize to me, Addi."

"I've put you through so much. I pushed you away. I ruined what we had."

His eyes are on fire, his gaze burning into my soul. "We both said and did a lot of things that were just fucking stupid. When I thought that the last thing I would ever have said to you was that we couldn't be together… that love wasn't enough… I was devastated. I don't care about any of that shit. We have a second chance to be together, to be a family, and to make the most of the time we have. It's a gift, Addi, and I'm not going to squander it. You're stuck with me."

"Fine by me. I love you, Carter. I noticed that all of the doctors and nurses think I'm your wife." He rolls his eyes in a playful way, before his face becomes pensive. He sits for a moment and then reaches into his pocket, pulling something out, holding it tight in his fist. His gaze locked on mine.

"Whether you ever get to the point where you let me sign a piece of paper to make it legal or not, you are already my wife, in every way that matters." He opens his fist to reveal a huge emerald cut ruby ring, set in platinum. "This isn't an engagement ring, Addi. I'm not asking you to marry me. I'm never going to ask that of you. If you want to make it official at some point down the road, then you'll need to ask me. As far as I'm concerned, you *are* my wife."

He slides the stunning ruby onto my ring finger on my left hand, before kissing the tip of my finger.

"You are mine, Addison Warner, and I'm yours. I vow to be the best non-husband, husband, and the best father I can possibly be. I vow to love and protect you and our precious baby girl with every last breath I have in my body. Nothing and no one will ever tear us apart. We are a family now. You, me, and Verona."

He moves his chair out of the way, dropping down to one knee.

"I'm here, on my knee, offering you every part of myself, Addi. I'm one hundred percent all in. Do you accept that?"

I'm overwhelmed by this amazing man, putting his heart on the line for me... again.

"Yes." It's all I can choke past the lump in my throat, but it's all he needs.

"I love you so much. I swear I'm going to chain you to my fucking side from now on, so I know you're safe. You okay with that?"

"Chains? You know I love it when you talk dirty to me!" I lighten the mood.

"Even when you're incapacitated you're still a hot little minx. I'm going to have the worst case of blue balls by the time I'm allowed anywhere near you."

"You're such a jackass." I can't help but laugh at the playful look on his face.

"But I'm your jackass, and you love me."

"That's true. I do love you, my non-hubby." I glance down at my non-engagement, wedding-type ring. "When did you buy this?"

"Remember when we were in Florence, on the Ponte Vecchio?"

"Oh My God. You've had it all this time?" There's a vulnerability in his smile and it completely slays me.

"Yes."

"You kept it, even when I walked out on you?" My heart breaks at how badly I screwed up.

"Of course. You're it for me, Addi. I held onto it, hoping like a schmuck that you would come back to me."

"You are the most amazing man I have ever met. Do you know that?"

"I am pretty awesome. You really are a lucky girl."

I slap him on the arm, sending shocks of pain through my aching body as my hand connects with solid muscle. "Ouch."

"Be careful, Addi. I know you love touching me, and you like it rough, but rein it in for a while, will you?" He wiggles his eyebrows suggestively, making me laugh, and I curl my arms around my stomach to curb the pain.

"Stop making me laugh."

The playfulness is gone from his face as he gently wraps his arms around me, holding my body against his. "Sorry, baby. I'm just so happy to be here, talking and joking with you. I'll take better care of you now. I promise."

The nurse arrives shortly after to administer my pain meds, which I take, gladly. Carter stays with me while I drift in and out, becoming drowsy, before falling asleep, our fingers entwined and our hearts full, grateful to have a second chance together.

CHAPTER 40

CARTER

VERONA IS SUCH AN AMAZING LITTLE GIRL. MY TINY TREASURE. MY Tesorina. I've been her daddy now for two weeks, and I can't remember what life was like without her in it. She's a strong little thing. A survivor like her mommy.

I've spent every available minute with Addi and Verona, savoring every moment with them. Addi is getting stronger by the day, which lets her spend more and more time by Verona's bedside. Every day I have to force her back to her room to rest, and every day she fights me on it.

Verona is improving. Her breathing is better and she's feeding well. She's charming all of the nurses in the NICU, having someone talk to her and coo over her every minute of the day. She definitely gets it from her daddy! I could spend every second of every day just staring at her, marveling at how amazing she is, and I would never tire of it.

Today is the day I get to take Addi home, as long as her blood results are good. She's got a long recovery ahead, especially after the hysterectomy, but she's so focused on Verona that it hasn't really hit her yet. She's managing the physical pain really well, but I'm worried about the emotional fallout for her. She still hasn't mentioned the fact that she miscarried once before, and I'm reluctant to bring it up in case it's just too much for her to handle at this point. All I can do is be here for her and love her, and when she's ready I can listen, and try to help her through it. I just hope she lets me, when the time comes.

I stayed at my place last night rather than the hospital so that I could get Addi's apartment organized for her coming home. It also gave me the chance to pack up my own essentials, so I can stay with her until she's fully recovered. I'm just praying that by then, she'll have come around to the idea of living with me. I don't want to be a part-time dad. I want to live in the same house as Verona, with Addi. I can't push her, though. I've inadvertently done that in the past and driven her away.

Stepping into her apartment last night was like walking into a haunted house. Xander and Lily took care of getting it professionally cleaned, but in my mind's eye, I could see the crimson trail of blood in the hallway. I could see Addi lying on the floor, her lips turning blue. I stood and watched it play out, like an out-of-body experience, seeing myself frantically try to revive her.

I stood frozen to the spot, staring at the floor until I heard a knock on the door behind me. The door was wide open, but I think Xander and Lily were worried they would startle me. They came to help me get the place ready for Addi, and I was grateful to have the company. We put up welcome home banners, put fresh covers on her bed, and we got a framed picture of Verona to keep her company until we get to bring her home.

I had asked Xander to get Lily's old room cleared out over the past few weeks, so I would have a blank canvas to turn into a room for our little princess. We spent hours last night building a crib, painting the walls pink, and filling it with all kinds of furniture and teddies, and pictures that Lily picked out for me. It was around 2 a.m. by the time we finished. I know it's going to be a while before Verona will be home with us, but I wanted Addi to see that I'm prepared for anything. I'm ready for us to be a family. If nothing else, I'm hoping it will distract her from the inevitable distress of walking back in here.

I was happy to get back to my apartment and crawl into my own bed. I don't relish the idea of staying in Addi's place for the foreseeable future, but I'll do it, for her. I want her to feel comfortable, surrounded by her own stuff.

~

WHEN I WALK INTO ADDI'S ROOM, I'M MET WITH AN EMPTY BED. IT'S only 9 a.m. and I know exactly where she'll be. I leave the bag I brought for her, with some clothes to travel home in, and make my way to the NICU. Sure enough, when I open the door, I see her sitting in the corner next to Verona's crib. What I'm not prepared for, is the tiny baby in her arms. I've never seen Verona out of the incubator, and the sight of her cradled in her mother's arms is… transcendent. I have never seen Addi look more beautiful than she does in this moment.

Our baby girl is still hooked up to tubes and machines, but today, she's also wrapped in a tiny pink blanket, sleeping like an angel. Her little hand is wrapped around Addi's finger, and as I crouch beside them, she turns to greet me, her face glowing.

"Hi, baby. They said she was strong enough for me to hold her for a little while this morning. She's doing so well. Look at her, Carter. Look at our baby girl. Isn't she the most perfect thing you've ever seen?" I'm mesmerized as she strokes Verona's cheek with her thumb.

"She's perfect. You're both perfect. God, I love you, Addi. Thank you so much for giving me a daughter. I promise I'm going to be the best dad I can be."

Addi gently caresses my face with her free hand, lifting my gaze to meet hers. "You already *are* the best dad. You didn't just save my life, Carter, you saved Verona's, too. I know she is the luckiest girl in the world to have you as her daddy. Would you like to hold her?"

"She's so small, I don't want to hurt her."

"You won't. Grab a chair and you can sit with her for a while." I do as she says, my adrenaline pumping as nerves spread throughout my entire body.

I've been waiting for this moment for two weeks, dreaming about what it will feel like to hold my daughter in my arms for the first time, but now that it's here, I'm scared that I won't know what to do, or how to hold her properly.

The nurse comes over to help, lifting Verona from her mother's arms, and placing her in mine. My breath catches in my chest, and my heart literally skips a beat when I feel the warmth of my daughter's little body pressed against my chest. She is so small, so fragile, and yet so strong, fighting for every moment she's had over the past two weeks.

As I lose myself in her, taking in every tiny detail, I am overcome with an all-consuming love. Her little fingers curl around my thumb, and I fall in love with her all over again. She is sweet and innocent and mine... my daughter, my tiny treasure.

"Ti amo, Tesorina. I hope you don't mind me stealing you away from mommy for a little while. I just wanted to give you a cuddle and tell you how much daddy loves you, baby girl." I study her face, enchanted by how much she resembles Addi.

We spend the entire day sitting by her incubator, watching the rise and fall of her chest, marveling at the cute noises she makes, and remembering how magnificent it felt to hold her in our arms, even if it was only for a little while. One day soon, we'll be able to take her home, and hold her for as long as we want, but for today, I will revel in the fact that I *can* take Addi home, and I *can* hold her in my arms as she falls asleep at night. It's hard for both of us to leave the hospital without Verona, and we feel guilty about it, but I need to make sure that Addi is fit and healthy for when we *do* get to bring our baby girl home.

I pull Addi close as we walk out into the fresh air together. "We'll be here all day every day until they let us bring her home, but please, Addi, let me take care of you. You need to rest. I almost lost you, Tesoro... I..."

She presses her finger over my lips. "Shh, baby. Please, take me home."

A wave of relief washes over me. "Your wish is my command."

THE DRIVE OVER HERE WAS QUIET, ADDI'S MOOD SOMBER. I WANTED TO carry her up from the car, but she wouldn't hear of it, insisting that she can manage the elevator ride up to her apartment. I can't help but notice the tension in her body and the slight shaking as she leans into my side, wrapping her arms around my waist. I know it must be difficult for her coming back here. I just wish I could make it better for her and she didn't need to face these demons.

I open the door and let her go at her own pace, slowly edging her way inside. She manages a small smile when she sees the banners, welcoming her back home. "You did this?"

"With a little help from Xander and Lily. There's more. Would you like to see?" She nods her head, making sure to avert her gaze from the kitchen. It kills me to see her like this.

She struggles down the hallway towards Lily's old room, and I don't know if it's the pain from surgery or the memories that are making it so hard. When I open the door to the new nursery, her face lights up, but it's tinged with sadness. I wrap my arms around her.

"She'll be home soon, Addi. She's doing great and she's going to keep getting bigger and stronger, and before you know it, we'll be in here at 4 a.m. in the morning, crying because we want her to go back to sleep and give us a break!" Her soft chuckle is a beautifully sweet sound.

"I can't wait."

I kiss her hair, drinking in her scent. "Me too, baby. Me too." She quietly sobs into my chest, and I can't do anything to make it better, so I just hold her, for the longest time. "You need to rest. Let's get you changed and into bed. I'll make us something to eat. We can watch one of your god-awful chick flicks while we eat. Sound good?"

She squeezes me a little tighter. "Sounds great."

I help her into the bedroom and get her changed into some comfortable pajamas with funny little minions on them. Nothing like the sexy lingerie I'm used to from her, but she pulls it off, looking adorable and gorgeous.

"You okay to go to the bathroom yourself?"

She rolls her eyes at me, full of mischief. "God, Carter, let's keep some mystery in the relationship, shall we? If you see me on the toilet I will officially die of embarrassment and we will *never* have sex again due to my immeasurable shame!"

"Well I know when I'm not wanted. Never having sex with you again is not an option, so I'm going to go start dinner, leaving you and the 'mystery' intact."

I force myself into the kitchen, busying myself preparing something simple but tasty for us to eat. I grab my phone and put on some music to cook to. It only takes about fifteen minutes to throw together a pasta dish, which I quickly plate up and head back to Addi's room. I guess it's sort of my room now, too, for a while at least.

As I open the door, all I can hear is Addi, sobbing her heart out. I dump the plates on the nightstand and scoop her gently into my arms. "What's wrong, baby? Are you sore? Are your stitches okay?" She doesn't speak, she just continues to sob into my chest. "Addi, talk to me, baby, please. What can I do?"

"I can't do it, Carter. I can't do it."

"What can't you do, Addi?" I try to lift her face to look at me, but she just burrows deeper into my chest.

"I can't stay here. I can see it everywhere, the blood. I can't live here anymore. I couldn't step over the threshold into the bathroom. I just stood there, reliving it. The hallway, the kitchen, all of it. I just can't."

I stroke her back, trying desperately to calm her, my heart breaking for her. "Shh, baby. It's okay. We don't have to stay here tonight. We can go to my place if you want. We can stay there for a while?"

She finally lifts her gaze, with tear stained cheeks and red eyes. "But you put so much work into the nursery for Verona."

"It doesn't matter. All that matters is that you're happy. We can live on the moon if it makes you happy. And when you're ready to move back here, then I'll make it happen. Whatever you want, Tesoro. You know that."

"I want to live with you, Carter... permanently. You, me, and Verona. You once asked me to move in with you and I ran away, so I understand if the offer is no longer on the table, but if it is, I want it more than anything."

I'm elated and deflated at the same time. Overjoyed that Addi wants us to live together as a family and devastated that she can't bear to stay in her own apartment anymore. "Of course the offer is still there. I need you to be sure though. It's what I want, more than I've ever wanted anything. You and Verona mean everything to me."

She cups my face in her hands. "I've wanted this since I came back to New York. I've wanted it since the first time you asked me, but I know I have to earn back your trust after everything I put you through."

I take her lips with my own, pouring all of the emotions I've been holding in, into this one kiss. "I was stupid, Addi. I should never have said those things to you. I didn't really mean them, and when I thought I'd lost you for good, I was devastated. You could have… you would never have known… I thought I wouldn't get the chance to tell you how sorry I am for pushing you away. Please forgive me."

She plants the softest kiss on my lips. "You have nothing to apologize for. I gave you good reason not to trust me. I broke your heart and when you trusted me with it for a second time, I took it for granted. I wasn't worthy of the faith you put in me and I'm so sorry."

"Tesoro…"

She stops me before I can continue. "Please, let me finish. I need for you to hear this. There are things you need to know." She's finally ready to talk to me, and I am ready to hear whatever she needs to say. "I've been punishing you for Gavin's mistakes. I've let the way he treated me influence my life for the past four years, letting it seep into every aspect of my relationships, or lack thereof. I thought I was dealing with it, moving past it, but then you walked into my life and changed everything. I didn't tell you everything about what happened with him. I've never told anyone what really happened. Carter, I've been pregnant before."

I pull her into my arms. "I know, baby. The doctor told me that the scarring from your previous pregnancy had something to do with the bleeding."

She stares up into my eyes, searching for… something. "Doctor Field told me she explained everything to you, but you never once brought it up. Why didn't you say anything?"

"I figured you would tell me when you were ready. You've been through enough, Addi. You don't have to explain anything to me."

"I want to."

Addi goes on to tell me the full, sordid, horrifying story of what really happened between her and Gavin. My heart shatters into a million pieces for the girl before me, sobbing her heart out as she tells me about him intentionally beating her, killing their baby. She talks of how she kept it to herself, feeling so ashamed that she couldn't protect her unborn child. My blood runs cold, filled with an all-consuming rage. I want to kill this pathetic excuse for a man I've never met. I want to avenge the Addi I never had a chance to meet. I want justice for the baby he wasn't man enough to love.

I pull Addi close, careful not to hurt her, forcing myself to stay calm, for her sake. "I can't believe you've carried this burden around with you for so long. No one should have to live through something like that alone. You amaze me, Addison Warner. You are the strongest woman I have ever met. The fact that you let me in at all, and you chose to love me, that you gave me a chance to be a dad… it blows my mind."

"I almost ruined it all. I almost lost our baby. When I was lying on the operating table, I was so scared I wouldn't get another chance with you. A chance to let my past go and give our future together a real shot. I was terrified that I hadn't protected our baby. That I would never get the chance to meet her. I love you so much, Carter. I won't ever take this chance for granted. You saved my life in more ways than one. I can never thank you enough."

Her broken sobs call to every protective instinct I have, every fiber of my being desperate to fix this. I need to kiss her and to feel her lips against mine, to feel the connection we share so deeply. "Tesoro, the fact that you are here with me, breathing, your beautiful heart beating in your chest, it's all I will ever need. I told you at the hospital, and I will continue to remind you every day for the rest of your life." I capture her mouth with my own, claiming what's mine. Mine to love, and mine to protect. I kiss away each and every tear from her cheeks, planting soft feather light kisses on her tear swollen eyelids. *"No one will ever hurt you like that again, Addi. Not while I have breath in my body."*

"Take me home, Carter. I want to leave all the bad memories behind. I don't want them to hold me back anymore. I want to make a life with you and Verona. *You* are my home."

"Il tuo cuore è la mia casa, Tesoro. Ti amo." *[Your heart is my home, Treasure. I love you.]*

CHAPTER 41

ADDI

Eight Weeks Later

TODAY IS MY DUE DATE. THE DAY VERONA WAS SUPPOSED TO BE BORN. It's strange. You have all these preconceived ideas of what it's going to be like when you have a baby and of what the birth is going to be like. You read books like *What to Expect When You're Expecting*, thinking that once you're past the first trimester, you have nothing to worry about. My main concern just before Verona was born, was what tracks I wanted on my birthing playlist. Never in my wildest dreams would I have come up with what actually happened to me.

I missed my daughter's birth. She was pulled from my body, distressed and premature. She wasn't ready to face the world, and I wasn't awake to reassure her that everything was going to be alright. I've replayed and relived that day so many times in my mind. The feeling of dread thinking I was going to die, waking up to find out that my baby was born prematurely, being told I would never have any more children. No one should have to deal with such a diverse range of emotions in such a short space of time.

There have been so many nights when I've cried myself to sleep over the loss of even the possibility of giving Carter a son. I would give anything to have a little boy who looked exactly like his daddy, and I'm struggling to come to terms with the fact that I can never give him that.

He has been amazing these past two months. So loving, patient, and understanding. When I finally broke down and told him my darkest secret, he opened his arms and loved me even more. He listened without judgment and looked for the positive. When I asked him to give me another chance and for us to live together, he didn't hesitate, not even for a second, giving me unconditional love and trust. I know how hard it must have been for him, but he did it anyway, for me, and for our daughter.

We have spent every day at the hospital, watching Verona improve with every tube and machine that's been removed and rendered unnecessary. We've celebrated these small victories in our daughter's little life. Every day we've gotten to hold her for longer, getting to know her better, seeing her tiny personality shining through, even in the face of adversity.

Over the weeks, I've become stronger, my body healing, my mind coming to terms with everything that's happened. Carter and I are closer than we've ever been. I've always used my looks with men, confident in the effect my body would have on them, and that has changed dramatically.

I struggle with my self-confidence. When I stand and stare at my reflection in the mirror, it feels like I'm looking at someone else's body. The scars from my emergency surgery are still red and tight. My skin looks different, the muscles underneath lacking any form of tone. I'm still carrying an extra ten pounds, but I'm so exhausted with the hospital visits and my own recovery that I've just let Carter feed me. He's an old Italian woman! Like his aunt—always trying to feed me something, telling me I need to keep my strength up.

The hospital said it would be at least six weeks before I should consider any sexual activity again, but that just wasn't realistic for us. Our connection is too primal for that length of time apart. Carter has been so careful with me, treating me like I could break from the slightest touch, but he's definitely creative when it comes to finding other ways to satisfy our desire for one another.

The night we first made love again was so special to me. I have never felt so completely loved and accepted for who I am. Carter made me feel truly beautiful for the first time in my life.

"Goodnight, Tesoro." He pulls me close against his naked chest as he breathes in my scent and kisses my hair. My heart is pounding in my chest, the ache between my legs growing with every day that passes. "Are you okay, baby? I can feel your heart racing."

I turn in his arms, nervous of what I'm about to say. "Make love to me, Carter."

His eyes are tender and filled with desire, searching mine to make sure this is what I want. "I don't want to hurt you. We can wait."

I grab his face in my hands, feeling the scruff on his jawline scraping against my palms, placing a soft kiss on his gorgeous mouth, before nibbling and sucking on his bottom lip. "I don't want to wait any longer. Please, make love to me." I'm underneath him in seconds, but he's careful not to put his weight on my stomach.

He starts at my neck, kissing just under my ear, before working his way down. I can feel my body start to tingle all over, the familiar jolt of anticipation coursing through my veins, and when his lips brush over the tip of my nipple I can't help but cry out with pleasure, moaning his name as I begin to writhe under his expert touch. He makes a move to throw the covers off of us, but I try to pull them back up without ruining the moment, conscious of my scars. He stops kissing me, lifting his gaze to mine.

"What's wrong?"

I throw my hand up over my eyes, trying to stop the flow of tears welling up inside. "My body. It's disgusting now. I have scars. I don't look the same."

I feel his warm, strong hand, pulling my arm down, forcing me to look at him. All I see staring back at me in his beautiful chocolate-brown eyes is love. "You are more beautiful to me now, than you have ever been, Tesoro. Do you know what I see when I look at your scars?"

"No." My voice is a whisper, thick with unshed tears.

"I see strength and courage. I see a survivor. I see the love of my life and the mother of my child. You're fucking breathtaking, Addi." I shy away,

shifting my head to the side, but Carter uses one finger to guide me back to him. "You need to wear these scars with pride. They're a part of who you are. You have come through so much, and you've done it by yourself. It's all you, cara mia. You are amazing and I'm in awe of you every single day. Please, don't ever think that you are anything less than stunning. I love your scars. Without them, we wouldn't have our precious baby girl and you wouldn't be here with me now. I will always love these scars. They mean... life."

He takes his time, kissing every inch of each scar, making me feel wanted and desired. He makes me feel whole again, and when he gently pushes inside of me I feel a wave of relief. My body responds to the physical connection I crave with every fiber of my being. There's some pain after my operation, but the pleasure of being connected to Carter again far outweighs any discomfort.

"Are you ok, baby?" His voice is low and tender, thick with his own desire.

"Yes. Please, don't stop." He slowly starts to move, rocking in and out of me, savoring each gentle thrust. The expert roll of his hips has me panting beneath him, perched on the edge of an explosive release.

"Come with me, Tesoro. I need to see you, to feel you come apart for me." He never loses control, pushing in and out of me in measured, leisurely thrusts, working my clit with his thumb, slowly building us higher and higher, until I can't take it anymore. It's like waves crashing over me, intense and profound, overwhelming me time and time again, over and over until I'm moaning his name as he growls mine, finding his own release, joining me in a sea of ecstasy.

"Addi... Ti amo."

I wrap my arms and legs around his body, holding him close. "I love you, too."

I will never forget that night for as long as I live.

IT'S TIME TO GO TO THE HOSPITAL AND BRING OUR BABY GIRL HOME. I'M nervous and excited, checking that we have everything we need at least five times before we leave. Carter is so adorable right now, checking and rechecking the car seat, asking if we need another blanket for Verona, or if the jacket and onesie we packed are going to be warm enough.

"Okay. Let's just stop. We've got everything we need. Let's enjoy this moment. We get to bring our princess home today. We are finally going to be a family, here in our home, together." He stops what he's doing, making his way over to where I'm standing.

"You're right, baby. We've waited long enough for this day to come. Let's enjoy it. I can't wait to have my two favorite girls under one roof. Let's go and bring our daughter home."

We arrive at the hospital to find all of the doctors and nurses who have helped Verona on her journey, gathered around her crib with balloons, teddies, and presents for her. She's made a lasting impression on everyone who has come into contact with her. A tiny person who has made a big difference to so many people's lives already.

When I lift her into my arms today, it feels different somehow. Knowing that I don't have to let her go. I don't have to say goodbye at the end of the day. She's finally going to be where she belongs—with Carter and me. It's a teary goodbye when we leave. So many people to thank for doing so much for our baby girl. Words could never really convey just how grateful we are for everything they've done.

The drive home is… slow. Carter's wary of every other driver on the road, slowing down to twenty miles an hour, just in case he needs to break for another car. We find ourselves laughing, knowing just how ridiculously over cautious we're being, but we get there in the end!

When he opens the door to our apartment, I feel the change as soon as I step inside with Verona in my arms. There is a tangible shift. Our home is finally complete. We have a quiet, wonderful first night at home together—our little family. Carter is lying on our bed with Verona sleeping on his chest, like a little starfish, her arms and legs spread wide, clinging to her daddy, perfectly content. I'm curled into his side, his arm wrapped around me as he watches our girl sleeping, transfixed by the tiny rise and fall of the cute little bundle on his chest. I am mesmerized by them both. There is something about watching a strong, alpha male like Carter, being so tender and loving with a baby.

It melts my heart. I never thought I would have this—a man who loves me unconditionally and a baby girl to love and cherish. They are such a gift in my life, and I am lucky enough to be here with them. It's the greatest gift I will ever have.

I spent the past few years of my life keeping people at arm's length, trying to fix what had been broken. The moment Carter walked into my life, he changed that, forcing his way into my heart, whether I liked it or not, relentless in his pursuit. I will always be grateful to him for not giving up on me, for continually pushing me to open up, to let him heal me and love me for who I am. It's been a long and bumpy road for us to get to where we are now, with a lot of heartache along the way, but we're stronger for it. He's given me more chances than I deserve. He believed in me, in us, when I didn't have the strength to. He saved my life two months ago, giving me the opportunity to raise our beautiful baby girl with him. I am his, in every sense of the word, in every way possible. Carter de Rossi is 'the one,' he is everything to me, and I will make sure he knows it, every minute of every day, for as long as we both shall live…

EPILOGUE

CARTER

Ten Months Later

The sun is shining in Central Park today, the birds are chirping, and I'm surrounded by family and friends to celebrate my baby girl's first birthday. I can't believe it's been a year since our life was turned upside down. It's amazing how much one tiny little human can change every aspect of your life.

Nothing can prepare you for how you're going to feel when you become a parent. The fear, the worry, and the love you feel for this helpless little baby from the moment you lay eyes on them—it's fucking amazing.

We had a rough start, with Verona and Addi fighting for their lives, but my girls are survivors, strong-willed, fierce and determined when they put their mind to something. Verona is so like Addi, not only in looks, but in personality. She has a tenacity that can be trying as a parent, but it will stand her in good stead when she's older. I swear she is going to be a real ball buster! I fucking love that about her.

Since we brought her home from the hospital, Addi and I have really found our stride. We've learned to trust each other again, far beyond what we ever had before. We rely on each other, we're a team. It's a joke of ours when Verona is giving us a hard time—*it's us against her*. We're a family.

Addi and I still share an intense and explosive passion for each other. It never seems to fade or falter. I always thought the fierce connection we share would be the death of us, because that level of passion can become toxic between two strong-willed people, but I was wrong. Our explosive connection is our greatest strength. It's an unshakeable foundation that will always be there. Embracing it has allowed us to build on it, to use it, and to cherish it.

Taking a step back from work and handing over the day to day running of the clubs was the best decision I've ever made. I get to spend so much time with my favorite girls. I have been there for all of my Tesorina's firsts—first word, first smile, first steps. You can't put a price on that, and I wouldn't change it for anything.

Addi decided not to go back into advertising. Instead, she spends her days with Verona, and she loves it. She set up a charity to help raise money and awareness for premature babies in the NICU and their families. She also started a website for young women who've had hysterectomies, which has been a great success, bringing women together from all over the world, giving them somewhere they can talk with others who understand what they're going through.

It was a major turning point for Addi when she started the website. It has allowed her to connect with and help so many other young women. It's still hard for her, and for me, to know that we can't ever give Verona a biological brother or sister, but we've spoken about adoption, and I think at some point in the future, we'll give a baby a home and a family, and a big sister who will love the crap out of them!

The party is in full swing, and Verona is being completely and utterly spoiled by everyone. It's a joy to watch her interact with her grandparents, and with our friends. She has funny little names for everyone, and her own special relationship with each and every one of them. Xander and Lily are Xan and Lelly—they dote on her and I wouldn't be surprised if Verona has a little playmate in the not too distant future. Vittoria is Aunt Tori, and Logan is Log. We don't get to see much of them with their work schedules, but when we do, Verona is mesmerized by her ballerina aunt, and she has a soft spot for Logan's charms. He's great with her, always ready with a silly game or a funny face to amuse her. I have no idea what is going on between Vittoria and Logan anymore. I don't think they're together, but I can see they still have feelings for each other. Addi made me promise not to beat the shit out of him, and to let Tori make her own decisions. I can't refuse her anything, so I agreed, but if he ever hurts my little sister, all bets are off, and I will bury him in a shallow grave!

Everyone seems to be enjoying themselves today, and most importantly, Verona is having the time of her life. Addi arranged for this little corner of Central Park to be turned into a princess paradise. Everything our baby girl adores. Cinderella and Snow White are entertaining all the kids with dancing, singing, and stories. There is a face painting station where all of the girls have been covered in glitter and pink! She even organized a princess makeover boutique. We now have twenty or so toddlers running around dressed in the smallest ball-gowns you've ever seen.

I've done my duties and mingled, saying hello and making small talk with all the dads, half of whom I've never laid eyes on before. My girls are social butterflies with their Gymboree and mother-toddler groups, but I try to steer clear of that whenever possible. I love my princess, but spending time around lots of tiny terrors at once is a living nightmare.

Everywhere I walk, and everyone I talk to today is just background noise. I can't take my eyes off of Addi and Verona. They are inseparable. The best of friends, they get up to all kinds of mischief together when my back is turned. It's fucking adorable. As I stand watching them, I can tell they're conspiring against me. Verona's perfect little cherub face keeps turning around to look at me, with a massive grin every time. Addi is crouched on the ground beside her, whispering in her ear, smiling over at me with feigned innocence. I'm close enough for her to see me raising my eyebrows, a questioning look on my face. She simply blows me a kiss, hands Verona something, and sends her my way.

My baby girl comes teetering toward me, her face covered in birthday cake, and her cute, chubby little hands holding an envelope out to me.

"Daddy, Daddy, Daddy!"

I scoop her up into my arms and plant a kiss on her sweet little cheeks. "What have you got here, Tesorina? Is this for me?" My name is written in elegant script with a purple ribbon wrapped around the plain white envelope.

She points her tiny finger towards Addi, standing next to the princess castle bounce house we had set up for the party. She looks breathtaking in a powder blue summer dress, her hair soft and flowing, her gaze fixed on me. The smile she flashes has my heart hammering in my chest.

"Did mommy give this to you for me?" She nods her head enthusiastically, proud of herself for doing what mommy asked. "Well done, baby girl. You are so clever." I nuzzle her cheek, drinking in her cute baby smell.

I tuck her into the crook of one arm so that I can open the envelope and see what Addi is up to. I peel off the ribbon and give it to Verona to play with, carefully opening the back so as not to rip the envelope. What I find inside is beyond anything I ever could have imagined. I pull out three plane tickets to Barbados in two weeks' time for me, Addi, and Verona. That in itself sounds amazing, but what I see glinting in the sunshine at the bottom of the envelope is so much better. There are two platinum wedding bands attached to a piece of card that says, 'READ THE INSCRIPTION.' I pull the larger of the two rings free and hold it up to the light.

Forever yours, Addi xxx

My eyes dart up to meet hers, our friends and family oblivious to what is transpiring between us in this moment. I'm transfixed by her, enchanted by her, and filled with desire. A sly grin spreads across her face as she presses her finger to her lips and gives me a wink, "Shh."

I close the distance between us in a few short strides, Verona bouncing in my arms, squealing with delight. I pull Addi flush against me with my free arm, sealing my lips over hers, tasting her sweet cherry mouth, lapping at her tongue with my own. She melts against my body, giving herself over to me completely.

"So, should I take that as a 'yes' then?"

"Yes! I want to shout it from the rooftops." I whisper in her ear.

She bites her succulent, pouty lip, slowly shaking her head. "Just you and me, baby... just for us... you, me, and V." I nod my acquiescence. I would do anything she asks to finally make it official.

She cradles my face in her hands, pulling my mouth down on hers in a fierce kiss. The feel of her tongue twisting and tangling with mine igniting a fire inside me, a passion so great that I will never get enough of this woman. My body is so attuned to her every move, her every breath. The slightest touch of her skin causes a thermonuclear reaction. Every fiber of my being vibrates when I'm in her orbit. No amount of time together will ever quench my thirst for her. My lover, the mother of my precious baby girl, my best friend, my Tesoro.

As I kiss the woman of my dreams with my sweet little Tesorina wriggling in between us, cuddling us as tight as her tiny arms will let her, I know, beyond a shadow of a doubt, this is what life is all about.

They say there are only two things in life that are certain—Death and Taxes. That's not true of my life. In my life, there are three certainties. Three things that are unshakable truths—death, taxes, and the fact that I will love and protect the two women in my arms with a ferocity unparalleled throughout the course of history. I will protect their hearts with my own. I will protect their bodies against anything that could harm them, laying down my own life in the process if necessary. But above all else, I will cherish the love they give me and I'll give it back tenfold in return, freely, unconditionally, and never-ending. They are my life's blood, the reason my heart beats in my chest. It will always beat for them, and them alone. My love for them is relentless. I miei per sempre tesori. [My treasures forever.]

THE END

ABOUT THE AUTHOR

I'm happiest when wandering through the uncharted territory of my imagi-nation. You'll find me curled up with my laptop, browsing the books at the local library, or enjoying the smell of a new book, taking great delight in cracking the spine and writing in the margins!

Eva is a native Scot, but lives in Texas with her husband, two kids, and a whizzy little fur baby with the most ridiculous ears. She first fell in love with British Literature while majoring in Linguistics, 17th Century Poetry, and Shakespeare at University. She is an avid reader and lifelong notebook hoarder. In 2014, she finally put her extensive collection to good use and started writing her first novel. Previously published with Prism Heart Press under the pen name *Sienna Parks*, Eva decided to branch out on her own and lend her name to her full back catalogue! She is currently working on some exciting new projects.

ACKNOWLEDGMENTS

First and foremost, I need to say a HUGE thank you to my husband. You have supported me 100% in my endeavors to become an author. You've been my strength when I had nothing left to fight with. I can't say thank you enough for putting up with me through this crazy process! When I've doubted my abilities, you've talked me up, when I've let the house descend into disarray while I spend time writing my fictional characters' lives, you've picked up the slack and encouraged me to write while the ideas are flowing. You are everything to me, and I love you more than ever. You and me against the world, baby.

Jaye—SDS. You are a rock star! You were able to jump into my mind and help me fight my way through the process of polishing *Relentless.* You have mad editing skills, my friend, and I feel very blessed to have you in my corner. Thank you for all your hard work, late nights, pep-talks, and for your unwavering belief that this book needed to be published. I can never repay you for your kindness. I'm honored to call you my colleague, and more importantly, my friend. Love you, bud.

To my betas—Where do I begin? You amazing ladies have not only given me your honest feedback when I needed it most, you have championed me every step of the way, loving Addi and Carter just as much as I do. You GET ME! That's a rare and wonderful gift, and I cherish it. You are my dearest friends, my life coaches when I'm having a meltdown, and I feel like the luckiest woman alive to have found you.

Sharron, we have had quite the crazy ride together. It has been a joy to spend time talking about my characters with a family member. I don't need to explain to you what that really means to me, because if I did, I'd ugly cry all over you! I consider it a privilege to have you in my life and your love and acceptance of my passion for writing is a gift I will never take for granted. Love your crazy ass, chick.

Maria, my amazing friend. It's been so fantastic getting to know you and share this experience with you. Your notes on every chapter I sent your way had me laughing, and at times, crying with your kind words. Your mad skills are second to none! Your constant love and support is something I hold very dear, and I look forward to the day when I finally meet you in person and sit down over a glass of wine and a good book. Love you hard, Ria.

Also, to the rest of the Alexander clan—you guys rock! Thank you so much for getting involved. I got a whole family of betas for the price of one!

Leslie. You're my girl. Your red/purple pen ensured that Addi and Carter's story is the best I could possibly make it. You've seen the good, the bad, and the downright ugly at times. You've been on this journey with me since the very beginning, when I was just an insecure girl with half a book and a dream of becoming an author! I'm still an insecure mess, but I know how much you love to stroke my "fragile author ego"—not! It's been a blast, and I've laughed my ass off more times than I can count. You push me when I need it, even when you know I'm going to text SHOUT or become crabby! We just… click! I love your guts, girl—always.

I would like to say a special thank you to Noemi and Diane. To see my words as you see them is a gift. You have been dedicated to helping me promote my work since the very beginning. Thank you so much. I love you both.

And last but by no means least, a *massive* thank you to you the reader. Thank you for spending your hard-earned cash on my book, thank you for all your kind words, messages, and reviews. You are the reason I get to have this amazing, dream job. Your support means the world to me and I hope you've enjoyed Carter and Addi's journey together. Thank You.

SOCIAL MEDIA

www.instagram.com/evahainingauthor

www.facebook.com/evahainingauthor

www.twitter.com/evahaining

www.amazon.com/author/evahaining

www.bookbub.com/profile/eva-haining

https://www.goodreads.com/author/show/20271110.Eva_Haining

www.evahaining.com

CPSIA information can be obtained
at www.ICGtesting.com
Printed in the USA
BVHW070302161221
624192BV00023B/741